THE
AWAKENING

By Nora Roberts

Homeport
The Reef
River's End
Carolina Moon
The Villa
Midnight Bayou
Three Fates
Birthright
Northern Lights
Blue Smoke

Montana Sky
Angels Fall
High Noon
Divine Evil
Tribute
Sanctuary
Black Hills
The Search
Chasing Fire
The Witness

Whiskey Beach
The Collector
The Liar
The Obsession
Come Sundown
Shelter in Place
Under Currents
Hideaway

The Born In Trilogy:
Born in Fire
Born in Ice
Born in Shame

The Bride Quartet:
Vision in White
A Bed of Roses
Savour the Moment
Happy Ever After

The Key Trilogy:
Key of Light
Key of Knowledge
Key of Valour

The Irish Trilogy:
Jewels of the Sun
Tears of the Moon
Heart of the Sea

*Three Sisters Island
Trilogy*:
Dance upon the Air
Heaven and Earth
Face the Fire

The Sign of Seven Trilogy:
Blood Brothers
The Hollow
The Pagan Stone

Chesapeake Bay Quartet:
Sea Swept
Rising Tides
Inner Harbour
Chesapeake Blue

In the Garden Trilogy:
Blue Dahlia
Black Rose
Red Lily

The Circle Trilogy:
Morrigan's Cross
Dance of the Gods
Valley of Silence

The Dream Trilogy:
Daring to Dream
Holding the Dream
Finding the Dream

*The Inn Boonsboro
Trilogy*:
The Next Always
The Last Boyfriend
The Perfect Hope

*The Cousins O'Dwyer
Trilogy*:
Dark Witch
Shadow Spell
Blood Magick

The Guardians Trilogy:
Stars of Fortune
Bay of Sighs
Island of Glass

*The Chronicles of
the One Trilogy*:
Year One
Of Blood and Bone
The Rise of Magicks

*The Dragon Heart
Legacy trilogy*:
The Awakening

**Many of Nora Roberts' other titles are now available in eBook and she is
also the author of the In Death series using the pseudonym J.D. Robb.**

NORA ROBERTS

THE AWAKENING

THE DRAGON HEART LEGACY

PIATKUS

PIATKUS

First published in the United States in 2020 by St Martin's Press
First published in Great Britain in 2020 by Piatkus

1 3 5 7 9 10 8 6 4 2

A CIP catalogue record for this book
is available from the British Library.

ISBN: 978-0-349-42637-2 (hardback)
ISBN: 978-0-349-42636-5 (trade paperback)

Printed and bound in Great Britain by
Clays Ltd, Elcograf S.p.A.

Papers used by Piatkus are from well-managed forests
and other responsible sources.

Piatkus
An imprint of
Little, Brown Book Group
Carmelite House
50 Victoria Embankment
London EC4Y 0DZ

An Hachette UK Company
www.hachette.co.uk

www.littlebrown.co.uk

For Colt,
my bright boy who adds more
light and love to our lives

PART I
CHANGES

A lie which is half a truth
is ever the blackest of lies.
−Alfred, Lord Tennyson

Presume not that I am the thing I was.
−William Shakespeare

PROLOGUE

VALLEY OF THE FEY

Mists, shimmering silver fingers, rose over the pale green water of the lake. They twined and twisted toward a sky quietly gray, while in the east, over the hills, a pink blush waited, like a held breath, to waken.

In the chill of dawn, Keegan O'Broin stood by the lake and watched the day become. A day, he knew, of change and choice, of hope and power.

He waited, like that held breath, to do his duty, and his hope was he'd be back at the farm before noon. Chores to do, he thought, and more training, of course.

But at the homeplace.

At the signal, he stripped off his boots and his tunic. His brother, Harken, did the same, as did near to six hundred others. They came not just from the valley, the young and the not-so-young, but from every corner of Talamh.

They came from the south where the Pious prayed their secret prayers, from the north where the fiercest of warriors guarded the Sea of Storms, from the Capital in the east, and from here in the west.

For their chieftain, their taoiseach, was dead, his life given to save the world. And as it was written, as it was told, as it was sung, a new one would rise, like those mists, on this day, in this place, in this way.

He didn't want to be taoiseach any more than Harken did. Harken, a cheerful boy of twelve years—the youngest allowed to participate in the ritual—was a farmer, blood and bone. Keegan knew his little brother thought of the day, of the crowds, of the leap into the lake as great fun.

For Keegan, today he would keep an oath given to a man dying, a man who'd stood as his father since his own went to the gods, a man who'd led Talamh to victory over those who would enslave them, though it cost him his life.

He had no desire to lift up the staff of the taoiseach, to take up the sword of the leader of the *clann*. But he'd given his word, and so he'd dive into the water with all the other boys and girls, men and women.

"Come on then, Keegan!" Harken grinned, his raven-wing mop of hair blowing in the spring breeze. "Think of the fun of it. If I find the sword, I'll declare a week of feasting and dancing."

"If you find the sword, who'll tend the sheep and milk the cows?"

"If I rise up as taoiseach, I'll do all of that and more. The battle's done and won, brother. I grieve for him as well." And with his innate kindness, Harken wrapped an arm around Keegan's shoulders. "He was a hero, and never to be forgotten. And today, as he would want, as must be done, a new leader comes."

With his blue eyes bright as the day, Harken looked around at the crowd on the shores of the lake. "We honor him, and all who came before him, all who will come after."

Now Harken jabbed an elbow in Keegan's side. "Leave off the brooding, it's not as if either of us will come out of the water with Cosantoir in our hand. More like to be Cara, as she's as clever in the water as a mermaid, or Cullen, who I know's been practicing holding his breath under the water these past two weeks."

"So he would," Keegan muttered. Cullen, as fine a soldier as was born, wouldn't make a good chief. He'd rather fight than think.

Keegan, a soldier himself at fourteen, one who'd seen blood, spilled it, knew power, felt it, understood that thinking mattered as much as the sword, the spear, the powers.

More, come to that.

Hadn't he been taught just that by his father, and by the one who'd treated him like a son?

As he stood with Harken, with so many others, all chattering like magpies, his mother moved through the crowd.

He wished she would dive today. He knew no one who could settle a dispute as handily, who could deal with a dozen tasks at one time. Harken had her kindness, their sister, Aisling, her beauty, and he liked to think he had at least some of her canniness.

Tarryn paused by Aisling—who chose to wait with her friends rather than the brothers she currently disdained. Keegan watched her tip up Aisling's chin, kiss her cheeks, say words that made her daughter smile before she moved on to her sons.

"And here I have a scowl and a grin." Tarryn ruffled Harken's mop, gave the warrior's braid on the left side of Keegan's head a light tug. "Remember the purpose of this day, as it unites us, and speaks to who and what we are. What you do here has been done by those before for a thousand years and more. And all who took the sword from the lake, their names were written before ever they were born."

"If the fates deem who rises, why can't we see? Why can't you," Keegan insisted, "who sees the before and the yet to come?"

"If I could see, if you could, or any, it would take the choice away." As a mother would, she put an arm around Keegan's shoulders, but her eyes—bright and blue like Harken's—looked out over the lake and through the mists.

"You choose to go into the water, do you not? And who lifts the sword must choose to rise with it."

"Who wouldn't choose to rise with it?" Harken wondered. "They would be taoiseach."

"A leader will be honored, but a leader carries the burden for us all. So they must choose to lift that as well as the sword. Quiet now." She kissed both her sons. "Here is Mairghread."

Mairghread O'Ceallaigh, once a taoiseach herself, and mother to the one now buried, had shed her mourning black. She wore white, a simple gown with no adornments but a pendant with a stone as red as her hair.

They seemed to flame—the stone and her hair—as if they burned away the mists as she walked through them. She wore her hair as short as that of the faeries who streamed in her wake.

And the crowd parted for her, the chattering ceased to silence that spoke of respect and of awe.

Keegan knew her as Marg, the woman who lived in the cottage in the woods not far from the farm. The woman who would give a hungry boy a honey cake and a story. A woman of great power and courage, who had fought for Talamh, brought peace at deep personal cost.

He'd held her as she'd wept for her son, as he kept his word again and brought her the news himself. Though she had known already.

He'd held her until the women came to comfort.

And then, though he was a soldier, though he was a man, he'd gone deeper into the woods to shed his own tears.

Now she looked magnificent, and he felt a shudder of that awe inside his belly.

She carried the staff, the ancient symbol of leadership. Its wood, dark as pitch, gleamed in the sun, through the mists that thinned and broke in pieces.

Its carvings seemed to pulse. Inside the dragon's heart stone at its tip, power swirled.

When she spoke, even the wind fell silent.

"Once more we have brought peace to our world with blood and sacrifice. We have, through all ages, protected our world, and through it all the others. We chose to live as we live, from the land, from the sea, from the Fey, honoring all.

"Once more we have peace, once more we will prosper, until the time comes round again for blood and sacrifice. Today, as it was written, as it was told, as it was sung, a new leader will rise, and all here will swear their fealty to Talamh, to the taoiseach who will take the sword from the Lake of Truth and accept the Staff of Justice."

She lifted her face to the sky, and Keegan thought her voice, so clear, so strong, must reach all the way to the Sea of Storms and beyond.

"In this place, in this hour, we call upon our source of power. Let the one chosen and choosing this day, honor, respect, and guard the Fey. Let the hand that lifts the sword be strong and wise and true. This, only this, your people ask of you."

The water, pale and green with its power, began to swirl. The mists over it swayed.

"So it begins." She lifted the staff high.

They raced toward the water. Some of the younger ones laughed or whooped as they dived, as they jumped. Those on shore cheered.

Keegan heard the din of it all as he hesitated, as his brother went into the water with a cheerful splash. He thought of his oath, thought of the hand that had gripped his in those last moments of life on this plane.

So he dived.

He'd have cursed at the cold slap of the water, but saw no point in it. He could hear others do so, or laugh, even kick their way back to the surface.

He shut off that part of him that could hear thoughts as too many of them crowded in.

He'd sworn he would take to the water this day and dive deep. That he would take up the sword if it came to his hand.

So he dived deep, deeper, remembering the times as a boy he'd done just this with his brother and sister. Children on a summer day hunting for smooth stones on the soft lake bottom.

He could see others through the water, swimming down or over or up. The lake would push them to the surface if the air ran out of their lungs, as it was promised this day no one who entered the lake would come to harm.

Still the lake moved around him, swirling, sometimes spinning. He could see the bottom now, and those smooth stones he'd gathered as a boy.

Then he saw the woman. She simply floated, so at first he thought her a mermaid. Historically the mers abstained from the ritual here. They already ruled the seas and were content with that.

Then he realized he only saw her face, her hair—red as Marg's, but longer and streaming back in the water. Her eyes, gray as shadows in smoke, struck some chord in him that was knowing. But he didn't know her. He knew every face in the valley, and hers wasn't of the valley.

And yet it was.

Then, though he'd blocked himself, he heard her as clearly as he'd heard Marg on shore.

He was mine, too. But this is yours. He knew it, and so do you.

The sword all but leaped into his hand. He felt the weight of it, the power of it, the brilliance of it.

He could drop it, swim on, swim away. His choice, so the gods said, so the stories said.

He started to loosen his fingers and let that weight, that power, that brilliance slide away. He didn't know how to lead. He knew how to fight, how to train, how to ride, how to fly. But he didn't know how to lead others, not into battle or into peace.

The sword gleamed in his hand, a shine of silver with its carving pulsing, its single red stone flaming. As he eased his grip that shine dulled, the flame began to gutter.

And she watched him.

He believed in you.

A choice? he thought. What bollocks. Honor left no choice.

So he pointed the sword toward the surface where the sun danced in diamonds. He watched the vision—for she was nothing more than that—smile.

Who are you? he demanded.

We're both going to have to find out.

The sword carried him straight up, an arrow from a bow.

It cleaved through the water, then the air. The roar came up as the sun struck the blade, shot its light, its power across the water.

He rode it to the thick, damp grass, then did what he knew he must. He knelt at Mairghread's feet.

"I would give this and all it means to you," he said, as her son had, "for there is none more worthy."

"My time is past." She laid a hand on his head. "And yours begins." She took his hand, brought him to his feet.

He heard nothing, saw nothing but her. "This was my wish," she murmured, only for him.

"Why? I don't know how to—"

She cut him off, a kiss to his cheek. "You know more than you think." She held out the staff. "Take what's yours, Keegan O'Broin."

When he took the staff, she stepped back. "And do what comes next."

He turned. They watched him, so many faces, so many eyes watching him. He recognized what churned inside him as fear, and felt the shame of it.

The sword chose him, he thought, and he chose to rise with it. There would be no more fear.

He lifted the staff so its dragon's heart pulsed with life.

"With this, there will be justice on Talamh for all." Now the sword. "With this, all will be protected. I am Keegan O'Broin. All that I am or ever will be pledges this to the valleys, the hills, the forests and ballys, to the far reaches, to every Fey. I will stand for the light. I will live for Talamh, and should the gods deem, I will die for Talamh."

They cheered him, and through the roar of it, he heard Marg say, "Well done, lad. Well done indeed."

So they raised him up, the young taoiseach. And a new story began.

CHAPTER ONE

PHILADELPHIA

Sitting on a bus that seemed to have a bad case of the hiccups, Breen Kelly rubbed at the drumming ache in her temple.

She'd had a bad day that came at the end (thank God!) of a bad week that had spilled out from a bad month.

Or two.

She told herself to cheer up. It was Friday, and that meant two whole days before she'd be back in the classroom struggling to teach language arts to middle schoolers.

Of course, she'd spend a chunk of those two days grading papers, doing lesson plans, but she wouldn't be in the classroom with all those eyes on her. Some bored, some manic, a few hopeful.

No, she wouldn't stand there feeling as inadequate and out of place as any pubescent student who'd rather be anywhere else in the universe than the classroom.

She reminded herself teaching was the most honorable of professions. Rewarding, meaningful, vital.

Too bad she sucked at it.

The bus hiccupped to the next stop. A few people got off; a few people got on.

She observed. She was good at observing because it was so much easier than participating.

The woman in the gray pantsuit, phone in hand, frazzled eyes.

Single mother heading home after work, checking on her kids, Breen decided. She probably never imagined her life would be so hard.

Now, a couple of teenage boys—high-tops, knee-length Adidas shorts, earbuds. Going to meet some pals, play some H-O-R-S-E, grab some pizza, catch a flick. An age, Breen thought, an enviable age, when a weekend meant nothing but fun.

The man in black, he . . . He looked right at her, looked deep, so she cut her eyes away. He looked familiar. Why did he look familiar? The silver hair, the mane of it, made her think: college professor.

But no, that wasn't it. A college professor getting on the bus wouldn't make her mouth go dry or her heart hammer. She had a terrible fear he'd walk back, sit next to her.

If he did, she'd never get off the bus. She'd just keep riding, riding, going nowhere, getting nowhere, a continual loop of nothing.

She knew it was crazy, didn't care. She surged to her feet, rushed toward the front of the bus with her briefcase slapping against her hip. She didn't look at him—didn't dare—but had to brush by him to make the doors. Though he stepped to the side, she felt that her arm bumped his as she passed.

Her lungs shut down; her legs went weak. Someone asked if she was all right as she stumbled toward the doors. But she heard him, inside her head: *Come home, Breen Siobhan. It's time you came home.*

She gripped the bar to keep her balance, nearly tripped on the steps. And ran.

She felt people look at her, turn their heads, stare, and wonder. That only made it worse. She hated to draw attention, tried so hard to blend, to just fade.

The bus hiccupped by.

Though her breath whistled in and out, the pressure on her chest eased. She ordered herself to slow down, just slow down and walk like a normal person.

It took her a minute to manage it, and another to orient herself.

She hadn't had an anxiety attack that severe since the night before her first day in the classroom at Grady Middle. Marco, her best friend since kindergarten, had gotten her through that, and through the one—not quite as bad—before her first parent/teacher conference.

Just a man catching the bus, she told herself. No threat, for God's sake. And she hadn't heard him inside her head. Believing you heard other people's thoughts equaled crazy.

Hadn't her mother drummed that into her head since . . . always?

And now, because she'd had a moment of crazy, she had a solid half-mile walk. But that was fine, that was all right. It was a pretty spring evening, and she was—naturally—dressed correctly. The light raincoat—there'd been a 30 percent chance of rain—over the spring sweater, the sensible shoes.

She liked to walk. And hey, think of all the extra steps on her Fitbit.

So it messed up her schedule a little, what did it matter?

She was a twenty-six-year-old single female, and had absolutely no plans for a Friday night in May.

And if that wasn't depressing enough, the anxiety attack worsened her headache.

She unzipped a section of her briefcase, took out a little pouch, and picked two Tylenol out of it. She downed them with water from the bottle in her briefcase.

She'd walk to her mother's, pick up and sort the mail—as her mother refused to have the post office hold it when she was out of town—shred the junk mail, put bills, correspondence, and so on in the correct trays in her mother's home office.

Open the windows to air out the duplex, water the plants—house and patio, as it hadn't rained after all.

Close the windows after one hour, set the alarm, lock the doors. Catch the next bus and go home.

Toss dinner together: Friday night meant a salad topped with a grilled chicken breast, and—yes!—a glass of wine. Grade papers—post grades.

Sometimes she hated technology because school policy demanded she post those grades—then deal with students or parents who objected to same.

She walked, ticking off items on her list while people around her headed toward happy hour or an early dinner, or anywhere more interesting than her own destination.

She didn't envy them—too much. She'd actually had a boyfriend, had worked dinner dates, theater dates, movie dates into her schedule. Sex, too. She'd thought it had all gone well, smooth and steady.

Until he dumped her.

That was fine, she thought. That was all right. It wasn't as if they'd been madly in love. But she'd liked him, felt comfortable with him. And she'd thought the sex had been pretty good.

Of course when she'd had to tell her mother Grant wouldn't escort her to her mother's forty-sixth birthday party, and why, the stylish, successful Jennifer Wilcox, Philly Brand advertising agency's media director, had rolled her eyes.

And done the expected "I told you so."

Hard to argue as, well, she had.

Still, Breen had wanted to lash back.

You got married at nineteen! You had me when you were twenty. And less than a dozen years later you pushed and pushed and pushed him out. Whose fault is it he walked away from me—not just you, but me?

Was it her own? Breen wondered. Wasn't she the common denominator with a mother who didn't respect her and a father who hadn't cared enough to stay in her life?

Even after he'd promised.

Old business, she told herself. Put it away.

She spent too much time in her head, she admitted, and felt relieved to find herself a block away from her mother's town house.

A pretty, tree-lined neighborhood. A successful neighborhood, one populated by successful people, businesspeople, couples who enjoyed urban living, close access to good bars and restaurants, interesting shops.

All those rosy redbrick buildings, the perfectly painted trim, the sparkling windows. Here people jogged or hit the gym before work, walked along the river, had elegant dinner parties, wine tastings, read important books.

Or so she imagined.

Her best memories bloomed from a tiny house where her bedroom had a slanted ceiling. An old brick fireplace in the living room—not gas or electric, but wood-burning. Where the backyard was as full of adventure as the stories her father told her before bed at night.

Magical stories of magical places.

The arguments had spoiled it—the ones she heard through the walls, the ones she heard inside her head.

Then he'd gone away. At first just for a week or two, and he'd take her to the zoo—she'd been desperate to be a vet back then—or on a picnic on his Saturday visit.

Then he simply hadn't come back.

More than fifteen years now, and she still hoped he would.

She took the key out of her change purse, a key given to her with a detailed list of instructions three weeks before, when her mother had left for one of her business trips followed by a restorative spa/meditative retreat.

She'd leave the key, along with a quart of milk and the other groceries on the list, after she picked up the mail the following Wednesday, as her mother returned Thursday morning.

She retrieved the mail from the box, tucked it under her arm before she unlocked the door, stepped into the foyer to deactivate the alarm. Closed the door, put the key back into her change purse.

She went back to the kitchen first, an HGTV contemporary marvel of stainless steel, white cabinets, white subway tile, farm sink, and walls the color of putty.

She dumped her bag, the mail on the central island, hung her raincoat over a backless stool. After setting her timer for an hour, she began opening windows.

Through the kitchen and great room, back to the living area—all open concept with glorious and gorgeous wide-planked flooring. Since the powder room had a window, she opened that, too.

Barely a breeze to stir the air, but the chore was on her list, and Breen followed the rules. Retrieve the mail to take upstairs. In the third bedroom, one her mother had redesigned into her office, she set the mail on the L-shaped counter that served as a workstation.

Café au lait–toned walls here, and chocolate leather for the desk chair. Ruthlessly organized shelves held awards—her mother had garnered quite a few—books, all work-related, and some framed photos, also work-related.

Breen opened the trio of windows behind the workstation and wondered, as she always did, why anyone would put their back to that view. All the trees, the brick buildings, the sky, the world.

Distractions, Jennifer told her when she'd asked. Work is work.

She opened the two side windows as well, the ones flanking a—locked—wooden filing cabinet.

Wide windowsills held thriving green plants in copper pots. She'd water those and the rest after she opened the other windows. Then she'd sort the mail, and wait out the timer. Close all the windows again, lock up, be done.

She opened them in the perfect, welcoming guest room—where she had never slept—in the guest bath, in the simple elegance of the master and its en suite.

She wondered if her mother ever took a man to that lovely bed with its summer-blue duvet and plumped pillows.

And immediately wished she hadn't wondered.

She went back downstairs, started for the patio door, then backtracked as the phone in her bag rang.

She glanced at the readout—never answer unless you know who was calling—and smiled. If anyone could make this crappy day a little better, it was Marco Olsen.

"Hi."

"Hi your own self. It's Friday, girl."

"I heard that." She took the phone outside to the patio, with its stainless-steel table and chairs and the tall, slim pots on the corners.

"Then get your well-toned ass down to Sally's. It's happy hour, baby, and the first round's on the house."

"Can't." She turned on the hose, began to water the first of the pots. "I'm at my mother's dealing with all that, then I have papers to grade."

"It's Friday," he repeated. "Shake it loose. I'm on the bar till two, and it's Sing-Out night."

The one thing she could do in public without anxiety—especially after a drink and with Marco—was sing.

"I've got another"—she checked the timer on her wrist—"forty-three minutes here, and those papers won't grade themselves."

"Grade 'em Sunday. You've had the brood on, Breen, and that Grant 'Asshole' Webber's not worth it."

"Oh, it's not just that—him. I'm in, you know, a kind of slump, that's all."

"Everybody gets dumped."

"You haven't."

"Have, too. What about Smoking Harry?"

"You and Harry decided, mutually, your relationship in that area had run its course, and are still friends. That's not getting dumped."

She moved on to the next pot.

"You need some fun. If you're not here in—I'm giving you three hours so you can go home and change, put some sexy on your face—I'm coming to get you."

"You're working the bar."

"Sally loves you, girl. He'll come with me."

She loved Sally, drag queen extraordinaire, right back. She loved the club where she felt happy, loved the Gayborhood. Which was why she lived in the heart of it in an apartment with Marco.

"Let me get done here, then see how I feel when I get home. I've had a headache for the last couple hours—not making that up—and I had a stupid anxiety attack on the bus here that made it worse."

"I'm coming to pick you up, take you home."

"You are not." She moved on to the third pot. "I took Tylenol, and it's going to kick in."

"What happened on the bus?"

"I'll tell you later—it was just stupid. And you may be right—I could use a drink, some Marco, some Sally's. Let me see how I feel when I get home."

"You text me when you get there."

"Fine, now go back to work. I've got one more pot out here, the plants inside, the stupid mail, and the damn windows."

"You oughta say no sometime."

"It's not that big a deal. I'll be done in under an hour, catch the bus home. I'll text you. Go pour some drinks. Bye."

She went inside, carefully locked the patio door before she filled the watering can to deal with the inside plants.

A breeze kicked up, had her standing by the window, eyes shut, letting it blow over her.

Maybe it would rain after all, a nice, steady spring rain.

It kicked up harder, surprising her because the sun continued to beam through the glass.

"Maybe we're in for a storm."

She wouldn't mind that either. A storm might blow the damn headache away. And since Marco had given her three hours when two would do, she could spend that hour starting on the papers.

Less guilt that way.

Carrying the watering can, she started back upstairs while the wind—it had graduated from breeze—sent the window treatments flying.

"Well, Mom, your house is definitely getting aired out."

She walked into the office, and into chaos.

The bottom filing cabinet drawer hung open—she'd have sworn it was locked. Papers winged around the room like birds.

Setting the watering can down, she rushed to grab at them, scoop them off the floor, snatch them from the air as the wind whirled.

Then died, like a door had slammed shut while she stood with her hands full of paperwork.

The ever-efficient Jennifer would be seriously displeased.

"Put it back, put it all back, tidy it all up. She'll never know. And there goes my extra hour.

"Sorry, Marco, no Sally's for me tonight."

She picked up empty file folders, scads of paper, and sat at her mother's workstation to try to sort them out.

The first file's label puzzled her.

ALLIED INVESTMENTS/BREEN/2006–2013.

She didn't have any investments, was still paying off her student loans for her master's, and shared the apartment with Marco not just for the company, but to make the rent.

Baffled, she picked up another folder.

ALLIED INVESTMENTS/BREEN/2014–2020.

Another listed the information with the addition of: CORRESPONDENCE.

Had her mother started some sort of investment account for her, and not told her? Why?

She'd had a small college fund from her maternal grandparents, and had been grateful, as it helped her get through the first year. But after that, her mother made it clear she'd be on her own.

You have to earn your own way, Jennifer told her—repeatedly. Study harder, work harder if you ever want to be more than adequate.

Well, she'd studied in between two part-time jobs to manage the tuition. Then took out the loans she figured she'd be paying off this end of forever.

And she'd graduated—adequately—landed an adequate teaching job, then added to the debt because she'd needed that master's degree to hold on to it.

But there were investments in her name? Didn't make any sense.

She started to sort through the papers, intending to make stacks that applied to each folder.

She didn't get far.

While she couldn't claim to know or understand much about investments or stocks or dividends, she could read numbers just fine.

And the monthly report—as it clearly stated—for May of 2014, when she'd been struggling to make ends meet, working those two jobs and eating ramen noodles, listed the bottom line in the account as over nine hundred thousand—*thousand*—dollars.

"Not possible," she murmured. "Just not possible."

But the name on the account was hers—with her mother's name listed as well.

She pawed through others, found a consistency of a monthly deposit from the Bank of Ireland.

She pushed away from the workstation, walked blindly toward the windows as she yanked out the tie holding her hair back.

Her father. Her father had sent her money every month. Did he think that balanced just leaving her? Never calling or writing or coming to see her?

"It doesn't, it doesn't, it doesn't. But . . ."

Her mother knew and hadn't told her. Knew and let her think he'd simply vanished, stopped paying child support, left them both without a thought.

And he hadn't.

She had to wait until her hands stopped shaking, her eyes stopped burning.

Then she went back to the workstation, organized the papers, read through the correspondence, studied the latest monthly report.

The resentment, the grief coalesced into a low and steady burn of fury.

Taking out her phone, she called the number for the account manager.

"Benton Ellsworth."

"Yes, Mr. Ellsworth, this is Breen Kelly. I—"

"Ms. Kelly! What a surprise. It's so nice to actually speak with you. I hope your mother is well."

"I'm sure she is. Mr. Ellsworth, I've just become aware that I have an account with your firm with funds and investments totaling three million, eight hundred and fifty-three thousand, eight hundred and twelve dollars and, um, sixty-five cents. Is this correct?"

"I can get you the account value as of today, but I'm not sure what you mean you've become aware."

"Is this my money?"

"Yes, of course. I—"

"Why is my mother's name also on the account?"

"Ms. Kelly." He spoke slowly. "The account was opened when you were a minor, and you expressed the wish to leave the account in your mother's hands. I can promise you, she's been scrupulous in overseeing your investments."

"How did I express this wish?"

"Ms. Wilcox explained that you had no desire to deal with the investments, and you never communicated with me or the firm to request the account be turned over to you exclusively."

"Because I didn't know it existed until today."

"I'm sure there's a misunderstanding. It might be best if I met with you and your mother to sort this out."

"My mother is out of town, currently at a retreat where she has no access to phone or internet." And some god somewhere had been looking out for her, Breen thought. "But I think you and I should sort this out."

"I agree, absolutely. My assistant's gone for the day, but I can set up an appointment for Monday."

No, no, she'd lose her courage over the weekend. It would drain. It always did. "How about now?"

"Ms. Kelly, I was on the point of leaving the office myself when I took your call."

"I'm sorry to inconvenience you, but I think this is urgent. I know it is for me. I want to talk to you, get a better understanding of this . . . situation before I contact a lawyer."

In the silence, Breen squeezed her eyes shut. Please, she thought, please, don't make me wait.

"It might be better if we met now, talked this all through. I'm sure, as I said, this is just a misunderstanding. I've been told you don't drive, so—"

"I don't have a car," she corrected, "because I can't afford one. But

I'm perfectly capable of getting to your office. I'll be there as soon as I can."

"I'll meet you downstairs, in the lobby. We're a small firm, Ms. Kelly. Most will have gone for the weekend before you get here."

"All right. Thank you."

She hung up before he could change his mind, and sat—shaking again.

"Get your guts up, Breen. Get your stupid guts up, and go."

She put all the papers she'd stacked in their appropriate files. She left the watering can, left the file drawer open, and went downstairs.

She thought of the bus, how long it would take her to get to the offices in City Center.

Then she did something she'd never done.

She took an Uber.

Traffic was horrible. But then again, it was Friday rush hour. The Uber driver, a woman about her age, chatted, then stopped when Breen just put her head back and closed her eyes.

She wanted to read through the files again, but she'd get carsick. Not a good way to meet the man who was, apparently, her investment broker for the first time.

She needed a plan, but couldn't think through the distress, the anger. Her schedule for the weekend included—or had—sitting down to pay bills, juggle funds, squeeze them. She'd planned that sad chore for after her workout. At home, as she couldn't afford a gym membership.

Not just couldn't afford, she admitted, but felt weird and uncomfortable working out with other people around.

Whatever came of this meeting, she still had bills to pay.

She opened her eyes to see they'd broken out of the worst of the traffic and made some progress along the river. The sun, dipping down in the west, still beamed, hit the bridges, the water, made it all shine to her eyes.

No rain after all, she thought, and realized she'd left her raincoat in her mother's kitchen.

Had she remembered to lock up, reset the alarm?

After a moment's anxiety, she closed her eyes again, walked herself back.

Yes, yes, she'd done that. All that was just autopilot.

When the car pulled up in front of the dignified brick building in the shadows of steel towers, she tipped the driver.

There went Sunday night pizza.

When she crossed the sidewalk, a man opened the door.

He stood, tall and lanky in a navy pin-striped suit, crisp white shirt, bold red tie. For some reason the gray, salted through his brown hair, made her feel easier.

~~He was older, she~~ thought. Experienced. He knew what he was doing.

She sure as hell didn't.

"Ms. Kelly." He held out a hand.

"Yes, hello. Mr. Ellsworth."

"Please come right in. My office is on the second floor. Do you mind the stairs?"

"No."

She saw a quiet, carpeted lobby with a glossy reception counter, several oversize leather chairs, a few big green plants in big terra-cotta pots.

"I want to apologize for any part I've played in this misunderstanding," Ellsworth began as they walked up to the second floor. "Jennifer—your mother—indicated you weren't interested in the details of the account."

"She lied."

That hadn't been in the plan—whatever the plan might be. But it came right out of Breen's mouth. "To you, if you're telling me the truth. To me by omission. I didn't know there was an account."

"Yes, well." Ellsworth gestured toward an open door.

His office, bigger than the living room in her apartment and airy due to the big windows, held an old mahogany desk beautifully refinished, a small leather sofa, two visitor chairs.

A counter held a fancy coffee maker. Framed photos—obviously family—covered a floating shelf.

"How about some coffee?"

"Yes, thank you. Milk, no sugar."

"Have a seat," he invited while he walked to the coffee machine.

"I have all the files," she began as she sat, pushed her knees together because they trembled. "From what I can see, the account was opened in 2006. That's when my parents separated."

"That's correct."

"Can you tell me if the deposits starting then were child-support payments?"

"No, they were not. I'd suggest you speak to your mother about that, as I can only talk to you about this specific account."

"All right. My mother opened the account?"

"Eian Kelly opened the account, in your name, with your mother as guardian. He made arrangements, at that time, to have a monthly deposit wired from the Bank of Ireland. For your future, your education, your financial security."

Now she gripped her hands together as they trembled, too. "You're sure."

"I am." He handed her the coffee, then took his own and sat, not behind the beautiful desk with its computer but in the chair beside hers. "I arranged it for him. He came into the office, opened the account. I've been managing it since that time."

"Has he—has he been in touch with you?"

"Not since that time, no. The deposits come. Your mother has overseen the account. She's been scrupulous, as I told you. If you've looked over the reports, you'll see she's never taken out a penny. We have quarterly meetings, more if there's something we need to discuss. I had no reason to think you were unaware."

"Do you have many clients— Am I a client?"

He smiled at her. "Yes."

"Do you have many clients who take no interest at all in an account worth almost four million dollars? I know Allied's a prestigious firm, and that's probably a small account, but it's still a great deal of money."

He took a moment, and she knew he chose his words with great care. "There are situations where a parent or guardian, a trustee, may be better suited to make the financial decisions."

"I'm an adult. She's not my guardian." She felt it, sensed it, knew it. "She told you I was irresponsible, unable to handle money."

"Ms. Kelly—Breen—I don't want to get personal. I can tell you, without hesitation, your mother has always had your well-being in mind. With your issues . . ."

"What are my issues?" The anger rose up again, so much better than the nerves. "Irresponsible. Not too bright either, am I? Maybe even just a little slow on the scale."

He actually flushed a little. "She certainly never said anything like that directly."

"Just implied. Well, let's get to know each other, Mr. Ellsworth. I have a master's degree in education—hard earned just this past winter, and for which I owe a mountain of student debt."

She saw the stunned look, nodded.

"I teach language arts at Grady Middle School, and have since I graduated from college—already with considerable hills of debt despite working two part-time jobs. I'm happy to give you the name of my principal, names of various professors."

"That won't be necessary. I was under the impression you didn't work, or hadn't kept a job."

"I've worked since I was sixteen—summers, weekends. I still work through the summer, to pay off that debt, and I private tutor two evenings a week for the same reason."

Tears began to swirl in her eyes, but they were hot, hot with anger. "I shop sales or thrift stores, have a roommate. I balance my bank account—such as it is—to the penny every month. I—"

"Here now. Here." He closed a hand over hers. "I'm very sorry there's been this—"

"Don't call it a misunderstanding, not when it was deliberate. My father wanted this money for me. Instead I waited tables and took out loans to pay for college when the money he sent for me would've—it would've changed my life. Knowing he sent anything would've changed my life."

She set the coffee aside, pulled in a breath to try to compose herself. "I'm sorry. This is my mother's doing, not yours. Why wouldn't you believe her? You said I was your client."

"You are, and we're going to fix this. When is Jennifer due back?"

"Next week, but I need to know something now. Is this my money?"

"Yes."

"So I'm authorized to withdraw funds, transfer funds."

"Yes, but I think it would be best to wait until your mother's back, for the three of us to sit down and talk."

"I'm not interested in that. I want to transfer funds, establish another account—in my name only. Can I do that?"

"Yes. I can set up an account for you. How much do you want to transfer?"

"All of it."

"Breen—"

"All of it," she repeated. "Or when I meet with you and my mother, I'll have a lawyer, and I'll sue her for, I don't know, embezzlement."

"She hasn't touched the money."

"I'm sure a lawyer will know what term to use. I want my money so the next time I sit down to pay bills I can pay off my student debt and take a full breath again. This money came from my father into your hands. He trusted you to do the right thing by me. I'm asking you to do the right thing."

"You're of age. You can sign a document to have your mother's name removed from the account. I'll need to see your identification, you'll need to fill out some forms. I'll need to call in one of our notaries and a witness."

He laid a hand over hers again. "Breen, I believe you. But would you mind giving me the name and number of the principal at your school? Just for my own peace of mind."

"Not at all."

CHAPTER TWO

By the time Breen walked into Sally's, the place was in full swing. Colored lights streamed over the crowded bar, the packed tables. The spotlight beamed on Cher—or Sally's version thereof—belting out "If I Could Turn Back Time."

Truer words, Breen thought.

She made her way through the enthusiastic crowd, even managed to smile when someone waved or called her name.

Marco caught her eye, bless him, sent her a quick salute as he mixed drinks.

He wore a spangled silver shirt—Sally's was a spangly place—snug black pants, and a silver hoop in one ear. Recently he'd started sporting a little goatee, and she thought it suited him, like the long braids he tied back. His cocoa skin gleamed.

Sally's was hot, in more ways than one.

"Geo, give our girl a seat."

"No, no, that's okay."

But Geo, small, thin, and resplendent in red, hopped right off the stool.

"You sit, sweetie pie. I gotta make the rounds anyway." He gave her a kiss on the cheek. "Our baby looks tired."

"I guess I am."

She took the stool while Marco filled an order. Then poured her a glass of white wine.

"You're late—and you didn't even change. That's some sad outfit, girl." Then his eyebrows shot up when she downed half the glass in one go.

"Okay, that looks like the end of a rough day."

"Rough, strange, scary, exhilarating."

And she burst into tears.

"Geo! I'm taking my break."

He rushed through the pass-through, grabbed Breen's arm, and pulled her with him into the backstage area.

A couple of the performers sat in front of the Hollywood lights on their makeup counters, gossiping.

"Ladies, we need the room."

One of them, done up gorgeous like Gaga, pulled Breen into an embrace. "There, baby girl! It's all going to be all right. You trust Jimmy now. No man's worth your tears."

Another kiss on the cheek, and with Sally moving into "Gypsies, Tramps & Thieves," Marco sat Breen down.

"What happened, honey? Tell me everything."

"I—my father—"

Marco gripped her hand tighter. "He got in touch?"

"No, no, but he—Marco, he's been sending money since I was ten. He started an account, an investment account with Allied, and he's wired money every month. She didn't tell me. She never told me, kept it locked in a drawer. And all this time . . ."

She looked down at her hands. "I forgot my wine."

"I'll go get it."

"Wait. It's . . . Marco, I have as of today, because there were dividends and—I have to learn about all of this. But as of today, I have three million, eight hundred and seventy-eight thousand, five hundred and ninety-six dollars and thirty-five cents."

He goggled at her. "Did you have a dream or something? Baby, you know sometimes you have those dreams."

"No. I've just come from a meeting with my broker. I have almost four million dollars, Marco."

"You sit right here—don't move. I'm going to get the wine. I'm going to get the bottle."

She sat, and caught a glimpse of herself in the mirror.

Really pale, she realized, eyes tired. She'd pulled out her hair tie, and the work she'd done that morning blowing it smooth was wrecked. And the brown rinse she used once a week to calm down the red—too much attention, too distracting—had faded to mouse.

Didn't matter, she thought. Just didn't matter. As soon as she unloaded herself on Marco, she'd go home, lie down. Grading papers had to wait until her head cleared. Since she intended to drink at least two glasses of wine before she walked home, it wouldn't be cleared tonight.

He came back with the bottle, two glasses, poured each before he sat.

"I think let's backtrack a little. How did you find out?"

"It's the strangest thing, Marco."

And she told him everything.

"I gotta go back here a minute," Marco said. "You went to this guy's, this broker guy's office, by yourself? That was brave, Breen."

"I didn't know what else to do. I was so mad."

"Who tells you you need to get mad more?"

A smile flitted. "You do."

"Like I'm saying now you need to stay mad when you talk to your mom."

"Oh God." She dropped her head into her hands—really wanted to drop it between her knees.

"Don't you go jellyfish now."

He glanced back as Sally, in full Cher, glided into the room. Salvador Travino put one hand on the hip of his knockoff Bob Mackie sequined gown, flipped back the waist-length fall of wig.

"They're backed up at the bar, Marco. What the fuck?"

"Sorry, Sally. Breen—"

Sally shot up a finger, heavily lashed eyes narrowing on Breen's face. "Are you sick, my darling girl?"

"No, no. I'm so sorry. I just . . ."

"You look sick." He cupped Breen's chin in his hand. "Pale as a genuine virgin on her wedding night. Is it that asshole, Grant?"

"No, nothing like that."

"Good, 'cause he's not worth it. When did you eat last?"

"I . . ." She couldn't quite remember.

"Just what I thought. Marco, you take our girl home, and get her some food. You got any red meat?"

"Um, probably not."

Sally shook his head, executed a perfect Cher-style hair flip-back. Then gave a come-ahead with one hand. "Give me your phone. I can't keep one in this outfit."

Taking Marco's phone, he tapped in a number, tapped his glittery gold stiletto. "Beau, you handsome bastard, it's Sally. I'm better than I look and I look fabulous. I need you to put a couple of your cheese-steak specials together for me, for pickup. Yeah, the works, my man. Put it on my tab. Marco's coming by for them. I'll see you soon, and give that pretty wife and gorgeous baby of yours kisses for me. And here's one for you."

He made a long smacking sound, then handed the phone to Marco.

"You go by Philly Pride, get those cheesesteaks. Then, Breen, you get out of those clothes and into some pj's. You should listen to Sally and toss those clothes right out the window for somebody with no fashion sense to pick up."

"I can't leave you in the lurch on a Friday night," Marco began, and got the withering eye.

"You don't think I can handle the stick? Boy, I've been handling sticks—of all natures—since before you were out of diapers. And looking as good as I do, I expect to rake in some fine tips. Take that girl home."

"Thank you, Sally." Rising, Breen went in for a hug, just laid her head on Sally's shoulder. The man had been more of a mother to her than her own for the last decade.

"We'll talk soon. And you call me if you need me. Not before ten in the morning unless it's an emergency. I need my beauty sleep."

"No, you don't. You're the most beautiful person I know."

"Go on. Take off. I've got a club to run."

They went out the back. Marco's arm automatically went around Breen's waist. Her head automatically tipped toward his shoulder.

"I'm so tired all at once, Marco. I don't know if I can eat."

"You'll eat, or I'll tell Sally. Then I'm going to tuck you into bed."

He walked her along the brick-paved streets under the rainbow streetlights.

The clubs, the restaurants, the cafés were all hopping, as they should be on a pretty Friday night in May.

"I just remembered I left the watering can on the floor of my mother's office. It's probably going to leave a ring."

"Aw."

"They're beautiful floors, Marco. None of this is their fault."

"They're your mother's problem, and there wouldn't be a ring on them if she hadn't hidden all this from you for, Jesus, sixteen years. So you stop, right now, or you'll piss me off. Tell me what you're going to do next."

"Pay off the student loans. Mr. Ellsworth said he was going to talk to someone—I can't remember, it's all so much—about that. And how I could probably get them down a little with a full payoff, if that's what I wanted to do. And I do. I want them off my head."

"Okay, I get that. But two other things. How you're going to talk to your mom and—maybe most important of all—what you're going to do for fun."

"I can't think about the fun."

"Fine. I will."

He swung into Philly Pride and the scent of grilled onions. She decided not to think at all while he picked up the food—and flirted harmlessly with Trace, the counter guy.

"Do you think I should ask him out?" Marco wondered when they walked outside again.

"Trace? No, he's too young for you."

"He's our age!"

"Chronologically. He'd bore you inside a week because all he'd want to do other than sex is play video games. You'd say let's check out this club, and he'd say maybe after I run up my score on *Assassin's Creed*."

"I hate you're right, because he's *mmmm*."

"But the *mmmm*—and it's there all right—wouldn't last that week. And you're bringing all this up to take my mind off things."

"It worked."

She started to tip her head toward his shoulder again, and caught a glimpse of the man—the silver hair, the tall, slender build in black—across the street.

"Do you see that man, Marco?" She grabbed his arm, then turned to point.

"What man?"

"I— He was just there. He must have turned that corner. He was on the bus today. He . . . I got a weird feeling."

Since he knew her weird feelings often panned out, Marco gripped her hand, jogged to the corner, peered down the side street.

"Do you see him? What's he look like?"

"No, he's just gone. It's nothing. I had that stupid headache, and that weird feeling. It just felt weird all over again seeing him so close to home. If I did," she qualified. "I just caught a glimpse. Never mind."

They walked the half block more to their apartment—a three-level walk-up. She loved the building, the old brick, the rainbow the owner had painted on the entrance doors, the music flowing out of the open windows on a happy spring night.

It made the climb to the third floor worth it.

The landlord kept the building, and the units, in good repair. The tenants kept it clean, and looked out for each other.

They walked up to the sounds of the Friday-night card game from 101, a fretful baby from 204, and soaring opera from 302.

Inside, Marco headed straight for their tiny galley kitchen.

"You go change out of those clothes—and I wouldn't mind one bit if you listened to Sally and tossed them out the window."

"There's nothing wrong with these clothes."

"The pants are baggy in the ass, the sweater's beige and washes you out, and, girl, don't get me started on those shoes."

Sulking a little, she walked back to her room with its neatly made bed, its small but organized desk, and its single window that looked out on all the color of her part of the city.

She stepped out of her shoes, then put them away in her broomstick of a closet. She stripped off the sweater she now hated, but tossed it in the hamper rather than out the window. Then did the same with the pants.

Maybe they were baggy in the ass, but they didn't draw any eyebrow wiggles from male students or staff the way Anna Mae's—US and world history—body-conscious outfits did.

She put on cotton pajama pants and a T-shirt. Took a look at her desk, where she should be sitting right now grading papers.

And walked back into the space that served as their living room, dining room, and her workout area.

It wasn't much, but since she'd let Marco have his way there, it had style.

Together they'd painted the walls a warm, spicy color that made her think of crushed chili peppers, hung a shelf that held colored bottles of every size and shape. Art—framed posters—ran the theme of musicians. Springsteen, Prince, Jagger, Gaga, Joplin.

They'd covered the secondhand couch in dark green and a lot of wild pillows. Their dining room table consisted of a repurposed door—another thrift-store find—bolted to old iron legs.

An artist friend had painted an orange and emerald dragon, in flight, on top of the old door as a birthday gift for Breen.

Marco set plated food on the table, lit the candles in their iron stands.

"Sit," he ordered. "Eat. No more wine until you get some food in you."

"I shouldn't have any more wine."

"Well, you're going to."

He turned on their shared iPod, eased the volume down so music whispered out.

She sat, and though she didn't have an appetite, picked up her sandwich. "You know, I couldn't get through life without you, Marco."

"Never going to have to. Eat."

She ate. Maybe she didn't have any appetite, but she could feel herself settling with the food.

"I want to quit my job."

The minute she said it, she dropped her cheesesteak, slapped a hand over her mouth. "Where did that come from?" she demanded.

"Could be it comes from you never wanting to be a teacher in the first place." He continued to eat placidly, but he had that tiny smile going.

"Well, I can want to quit, but it's crazy and stupid. Yes, I've fallen into a lot of money out of nowhere, and it can last me a long time, even grow if I'm careful. Quitting a steady job, one I studied for, paid for—or will shortly pay for—isn't the way to handle this."

"You wanted to be a vet."

"I wanted to be a vet. I wanted to be a ballerina. I wanted to be a rock star, and I wanted to be J. K. Rowling. I'm none of those things, and won't be."

"You're a really good writer, girl."

She shook her head, went back to eating. "That's an old dream. I have to think of now, and next."

"Quit your job."

"Marco—"

"You hate it. You never wanted to be a teacher. That's what your mother wanted you to be, that's what she convinced you you had to be. Like it was your only option. Pay off the debt, quit your job, and give yourself some time to figure out what you want to do, want to be."

"I can't just—"

"Yes, you can. It came out of your mouth because it's what's in your heart and your mind. Now's your chance, Breen."

"But I don't know how to do anything else."

"Because you never had the chance. Take some time to find out. You could write, I'm telling you. Or if that ain't the thing, you could start a business."

"Me?"

"Yes, you. Damn it, Breen, you're smart and organized." Scowling, he poured the wine now that she'd eaten a little. "You could do design work, and don't say 'me' in that dumbass tone. I didn't put this place together alone, and it looks damn good. We did it. You've got a voice, and play the piano. You could do that.

"You let her put you in a box," he continued, revved up now, "and now the top's flown off. Don't you dare slam it shut again."

"I . . . Just go in Monday and tell the principal I won't be back in the fall. Just like that?"

"Yeah, like that. You take the summer to figure out what you want to do, or try to do."

"That's pretty terrifying."

"I'd say liberating. Name one thing—the big thing—you really want to do now that you can. You have time, some money. What do you want to do most? Don't think, don't try to figure out what makes the best sense. Just say it, like you said you wanted to quit. Let it come."

"I want to go to Ireland. Oh Jesus, oh God, that's what I want. I want to go see where my father came from, see what pulled him back there and away from me. I want, if I can, to find him, to ask him why. Why he left, why he sent money. Just why."

"Do it. That's a great one thing. Spend the summer in Ireland, let yourself have that time, that place to figure the rest out."

"The summer?"

"Why the hell not? When's the last time you had any sort of vacation?"

"When we graduated from college and took a bus to the Jersey Shore for a week."

"We had a great time," he remembered. "And that was a time ago, Breen. Long time ago."

She picked up her wine, drank deep. "Go with me."

"To Ireland?"

"I'd never do it alone. Go with me. You're right, you're right." She pushed away from the table, whirled around the room. "Why the hell not? It's what I want. The one thing I really want. We'll fly first class this time, and stay in a castle. At least one night in a castle. We'll rent a car and drive on the wrong side of the road. We could—we could rent a cottage. An Irish cottage with a thatched roof."

"You maybe had too much wine."

"I haven't." She laughed now, eyes dancing. "Go with me, Marco, and share my one thing."

"I can't go off for the whole summer. Sally and Derrick, they'd be cool with it, but I've got a day job I gotta keep."

"You hate your day job. You hate working in the music store."

"Yeah, but nobody slapped me with four mil. But I could go for a couple weeks, get you started. Jesus, I've never been to Europe. What a kick in the ass it would be."

"I'll kick yours, you kick mine. Deal?"

He sat back. He loved her, more than anything or anyone in the world. And he couldn't put out that light in her eyes. But he could sure as hell bargain.

"I have conditions."

She plopped back down. "Name them."

"I can't afford first class, so fine, that's on you. But I pay my share of the rest."

"I don't care about that."

"Yeah, because you're a freaking millionaire."

She threw back her head and howled with laughter. "I'm a freaking millionaire."

"That's one condition. The others are just as solid from my side. When you finish eating, you're going in there and washing your hair until you wash that stupid-ass brown shit out of it—for the last time. And you're tossing that stupid-ass hair dryer out, the one you spend an hour with every morning blowing your gorgeous curls straight."

He shook his head when she opened her mouth to object.

"You're going to Ireland. Bet you won't be the only redhead there."

"I'm not the only redhead anywhere."

"That's right, but you let yourself be convinced the hair, your hair, made you look, what, frivolous? That it attracted attention—and why the hell shouldn't it? Fuck that, Breen."

"You'll go with me, at least two weeks, if I go back to my natural hair."

"That's right."

"Deal."

"Not quite there yet. I have one more."

"You're a hard sell, Marco Polo."

"I ain't no pushover. This one's important, it might be key." He leaned forward. "Tomorrow, we're going shopping because tonight we're bagging up damn near everything in your closet. We'll drop it by the Goodwill tomorrow, then you, being the lucky woman with every woman's dream of a gay best friend, are going to let me help you buy clothes that don't hurt my heart when you wear them."

"My clothes aren't that bad."

"Sad and pitiful is what they are, and you are not. You've let yourself think you need to be, or need to be goddamn beige. I'm not going to talk against your mama, because that's not how I was brought up. But I am going to say, when you go talk to her next week, you're going to look like what you really are: strong, capable, beautiful, and smart. And we're buying some good makeup while we're at it, too."

"That's a lot of conditions."

"It is what it is. I love you, Breen."

"I know you do, and so . . ." She held out a hand. "Deal."

"That's my girl!"

CHAPTER THREE

In another series of firsts, Breen took off work on the day of her mother's expected arrival. She'd bought the listed groceries, put them away. After all, she'd agreed to do so.

She opened the windows, watered the plants, sorted the mail.

She had a calm, and firm, monologue in her head. In fact, she'd written out what she intended to say to her mother. She'd edited and revised it several times. Practiced it in the mirror.

Then she'd practiced it without the mirror, as she didn't altogether recognize the person looking back at her.

She knew the drama of the change if only from the looks, comments, even compliments at work, on the bus.

The hair, flaming curls well beyond her shoulders—and Marco had vetoed her option of having it cut—made the statement. She wasn't sure, yet, what the statement was, but it made one.

No chance of fading into the background now, she thought. She'd see, that's all, she'd just see how she felt about it in a week or two.

But she knew already she liked her new—if limited—wardrobe. A few strong colors, some spring pastels—no beige. Pants that fit, a couple of simple, and pretty, dresses. One business suit. New shoes—she'd held the line at three against an enthusiastic Marco. And with Ireland in mind, a good pair of walking boots.

She'd stuck with sales, and had still spent more money in a single day than she spent on herself—just Breen—in six months.

More.

Maybe it had been the rush of it all that had weakened her enough to let Marco talk her into getting her ears pierced.

She fiddled with the little silver stud as she looked at the latest text from Marco on her phone.

It said: Courage.

And as she saw the cab pull up outside, she tried to take it to heart.

Going with instinct, she went to the door, stepped out.

Because her eyes were trained on her mother, she didn't see the man with the silver hair glance her way as he strolled by across the street.

Jennifer Wilcox looked, as always, perfect in trim gray pants, a light jacket in bold red over a soft white shirt. Her hair, richly brown, expertly highlighted, complemented her sharp-featured face with an angular wedge.

Breen saw the surprise—and, oh yes, the quick disapproval—as she walked down to help with the luggage.

"I've got this," Breen said as she took the handle of the large wheeled Pullman.

Jennifer shouldered the matching tote and her computer case.

"I didn't expect to see you here. Why aren't you at work?"

"I took the day off." Battling back the knee-jerk anxiety, Breen rolled the suitcase to the door and inside.

"That certainly wasn't necessary."

"It was for me."

"Are you ill?"

"No." She wheeled the suitcase to the base of the stairs, realized she'd started to take it up. Stopped herself. "I'm absolutely fine. In fact, I'm just terrific."

"A new boyfriend, is it?" Jennifer set down the tote, gestured at Breen's hair. "Is that was this is all about?"

"No, no boyfriend, new or otherwise. I'm a redhead," she heard herself say. "I've decided to embrace it."

"Your choice, of course, but no one's going to see past your hair. How do you expect your students to take you seriously when you look frivolous?"

"That won't be an issue much longer. I'll finish out the school year, but I turned in my resignation on Monday."

The fact Jennifer stared, just stared, brought Breen a dark satisfaction.

"Have you lost your mind? You need to rescind that resignation immediately. You're not going to throw away your education, your security, your future."

"I never wanted to be a teacher."

"Oh, don't be ridiculous. And I don't have time for this nonsense. I need to unpack, check in with the office." She looked at her watch. "You have plenty of time to get back to school, apologize to your supervisor, and fix this."

"No."

Jennifer's eyes, a changeable hazel, narrowed with temper. "I beg your pardon?"

"I said no, and you're going to need to take some time out of your busy schedule to talk about Mr. Ellsworth and my Allied Investment account. And my father."

The color, rising hot in Jennifer's cheeks, leached away. "How dare you! You went into my private papers?"

"My papers, but no, I didn't. And that's not the point. You lied to me, that's the point. You lied."

"I didn't lie to you. I did my job as a parent and did what was best for you. I looked out for your future."

"By making my past and present a lie, and miserable. He sent that money to me, for me. You let me believe he just left, he didn't care."

"He did leave, and I invested the money. You were a minor—"

"I haven't been a minor for a long time."

"You've never shown any skill or interest in handling money."

"I'm not taking that." Fury just erupted inside her. "That's bullshit."

"Don't you dare take that tone with me."

"I'll take whatever tone I like. I worked two jobs, took out loans, did without, all so I could get degrees I didn't want. So I could become a teacher because you hammered it into me that's all I could be. Not that it's a vital, honorable, incredible profession and vocation, but that those who can't do, teach. How many times did I hear that, Mom?"

"You don't have any other skills. And you'd better calm down."

"I'm way past calm. I could've taken a couple semesters to explore, to try to figure out what I wanted to do, to be. I could have tried writing."

"Oh please. Stop being childish."

"You decided what I should do, how I should do it. How I should dress, how I should wear my own hair, for God's sake. And you kept what was freedom for me locked in a file cabinet drawer."

"I protected you! I've spent my life protecting you."

"From what? From living my life? You told Mr. Ellsworth I had no interest in handling the money, you let him think I was incapable of handling it."

"Because you aren't capable, Breen." Jennifer brushed back her hair, and her voice took on that irritatingly, endlessly patient tone.

"Look at you, right now. You find out there's some money, and the first thing you do is quit your job. How is that responsible?"

"You know what I think's irresponsible? Slogging through a job you hate day after day. Covering up who you are, or who you may be given the chance to be, because your mother's made you feel inadequate."

"I've never said you were inadequate. That's not fair."

"No, you're right. Adequate was the line. Just barely adequate. And you know, maybe you're right. Maybe it'll turn out that's all I am. But I'm going to find out."

She took a breath. She could see, clearly, her mother looked ill, but she couldn't stop. "You knew how anxious I was about the student debt, how I had to juggle my paycheck, take extra work to keep treading water. And you kept the money that would have let me take a good, clear breath secret."

"It's important to learn how to budget."

Jennifer walked away to drop down in a chair. "Your father was a dreamer, and you took after him. You needed to learn how reality works. I did my best for you, always."

"Where is he?"

"I don't know." She pressed her fingers to her eyes. "I don't. He chose not to come back, you remember that when you slap out at me. He chose not to be a father to you. I never stopped him from seeing you. I wouldn't have."

She dropped her hands again. "I'm the one who was here. The one who made sure you had a stable home, who took care of you when you were sick, who helped with your homework, who was a mother while building a career so we could have that stable home."

"Yes, you did all that, but you left out one thing. You spent a lot of time and effort trying to mold me into what you thought I should be, and none letting me be who I wanted to be."

"Everything I did, everything, was to keep you safe, to give you stability, to teach you how to live a normal, productive life."

"As an unhappy, anxious middle school teacher who covered up her red hair with a brown rinse and wore a lot of beige so nobody noticed her."

"You're safe," Jennifer insisted, "you're healthy. You have an education and a profession."

"That's not enough. It hasn't been enough for you. You have a career, take vacations, go to spa retreats."

Hints of anger flashed through the patience. "I worked for it."

"You did, you did." For a moment, Breen sat across from her mother. "Nobody pushed you into becoming the media director of a successful ad agency. You had the skills, the determination, and you went for it. You worked and work hard. I admire what you've made of your life, and you're entitled to the rewards. I'm entitled to try to do the same."

Breen rose. "I've had your name taken off the account. Mr. Ellsworth should contact you tomorrow to discuss if you want another firm or another account executive to handle your investments. The groceries you asked me to get are put away. I watered the plants, sorted your mail. And, as you can see, the windows are still open. You'll have to close them yourself. It's the last time I'll serve as your general dogsbody."

She hesitated, then decided to say what she felt. "I'm sorry you're upset, but you were dishonest, and what you've done hurt me. It hurt me, Mom."

"I never wanted to hurt you."

"Maybe not. Maybe that's true but, like you always say, that's reality. I need to go. I'm meeting Marco."

"What are you going to do? What are you going to do, Breen?"

"Well, to start, the day after the last day of classes, Marco and I are flying to Ireland. I'm going to see where my father came from. I'm going to try to find him."

"You won't." Jennifer pressed her fingers to her eyes again. "You won't."

"I'm going to try. Either way, for the first time since he left, I'm going to have an adventure."

"Don't do this, Breen. Take time to think, not just react."

"You should close the windows. It looks like a storm's coming."

She walked out and kept walking, past the bus stop as the clouds thickened overhead.

The man in black strolled behind her. He carried a black umbrella, as it would rain, he knew, in sixteen minutes.

He hadn't expected things to move so quickly, so smoothly. Of course, they still had a ways to go, but the first steps had been taken.

He'd assumed he'd have to give the girl a few little pushes. But the one, it seemed, had been quite enough. And if she wavered on the following through, then push he would.

But for now, he could enjoy this visit to Philadelphia, a city he found full of fascination. The food—he particularly liked the soft pretzels, though he'd found the candy billed as Irish potato a disappointment.

He liked the neighborhoods, little communities, and the mix of architecture. He'd taken a tour or two, found himself amused when the guide spoke of old and history.

They knew nothing of old in the grand scheme, or of the long, long road of history.

But, all in all, he found it charming in its way.

The country had formed its government here, and they were so proud of it. Of course, the government was more than a bit of a mess, but these things did ebb and flow over time. And they were so very young yet.

And stubborn, and violent, and too often greedy.

And still there was heart and hope. Much could be done with both.

He thought the girl had it—and would need it—though she'd buried it for most of her time in this world.

She walked and walked—and good for her. He much preferred it to the buses. Though he did like the trains, and very much. However, if she kept walking, she'd end up very wet.

Then she stopped, studying some sort of shop. Started to walk on, walked back again. Stopped. He was about to tap into her thoughts, when she walked—quick, determined—inside.

He strolled along, paused to study the sign. Puzzled over it for a moment.

Then laughed and laughed as he opened his umbrella. The rain came down—exactly on time—and in a thunderous torrent. Delighted by the way things progressed, he wandered off to find a bite to eat. He had a yen for a hoagie, and thought he'd miss them when he went home again.

Two hours later, when Breen walked into the apartment, Marco was waiting. Saying nothing, he simply walked to her, wrapped around her, swayed.

"It was awful."

"I know. Wine or ice cream?"

"Why not both?"

"You got it. Sit down, let Uncle Marco fix everything." He brushed a hand over her hair. "Got caught in the rain."

"A little bit." She did sit. Now that she'd gotten home, exhaustion dropped down like broken bricks. "Don't you have to go to work?"

"Not for an hour or so," he said from the kitchen. "Time for wine, ice cream, and venting. I guess she didn't take it very well."

"She led with the insult I'd go through her private papers, harangued me for quitting my job, using that as evidence I'm irresponsible and can't handle my finances. She kept the money, and the fact my father sent it, from me to protect me."

Being Marco, he brought two bowls of cookie dough ice cream, two glasses of chilled pinot grigio on a bamboo tray, with cloth cocktail napkins.

"From what?"

"Myself, I guess, since I'm stupid, irresponsible, and incapable of making my own decisions."

Marco sat, picked up his spoon, spoke carefully. "I love your mother."

"I know you do."

"I love her because she was always good to me. I love her because when I came out, she accepted me in a way my family couldn't, and never has. It mattered."

"I know."

"I can love her and still say she's wrong, really wrong. No-excuses wrong, and I'm sorry."

"She was upset, genuinely. And not just because I caught her in this lie—and it is a damn lie, however she tries to spin it around. It was almost like she was somehow upset and worried I'd just sealed my doom or something."

He smiled as he ate ice cream. "Maybe overreacting a little, Breen?"

"Maybe, but it felt like that to me. She said she doesn't know where my father is, and I believe her. I think she was too upset to lie. We argued—fought really—most of the time. But she kind of gave up, if you know what I mean. Just gave up."

"Did you tell her we're going to Ireland?"

"Yeah, and all she said, basically, was I wouldn't find him." Breen picked up her wine now. "She never once, not once, said she'd been wrong. Never once said she was sorry. Why couldn't she just say 'I'm sorry'?"

She shook her head before Marco could speak. "Because she doesn't think she's wrong, simple as that. She's not going to apologize for being right, is she? Jennifer Wilcox is always right."

"Not this time."

"It doesn't matter." She went back to the ice cream. "I said what I had to say, and I'm doing what I have to do. Want to do. I don't have to prove myself to her."

She caught the look he gave her, sighed. "Okay, part of me wants to, but most of me wants to prove myself to me. That comes first. Oh." Breen wagged her spoon. "She disapproved of the hair, and it hit me as I was walking—and walking—I got my hair from my father. Bright red and curly. So maybe it's too much of a reminder, but you know what?"

"What?"

"It's my damn hair, and she's supposed to love me as I am. So she can just get the hell over it."

"That's the way." His quick grin turned to distress as he grabbed her hand. "What did you do? You hurt yourself."

"Oh, well, not exactly." Hastily, she picked up her wine again while Marco shoved up her sleeve to examine the bandage over her wrist.

"What exactly?"

"I was so mad. I walked right by the bus stop, then the next bus stop. I was going over and over the whole argument again in my head. It was so insulting, Marco, on top of it all, just insulting. And I remember how I used to take ballet, and how I loved it."

"You looked really cute in your leotard and tights."

"I had such fun with it, and Dad called me his Tiny Dancer, and when he left . . . She said we couldn't really afford the lessons anymore, but I shouldn't be sad because I was only average. I'd already gotten all I could get out of the lessons—the poise, the posture. She'd manage the piano lessons for another year, but that was all."

"You never told me."

"It hurt so much. It wasn't as if I had any illusions about becoming a prima ballerina—or not since I was about seven. I knew I was only average, but I loved it—the dancing, practicing with our little troupe, being a part of it. Doesn't matter now, and not the point. It's just that I remembered that, and other things. And I remembered I never fought back, never stood up for myself. And it made me mad all over again."

"So you cut your wrist?"

"I didn't cut my wrist. I was walking and thinking of all the times I gave in, didn't fight. And I saw this sign. Express You. And wasn't that what I needed to do? Express me? So I went in, and . . ."

She puffed out her cheeks, blew out air.

"Jesus my ass, Breen. You got a tattoo!"

"It was impulse. It was temper. It was revenge or something. And by the time I calmed down, it was too late to stop."

"What'd you get? Lemme see! Why didn't you text me to come? We would've gotten one together. That was the plan."

"We never had a tattoo plan."

"We would have if you'd ever said you wanted one. What is it? When can you take the bandage off?"

"It's not really a bandage, and I can take it off now. I started to get it on my biceps, then I thought no, if I have it on my wrist, I can turn it over and look at it whenever I need it. Which is more stupid."

She took the protective gauze off, turned up her right wrist.

"It's beautiful lettering, like what they carved in old stones, and I like the color—dark, dark green that's almost black but isn't. But what the hell is *misneach*?"

"It's pronounced 'misnaw.' It's Irish for 'courage'—I looked it up. And it's your fault I have a tattoo on my wrist."

He had her hand, turning it this way, that way, his big, beautiful eyes examining each letter. "How's it my fault?"

"It's what you texted me just as my mother got home. Courage. It's what I needed, and it's what I thought of when I saw that damn sign."

"I'm taking the credit because this is so cool. Let's go back tomorrow so I can get one. No, wait. I'll get one in Ireland—cooler yet. And you can get another."

"I don't think I'm up for another. You go right ahead."

"Did it hurt?"

"I was too mad to notice, then yeah, some when I came back down. By then, too late. Maybe I am irresponsible."

"You are not. You made a statement. I love it. Why don't you come into work with me, show it off?"

"I'm going to stay right here, do my lesson plans. And I'm going to start looking for a cottage for rent in County Galway."

"We're really doing it."

"We're really doing it." She turned her wrist over, thought: Courage.

Dutifully, as Breen believed in duty, she went to school every morning and did her best. She graded papers, found some satisfaction when she saw some improvement in certain students.

In the evenings, on the weekends, she prepared for the trip of her lifetime. She found a cottage in Connemara—a district in County Galway—exactly what she was looking for. It was just a few miles from a quaint village and there were acres to explore, and it even had a bay and mountain view.

She considered it another sign—like the tattoo parlor—that previous bookings fell through. So she snapped it up for the summer.

And struggled against the anxiety of making so big a commitment.

Before she could falter—courage!—she booked three nights in Clare at Dromoland Castle, then booked the flights.

Done.

Now she had to wait for her passport and Marco's to arrive, buy some Dramamine. She didn't know if she got airsick, since she'd never flown. But better safe than sorry.

She bought guidebooks and maps, rented a car—and spent a sleepless night worried about driving in Ireland.

She had two meetings with Ellsworth, who arranged for a thousand euros—dear God, a thousand.

It all seemed like a strange dream, even the packing.

When she walked out of school for the last time, she felt as if she walked through someone else's dream.

She walked to the bus stop, another last time, and thought it was like closing a door. Not locking it, not pretending it wasn't there, just closing it and moving into another room.

No, like moving out of a house where you'd never felt quite right, and hoping the next one fit.

And at this time the next day, they'd be on their way to the airport. They'd fly through the night to another world. And, for the first time in so long she couldn't remember, she wouldn't have to answer to anyone but herself. No schedule, no lesson plans, no alarm set for work.

What the hell was she going to do with herself?

Find out, she thought. And turned her wrist over. Gut up and find out.

She pulled out her phone when it rang.

"Hi, Sally."

"Breen, my treasure. I have to ask you for an enormous favor. I know you're busy."

"Really not. Everything's done."

"That makes me feel less guilty. I'm in a bind. Could you give me a few hours tonight? I've had three servers call in. Some sort of stomach bug, and I'm short-staffed."

"Sure. No problem."

"Bless your heart. I had to ask Marco, too. I'm so sorry, but—"

"Don't be. It'll be nice to see everybody before we leave. What time do you want me?"

"Can you make it by six?"

"Sure. I'm about to get on the bus home now. I'll obsessively check my travel list, again, change, and be there with Marco at six."

"I owe you both, big. Love you, girl."

"Love you back."

And good, Breen thought as she got on the bus. It would keep her mind off air travel, airport security, crashing into the Atlantic, driving on the wrong side of the road, and every other worry she'd conjured up over the last weeks.

She'd work the six to two, go home and drop into bed, and, please God, sleep and sleep late.

Before she knew it, she'd be on the plane and gone.

She started to settle in, glanced out the window.

There he was—the man with the silver hair. Just standing on the sidewalk, smiling at her. She'd lost track of the number of times she'd seen him since that first day.

At the market, outside Ellsworth's offices, even at Sally's one other night she'd helped out.

Every time she worked up the nerve to go closer, he just vanished. Not like poof, she thought. That was ridiculous, but he simply evaded her.

Just someone from the same neighborhood—and yet, she'd seen him in the city, too.

It didn't matter, she assured herself. She'd soon leave him behind—thousands of miles behind.

One more day, she thought as the bus rumbled along. Just one more day before the rest of her life began.

CHAPTER FOUR

Back in her apartment, Breen did just what she'd said she'd do. She obsessively checked everything.

Suitcases, recently purchased on sale—a half-price sale, maybe because they were turquoise. Neither was close to full, but she'd have room for souvenirs, gifts, and whatever else she purchased on a nearly three-month stay.

She'd opted to use her backpack for her carry-on—one she'd had since college. Though battered and worn, it would come in handy for hiking. At the moment, it held her guidebooks, maps, eye drops, Dramamine, ibuprofen, Band-Aids, her tablet, laptop, charging cords, pens, a notebook, two books, a toiletry and makeup bag.

She had a small, efficient cross-body bag that organized her passport, tickets, ID, credit card, cash.

When she reached the point she had to admit she had nothing left to do, she set the alarm on her phone for thirty minutes and stretched out to take a nap, since she'd wait tables until after two in the morning.

She had to turn off her mind first, as her thoughts insisted on conjuring worst-case scenarios.

Either she or Marco would contract a serious illness—or have a terrible accident—overnight and have to cancel.

They'd learn all flights to Ireland had been canceled indefinitely because . . . reasons.

They'd fly all the way to Ireland only to learn their passports were invalid. They'd be deported immediately.

The aliens finally invaded.

The Walking Dead became reality.

As she wasted nearly five minutes entertaining all the tragic possibilities, it was hardly a surprise her short nap was neither quiet nor restful.

She found herself alone walking on thick green grass under skies the color of pewter. Though gray, the sky carried a glow as if the sun pressed and pressed its light and heat behind those layered clouds.

A kind of inlet wove, a slow snake, between the land and the wider bay. She could see stubby green knuckles punching up through the still water, and fuzzy white sheep with black faces on the far hills.

The air, moist and cool, fluttered through the trees, shivered over a garden alive with bold, almost insolent color.

She heard birdsong and the musical notes of the chimes—dozens of them—hanging from the branches of a tree at the verge of the woods.

She walked that way, where the thick grass led to a soft brown path, narrow as a ribbon, and the light turned to a wonderfully eerie green. Moss, thick as a carpet, blanketed the wide trunks of trees, coated their curving branches, smothered rocks that heaved out of the ground.

A stream rushed by, burbling and spilling over rock ledges. She thought she heard murmuring, and laughter.

The water, she thought, or the wind chimes at the start of the path.

She walked on, caught up in wonder and delight.

A bird whizzed by, green as an emerald. Then another, ruby red, and a third, like a sapphire on the wing.

She'd never seen anything like them—so jewel-like, so iridescent—and followed the path of their flight.

And in the green shadows and light she heard them call, a young sound and somehow fierce. With it came the drumbeat of water striking water and rock.

The waterfall spilled from a dizzying height, had her heart leaping at the sight of it.

A thunderous fall, white as snow into the winding stream, where it turned pale, pale green.

The birds swirled around the fall of water, the three and more. Topaz, carnelian, amethyst, cobalt in a dazzling display. Dipping, diving, dancing.

One swooped to her, wings fluttering as it hovered inches from her face. She saw its ruby-red wings tipped with gold like its—his, she knew, his—eyes.

Not a bird, not at all, but a dragon no bigger than the palm of her hand.

"Hello. You're Lonrach, because that's what you are. Brilliant." She held out a hand, thrilled when he settled on her palm. "And you're mine."

She walked with him, drawn to the falls, the dance of the little dragons.

She realized she could see through the white water, as if it became moving and translucent glass.

And through it, she saw what seemed to be a city, gray and black, towers and spears of buildings rising into a sky more purple than blue. Like a healing bruise.

The greatest tower, a black glass spear, grew from an island of rock. A bridge, narrow, swaying, spanned over the crashing sea to connect it to the city on the cliffs.

She thought she heard weeping, war cries, and inhuman screams, the clash of steel to steel, the thunder of hooves.

Though it made her heart pound, she moved closer, saw swirls of light, explosions of it.

Was she supposed to go through, leave this wonderful place for one of weeping and war?

Why would she? Why would anyone?

Still, she found herself drawn closer as the dragon calls turned thunderous and the fall of water rocked the ground.

The dragon winged away to join the others. She tried to call him back but how could he hear over the din?

Then in the stream, in a pool of pale green, she saw the gleam of red and gold. For an instant she feared the dragon had fallen in, drowned, but he circled above her head, those gold eyes watchful.

A stone, she realized, big as a baby's fist, with dozens of smaller ones glinting on the gold links of the chain. And the clasp, clear through the water, a dragon in flight.

Someone had lost it; someone had dropped it. Anyone could see it was important. She'd climb down, wade through, and retrieve it.

As she inched her way down the bank, the air began to pulse, to beat like a heart. It seemed the central stone pulsed as well.

The moss-covered trees whipped in a rising wind. Lightning flashed, so strong, so fierce, the world went white for an instant. And the following clap of thunder stole her breath.

A storm, she thought. No one sensible walked in the woods during a storm, or reached into water when lightning cracked.

She'd come back later. She'd go home now, where it was warm and dry and safe, and leave it to someone else to find the pendant.

But if she just reached down, reached out, she might be able to snag the gold chain and . . .

She tumbled. Instead of into a shallow pool, she fell what seemed like fathoms deep, deep into the pale green water.

She tried to kick to the surface, but her hand met a wall, solid as steel.

She swam right, met another. Left, yet another, and realized she was trapped in some kind of box under the water. She saw the sky overhead, the fury of the storm that broke with blackening skies, flashes of lightning.

She beat against the walls until her own blood threaded through the water.

I can't breathe, she thought. Let me out. Let me out.

You are the key. Turn it. Awaken.

As her vision began to dim, she saw a lock. It glittered silver with jewels crusting it.

Too far away, she thought as she flailed.

Her heart banged; her body shook.

Marco yanked her up as her phone alarm beeped.

"Jesus, Breen, Jesus. I thought you were having a seizure."

"I . . . I was drowning. I was in the stream, but it was too deep, and . . . Oh my God, that was awful."

She pushed at her hair as he wrapped around her. "I was in someplace wonderful. It's all blurry now, but I was in a beautiful place, then I was in the water. Something I needed in the water, then I was drowning."

"You're shaking, girl." Shaking himself, he pressed his lips to her forehead. "Breathe it out now."

"I'm okay." She blew out a breath as he kept an arm around her. "The queen of all anxiety dreams, I guess."

"Worst one ever. You were shaking and choking and your eyes were wide open. You scared the ever-fucking crap out of me."

"Me, too." His shoulder, always there for her, made the perfect rest for her head. "Sorry, really. My own fault. I let myself get wound up about the airport, the flight, about every damn thing. I'm going to stop, because wherever the wonderful place was, that's where we're going."

"I'll sure as hell be glad when we get there. Don't do that to me again." He held her shoulders, took a long look at her face. "You're still what my granny used to call *peaked*. You're the poster girl for peaked. You want me to call Sally, tell him you can't make it?"

"Absolutely not. It was just a bad—a really bad—stress dream. Work and Sally's will take my mind off the ten thousand things I can dream up that could go wrong."

"Then go fix your face."

"What's wrong with it? Besides peaked."

"Put some smolder on those long gray eyes, girl. Didn't I show you how? I'm going to go put on something sexy that says your bartender deserves big-ass tips. You get the bathroom first." He walked out, called back to her as he went into his own room to change.

"How was the last day of the old life?"

"It was okay. More than okay. I'm ready for the new one."

Later, when they walked together to the club, Breen slipped an arm around Marco's waist.

He wore a snug red tee that showed off his slim build and gym-fit arms, and matched his belt, his high-tops.

The color made her think of the dream, but she shoved it aside.

She had reason to know she wasn't the only one with some anxiety.

"Do you not want to talk about going over to say goodbye to your mom and dad?"

"What's to say?" He shrugged. "We were all polite. My dad told me to have a good trip, then went down to his workshop. My mom gave me a Coke, told me how there were lots of churches in Ireland and she hoped I'd spend some time in some of them. She still believes I can pray away the gay."

"I'm sorry."

"Hey, we were polite, so that's something. Since I knew that wouldn't happen with my brother, I didn't go by to see him. I talked to my sister—she was swamped at work, but we had a good talk."

"You can always count on Keisha." She squeezed him as they walked. "We're the family misfits, Marco, just like always. I'm feeling okay about that. You always have, but I'm getting there, and even kind of liking it. And tomorrow, when we get on the plane, nobody knows us. We can be whoever we want to be."

"What's your choice?"

"I work for MI6, so I can't talk about it."

"That's a good one. I'm a young, billionaire philanthropist songwriting sensation who's having a secret affair with a certain hot music and movie star."

"Who would that be?"

"Can't say, because secret. But his name rhymes with Moodacris."

"As an agent for MI6, I can decipher your clever code. He is hot."

They turned toward the club, and Marco paused at the sign in the glitter frame posted next to the door. "Did Sally say anything about a private party?"

"No. Huh. Well, tips are always excellent with the privates."

They went inside. A club full of people let out a cheer.

Breen thought it looked like St. Patrick's Day—one of the many holidays Sally revered—had exploded.

Shamrocks, rainbows, winged faeries, leprechauns—not a single Irish cliché missed.

She heard Marco say, "Holy shit," and let out what was definitely a giggle.

Derrick Lacross, Sally's smoking-hot longtime love, headed toward them with a glass of champagne in each hand. He wore a green leather vest over his very impressive pecs and a tiny, adorably ridiculous little leprechaun hat cocked over his surfer-streaky blond mane.

"You didn't think we'd let you leave without a send-off, did you?"

He handed them both champagne, grabbed another from a tray, then turned to the club full of people.

When he raised his glass and everyone shouted, "*Sláinte!*" Breen let out a giggle of her own.

"This is amazing," Breen managed. "This is just amazing."

"We haven't even started. Drink up, my children."

Irish music blasted out of the speakers as Sally, his short, spiky hair dyed green for the occasion, glided over. *Glided* suited, as he wore a long, sparkling white dress and fluttering green wings.

"As if I'd ask you to work the night before you leave." He rolled his eyes before he gave them both cheek kisses. "You"—he handed Marco a high-crowned black hat with a shiny green band—"go eat, drink, and be merry. And you"—he took Breen's hand—"come with me."

"Sally." Marco moved in for a hard hug. "You're the best. Man, you and Derrick are the best."

"No question of that. Your sister had a meeting, but she'll be here in about an hour."

"Really? That's—that's just great."

"Now you run along with Derrick. Breen's not quite ready for party time."

Keeping a grip on Breen's hand, Sally wove through the crowd. "She'll be back, ladies and gentlemen. Enjoy, enjoy." He waved his free hand as if parting the sea. And some clever soul put a flute of champagne in it.

"Sally, this is the best surprise ever, and so sweet of you. So sweet."

"Oh, you know me, any excuse for a party." He led her backstage, into the communal dressing room. "But you and Marco are special to me, to Derrick.

"Now." He walked to one of the costume racks. "We're going to get your party on."

He pulled out a dress—short, as green as his hair. The deep vee in the back dipped to the waist.

"It's beautiful, but—"

"It's yours. Derrick, who obviously has exquisite taste in all things, picked it out for you."

"You bought me a dress."

"A party dress, which, despite your windfall, you haven't bought for yourself. And shoes, which I—also with exquisite taste—selected."

He held out a pair in glittering gold with open toes and ankle straps.

"Those heels are really high."

"You can handle them. You can handle anything. Now strip down, girl. The party's started without us."

Since the music, the voices, the laughter all pulsed against the walls of the dressing room, she couldn't argue.

Breen took off her shoes, her T-shirt, shimmied out of her pants.

"Lose the bra, sweetie. It only makes me sad."

Breen stood in her plain white bra, her practical white cotton panties. "No bra?"

"The dress has self-support, but your girls are young and perky anyway—and that sad bra deserves a decent burial. Flaunt your girls while you've got them."

"Okay. One more first for me."

She took it off, wiggled into the dress. She lifted her arm so Sally could deal with the side zip. "It fits."

"In every single way. Sit. Shoes."

She sat, slipped them on, struggled a bit with the straps. "You invited Marco's parents."

"It would've been rude not to."

"They declined. So did my mother when you invited her."

Sally knelt down to help Breen with the straps. "It's their loss. It hurts my heart to see people lucky enough to have beautiful children, inside and out, who can't bring themselves to accept those children for who they are."

Sally patted Breen's foot. "Girl, take it from an old queen: be who you are and the hell with the rest."

"You're not old," Breen said, and made Sally laugh.

"And you need a pedicure. Get some color on those pretty toes."

"I'll get one in Ireland."

"And buy some pretty underwear, girl." Before Breen could object, Sally hooked a finger in the discarded bra's strap, flung it away. "What are you going to do when you find some Irish hottie and he sees that mess?"

"I think I'd better find myself before I think about any Irish hotties."

"You're a smart woman. Find what makes Breen happy with Breen, then move to the rest."

"I love you, Sally."

"Oh, my baby girl, I love you, too. Now stand up, take a look at you."

She saw a woman with fire-red hair cascading in curls wearing a bold green dress that showed a great deal of leg standing in shoes fit for a princess.

"I look . . . sort of sophisticated."

"Straight lines, no frills, that's what suits you." Sally circled a finger in the air. "Give us a twirl."

"I might break my ankle."

"You've got better balance than you think."

She did the twirl, caught a glimpse of the back of the dress. Said, "Oh, wow."

"That's one sexy back you got there, girl." Sally put her hands on Breen's shoulders, smiled nearly cheek to cheek. "And there you are, Breen Siobhan Kelly."

"Even when you're not wearing wings, you're my fairy godmother, Sally."

"My favorite purpose of being a fairy. Now grab that champagne and let's let everybody get a load of you."

That night, Breen slept the sleep of the happily exhausted with no stress dreams, her new dress and shoes packed for Ireland.

All the stress tumbled back the next day. She reconfirmed all her reconfirmations of all her bookings, rechecked the contents of her bags. Studied her passport, looking for any possible flaws.

Then she harangued Marco to be sure he had everything in place. "You're sure you stopped the mail?"

"I stopped the mail, even though we hardly get any. And I took any perishables in the kitchen—also hardly any—over to Gracie across the hall. And yes, I gave her a key so she can water the couple of plants we've got, turn the lights off and on sporadically in case somebody wants to rob us of basically jack shit."

"And you put your euros in a safe place?"

"Yeah, yeah. Including the five hundred Sally and Derrick gave me last night."

"What? They gave you five hundred euros?"

"They wouldn't take no. I'm supposed to use part of it to take you to a nice dinner so you can wear your new dress."

"That's so . . . them."

"I got more if you've finished freaking out, because it's starting to make me freak out."

"What more?"

"We're taking a limo to the airport."

"Marco, we can't waste money on a limo."

"We're not. The gang at Sally's got it done. You know Reno's brother drives a limo. They worked it out. And he's going to be here in an hour, so I'm going to take a shower and get my I'm-a-world-class-traveler on. Is that what you're wearing on the plane?"

She looked down at her black yoga pants, the simple black sweater.

"We're going to try to sleep on the plane. This is comfortable and practical."

"It works. Makes you look like you do this all the time. But change the black shoes for those red kicks I talked you into. Just a little flash."

"Fine."

She changed her shoes, checked the ID cards on her luggage, got the black jacket. She'd checked the weather at Shannon Airport: sixty degrees and cloudy—40 percent chance of rain at the time of their arrival.

Marco—jeans, olive green T-shirt—looked out the window.

"Woo! Big black limo pulling up."

"Oh God, oh God, it's time! We need to get the bags down."

That equaled a process, due to the steps. By the time they got down three flights with one of Breen's suitcases, her backpack, and Marco's suitcase and carry-on, the uniformed driver walked up.

For the life of her, Breen couldn't remember Reno's—an amazing Tina Turner—brother's name.

"Hold on there, let me get some of that. Frazier," he said. "Got your ride outside."

"And it's a fine ride," Marco added.

"That she is."

"I'm sorry, there are a couple more bags upstairs."

"Don't you worry about it," Frazier told Breen. "Let's get these loaded up. We'll get the lady settled in the car, brother, and you and I will get the rest."

It was like a dream—the long car, the smooth leather, a white rosebud in a clear vase. Frazier offered her a bottle of water. She used it to down the Dramamine she didn't know if she needed.

When they glided away from the curb, and Marco played with the lights, the music system, she looked out the window.

She was leaving Philadelphia for three months. Everything and everyone she knew was here. And—if she stuck with the plan—after two weeks, Marco would come home.

She'd be on her own, really on her own, for the first time in her life.

No parent telling her what to do, no best friend beside her, no Sally to lean on. No supervisor, no job, no schedule.

She could find work if she needed to fill time. Her father had been an Irish citizen at the time of her birth, so she qualified for dual citizenship. And that meant she could work in Ireland if . . .

"Stop worrying," Marco ordered. "You're bringing yourself down."

"No, I was just thinking if I wanted to, I could work part-time over there. Maybe in a pub—really soak it up. Or a shop. Or a garden center. I'd like to learn how to plant and grow things. I think my father grew up on a farm. I think. So many of the stories he told me get mixed up in my head, but I think he grew up on a farm."

"They got plenty of them."

"Anyway, I'm not worrying." Absolutely not, she swore to herself. "I'm nervous, but that's different. Aren't you nervous?"

"Nope. Juiced. You and me, Breen, we've barely been out of Philly our whole lives. And look what we're doing. I'm really grateful you're giving me this chance."

"I couldn't do it without you. Literally. I'd never get on the plane."

"Get ready, because we're nearly at the airport."

Her hand reached automatically for her purse, and Marco closed his over hers.

"You've got everything, honey, including your passport. We're cruising in a freaking limo. Savor it."

"You want to savor?" She took out her phone, snuggled in next to him. "Limo selfie time."

"Send it to me. I'm Instagramming it, tweeting it, too. Hashtag BFFs, hashtag on our way, hashtag—"

"That's enough," Breen said with a laugh.

"Hey, you need to do a travel journal—day by day. We'll put up a blog."

"I don't know how to do a blog."

"You know how to write. I know how to set up a blog." He slid on the Wayfarers he'd splurged on. "We just need a name for it. You have to keep it up after I leave, so— Shit we're here. I'll think about it."

If the limo equaled another world, the airport ranked as another universe. So many people, so much noise, so many signs.

They checked in, and she tried not to panic when she watched her bags ride away on the belt and she was left with her backpack and little purse.

Lines everywhere! Getting through security brought on more low-grade panic, but nobody got arrested.

They followed the signs for the first-class lounge as directed.

"So many people going somewhere, or coming back from somewhere."

"So are we, going somewhere." Grinning, bopping a little, Marco grabbed her hand, swung their arms. "Maybe we should get a drink, or a snack. We got the time."

"Let's just check in to the lounge first. That's what they said to do." She didn't know if she could eat anyway, but knew she wanted somewhere quiet just to settle herself.

She saw whole families—babies, toddlers, grandparents. Business types strode along, checking their phones. Some people dozed in chairs at gates. A lot of people looked bored.

How could anyone be bored when they were about to fly?

She saw people watching TV, reading books, reading their tablets. She saw . . .

The man with the silver hair.

That couldn't be, but she saw him standing in line at one of the gates.

"Marco—"

"There it is, there's the lounge."

"Marco, I saw . . ."

But he was gone.

"Nothing," she mumbled.

Her imagination, stress, sensory overload.

They walked through the marked doors and into the quiet, into the smell of citrus. A white orchid bloomed on a glossy counter where a woman sat smiling.

"Good evening. May I see your boarding passes?"

"I don't know if we're in the right place," Breen said as she fumbled them out.

"You certainly are. We'll announce when it's time to board. Go right in."

They walked into a large room, another quiet one where people sat in chairs or at tables, enjoying drinks or snacks, paging through magazines.

Not at all sure what to do, Breen sat, looked wide-eyed at Marco.

He looked wide-eyed back at her. "People live like this, Breen. Think about it! They got shrimp up there—did you see that? They got cocktail shrimp. I'm getting us some."

A uniformed man stopped. "Would you like a drink?"

"I . . ."

"Can we get champagne?" Marco asked.

"Of course."

She drank champagne, ate cocktail shrimp. And didn't blink when Marco put a couple of apples in his carry-on along with a bag of chips, a Coke, a bottle of water.

The adventure begins, she thought, and realized she could do a daily journal. It could be fun—and she'd want these memories to look back on.

Two glasses of champagne quelled the nerves so she felt only a dreamy eagerness as their flight was called. She learned first class meant they basically walked right onto the plane.

And there discovered their seats were like futuristic pods.

"We got our own TVs, girl, and a shitload of movies—free! And lookie here. These chairs go all the way back like beds. Hey, we got these cool bags full of stuff. Toothbrushes and face mist and sleep masks. Socks! How cool is all this?"

"It doesn't seem real."

"It's real as fuck. Selfie."

As he pulled out his phone a flight attendant came by. "Can I get you some drinks before we leave the gate?"

"Champagne," Breen said and beamed. "We're drinking champagne all the way."

In the terminal, the man with the silver hair watched the plane pull away from the gate. And sighed.

His task here, complete and successful, meant his time had come to an end.

He'd miss Philadelphia, and the pretzels, the colors, the great groups of people.

And still, he'd be happy to be home again.

Not quite yet, he reminded himself. Another stop to make, another task to complete.

He strolled away, joined the throngs coming and going.

And, turning a corner, vanished on his way to the next stop.

CHAPTER FIVE

Breen discovered something. She liked flying. She hadn't expected to, had prepared herself to spend hours pushing down nerves.

Instead, she found the entire experience amazing. She had food, drink, entertainment, and Marco. More, she loved looking out the window. Nothing but night, but she imagined the ocean below, ships plying the waters, little islands floating, and all while she streamed through the air.

Flying first class may not become her routine—she had to be practical—but she decided she'd no longer feel tied to the ground. Maybe, just maybe, once a year she'd pick a spot on the map, pack her bags, and go.

Wouldn't that be incredible?

She hadn't expected to sleep either, but the wine, a movie with Marco, the quiet hum of engines did its work. With her earbuds plugged into her playlist of Irish ballads—might as well get in the mode—she lowered her seat back all the way, snuggled into the provided blanket and pillow, and slept.

She dreamed of green fields and blue lakes, of thick forests and rising hills. She dreamed herself riding a red dragon over those fields and lakes and forests, and dreamed so deeply she felt the wind rushing over her face.

She dreamed of a stone cottage by a stream where the woods crept in at its back and a garden rioted at its feet. And nearby, as the dragon flew, a farm with green fields and stone fences where a man plowed brown rivers through the green behind a muscular brown horse.

Deep, so deep was the dream that she heard his voice as he sang of love and loss.

She dreamed and flew through the night where the red dragon sailed a sky gasping with stars. And two moons, one full and white, the other a glowing half slice, watched over the world.

As the sun rose over the green hills, spreading light in reds and golds, she flew down. She landed by the lake, by the man who stood, a sword at his side, a staff with a gleaming red stone at its tip in one hand.

In the other he held the reins of a black horse. Hair, black like his horse, fell waving beyond the collar of his shirt, with a thin braid woven in to stream down the left side. His eyes, green as the hills, bored into hers.

"Dreams aren't doing. Awake and take, or sleep on and show his sacrifice means nothing to you."

Fury and shame, thick ropes, snapped into a hard knot inside her. Overhead, the dawn sky roiled black. The wind lashed, knife sharp. Lightning cracked through the black with a bolt that landed inches from the man's feet.

Neither the man nor the horse flinched.

But he smiled. "Awake then, and prove me wrong. Awake, Breen Siobhan O'Ceallaigh, and be."

She woke, groggy, disoriented. She swore she could smell the ozone, the grass. She lay still in the darkened cabin trying to hang on to the details of the dream.

Write it down, she decided.

She pushed up, switched on the reading light, dragged out her laptop. Maybe her brain still had a curtain of fog, but she'd write down everything she remembered. All in all, she thought it a wonderful dream, a fun dream. Even the man—soldier, she wondered, king?—had been fascinating. She wondered what he represented in her subconscious.

She could figure out the rest easily enough—the dragon grown up from her other dream, flying, just as she was flying now. The freedom of it. Her admittedly postcard image of Ireland.

The two moons? Maybe representing she'd left one place (world) for another. Who knew?

The cottage equaled the one she'd booked in Galway. The farm because she'd talked about her father growing up on one. The farmer? Her father? He'd sang, and her father had sung. An Irish tenor, like the farmer, but no, not her father's voice. She knew Eian Kelly's voice well, as she had recordings and had listened to them when her mother wasn't around.

But it was probably representative.

The angry man? Tall, muscular—but not bulked like Derrick, for instance. Those sharp green eyes, the black hair—long, a little wavy, with a braid down one side. Outfitted, she remembered, sort of like *Game of Thrones* or a King Arthur movie. The staff—power, right? Like the sword was warrior or soldier. And the stone, like the one in her other dream.

The storm, probably representative of her own temper in being told what to do. She was so beyond being told what to do.

Yes, all in all, a pretty cool dream, and worth documenting.

And so was the journey, she thought now. She didn't know about the whole blogging thing, but she opened a new document and after a moment's thought, titled it:

Finding Me

She wrote for nearly an hour as others in the cabin began to stir, as other lights came on. The flight attendants began to make the rounds, murmuring voices offering coffee, breakfast.

So she read over and edited—jeez, five pages!—while she drank coffee.

She took her complimentary toiletry kit and her own into the bathroom. When she got back, Marco sat up with his own coffee, reading her journal.

"Hey."

"You left it right here. This is really good, Breen."

"I haven't finished, you know, polishing it."

"It's good. It's like, conversational, funny, and it really gets the details. It's just what you want for a blog. I'm setting it up."

"Marco—"

"And I ordered us omelets, bacon for you, sausage for me. I thought about Bloody Marys or mimosas, but we're going to be driving pretty soon. Carla the flight attendant said we should be landing in about forty-five minutes."

He worked on her laptop as he spoke. "What do you want for your domain name?"

"I don't—"

"Let's keep it simple. BreenSiobhan.com—we'll keep your last name off it for now. I'm setting it up so it keeps your personal details private, and you'll be self-hosting. I'll help you with that. It'll send you updates when you get comments and all that. We're going with simple and classy for the look, and we'll keep it mobile-device friendly."

He liked to play with tech, she thought. So she'd let him. "Nobody's going to read it."

"Everybody at Sally's will. It's a great way for them to keep up with what we're doing, seeing, am I right? And for all of us when I go back home."

He smiled at her. "You write it, I do the tech stuff. I'll show you how to upload photos, upload your daily journal. If it's not fun for you after a couple weeks, you ditch it. You want to pick a font?"

"You pick." She wasn't going to worry about it. She'd consider the entire thing long postcards to friends.

"Great. I'm going to send a group email with a link once I have it set."

Once he had, she decided it was time to start worrying about getting through the airport, getting to the car rental place, actually driving. Though Marco had lost rock, paper, scissors and would take the wheel first.

But she looked out the window on the descent, and through the clouds saw the green fields and hills of her dream. She saw the patchwork of that impossible green with the richest of browns, the deepest of golds all glowing under a somber sky of pale gray.

Something in her heart sang, a note so sweet and clear her eyes stung from it.

"Oh, Marco, look!"

"I am." More, he leaned in with his phone, angling for photos. "It's like the pictures, but it's real. It's really real, Breen."

"I dreamed about it, about all of this. I wrote it down."

"It wasn't in the blog."

"No, I wrote it separate from that. I'll show you later. We need to get ready. We need to—"

"We are ready." He took her hand.

It wasn't so hard. Follow the signs, show your passport—again, not arrested—retrieve the luggage, then haul that over to where they'd booked a car.

Since Marco would take the wheel, he went off to get the car, and Breen took the luggage trolley outside for her first gulp of Irish air.

It was different, softer, as was the light. The rain held off, but she felt it in the air, the damp touch of it. The voices, some American and some with that lovely lilt that made her think of her father.

Would she find him? Would he be happy to see her? Would he tell her why, why, he'd stayed away so long?

She wanted to forgive him. She hoped, one day, she could forgive her mother.

But today, she told herself, today is for me. I opened a door, and today I walked all the way through.

She watched the little black car creep its way up, spotted Marco through the windshield. He looked like a man carefully, meticulously defusing a nuclear device.

She thought: Better him than me.

He stopped, got out. "Made it this far. No loss of life."

"Is it scary?"

"Yeah, some. Good thing it's not too far to the castle. I said 'castle.'" He grinned as they began to load the luggage. "The guy helped me program the GPS, so we've got the directions."

"I have the map—and I printed out directions."

"So we're covered." He started to get back in, realized he was on the wrong side. "I was being a gentleman, opening the door for you."

"Yeah, we'll both believe that." She got in, strapped in. Took a deep breath. "We can go really slow."

"Just yell if I screw up. No, don't yell. Calmly say: Marco, my friend, you are now on the wrong fucking side of the road. Cut that shit out."

"Got it."

"Okay, here we go." He started the car, grinned at her. "Let's go storm the castle!"

He did okay—better than, Breen thought. She had to stop herself from taking big eye gulps of the scenery, and keep her eyes on the road in case she had to tell him to cut that shit out.

But he did fine, even on the scary circles—roundabouts, she corrected.

"I'm driving in Ireland, girl."

"Yeah. Eyes on the road. We're almost there."

"You know, you've got to do it next time. That was the deal."

"Lots to do at the castle. Maybe we'll just stay there for three days."

"No chance. We're going to pubs, we're going shopping. We're going to see stuff."

"There's stuff to— Oh, that's Bunratty Castle. It's really close to where we're staying. I could manage that. I read about it. We can take a tour, see stuff, shop. I don't know if there's a pub. It's all so beautiful, Marco."

"Never seen anything like it outside of movies and books."

When he turned at the signpost for Dromoland, trees, great, huge, gorgeous trees, smothered both sides of the road. They wound through when it opened up to green again, with a pond on one side where ducks waddled.

As Breen let out a gasp, Marco stopped the car.

"I gotta stop. God, Breen, that's a damn castle. An honest-to-God castle."

Proud and beautiful, it ruled the rise with its majestic spread of gray stone, with its spears of towers, its turrets and battlements. Its flags waved in the wind.

"I saw pictures," she said. "I researched, and I still didn't really believe it would look like this."

"This is a day, Breen. This is a damn day."

"We're going to be too early to check in, but they'll take the luggage and store it. It's got acres and acres we can walk."

He inched the car along. "Could use some walking. Looks like it's going to rain, but that won't bother us."

"No, it won't bother us."

As they pulled up in front, a man in uniform walked down to open the car door for Breen. "Welcome to Dromoland. Are you checking in?"

"Yes. Yes, we're checking in."

It couldn't have gone smoother, Breen thought. Everyone was so friendly, so helpful. The grounds she walked with Marco were beyond magical.

When the rain came, and decided it meant it, they walked back, wet and happy, to explore the castle.

They found suits of armor, simmering fires in stone hearths, a couple of pretty shops, and dozens of brochures on the area that Breen snapped up.

They had a drink in the bar, a light lunch before someone came to escort them to their rooms.

Lovely rooms, Breen thought, with big beds and snuggly throws, with whiskey for those who'd want it and views of the hills.

"I am the king of the castle," Marco said, and bounced on the bed in his room.

"Okay, Your Majesty, the plan is unpack, then an hour's nap. We're following the rules of battling jet lag. We've had the walk, the food, now one hour's sleep. Adding in time to shower, change, blah, blah, we meet up at . . . five fifteen."

"Cocktail time. So the bar."

"That'll work, and we'll plan out what we want to do tomorrow." She walked to the door. "Unpack first, and set an alarm."

He saluted her. "Roger that. Hey, do the *Die Hard*. Take off your shoes and make fists with your toes."

She walked to her own room, simply wandered the space, touched fabric, furniture. She unpacked the suitcase she'd earmarked for this part of her journey. She considered a shower before her nap, but remembered her hair.

So she stretched out on the big bed under the soft throw, and with her face turned toward the window, drifted off.

There were dreams, but when her alarm beeped, they blurred. She pushed herself up in bed, decided the jet lag advice might not always work.

However lovely the room, it still felt like the middle of the night to her body. She tried the *Die Hard* thing before she dragged that body up and into the shower. She yearned for a Coke, something to jump-start her system, and remembered the minibar.

Wrapped in the hotel robe—and what a luxury that was—her hair like wet ropes, she opened the bottle, drank half of it.

Better, she decided. Definitely better.

It took her until five thirty to make herself presentable and find the bar again. There Marco sat, flirting with the sandy-haired bartender.

"Here's my best girl. Isn't she a looker, Sean?"

"She is indeed. Good evening to you, miss, and welcome."

"Thanks. Sorry I'm late."

"Worth the wait."

"And what can I get for you?" Sean asked her.

She eyed Marco's beer, knew she couldn't drink a pint of anything. She'd float away.

"Kir Royale," Marco decreed. "Breen looks like a woman who should be drinking Kir Royales."

"Will that suit you?"

"I've never had one."

"Well then, you must, of course. And Marco tells me it's your first time in Ireland, though your father was born here."

"Yes. It's as beautiful as he always told me. He was from Galway."

"Ah, a lovely place is Galway."

"Sean's from right here in Clare, and he's given me some places we need to see. Meanwhile." Marco took out his phone. "You've got twenty-two comments and eighty-four views on your blog."

"Oh, I do not."

"Look for yourself." Smug, he passed her the phone. "Breen's started a blog, about the trip, and life in general."

"Is that the truth? I'd love to read it myself, if you'd send me a link."

"Glad to."

Sean set a flute in front of her, a red-gold liquid with raspberries swimming in the bubbles.

"It's mostly the usual suspects."

"But not all—not in comments or views."

Reading, she picked up the flute, sipped. Looked up. "I definitely like this drink. Where's it been all my life?"

"Today's the first day of the rest of it."

Marco tapped his glass to hers.

She had two, stuck with water over fish and chips. They took another walk, then watched a family from Baltimore play snooker.

"I'm fading, Marco, and by some miracle I've made it until ten thirty."

"We could have a nightcap."

"I've had more to drink in the last few days than I do in a year. Besides, you can go back and flirt with Sean without the third wheel."

"Girl, he's adorable, and straight as a ruler. I was softening him up for you."

"Not looking for a flirt or a fling."

"Why do you make me so sad?"

"I'm calling it." She stifled a yawn. "Remember, breakfast at eight, then we head out. We're packing a lot in tomorrow."

"And you're driving."

"To. You drive back."

"I got it. I guess I'll call it, too."

As they walked back to their rooms, she dipped her head toward his shoulder. "It's been a really good first day."

"And don't you forget to write about it—push hard on my exceptional driving."

"Naturally. And tomorrow we end with dinner and music at a pub. Who knows? Maybe somebody'll remember my father. He used to sing in pubs."

"I remember. You said that's how your mother met him."

"Yeah, on a trip with friends when she was in college. Here in Clare, so maybe he still sings around here. Or in Galway."

"I hope we find him, but either way . . ." He walked her to her door. "Remember the name of your blog."

"Finding Me."

"That's the first thing. See you in the a.m."

"Night, Marco."

She woke at four thirty. She stumbled out of bed, grateful she'd left the bathroom light on so she wouldn't run into anything in the dark.

She grabbed her laptop and, taking it back to bed, tried to document the already fading dream.

> I was in a big building, a ruin, I think. Stone walls, windows without glass, some no more than slits. There were carvings on some of the walls and—are they lintels?—over doorways. No doors, just openings into what must have been other rooms.
>
> Some of the walls had niches where something must have stood at some point. I could see the sky overhead—blue—a lot of clouds, but white ones.
>
> Everything echoed so I could hear my own footsteps. But it was more than that. Sort of like there had been voices and they still echoed inside the building.
>
> There were stone markers on the floor, and I think carvings there, too. I can't see them now, but I knew they were graves, like the big stone—coffins?
>
> There was a kind of courtyard surrounded by stone

columns where the grass grew—green and tall with little white stars of wildflowers.

And stone steps, pie-shaped, forming a curve, that led up.

I went up, I don't know why. I wasn't really afraid, but I want to say I could feel the air thrum, I could feel it beat on my skin.

I stepped out, and could see a round tower with a pointed cap, the hills and cottages in the distance. Even smoke rising up from chimneys. Below I saw sheep with their thick wool and black faces grazing on the grass.

And a graveyard with stone markers, and beyond it, beyond the round tower, one of those stone circles. Not like the pictures I've seen of Stonehenge, but much smaller. Beyond it a river snaked toward a bay. The sun was strong enough to dance light over it, like the white starry wildflowers.

It was all beautiful. The wind was in my hair, but warm and soft.

I think I was happy.

Then I watched a rider come. A brown hooded cloak, a white horse with its hindquarters dappled with black. She rode to the graveyard, dismounted. She held flowers. I can't remember if I knew what kind, but I think they were white.

She walked to one of the graves, laid the flowers there, and stood with her head bent.

It felt like intruding, so I started to step back, but then she pushed off her hood. She looked up at me.

She looked like me. Or how I might look when I'm older. And I could see the red stone pendant I'd seen in the forest/waterfall dream around her neck.

She spoke to me. I wish I could remember more clearly, but I think she said something like: You have to look to find. You have to ask to have the answers. You have to awaken to become.

Breen sat back, thought it through. She'd had vivid, unusual dreams as a child. Unicorns, dragons—she'd always had a thing for dragons—dancing in the air with butterflies. She'd dreamed of riding white chargers and faeries, and all the wonderful things her father had wound into his stories.

But that had all faded, even—she thought—before he'd left. Then she'd replaced those fanciful dreams with anxiety dreams. Schoolwork, college courses, teaching.

She found it interesting, even comforting, they'd come back.

Maybe she'd buy a book on dream interpretation.

Since it was still far too early for breakfast, she settled for a Coke, and writing her daily blog.

It was fun to recount the day, the arrival at Shannon, the drive, the castle, all of it. When it satisfied her, she followed Marco's instructions carefully, uploaded some of the pictures, and put it all up.

Out of curiosity she brought up the previous blog, then goggled.

She now had forty-six comments, and two hundred and two views.

More than two hundred people read what she'd written, and forty-six of them had taken the time to comment.

Because it's new, she decided—and Sally spread the word. Still, it was just wonderful.

Hell, in a full week of teaching, she'd been lucky to get that many students to raise their hand in class.

Charged, she changed into workout gear, chose one of her videos to stream.

She knew the castle had a fitness center, but she wasn't ready for that.

Even when she finished, dressed in what she thought of as her Irish adventure wear—boots, jeans, a navy V-neck sweater over a white tee—she had time on her hands.

It was as if every day was a Sunday, only better, as she didn't have a single chore on her list. She grabbed her phone, her key, her crossbody bag, and her jacket and set out on a dawn walk.

The sky, pale, pastel blue, cupped over the hills. It had lovely clouds streaked with roses and reds where the sun topped their rounded tops. Everything smelled fresh and new and possible.

She walked along the paved path, up green rises and stone steps where morning birds sang in the trees. She walked, prizing the quiet and solitude, pausing to take pictures of the castle as the sky brightened, or a tree that looked like something out of a fairy tale.

She found herself at the stables, where a brown horse watched her approach. Since she'd only ridden horses in childhood dreams, she kept a wary distance.

"Hi there. You're very handsome."

She stepped a little closer, and when he blew air out of his nose, she all but heard him think: *Come and pet me.*

But she decided close enough.

"Maybe tomorrow," she told him.

She took his picture, checked the time, and started her walk back imagining what it was like to work in such a place.

She could do that. Maybe she'd apply for a job. After Marco went back, she could think about it. Maybe here, maybe some historic hotel in Galway.

Before she went back, she opted to detour to the walled gardens.

And there her heart simply soared.

A vined archway welcomed her. The beds beside the stone paths simply thrived with flowers. She recognized some, but most were a lovely mystery. She wanted to know more, made a mental note to get a book on flowers as well as dreams.

She could learn to do this, couldn't she? Learn to plant and grow and tend? To make something beautiful. While she watched butterflies flutter and bees buzz by, she bent down or over to sniff.

She smelled sweet and spicy, earthy and light, marveled at the textures and colors, the spreads, the spears. And at the skill and knowledge to create something that looked as if it had grown entirely on its own.

She could learn. She sure as hell knew how to study, as she'd spent her entire life doing just that. She'd study what she wanted to study this time around.

She sat on a bench to soak it all in while clouds, puffy and white as sheep, grazed over the blue. And shook her head at herself.

"Waiting tables in a castle one minute, a gardener the next."

Pretty clearly she didn't know what to do with herself.

She rose, reluctantly, to go back and meet Marco, but paused one last time to take a close-up picture of a luscious spread of deep purple flowers.

Enchanted, she brushed her hand over them.

They vibrated.

She snatched her hand back, imagining angry bees or snakes. Ireland, she reminded herself. No snakes.

But something.

But nothing moved, and everything went so very quiet.

Carefully, she touched her palm to the clump again, felt that odd hum under her skin.

"That's weird, right? It's like . . . it's growing. Even I know it doesn't work that way. Time for coffee," she told herself. "It's obviously time for coffee."

Rubbing her palms together, she walked away.

And didn't see the new flowers spread up from the bed and reach for the light.

CHAPTER SIX

Breen approached driving the way she'd approached oral exams. With terror and determination. Her hands might have clutched the wheel like a woman clutching a life buoy in a raging sea, but she navigated the skinny, twisty roads with steely eyes.

She'd never really been a tourist, so she approached that new designation by diving in headfirst.

She made her list, mapped out the routes. There were ruins to explore and wonder at, the Cliffs of Moher to marvel over. There was the edge of the world to dare at Loop Head, old abbeys and round towers, graveyards.

Lunch in a pub with a peat fire simmering, brown bread and farm butter.

While she didn't find a book on dreams, she found one on flowers when they shopped in Ennis, where baskets of flowers hung and the narrow, winding sidewalks begged to be explored.

She bought a scarf of rainbow colors for Sally, and one of greens and ambers for herself. She ate strawberry gelato in a sugar cone, lit a candle in a beautiful old church that smelled of peace.

When it was her turn behind the wheel again, she managed to drive into the little village of Doolin and park.

"More awesome views," Marco declared. "But before we get out and hike—again—I gotta tell you, Breen, you handle the driving better than me."

"My palms are still sweaty."

"Maybe, but you've got it down."

"You're the most excellent navigator. And still, walking's a big relief."

"Prepare to be relieved."

Out of the car, she lifted her face to the sea breeze before hitching on her battered backpack for the cliff walk. One thing she'd learned on this momentous first full day—she wasn't troubled by heights.

The cliffs speared up, dramatic and sheer above the wild waters of the Atlantic on one side. On the other, the pretty little village spread its color and charm ahead of the green fields and farms.

They walked the trail while the cliffs made their steady rise and the waves crashed.

"Can you imagine seeing this every day?" And she couldn't see enough. "I can't believe you'd ever get used to it."

Gulls streamed, feather white, smoke gray, and called to the wind. With Marco she hiked the gravel path, took the rough flagstone steps, and just stopped to bask and wonder.

"Oh, look at the wildflowers. Wait, I know that one—I think." She nearly reached in her pack for her book, then did a little hip wiggle as she remembered. "Thrift. That's thrift."

She hunkered down to take a photo. "Isn't it amazing how it pushes up through the limestone, so pink and pretty? I swear I'm going to start growing plants—nice potted plants when we get home."

"You figure you'll stay in the apartment?"

She looked up. "Marco, what would I do without you?"

When she straightened up, they walked again. "We could think about finding another place, same neighborhood," she considered. "With a little balcony. Or a garden apartment with a little patio."

"I wondered if you'd think about moving out, maybe getting a house or something."

"A house." She said it like a sigh. She'd never dreamed that big. "I could get a house, with a yard—for a garden. For a dog!"

"Now you're thinking."

"Now I'm thinking. If I get a house, you're coming with me. But you know what? Today's today. And look where we are. God, look at the cliffs! We were over there just a couple hours ago. From here they look like some ancient giant hacked them into being with his axe. It's all drama and ferocity. Then you look that way."

She turned her back to the sea. "And it's so peaceful, all pastoral. Like some quiet painting done in saturated colors."

She rolled her eyes when she realized he'd taken her picture.

Satisfied, he nudged his Wayfarers back down. "That one's head-lining the blog."

They hiked across fields, along rises, and she soaked up every-thing.

The sun beamed so bright, so clear, she took off her jacket to tie it around her waist.

"You can see for miles! Those islands out there."

"Aran Islands," Breen said when Marco pointed. "I read people there still speak Irish, and some plow the land with horses. I think I dreamed about it. Did I tell you?"

She told him about the dream of the forest and the fields and cot-tages, and the one where she rode a flying dragon.

"How come I don't dream cool shit like that? I've gotta work on it. It's like a dream, all of this. I mean, who'da thought, Breen, you and me, hiking cliffs anywhere, much less here."

"We're going to start traveling more, doing more. It may not be castles and the Wild Atlantic Way, but we're getting out of the rut, Marco."

"I'm for it." He held out his pinky. "Breen and Marco see the world. Or at least the East Coast. We can get ourselves a car next summer, drive up to Maine or down to Key West or anywhere in between. But no more just working and thinking about doing and going."

"No more."

On the cliffs, above the crash of waves, they pinky swore.

They logged a solid five miles by the time they looped back to the village.

"How're your boots holding up?" Marco asked her.

"Fine." She glanced over, narrowed her eyes. "Yours?"

He had the grace to look sheepish. "I maybe might've worked up a blister, and yeah, yeah, I should've used that glide stuff you offered me."

"I have moleskin in my pack."

"Course you do."

She just pointed at the car. "Sit, take off the boots and socks. We'll fix you up."

"It's not bad. I just started feeling it in the last mile."

He had indeed worked up a small blister on each foot.

"This'll cushion them," she told him as she applied the moleskin. "And since it's pub time, you'll be sitting down awhile."

"I'm ready for pub time." He wiggled his toes before sliding on his socks. "It's sure nice going into a bar and not working it. Music, too, right?"

"Absolutely music, too. And I'll be designated driver."

"It's my turn."

She just shook her head. "I've still got the keys."

She'd researched the pubs and figured they could do a crawl or settle into one—with her sticking to soft drinks and water.

She wanted the atmosphere, the music, but also wanted to try for the long shot. Doolin was famed for its traditional music, and her father had made his living playing that music.

Wouldn't he have, at some point, played here?

He might play here still, she thought.

When they walked into the pub, Breen decided they'd made the perfect choice. It held a long bar of dark wood backed by an old stone wall where shelves held a myriad of bottles and jugs.

Most of the stools there were already occupied, as were the scatter of low tables. The music of a bright fiddle played out of the speakers as people ate, drank, talked.

A low fire burned, red at its heart—a peat fire, which made it all the more perfect. On the wall crowded old photos, signs for Guinness and Harp and Jameson.

It smelled just as she thought an Irish pub should, of peat smoke and beer and food fried in the kitchen.

One of the waitstaff, a woman with stick-straight black hair in a bouncing tail, paused on her way to the bar with a tray.

"Are you after a table then?"

"Yes, please."

"Take your pick, but for the one in the corner there. That's for the musicians."

They grabbed a two-top.

"It's kinda like a movie, right?"

Breen could only grin. Lunch at a pub had been wonderful, but this? A perfect cap to a perfect day.

"It's everything I wanted."

"You gotta have one beer," he insisted. "It's like sacrilege or something otherwise. We're going to eat, stick around for music. We probably won't drive back for hours."

"A half pint," she agreed. "My dad drank mostly Smithwick's, so I'll have a glass of that."

The same waitress came back to them.

"And how's it all going then?"

"As good as it gets," Marco told her.

"That's lovely to hear. Americans, are you?"

"Philadelphia."

"Philadelphia," she repeated, and made it sound as exotic as the cliffs. "I've not been there, but been to America twice. Once to New York City to visit cousins, and to Wyoming."

"Wyoming?"

The waitress smiled at Breen. "I wanted to see cowboys, and so I did. A vast place is Wyoming. And so I'm Kate, and I'll be serving you this evening." She handed them menus. "Can I get you some drinks?"

"I'll have a pint of Guinness, and my friend wants a half pint of Smithwick's. I bartend at home," Marco continued.

"Do you now? Well then, we may call on you to pull some pints once the evening rolls on. The Cobblers Three are popular, and will fill the place before we're done. You're fortunate to have come early enough for a table. I'll get those drinks for you."

Marco, being Marco, picked up the menu. "That hike gave me a serious appetite."

"Waking up in the morning gives you a serious appetite." But she glanced at the menu herself. "I'm going to try the shepherd's pie."

"I'm going for the mussels for a starter. Want to split?"

"Have you ever known me to eat a mussel?"

"More for me. And they've got Irish lasagna. What makes it Irish? I need to find out. Man, I haven't checked your blog since lunch."

While he did, Breen just sighed into the moment.

"Breen, you got sixteen more comments on yesterday's, and you're up to fifty-eight on today's."

"Really? What do they say?" She scooted her chair over to read with him. "They really seem to like it."

"Damn right. Wait till they read what you write about today. What are you going to write about today?"

"I—I don't know. It's getting real."

"Don't start." He knocked his knuckles lightly on her forehead. "Just keep it up. I like how my best friend's a blogger."

"A couple of blog posts don't make a blogger. Let's see how it goes when I've got two weeks."

The waitress brought their beers, nodded toward the menus. "Have you decided what you'll have?"

"I'll try the shepherd's pie."

"You can't go wrong with it. And you, sir?"

"I'll start with the mussels, then go for the Irish lasagna."

"There's a treat. My mother's recipe, cobbled from my two grannies. Hers being from Italy, and my da's from right here in Clare."

"Your mom's the cook?" Marco asked.

"She is, yes, along with my brother Liam. The pub was my grandparents', you see, and now my parents have it. It's family."

"Speaking of family, Breen's father used to play in pubs like this. Maybe even here."

"Is that the truth?"

She'd intended to ease into all of that, but Marco liked to wade straight in.

"Yes. He was born in Galway, but I know he played here in Clare, as that's where he met my mother. It was all before I was born, so you wouldn't know. But he might've played here."

"My father might remember."

"I don't know the name of the band. He's Eian Kelly."

"If a man played in Clare, he likely played in Doolin. If he played in Doolin, he likely played in Sweeney's. I'll put your orders in for you."

Marco hefted his beer, tapped it against Breen's glass. "To another best day ever."

"Who wouldn't drink to that?" She took a sip of beer to prove it. "Do you want to hear what I've mapped out for tomorrow?"

He shook his head. "Still into today. You can surprise me. I never thought about coming here, you know? Like when I made my if-I-could-go-anywhere lists, it was usually Paris or Rome or Maui. But this really hits it, Breen. Who knew?"

She had—for herself—as long as she could remember. "I never thought I'd go anywhere. Just work through the day, the week, the year. And maybe one day find somebody, get married, have kids. Then we'd go places, pile everybody in the minivan and drive to Disney World or the beach, wherever, so they didn't feel so stuck in one place."

She looked around, families at tables, friends at the bar, the fire simmering. "If I ever have kids, I'd bring them here. It's heritage, and I'd want them to have that. I'm glad I'm taking mine back."

She glanced up as a sandy-haired man with a barrel chest and bright blue eyes stopped by the table.

"I'm Tom Sweeney. My daughter tells me you're Eian Kelly's girl."

"Yes. I— You know my father?"

"He and his mates played right over there." He gestured to the corner. "Sorcery they called themselves, and that's what they were with the music. Too many years ago to count," he said with a wide smile. "And how he is then, your da?"

"I don't actually know. He and my mother . . ."

"Ah, that's a sad thing to hear. And lost touch, have you?"

"Yes. I'm hoping to find him while I'm here, or at least find out more from people who knew him."

"Well, I can tell you a story or two if you like."

"I really would."

"I'll get you a chair." Marco popped right up.

"Thanks for that. Darling!" he called to his daughter. "Bring your old da a pint."

"I'm Marco, this is Breen." Marco pulled a chair over.

"More than pleased to meet you. I can see him in you," Tom said as he sat. "Your hair, bold red, your eyes, soft gray. That's Eian Kelly all over. Are you musical?"

"Not very."

"Your da never met an instrument he couldn't play, and like a magician, he was. Strong, clear voice as well. Close of age I'd say we were when I tended the bar here and he and his mates played." He grabbed his daughter's hand as she brought over his beer. "I have this one, her two brothers, and her sister because of Eian Kelly."

Marco grinned at Tom, at his daughter. "This is going to be a good story."

"Oh, he's no lack of them." Kate kissed her father on the top of his head, then went back to work.

"Well, I'll tell you. I was shy in those days. Not of people, but of girls. Never could get my tongue untangled around a pretty girl. And there was one in particular I had such a pining for. Sarah Maria Nero with her raven hair and gypsy eyes. Should she walk into the pub or should I see her on the street or in the market I could barely remember my own name much less speak to her.

"And then." He paused, drank, sighed a long sigh. "In she came one night with her friends—for she was a girl with many friends—to hear Sorcery. I pulled their pints, listened to her lovely, lively laughter, and suffered knowing she was forever out of my reach."

"It's hard being shy," Breen said. "And believing you're not quite good enough."

"It is that." His bright eyes held hers as he nodded. "It was during a break Eian Kelly came up to the bar, and he said to me, 'Tom,' he said, 'tell the girl you like her sweater.' I make a business of not knowing who he means, but he leans in. 'She fancies you,' he tells me. 'She wonders why she can't get you to say more than two words to her.'

"And I'm bumbling on how he couldn't know such a thing, and she doesn't so much as know my name. He tells me to trust him on this, and I won't be sorry for it."

"What color was her sweater?" Marco wondered, and made Tom laugh.

"Blue, all the blues from the palest to the deepest, one bleeding sweet into the next. And up she comes to the bar. I could all but hear Eian's voice in my head. 'Don't be a git,' his voice said. 'Talk to the girl.' So out the words popped, and she smiled at me.

"Oh!" Tom slapped a hand on his chest. "My heart near to burst. She said something, and I answered, but to this day I can't tell you what the words were with my heart beating so loud in my ears. Later, she stayed for more music when her mates went on. And Eian whispered in my ear to walk her home. I asked her if I could, and so I did. Eight months, two weeks, and four days later, she was my bride. I've had twenty-eight years with the love of my life because Eian Kelly told me to talk to the girl."

"That's a wonderful story."

It had tears stinging the back of Breen's eyes as it made her father real again.

"He had a way, Eian did, not just with music, but people. When he said trust me, as he did to me, you did just that. It wasn't long after that night, I heard he went back to Galway, and it may be other parts, for it was a year or so before he returned. I wanted to invite him to the wedding, and to book Sorcery into the pub again, but we couldn't reach him. Then back he came, and we had Sorcery to play. That was the night he met your mother."

"Here?" Her dreamy, weepy mood snapped into shock. "They met here?"

"Here, on a stormy summer night."

"Are you going to talk their ears off?" Kate set Marco's mussels on the table along with a basket of bread.

"Her mother's daughter she is. I'll let you eat in peace."

"No, please." Breen reached out to lay a hand on Tom's arm. "I'd really like to hear more, if you have time."

"I have that and more for Eian Kelly's daughter. You eat then, and I'll tell you."

So he settled back once more with his pint.

"She walked in, your mother, with a group of others. Four, maybe five of them. College girls from the look, on a holiday tour. Well into the evening we were, as I recall, and not a table left to be had. They all crowded up to the bar. Your father was singing . . . 'Black Velvet Band,' it was. Yes, I'm sure of it. And the wind blowing, thunder rolling, rain lashing. And I happened to see—I could never tell you why—the minute their eyes met.

"'No sooner met but they looked.'"

"'No sooner looked but they loved,'" Breen added.

"Might've been written for them. The lightning flash of it. With me and mine, it was a slow yearning, cautious steps. But this, a rocket launched. When he returned in three days' time to play again, she was with him. And the same two weeks later. I heard they went back to his homeplace to be married, and it was my thought they settled there or went to her home in the States, for I never saw him again."

"We lived in Philadelphia."

"And did he play still?"

"Yes, he did, and it meant traveling. I guess it was a strain, the traveling. They divorced when I was about ten. Then he left to come back to Ireland about a year later. He told me he'd be back, but . . ."

Tom put a hand over hers. "I'm sorry to hear it, and just as surprised. He's a good man, and I'd swear to it. And it was love he felt for your mother. A man as in love as myself sees it and knows it in another. Not just the heat but the love. We talked, Eian and myself, here and there during the time. He said he was taking— I've lost your mother's name along the way."

"Jennifer."

"Ah, yes. Jenny, he called her. He was taking Jenny back home, and there to be wed. We talked about me soon to be a father, and how much he looked forward to having children, a family. He talked of his farm back home, and raising a family there with Jenny, and how he wanted to settle, a family man, on his own land."

Now he gave Breen's hand a pat. "I hope I haven't made you sad with all this talk."

"No. Mr. Sweeney."

"Tom."

"Tom. You've given me pictures of my father I never had. He is a good man. I remember him as loving and patient, and fun."

"I hope you find him, and if you do, tell him Tom Sweeney wants to stand him a round. Now here's our Kate with your mains. You eat, and well, and it's on the house."

"Oh, but—"

"Eian Kelly's daughter doesn't pay for food nor drink under my roof. And I'll have my bride light a candle for your safe journey, as she's got a strong connection with such matters."

"Thank you so much."

"Pleasure." He rose. "The music will start soon. They're not Sorcery, but they're good craic. Marco, is it?"

"Yes sir."

"Look out for my old friend's daughter now."

"I will."

Marco waited until they sat alone at the table with Breen staring down at her food.

"You okay?"

"Yes. Better than okay. It's just . . ." She looked up, and though she had tears in her eyes, he knew they weren't grieving ones. "It's so much. We came into this town, into this pub, and we find someone who knew these wonderful things about my father. Things I've never heard. And I can picture him. It feels as if maybe I can actually find him. But for right now, listening to someone who knew him back then, before I was born, who thought of him as a friend, it's just so much."

"You know he made a big difference in somebody's life. That's seriously cool."

She looked around the pub, imagined her father and his band-mates filling the air with music.

"He gave up his life here for her, and for me. Maybe that's making him into too much of a hero, but hearing he wanted to raise his family on his farm, I believe that just from the way I remember him talking of home. Before he stopped talking much about it. The stories he'd tell me when I was little. But they went back to Philadelphia, tried to make a life there. It didn't work, but I know they tried."

She picked up her fork. "Yeah, I'm more than okay."

They ate, listened to music—and it was good craic. She didn't think her spirits could rise higher. Then Tom came back to the table with a framed photo.

"I forgot we had this on the wall—all these years. It's your father and his mates, right at that table."

It struck her heart.

He sat, a fiddle cocked on his shoulder and a dreamy look in his eyes. So young! she thought, with his mop of red hair, his worn boots. Younger than she was now, she realized. Slim and handsome in a black sweater and jeans frayed at the cuffs.

There were pint glasses on the table, three others playing instruments, but she saw nothing but Eian Kelly with his dreamy eyes and quiet smile, with a fiddle in his hands.

"You take that now. You should have it."

She pressed it to her heart before she rose and did what usually felt awkward. She hugged, hard, someone she barely knew.

"This means so much."

"I'll be hoping you see him in person before much longer. If you make your way back this way, come see us."

"I will."

That night she set the photo on the table beside her bed.

And she dreamed a pretty dream of the man in the photo with a red-haired baby on his hip standing in a green field as butterflies, a rainbow of colors, danced around them.

In the dream, he said, "This is home, my own darling. It's for us to keep it, and all in it, safe. It's for me to teach you how. That's joy and duty."

She squealed when he lifted her high, when he spun her around and around and the fluttering rainbows spun with them.

When he held her close again, she felt his heart beat against her and knew love absolute.

CHAPTER SEVEN

Up before sunrise, Breen wrote her blog. She spent some happy time selecting the pictures to go with the text, and made a note to do one of those personalized photo books for Marco for Christmas.

Energized, she dressed for the day and set out on another early walk. It still amazed her that her life could include such simple luxuries as a morning walk.

More confident, she decided to take one of the paths into the woods where the soft light dappled through the trees, and the air smelled quietly of earth and pine.

She felt alone in a wonderland, and marveling, walked deeper than she'd intended. When she caught sight of a river, mists rising, fingers of smoke through the trees, she wandered closer.

A little wooden boat with a pointed bow rested on shore, its oars crossed inside. She imagined what it might be like to float over the water, through those mists where a few lazy ducks glided along. Around the curve of the river, she calculated, the castle would come into view, as it had for hundreds of years.

She pulled out her phone, took a picture of the misty river, the little boat. From the left, she heard a rustling.

As she turned, she saw the bird perched on a branch looking down at her with gold eyes. A hawk—at least she thought so, as she'd never seen one up close. She knew the castle grounds held a falconry school, so a hawk made sense.

"Well, hello," she began, then froze in place when it swooped down to land at her feet.

Head cocked, he continued to study her.

"Pretty big bird," she murmured. "And really beautiful. Handsome? Whichever."

Fascination overcame nerves so she crouched down.

"Do they just let you out? I don't know how it works, but you look too smart to be lost."

"Oh, he knows what he's about."

The voice startled Breen, had her springing up. The hawk just watched.

With a quick laugh, the woman stepped out of the trees onto the path. She wore rough brown trousers, a forest-green jacket, a brown cap over sunflower-blond hair in a long, thick braid. And a falconer's glove on her left hand.

"Sorry. Amish wanted a flight, and I a walk, so here we are. Good morning to you."

"Good morning. Am I not supposed to be here?"

"Sure and you can come and go as you please. It seems Amish has taken a fancy to you. I'm Morena, and I'm with him."

"I'm Breen. He's gorgeous."

"And knows it as well." Morena gave a hand signal that had the hawk rising back up to take the branch. "Are you enjoying your visit to the castle then?"

"Very much. It's magical."

Morena's smile flashed again, her blue eyes bright with it. "Magic's where you find it, isn't it now?" She produced another glove, held it out. "Would you like a bit of a hawk walk?"

"Really? I can just . . ." She trailed off to look back up at the hawk.

"Well, as I said, he's taken a fancy to you, so let's both of you have a treat." She slid the thick glove on Breen's hand herself.

Over it, their eyes met again. Breen felt some sort of click, but couldn't understand or describe it.

Then Morena stepped back, and the moment slid by like the river.

"We'll walk a bit along the river so you can see how our boy does things. It should be good weather for you today, just some spots of rain in the afternoon, but plenty of bright."

"I don't mind the rain."

"That's a happy thing, considering. Here now, you take this bit of chicken in your hand, and turn it. You'll hold your arm up like this, elbow cocked. Well done," she said as she positioned Breen's arm. "Now watch him come."

Come he did.

It stole her breath, that spread of wings, the rich color catching just a quick strike of sunlight. He glided, all silent grace and power, to land on her gloved arm.

And now those eyes stared into hers, close, gleaming.

"Well done indeed," Morena said. "Now then, just turn your hand up, open your fist. He wants his reward."

He gobbled it, waited.

"That's just amazing."

"Magical," Morena said. "Give your arm a little push in the air, and watch him go."

They did it twice more, with the hawk soaring and diving through the trees, gliding from branch to glove, and into the air again.

"You did very well. That's enough breakfast for our boy, and I imagine you're wanting your own by now."

"This was the most incredible experience." With regret Breen watched the hawk hop from her arm to Morena's. "Thank you so much. Do I go to the school to pay?"

"Oh, there's no payment for this, not at all. A treat for you and my boy here."

"More treasure than treat for me."

"It's kind of you to say so. There's your way back," she added, and pointed with her free hand. "I wish you a fine day, and a happy journey."

"Thank you, Morena, for a morning I'll never forget."

"You're more than welcome." She turned in the opposite direction, moved into the trees before she stopped, looking over her shoulder.

The click came again, quick, distinct, then gone.

"We'll see you again, Amish and I, when you reach the homeplace."

"The homeplace?"

But Morena and the hawk slipped into the trees, into dappled light and shadows.

Since the unexpected encounter added time to her walk, she had to hurry back to meet Marco for breakfast.

She rushed into the dining room, where he already sat, coffee on the table as he read something on his phone.

"I'm late, but—"

He held up a hand to stop her, kept reading. With a shrug she poured herself some coffee. When the waiter came to the table, she ordered bacon, scrambled eggs, whole wheat toast.

"I'll take the full Irish, eggs over easy," Marco announced, still reading. "I could eat the full Irish every day for the rest of my life."

Then he put his phone down, looked at Breen. "I was reading your blog."

"Oh. What do you think? Too personal? I was worried I got a little too personal, thought about taking it down and—"

"Not a chance. Sure, it's personal, but it's . . . Damn, girl, it choked me up. I mean, I was there in the pub, and reading it still choked me up. You did a great job with the day, right? The driving, the scenery, the cliffs, and everything. Took me right back to it all. But when you got to the part about meeting Tom, and how he knew your dad, and all of that? The picture he gave you? It freaking killed me."

"In a good way?"

"Cut it out. You know when something's good. Only thing missing is the picture. I'm going to see if the hotel can scan it so we can get it on the blog. It's a long shot your dad would see it, but hey, who knows? Somebody who knows him might see it, and tell him."

"I never thought of that." She sat back as hope bubbled up. "Marco, I never thought of that. It's brilliant."

He tapped his temple. "I got the cells. You posted it over an hour ago. What've you been up to?"

"Oh my God, the best!"

He listened, then held up both hands. "You had a big-ass bird on your arm?"

"I did, and it was fantastic. Marco, he looked right at me. I mean right into my eyes."

"You didn't freak? I'm freaking just hearing about it. Big-ass birds got big-ass claws—"

"Talons."

"Sharp whatever you call them, and big-ass beaks that can poke your eye out. Big-ass birds give me the willies. Flamingos? Sure, pink, and people think goofy, but I bet they could tear you a new one. Remember that parrot they brought in when we were in third grade?"

He held his hands apart to a height easily twice as big as the African gray had been. "Hearing that bird talk while he gave you the side-eye? Saying things like 'Time for dinner' and 'Let's party'? That ain't natural, girl. Gave me nightmares."

"I remember. This bird didn't talk, and he was gorgeous and graceful, and the falconer, Morena, showed me how to call him to the glove, give him raw chicken parts."

"You fed him raw chicken?"

"I didn't have time to sauté it."

"Okay, glad you had fun, glad I missed it. I might have nightmares anyway."

"You're up for the most disgusting horror movie they can make, but a bird over the size of a sparrow gives you nightmares."

"They're fine up in the sky where they belong. I don't want a sparrow landing on me either." He shuddered.

They dug into breakfast, went over plans for the day.

"Before we go from this castle to the next castle, let me take the photo, ask them to scan it for me. If they can't, I can try to take a picture of it."

Back in her room, Breen took it out of the frame. "Look, it's got their names on the back. Sorcery. Eian Kelly, Kavan Byrne, Flynn McGill, and Brian Doherty."

"Better yet. When I add it to your blog, I'll put their names under it. Adds chances somebody'll know one of them, right?"

"It feels like it." She touched a fingertip to her father's face. "It was a long time ago, though."

"We're standing in a castle that's hundreds of years old. That says time's relative, right? Think positive, girl."

"Done. I'll go with you. We'll do this, then head to Bunratty for a good taste of the way back."

They toured the castle first, the dominant stone structure that lorded over the river. With Marco she walked its enormous dining hall, imagining the banquets with lords and ladies in their finery, the fire roaring while servants poured ale and mead, carried in big platters of meat.

Musicians would have played on the balcony above, and candles would have thrown gold light over the heavy tables and chairs, on the walls with their tapestries.

Stone stairs curved up to bedchambers, garderobes, salons where women would have sat to sew and spin, more where men planned battles.

"Freeze your ass off in the winter," Marco decided.

"But look at the views."

"Views are chill, yeah. But gimme central heating and a working john."

She poked him with her elbow. "It's romantic."

"Can't say it's not, but I'll take my romance knowing the toilet's going to flush. Still, it's seriously sick, because it was really real. People lived here, and worked here, and had all kinds of sex here. Then they shot arrows or dumped rocks on other people who tried to take over."

"A clan's a family. You protect your family."

Marco slid an arm around her waist when they walked back out. "Sister, I'd dump rocks on anybody who tried to hurt you."

"I appreciate that."

She loved the castle, but fell in love with the folk park. The thatched-roofed cottages and shops, the costumes, the music, little farms and village streets—that equaled the really real to her. It showed her how people—regular people like her—lived. Where they slept, how they cooked, how they raised their children.

She liked the little donkeys and the geese, the fiddler outside the pub—all of it representing to her the ins and outs of daily life in another world, another time.

"I know it couldn't have been as simple or as charming as it looks, but it feels like it. And it feels sort of familiar. I guess with movies and books you have a sense, but this is laid out with actual places and people."

And strolling along, she felt as though she could slide right in—into a cottage for a seat by the fire, into a pub for a pint.

"It gives me this weird kind of déjà vu."

"Keep your déjà with you," Marco decided. "It's cool to see, but I'll stick with the internet and loaded nachos, pillow-top mattresses and an ice-cold beer on a hot summer night. Not to mention LGBTQ rights and, you know, penicillin."

"On the other hand, no nuclear warheads."

"You'd have to learn to milk a cow. Maybe a goat."

"No air pollution or climate change."

"No AC in the hot, no heated-tile floors in the cold."

"We don't have AC or heated-tile floors," she pointed out.

"But they exist, am I right? And my rich bestie could afford both if she wanted them."

She laughed as he gave her a quick squeeze. "I guess I could."

They wandered into a gift shop, nearly wandered out again. But she stopped, pointed. "Look, a hawk pin. I'm going to buy it as a thank-you for Morena."

"The bird lady?"

"Yeah, the bird lady. It's perfect, the way the hawk's wings are spread inside the circle."

"You do that, then let's find some food. It's been a long time since breakfast."

She bought the pin and a card to write a thank-you note.

"Two more points of interest on the list, with a village for food and poking around. I'll navigate," she told him.

Then she froze. It struck her as impossible—and because it was impossible, as terrifying. But she saw him, she saw the man with the silver hair.

And as he had for that moment the first time on the bus, he looked right at her.

"There he is!" She clawed at Marco's arm as the man sauntered—that was the word for it, *sauntered*—away.

"Who? What?"

She just shoved her gift bag at Marco and ran. Not away, not this time, but after. That struck her not as impossible, but as liberating.

She sprinted—or tried to—in and around people who admired the village, those taking videos and snapshots, or kids racing to see the donkey.

She kept him in sight, was no more than seconds behind him when he turned a corner.

She turned it.

And he was gone. Simply gone.

Not possible, she thought, fighting to catch her breath. Just not possible.

"Breen." Marco raced up to her, grabbed her arm. "WTF!"

"I saw him, Marco, I swear I saw him."

"Who? Plus, you just reminded me why I used to push at you to join the track team. You've got some fast feet, girl."

"The man—the man on the bus, and outside the apartment, and at Sally's. At the airport, too. I just saw him again."

"Breen—"

"I know how it sounds, Marco." She shoved a hand through her hair. "I know, but I also know what I saw. He's about six feet—maybe six-one or -two, and lanky. He's always in black, and he has silver hair—not white, not gray, it's shiny and luxurious."

Marco put an arm around her, a protective gesture that wasn't lost on her. "But you don't see him now?"

"I'm not crazy or delusional. I chased him to this corner, and he went around the side, and . . ."

Vanished like a puff of smoke, she thought.

"I don't know where he went. There are a lot of people. But I saw him, and it doesn't make sense."

"Okay. Let's walk." He kept his arm around her as he drew her away. "You're shaking."

"It's not anxiety. I'm pissed off," she realized. "I'm really pissed off. It feels like he's taunting me. It feels so arrogant."

"I can dump rocks on him if you see him again."

She didn't laugh, but she did tip her head toward his shoulder. Then she straightened. "Would my mother have someone follow me?"

"I didn't think of that." Now he did as he guided her along the path. "I guess she could, but why?"

"I don't know, just to keep tabs. But that doesn't make sense, since I saw him on the stupid bus before I found out about the money. And hell, she could read my blog if she wanted to know what I was doing. She could just freaking ask if she wanted to know."

As they walked, he rubbed her back in that soothing way he had. "It's a wide world of coincidence, but you said you saw him at the airport."

"I did." Or she thought . . .

"I bet we're not the only people from Philadelphia in Ireland, or even in this park right now."

"He looked at me like he knew me," she added, then shook her head. "Maybe because he recognized me like I did him. Maybe. The first time, on the bus, it felt like he looked at me, but I was already worked up. Getting dumped, hating my job, hating that I was on the bus going to my mother's. But I guess—in the wide world of coincidence—he could have seen me today and thought: Hey, she looks familiar."

She didn't believe it. She realized as she said it, she didn't believe it at all, but there was comfort in saying it.

"We could walk around more, see if you spot him again."

"No, it's silly. Let's go get some fish and chips."

"I'm all about it."

But he kept his arm around her as they walked back to the car. And he kept his eye out for a man with silver hair.

She put it behind her, and with Marco revived from lunch, explored ruins and round towers, explored another castle in the rain that swept in, and out again just as quickly.

She sat on a seawall with the Atlantic wind in her hair, walked the moonscape of the Burren. They rounded it out with another pub meal and music before taking the winding roads back to their last night at the castle.

"It's still light out. Let's have a drink in the bar. You've earned another Kir Royale on me. Last night here," Marco pointed out before she could make an excuse.

"You're right—last night, and I earned it. I'm just going to drop Morena's gift at the desk, then change my boots. Meet you there."

She detoured to the desk.

"Good evening, Ms. Kelly, and how was your day?"

"It was wonderful. I wonder if I can leave this with you to send to the falconry school? It's a little thank-you for Morena—I didn't get her last name. She let me do an informal hawk walk this morning when I met her and Amish—the hawk—in the woods."

"Isn't that lovely?" The young brunette on the desk took the gift bag. "I'd be happy to, of course. Enjoy the rest of your evening."

She intended to. She walked to her room, pried off her boots, let out a long sigh as she wondered how many miles she'd put on them—and her feet—in the last two days.

Worth every step.

Since it was the last night, she decided she could take a minute or two to freshen her makeup.

As she checked the results, a knock sounded on her door.

"It's been five minutes, Marco," she muttered. "Okay, ten."

But she opened the door to the brunette from the desk.

"Sorry to bother you, miss, but I checked with the falconry school—with my cousin, as it happens, who works there. He tells me they have no Morena, nor a hawk called Amish."

"I don't understand."

"It may be you misunderstood the names. My cousin would be happy to check in the morning if any of the falconers met with you, though no one mentioned it through the day. I didn't want to keep the gift until we find the right person, you see."

"Yes, of course, thank you."

"Anything more I can do for you, Ms. Kelly?"

"No, no, thanks. Sorry for the trouble."

"No trouble at all. Have a lovely evening."

But she hadn't misunderstood the names, Breen thought as she shut the door. And she sure as hell hadn't imagined the experience.

Morena and Amish—she could see, and hear, them both perfectly. She could remember the thrill of watching the hawk fly to her glove, and the way he'd looked right into her eyes.

Then again, Morena hadn't specifically said she was with the school. Wasn't it possible she decided to fly her own hawk on castle grounds?

Breen thought that might be frowned upon, even illegal. She wouldn't push it, she decided as she tucked the bag in her suitcase. She could get the woman in trouble.

And she remembered the way Morena had looked back at her, told her they'd see each other again.

Then she'd just . . . melted into the trees. Just disappeared.

Like the man with the silver hair.

"Maybe I'm losing my mind." Feeling the pressure in her chest, she closed her eyes, forced herself to breathe through it. "Maybe I imagined it all."

She opened her eyes again. "But I didn't. I absolutely didn't."

So she wouldn't worry about it. She'd go have that drink with Marco.

And she didn't see any point in mentioning any of this to him.

That night she dreamed herself a child, one of no more than two or three. She sat, crying, inside a cage with glass walls. Outside the cage the water flowed, pale green.

She cried for her mother, and her father, but they didn't come. She cried for someone she called Nan, but no one came.

Outside the glass walls in that flickering light stood a shadow she knew to be a man. But she couldn't see him. She didn't cry for him because she feared him, even as a child of no more than two or three.

When he spoke, his voice was smooth and sweet as music. And false, somehow false.

"There now, my child, my blood, my own, your tears are foolish and weak, and no one can hear them. You have lessons to learn, to carefully learn. I'll teach you to be all you are, and you'll have toys, shiny and bright, and sweets, all the sweets your heart desires."

"I want my ma, I want my da, I want my ma, I want my da. I want—"

"Silence!" Not smooth and sweet now, but a boom of thunder. "I'll teach you what to want. I'll show you what you can have. I am your mother, your father, your all now. Heed me or you'll shed more than tears. Lessons to learn, and the first is obedience."

As the shadow moved closer, she screamed. She screamed first in fear, then in the rage only a child can feel.

And with that scream, with that fisting of her hands, the glass shattered.

She was in her bed in the room with the sloped ceiling in the little house in Philadelphia. And a child still, a bit older, but a child still, she clung to her father as he stroked, rocked, soothed.

"Just a dream, *mo stór*, only a dream. Da's here, right here. You're safe and well and I'm right here. He can't hurt you. He'll never touch you again."

But as she tried to claw herself out of the dream, Breen thought he could.

She thought he would.

CHAPTER EIGHT

She decided not to tell Marco about the dream, and she certainly wouldn't blog about it. But she wrote it out in what she now thought of as her personal journal.

Since the best explanation for Morena and her hawk equaled trespassing, she didn't see any reason to mention it.

She wrote her blog, concentrating on the positive and happy—and found that made her feel more positive and happy.

Following habit, she streamed a workout, then took herself out for her final morning walk at Dromoland. The walled gardens offered peace and beauty, so she took it, pulled it into her like the positive and happy.

Bad dreams were just that—dreams—and since she'd been plagued by them most of her life, she wouldn't dwell on them during waking hours.

Not when she had flowers and birds and soft sunlight through layered clouds. Though what she had left to pack would take about five minutes, she told herself she'd go back in, get it done. Then admitted to cowardice and pushed herself to take a path into the woods.

Nerves bubbled up and, annoyed by them, she pushed herself to take the same route she had the day before. But this time, she walked alone.

She wound her way back as those layered clouds began to drip.

The plan, loosely outlined, put her at the wheel for the first leg north. So with the little car loaded and Marco beside her, she drove away from the castle in a thin, steady rain.

"We slept in a castle, Breen."

"We slept in a castle, Marco. Now we're going to take our time and our wandering way and see more on the road to our cozy Irish cottage."

"How many people do we know who can say what you just said?"

"Absolutely no one."

They headed north, then west toward the coast, adding gorgeous miles to the journey. In and out of rain, into a patch of strong sun that had cloud shadows sliding over the fields, they pulled off and stopped where they pleased.

On foot, they crossed a field wild with buttercups to explore a ruined keep while behind a fence a little gray donkey watched them. When Marco jogged over, the donkey stretched her head over the fence in invitation.

Gingerly at first, Marco tapped his hand on the donkey's head. "Look at that. She likes it."

"Turn around. I'll take your picture. Urbanite Meets Donkey."

"I'll do better."

To Breen's astonishment, Marco vaulted over the fence.

"I don't think you should—"

"It's not hurting anything, and look, she likes it."

He actually put an arm around the donkey's neck, who proceeded to rub against him like a cat.

"That's something you don't see every day," Breen murmured, and immortalized it.

"Come on over. She's really sweet."

Though she hesitated, Breen lectured herself on cowardice and moved to the fence. She had to push herself as she had that morning to climb over. And when the donkey turned its head toward her, she let out a muffled squeal that made Marco laugh.

"Gut up, Breen. She's not going to eat you."

"She could bite. What do either of us know about donkeys?" But she put a tentative hand on the donkey's head. "There, done. Now we should get back on the road."

"Wait. I need to get your picture with her, too. Think of the blog," he added.

"Think of the blog." She muttered it, but put her hand back on the donkey. It looked at her, right at her, just as the hawk had done.

"She is sweet, isn't she?" Now she stroked as she might a friendly dog. "She likes the company. She gets lonely out here when the sheep aren't around. Isn't that right, Bridget?"

"Breen, you're not going to believe this."

"What?" Smiling at the donkey, stroking its rough hair, she imagined a farmhouse, and a boy with messy brown hair who came out to brush her.

"There's a butterfly on your shoulder. Don't jerk! I got a great picture already, but just turn your head to the left. Slow."

Heart thumping, she turned her head. The butterfly perched, wings as yellow as the buttercups, spread. Astonished, she stared while those wings, dappled with black dots, closed and opened.

Then it flew, a delicate blossom riding the air.

"That was major cool. Here, look at the pictures I got."

He held out his phone, slowly swiping through, as he'd taken several shots of Breen smiling at the donkey as if they were old friends, and a butterfly on her shoulder.

And the one he'd managed to get after she turned her head. And there she didn't see shock on her own face, but absolute delight.

"I didn't know they did that—landed on people."

"Neither did I." She touched a hand to her shoulder.

"I think I'd've freaked. You didn't."

"Inside a little."

"Didn't show. That's sure as hell something to blog about. Gotta book it, girl." He gave the donkey a last pat. "Bridget?" Grinning, Marco looked back at Breen. "Where'd you get all that?"

She didn't have a clue. "I guess she looks like a Bridget."

"We'll go with it. Nice to meet you, Bridget."

Marco took Breen's hand when they climbed over the fence, swung it. "My turn to drive."

They crossed into Galway, navigated their way with considerable stress to a car park in Galway city.

"You did great." Breen rubbed the tension out of the back of her neck.

"Got us here. We need a break, and food. And anyplace that has a street called Shop Street deserves my attention."

Breen soon discovered it deserved a lot of people's attention. The crowds seemed huge after a full morning of no one, but Marco jumped right in. Pulled in his wake, she cruised the shops, resisted everything until she came across a piece of framed ogham script. Beneath the script it read: COURAGE.

"I sense a theme."

"It's a good one. And this is small enough to pack easily when my time's up."

"I'm getting one."

"Which one?"

"No, not the art. Or not the wall-hanging art. Ink. What should I get?"

"That's on you, in every way."

"Ha-ha. We'll talk about it over lunch. I'm starved."

"You could get that tattooed so you'd just have to point at it several times a day."

"And she hits with another one. Something Irish," he said as they wandered out to pick a lunch spot.

She looked at him, her Marco with his golden brown skin, his riot of dark braids down to his shoulder blades, the meticulously groomed goatee.

"You're not Irish."

"But I'm getting it in Ireland, right?"

He decided on an Irish harp. Maybe he wasn't Irish, but he was a musician. Plus, he liked the look of it.

"Now, where should I get it? On me, I mean. I can google where in Galway."

Because she still didn't take him seriously, Breen only smiled. "You've got a great butt."

"I really do, but then only the chosen few would see it. Biceps seem, like, usual. Though . . ." He flexed.

"Yes, Marco, you have great bis, too."

"I'm going with the usual. It's a manly choice, and look here, this place gets solid reviews." He studied his phone. "Done. Let's do this."

When he rose from the table, Breen blinked at him. "You're serious?"

"You're not getting one up on me, girl. You got ink, I get ink."

"Marco, you need oxygen when you watch a hospital show and somebody gets a shot."

"You're going to hold my hand."

She held his hand—and watched his eyes widen at the first prick of the needle.

"Holy shit. Distract me."

"Multiplication tables?"

"Jesus, not math. Sing."

She started to laugh, but he sat in the padded chair, eyes huge, his hand clamped on hers as a guy named Joe with complex and colorful tattoo sleeves meticulously worked the outline of a harp into his skin.

She started with "Molly Malone" because the melody struck her as soothing. Joe, the tattoo guy, shot her a grin, then joined her with a very nice baritone on the chorus.

"Is it finished?"

"No, honey."

"You're doing brilliant, Marco," Joe told him.

Marco just closed his eyes. "Keep singing."

She went with "The Wild Rover"—a brighter tune—and a woman of about fifty in the middle of getting a Celtic spiral on her forearm picked it up.

Because he'd heard it a few times and knew the words, Marco—eyes still firmly shut—added some harmony.

"That was grand!" The second tattoo artist, a woman of maybe thirty, stopped to applaud. "Are you professionals then?"

Breen shook her head, wondered if she'd ever have full use of her hand again.

"You should be, for you have lovely voices. Let's have another. Do you know any Lady Gaga?"

"Do we know Gaga?" Marco managed a smile—eyes still closed. "'Born This Way,' Breen."

She sang as the harp took shape, and since watching the actual process made her a little queasy, kept her eyes on Marco. At some point his grip loosened enough for her to flex her aching fingers.

But she held on, because he needed it.

"And there you have it, mate." Joe patted Marco lightly on the shoulder. "You can have a look now if you want to."

"Okay, just breathing first." He opened his eyes, looked at his biceps, and the harp with its bold green shading. "It's awesome! Look at that, Breen. I got a tat, and it's awesome."

"You come back for another sing-along anytime. I like yours," Joe told Breen.

"Thanks."

"If ever you want another, come see me."

"I think one's going to be enough."

He grinned at her. "That's what they all say."

"I got a tat," Marco said when they walked out. "I got inked in Ireland."

"Yay. You seem a little wobbly."

"Legs feel shaky yet, but I did it. You're driving now, right?"

"You can count on that."

"Next time, we do it together."

"Right." She mentally rolled her eyes. "Next time."

When they reached the car, Marco folded her into a hug, swayed with her. "I love you, Breen. You never let go."

"Never will."

"Don't make me sound like a pussy when you blog about it."

"As if." She got in, waited for him to take the passenger seat. "You may need to sing until I get through the traffic."

"You got it."

But it wasn't as bad going out as it had been coming in.

As she took the route to Connemara, through and around villages, she could count more sheep than cars.

And Marco dozed, likely worn out, she thought, from tattoo trauma.

She settled into the quiet of it all, the lack of urgency, the knowledge she could stop anywhere she pleased and no one would tell her she had to do something else, be somewhere else.

She saw signposts for sites she wanted to visit, but as Marco slept, she told herself she—or they—could come back on a day trip.

She looked out over Lough Corrib, wondered if she'd enjoy a boat trip. She could cross over to Mayo, see sights there, too. She had weeks and weeks to do just as she wanted, when she wanted.

Freedom, heady and sweet.

If she ever did get another tattoo—not likely—she'd choose *Freedom*.

She passed cows and sheep and hills and fields and rising cliffs that all burned their beauty into her heart.

Marco stirred, rubbed his eyes. "Man, I went out! Where are— Holy wow!"

"They're called the Twelve Bens." Her voice was soft, tight with emotion. "We're in Connemara. It's like something that just froze in time, at exactly the right moment. You missed the lake—God, it was beautiful, Marco. We'll come back."

"How long was I out?"

"I don't know. It's all timeless here. Oh, do you see that?"

He straightened, looked where she pointed. "The big hole in the ground? What are those things stacked up?"

"It's peat. They're drying it. They dig it, cut it, and dry it in the wind."

"The stuff they burn, seriously?"

"Yes, my father told me about it. I'd forgotten so much he'd told me, and it's coming back now. When I see things, I remember. They had a peat bog on the farm where he grew up. It might even be around here. He must've told me where, but I can't remember."

"Bet you will."

"I hope so, but I know this feels . . . almost like home."

"Sense memory. I read about it." He pulled out his phone to take pictures out the window. "It's, like, in your blood, right? Your dad, and your ancestors and all. So you sense it, feel it."

"It's like that. Smell the air, Marco."

She all but drank it.

"You can smell the peat and the pine, and I swear, you can smell the green."

"I can drive if you just want to soak it up."

"I'm fine. We're nearly there."

"Good, because I'm—"

"Starving."

"Could use a snack. Hold on." He dug into the bag at his feet.

"Got chips and Cokes. Road food."

"Crisps over here," she reminded him, and took one. "You've got the contact for the rental manager, right?"

"Yep."

"Go ahead and text her. She said to do that when we were about thirty minutes out. I think that's about right."

"Don't we need to stop for supplies?"

"Let's get there first, take some stock, make a list. There's a village not far from the cottage—a couple of them."

"She's fast." Marco read the return text. "She'll be there to welcome us, she says."

"Perfect." She glanced over to grin at him. "It's all just perfect."

When she turned onto the skinny, snaking road boxed in with hedgerows, Marco shifted in his seat.

"You're sure this is right?"

"Yes."

"I thought it was on the water, with a mountain view."

"You have to get to it first."

"Okay . . . I'm just saying there might be a reason it was available for the whole summer."

"Have some faith."

Maybe she was a little nervous herself—and not entirely sure two cars could pass each other on this tiny road—but they had nowhere to go but ahead.

"It's remote-ish," she added to reassure them both. "Private. I wanted private."

"There's private and there's Bumfuck. This is feeling like Bumfuck. You said there's a village."

"Yes, only a couple kilometers. Walkable."

"Anybody who walks on this road has a death wish. How about I text—what's her name?—Finola McGill—which sounds made-up—just to be sure we didn't take a wrong turn onto somebody's cow path?"

"If you think— Wait, there's the turn—it said to turn right—and it'd be signposted. See? It says Fey Cottage. That's us."

She turned and the world began to open up. Though the road stayed narrow, a field stretched on the right with the mountains rising. She caught her first glimpse of the bay.

"It's weird. Before you turned it was like we were hedged in. Get it—hedged."

"Not anymore."

The field gave way to the forest—fairy-tale green and shadowy. And there, between the forest and the bay with the majesty of the mountains rising, sat Fey Cottage.

Flowers all but exploded at its charming feet with white paths winding through them. Its sturdy gray stone walls rose two pretty stories under its thick thatched roof. Its windows sparkled, flashing jewels in the sun.

"Okay, I take it back. It's no castle, but it's like something out of a movie, and man, those views."

When she said nothing, he glanced over to see her staring with tears in her eyes.

"Hey, girl."

"This is what I wanted. The castle—I wanted that, wanted the experience, but this . . . This is what I wanted. A cottage near the woods and the water, with flowers everywhere."

"And that's what you got." He took her hand, pressed it to his cheek. "You deserve getting what you want."

"I have it because of my father. I'm not going to forget that, no matter what."

"You had the chance to have it because of your dad, and that's a big. But you took the chance. Don't you forget that."

"Right." She swiped her hands over her face.

As soon as she got out of the car, the front door—white as the paths—opened.

The woman who stepped out wore a bold orange sweater and trim brown pants over a curvy body. Her hair, the color of roasted chestnuts, swept back from a pretty face of rose and cream where dimples flashed with her welcoming smile.

"And here you are! Welcome to Fey Cottage. Ah, Breen Kelly." She extended her hand—a strong, confident grip—then laid her other hand over Breen's for a long squeeze before she turned to Marco. "And Marco Olsen. What a handsome one you are. I'm Finola, and I'm delighted for certain to meet you both. You've had a long journey, so come in, come in. We'll have you settled in no time."

"Thank you. It's so beautiful. It's all so beautiful."

"I couldn't be more pleased to hear you say so. Come in, come in, and I'll show you around before we deal with your bags and so on. What a fine day we're having for your welcome home."

She whisked them straight into the living room, one centered around a stone fireplace where logs stacked. The wide mantel gleamed and held a trio of fat white candles.

A rug decorated with a central trinity knot spread over a floor of the same gleaming wood as the mantel. Its forest-green motif picked up the color of the sofa with its fat cushions. A throw artfully arranged on the back of the sofa was the color of top cream and looked soft as clouds.

Shelves held books—a world of books. Tables held pottery vases filled with flowers. Crystals dangled from windows to shoot rainbow light into the room while the sparkling glass opened it to more flowers dancing in the sun and the sloping green that led to the water.

Water as blue as summer and so clear it caught the reflection of green hills on its surface.

Everything spoke of welcome and comfort.

"It's wonderful," Breen murmured. "It's just wonderful."

"A bit warm for a fire on such a fine day, I thought, but it's laid so you can enjoy it tonight. As you see you have what they call the 'open concept,' so if you've a mind to cook you're not cut off from the rest."

Though cooking wasn't her strong suit, Breen wandered in. The kitchen was separated from the main room by a breakfast bar the color of slate.

A little table, already set charmingly for two, took center. The counters held a little coffee maker—thank God—a stoneware bowl of fresh fruit, more flowers, a toaster.

A bright red kettle sat on the range Marco already beamed at.

"That is top-of-the-line," he announced.

"And do you cook?" Finola asked him.

"Yeah, I do."

"Clever as well as handsome then. Aren't you lucky to have such a friend? You have a nice pantry, I think, and it's stocked, as is the refrigerator with what we thought you'd want."

"Oh, we never expected—"

Finola brushed Breen's surprise away. "We can't have you troubling with such matters on your arrival. I've brought you a round of brown bread, baked myself fresh for you. It's in the bread drawer there. And biscuits in the jar. Not store bought," she added with a wag of her finger.

The warmth, the welcome simply stunned her. "It's so thoughtful of you. Thank you so much."

"Sure it's little enough. And right through there you have the little room with the washing machine and drying machine, though there's a line out the back for hanging on a sunny day.

"Now, there's the bedroom down here, and what I like best about it is it has its own door so if you wake and fancy a walk, there you have it."

Breen walked through in a haze of wonder and delight. If she'd designed a cottage for her stay, this would be exactly it.

She'd set up her office/gym in the main-level bedroom. When she wanted a break, she'd just step outside, into the gorgeous gardens, or beyond to the water, around to the woods.

She'd learn to cook more—and better. Marco could help with that. And in the evenings she'd curl up in front of the fire with a book.

Finola led them upstairs. Doors stood open on either end of a short hall. In the center of the hall, a narrow table with curved feet held more flowers, more candles. Breen ran her fingers over the intricately carved surface, a dragon in flight.

"This is stunning. What beautiful work."

"It is, isn't it? I'm proud to say I know the artist well—I should, as we've been married these forty-eight years. When she who made the cottage asked for something special, he crafted this."

"It's . . ." Breen, fingers still on the carving, turned. "Wait."

"That didn't get by me either," Marco added. "Did you get married before you were born?"

Finola's cheeks pinked as she laughed. "Ah now, listen to you! I've a granddaughter your age, and three more besides."

Marco, in his Marco way, grabbed both her hands. "Tell me your secret. I'll do anything short of sacrificing a chicken."

"Oh now. We'll say living happy as you can, loving hard as you can. Taking care when care's needed. And a good cup of wine of an evening."

"I can do all of that. All of that is now on my daily regimen."

"And this is a good reminder." Finola took Breen's hand, turned up her wrist to tap the tattoo. "To have the courage to do all of that, for all but the wine take courage."

"You read Irish."

"As I was taught."

A little unnerved by the direct look—Finola's eyes were a steely blue, and somehow strong—Breen eased her hand away. "Marco got a tattoo this afternoon."

That strong look softened into flirtation as Finola turned to Marco. "Well then, let's have a look at it—wherever it might be."

He shoved up the sleeve of his sweater. "It's still a little red."

"An Irish harp! And very nicely done as well." She put her thumb and forefinger on either side of it to give his biceps a little squeeze. Winking, she said, "Woof!"

The usually unflappable Marco flushed.

"And now you'll have to learn to play the harp."

"Marco's a musician."

"When I'm not being a bartender."

"Handsome, clever, and musical? What a catch you'll be for some lucky boy. Now let me show you the bedrooms, and we'll see if I guessed right. I've pegged this as yours, Marco, but don't fret if I've got it wrong."

She backtracked to the room at the top of the stairs.

The bed, plumped with pillows under a fluffy duvet, faced the windows. Its heavy head- and footboards boasted carvings of flutes and fiddles, harps and harpsichords, *bodhrán* drums and dulcimers.

"Wow" was all Marco could manage.

"Is this your husband's work, too?" Again, Breen traced her fingers over the carvings. "It's fabulous."

"It is, and thank you. You've a fine view of the bay, and its roll to the sea, of the mountains as well. A good, sturdy chair and the chest of drawers as well as the closet. Your own bath, of course. The blanket— or *throw* is the word—is the work of my dearest friend. I think she's made all those shades of gray warm rather than somber."

"Marco, your view! You're going to see this every morning."

He walked to the window, stood shoulder to shoulder with Breen. "It's like a painting. You can have this room if you like it better."

"No." She tipped her head toward his shoulder. "It feels like you."

"It's lovely, it is, to see friendship so true. I know it myself, and what it means to the heart. Why don't I show you the other bedroom? I think you'll be happy with it, Breen."

"If it's anything close to this, I'll be ecstatic. Does your husband work nearby?" Breen asked as they walked down the hall again. "If he'd ship to the States, I'd love to have a piece he made. I'm going to be in the market for some new things."

"Oh sure, it's not far as the crow flies. We can talk about all that when you're well and settled."

She gestured Breen into the room.

Carved faeries danced on the headboard. Dragons flew and flowers bloomed. The throw at the foot blended hues of green, from shadowy forest to soft sea. The desk in the corner held more flowers, an antique inkwell, and a dark green bowl of colorful tumbled stones. The art on the walls carried the theme of the bed with flowers and faeries, and a striking one over the bed of a woman—her back to the room as she faced a misty lake, her long white dress painted as if to ripple in the wind, her fall of red hair streaming in curls.

But Breen could only stare at the view that swept outside the windows.

The forest crept in, full of glorious secrets; the water rolled and rolled. She saw a pair of swans gliding near the shore.

And under a sky gone blue and bright with a summer day, the mountains.

"I think she's pleased," Finola said to Marco.

"Oh yeah, she is. You've got a fireplace, Breen. We built our dream houses—in our heads—when we were kids. Breen always had a fireplace in the bedroom."

Small, stone, the split logs laid, it murmured cozy nights.

"The pictures—I saw pictures online."

"Oh, we did a bit of decorating since. We need to—what is it?—update all that." Finola merely smiled as Breen turned to her. "Will it do for you then?"

"Ms. McGill—"

"Oh now, it's Finola to you and yours."

"I cried in the car," she heard herself saying. "Because when I saw the cottage it was so much what I wanted. And now this? It's everything and more. I'll take good care of it, I promise."

Those strong, direct eyes softened again. "I've no doubt you will. Now if we could take a quick walk outside? I've keys for you, of course," she began as she walked out, and down the hall to the stairs. "I can promise you'll have no trouble here, but you lock up if you feel the better about it. There's a little veg garden, and you should help yourself to that, to the flowers and the herbs. You'll have Seamus coming by early once or twice a week to tend to things," she continued as she led the way back to the kitchen and out its door to the back.

"The flowers are just amazing."

"Well now, Seamus has the touch for certain."

"I'd really like to learn how to garden. Would he mind if I asked him questions?"

"Talk your ear off more like than mind. You ask away. Now, as you can see, there are paths going into the woods, down to the bay. You can walk and wander where you please. There's a path through the woods to the near village. And there you see you've plenty of wood for the fire under the lean-to. If you need more, just tell Seamus and we'll see to it."

Breen thought if she could have any house in the world with any view in the world, it would be just this.

"Now, you won't always have so fine a day as this," Finola continued. "It's Ireland, after all—but when you do, you might sit there at the little table and enjoy the air and a nice cuppa or that glass of wine. Oh, I all but forgot! You've got the internet service. The password there is 'magic one.' That's altogether—one word, I'm meaning—and written out, not the number itself."

Marco took out his phone. "Got it. We'll need that. Breen's a blogger."

"Is that the truth?"

"I'm new at it."

"I'll send you a link," Marco told Finola. "You can bet she'll be blogging about the cottage."

"That would be lovely. Now, is there anything else I should tell you? Are you wondering about anything at all?"

"I can't think of a thing. Honestly?" Breen looked around, tried to see it all at once. "I'm dazzled."

"Then I'll be on my way so you can relax after your journey. My nephew will have taken your bags up to your rooms by now. He's a good lad, is Declan."

"Oh, you didn't have to do that."

Once again, Finola waved it away as she went back inside. Now a bottle of wine stood on the counter.

"Enjoy the first evening of many." She set keys beside the wine.

"You can bet we will," Marco told her. "Why don't I open this, and you can join us in a glass?"

"Aren't you the sweet one, and I thank you. But I have to get on my way. No, no, now, open that wine. I'll show myself the door, as I know where it is." She waved them away, walked to the door. And paused, looked back. "*Fáilte. Déithe libh.* A welcome and a blessing to you both."

"Okay, this is awesome. I gotta say I figured on a cottage deal for you, girl. Now I'm all in. And I'm opening this wine right now."

"Yes, do that. It is awesome. And she was awesome. Did you see her skin? She has to be at least sixty, even if she got married as a teenager, and she's . . . I figured she was maybe forty."

"If she had work, it's top-of-the-line. Just like this stove, where I'm going to cook us a hell of a meal later. You've got to blog your fine ass off about this place."

"I will in the morning, after I sleep in that amazing bed. Pour really big glasses, Marco, and let's take them and walk down to the water. I want to take my shoes off and put my feet in the bay."

"Put them in, hell. We're going to take off our shoes, drink big glasses of wine, and dance in the freaking bay."

"I'm in."

CHAPTER NINE

Breen woke as the first soft light of morning slid into the room. She'd slept deep and—as far as she remembered—dreamless. She wondered if the crystal of pale pink hanging over the bed— one she hadn't noticed until she'd climbed in—had anything to do with it.

She'd known a girl in college who'd sworn by crystal power. Not that she believed any of that.

All she knew for certain was she felt rested, energized, and stupidly happy. She plumped her pillows up, settled back to bask in the room, the view coming to life outside the windows, and the fact she was, for the rest of the summer, home.

Because she caught herself already writing the blog in her head, she bounded up. She pulled a sweatshirt over the T-shirt she'd slept in, thick socks on her bare feet, and went downstairs to make coffee.

She took a big white mug of it into the main-level bedroom, settled down at the laptop she'd set up on the desk.

Then just sipped coffee and sighed at the rioting flowers outside the glass door.

They'd already agreed on a day at the cottage, a lazy one. Marco would sleep in, no question. They'd explore the area—together or separately. And maybe she'd settle in for a couple of hours and work on what she thought might be a short story, or a novel, or nothing at all.

But she wanted to try. Blogging had opened the door—as she now suspected Marco had meant it to.

She booted up her laptop, then took a deep breath.

> A thin, soft rain fell as we left the magic and wonder of
> Dromoland, she began.

More than ninety minutes later, almost without pause, she finished:

> I feel more at home here, sitting at this pretty little desk,
> looking out at the glorious garden a man named Seamus
> tends, than I have anywhere in my life. If the purpose of all
> of this really is Finding Me, I think I've begun to.

She got another cup of coffee before she went over it all, chose and added photos. Agonized over whether she could and should do better. Lectured herself, then put it up.

Back upstairs, she put on workout gear, then used the dual purpose of the room for a solid forty-five minutes.

When she heard clattering in the kitchen, she bounded out to find Marco fumbling at the coffee machine.

"Good morning!"

He gave her a grunt.

"I've done the blog, worked out. I'm going to cook breakfast—which I can actually handle—then shower, change, take a walk. What are you going to do?"

"Drink coffee. And try to ignore my overly perky roommate."

"I've got all this energy!" To prove it, she turned two tight pirouettes.

He answered that with a sleepy, sour look.

"I'll go shower and change first. That'll give you time to wake up before bacon and eggs."

"Deal. Take your perky self upstairs. I'm going to take this coffee . . ." He circled a finger at the door.

"Outside."

"Yeah, there." He rubbed his eyes, managed a smile. "It's annoying as fuck, but perky looks good on you."

"Feels good. Breakfast in thirty," she called out as she bounded from the room.

She served it on the patio. It might've been a bit chilly, but not too. And it wasn't raining. Yet.

"Blog's good, Breen." He shoveled eggs in his mouth like a man starving. "Just gets better and better."

"Because everything's better and better." She looked out at the water, softly blue as the sun pushed light through the clouds, and at the birds that skimmed along, the boat—red as a stop sign—plying its way.

"I love it here. I know it hasn't even been a day, but I love it here."

"It suits you." He studied her as he bit into a slice of the brown bread she'd toasted. "What you wrote at the end of your blog? I think that's true."

"I hope it is. I do want that walk—and I need to get a bird book to go with my flower book. There are so many of them, and I want to know what they are. And it's a little scary, but I want to sit down today and try to write. Not blog, but write a story. Or start to."

He hefted his coffee mug, tapped it to hers. "Then that's what you'll do."

"You aimed me that way, toward writing. Trying to."

"Maybe." Then he grinned at her. "You can give a girl a nudge, but she has to take the step, right? Anyway, I'll stay out of your hair so you can concentrate. I think I'll take a trip into the village. I can poke around, scout out someplace we can go when we want to eat out, where there's music."

"That would be great. There are lots of places to see, and we can plan routes."

"But not today." To prove it, he shot out his legs, crossed his ankles. "Close to home today."

"Exactly. Remember that pledge we made the night we moved into our apartment?"

"Oh yeah. If neither of us find the love of our lives, you and me live together forever."

"Still on?"

"Damn straight, girl."

She'd be happy with that, Breen thought as she set out on her walk. In a lot of ways, Marco was the love of her life. Just minus the sex. And sex wasn't that big a deal—especially when you weren't having it anyway.

She walked along the narrow strip of beach first, letting the wind stream over her hair, her scarf, her jacket. And letting her mind roll toward the story she wanted to tell.

Maybe she didn't know exactly how to start, but it was time to sit down and try. In fact, it was past time. Though she looked with considerable yearning toward the woods, she walked back to the cottage.

No excuses, she told herself. She had an empty cozy house without distractions and a solid space of time. Maybe it was good the entire idea of trying to write, of trying to be a writer made her anxious.

Maybe she'd write better nervous.

She took a jug of water to her desk, opened her laptop.

She spent what felt like hours staring at the screen, fingers poised on the keyboard.

Then her fingers began to move.

> A blue moon rose the night the visitor came to call, and
> Clara's life changed forever.

That first sentence cracked open a dam inside her, and Breen wrote in a flood for two hours.

When she surfaced, she found herself astonished to see she'd filled eight pages with words.

Some of them—most, she thought—were probably terrible. Or worse, even worse, just silly. But she'd written them.

She poured a glass of water, downed it. She got up, paced the room, walked outside, paced some more. And realized she wasn't done.

This time she got a Coke to fortify her, used the little buzz to write for another two hours.

Though it terrified her, she went back to the beginning, began to read. She caught herself second-guessing, fiddling, even considering tossing it all out and starting again.

Then realized she had to stop, step away, let it all just sit. She'd pick it up again in the morning, just start again where she left off.

Because it was amazing to ride along on the current of the story, and she didn't want to give that up.

Dazed, she walked out to find Marco at the stove, something in a pot filling the air with delicious.

"I didn't hear you come back."

"You were in deep, girl. I've done made us some potato and ham soup, got the fire going—it's raining and cooled down some, and I'm trying my hand at making soda bread. Don't judge it harsh, as I'm a bread-baking virgin."

"I didn't help. What time is it?"

"It's glass of wine time for you."

She glanced at the time. "Holy crap! I didn't realize. You didn't have to do all this, Marco. I figured we'd go into the village for dinner."

"I had my fun, and I've got a couple spots picked out for tomorrow night." He poured her a glass of wine from the bottle he'd set on the counter. "You know I like to cook it up when I've got the time, and this Philly boy ain't never made potato soup and soda bread."

She had to admit he looked as happy as happy got as he topped off his own wine.

"I had a sandwich the size of Utah in a pub," he continued, "and lots of conversation. Did a little shopping. Found a bird book for you, a cookbook for me—and used my book to try out what's for dinner."

When he uncovered the shaggy round of bread with a deep X in the center, she studied it.

"You actually made bread. From . . . flour."

"Buttermilk, too. I bought freaking buttermilk. Looks pretty good, right?"

"Looks great, smells great. Why aren't we eating it?"

"Because this soup needs more time, and we're going to use that to sit by the fire, drink some wine while you tell me about your writing day."

"Actually, I think I went into a fugue state."

He covered the bread again before giving the soup another stir.

Then he took her hand, grabbed the wine bottle, and steered her into the living room.

"Like I said, you were in deep when I poked my head in."

"I wrote fifteen pages, Marco."

"That's a lot. That feels like a lot. Can I read them?"

"I . . . not yet. I haven't even read them. I started to." Like him, she propped her feet on the coffee table. "Then, I don't know, I felt like I should just walk away for now, let it all . . . simmer like your soup, I guess."

"Sounds smart. You're going to be a natural at this."

"I don't know about that, but it felt good, and that's enough for now. It all feels good."

So did eating soup and bread in the kitchen, and snuggling up with a book in front of the fire. And waking up in the morning to another day.

She wrote her blog, thinking of it as a warm-up act, then spent an hour on her book. Only an hour, as she set a timer. She'd have weeks and weeks of alone soon, and didn't want to miss the time she had with Marco.

They ventured out, visiting sights and villages, then had dinner in a pub in Clifden with music—and conversation.

She found two people who remembered her father, and his music, but not with the clarity of Tom from Doolin.

They fell into a routine. Breen rose early to write, then they'd have a day out to ramble with a pub meal and music, juggled with days closer to the cottage and dinner at home with Marco walking her through simple recipes.

No matter how hard she tried to stop time, the ten days flew.

On a drippy day that mirrored her mood, she drove her best friend back to Shannon Airport.

"I don't know what I'm going to do without you, Marco. Maybe I should—"

"Don't you even start to say maybe you should go back to Philly, too. You just gave me the best two weeks of my life. Don't go spoiling it."

"It's one thing to talk about spending a whole summer here, by myself. It's another to actually do it."

"You're going to be more than fine. You think I could go if I didn't know that in my gut? And I'll tell you what you're going to do. You're going to write your ass off, learn to cook some more—you're doing okay there."

"Because you stop me before I screw up."

"Screw up, eat a sandwich," he said with a shrug. "You're going to take those crazy long walks you love so much, text me every damn day. And find you. You do that for me, Breen." He squeezed her hand. "You find you, then you can bring you home because I'm going to miss the hot holy hell out of you."

"I already miss you. I couldn't have done any of this without you."

"That goes both ways."

Her heart sank, just sank out of her body when she made the turn for the airport.

"You're going to drop me at the curb, like we said."

"I can park and come in, and—"

"No way. We'll both cry like babies. I got myself a manly tat, I can't be crying like a baby."

"I'm going to cry anyway."

"Do me a solid, Breen."

Already sniffling, she drove toward departures. "You know I will."

"Have fun with all of it. Just let go and have fun. I want to picture you sitting at that desk writing and having fun with it. Sitting outside with some wine, looking at the water, and having fun with it. Maybe getting yourself out for a night at the pub and flirting with some sexy Irish guy, and having fun with it."

"I'm going to try."

"I'm gonna Yoda you. There is no try. Okay now, you've got Finola's number if you need anything at the cottage, and you know how to work the stove and oven. Don't forget to lock up at night even though."

"I won't. Don't worry about me, Marco."

"Shit, course I'm going to worry about you some. It's part of my job."

She pulled up at the curb, remembering how thrilled they'd both been when they'd arrived. "You've got your passport, your tickets, your—"

"I got it all."

He got out to retrieve his bags while she got out and tried not to wring her hands.

"Text me as soon as you land. The minute."

"I will, and you text me when you get back to the cottage. I'll be in that first-class lounge, thanks to my best girl." He set down his bags to grab her into a hard hug. "If you can't sleep or you get nervous, you call me—right out call. Okay?"

"I will. I love you. I'll miss you."

"I love you back, and I'm going to miss you so hard. Now I'm going before I start blubbering." He kissed her, squeezed her again, then grabbed his bags.

He hurried toward the doors, then turned around once. "You have fun, girl, or I'm gonna be really pissed."

Then he was gone.

She drove through rain and tears back to the solitude she didn't know if she was ready for.

The sun broke through minutes before she reached the cottage. And the rainbow shimmering over it had tears flowing again.

She wanted Marco to see it, so she got out of the car, used her phone to try to capture it. Standing there, she sent it with a text.

> A good omen for your safe travel, and my next phase.
> I love you a rainbow's worth.

He responded:

> Love it—def blog worthy. Sitting here like a rich bastard
> drinking a beer and eating freaking canapés. Go take a
> walk under the rainbow. Love you.

Okay, she thought, maybe I will.

She grabbed her purse to take inside, and there changed into the classic Wellingtons Marco had talked her into.

Two steps out the kitchen door, she let out a muffled squeal.

The man wore Wellingtons like hers, rough brown trousers, and a work jacket. Tufts of gray-streaked yellow hair stuck out from under a blue cap.

He was bigger than a leprechaun, but not by much, and his round Irish face, merry blue eyes, and pug nose made her think of one.

He tossed a handful of what she assumed were weeds into a black tub, then tipped his cap at her.

"Good day to you, miss! I'd be Seamus, here to see to the garden if it pleases you."

"Yes, of course. Finola said you'd be by. We must have missed you before."

His smile, charmingly crooked, beamed warmth. "It would seem so. And how are you enjoying your stay?"

"Very much. I—I just dropped my friend off at the airport for his flight home."

"Ah, and that makes you sad, of course. Friendship's the bread of life, isn't it now? Well then, I wish him a fair journey."

"Thank you. The gardens, they're just beautiful."

"Flowers are one of the gifts the gods give us, and tending them a pleasure and duty."

"I've been trying to learn about them—flowers and plants."

He just beamed at her again. "Have you now?"

"Yes, I have a book."

"Books are fine things, one of the finest for certain. But then doing's a good teacher as well."

"If I wouldn't be in the way, could I ask you some questions?"

"Sure and you can ask all you please. The roses there need deadheading. I can show you how it's done, and you can have a go at it if it pleases you."

Between Seamus and the rainbow, her mood lifted. "I'd love to try."

He spent a patient hour with her, naming flowers and plants, explaining growth cycles, guiding her hands to pull a weed or dead-head a spent bloom.

He showed her what flowers to harvest from what he called the cutting garden to make a nice display inside.

When she offered him tea, he thanked her but said he had work elsewhere. So he tipped his cap again before he walked away and left her with a handful of flowers and a feeling of fresh optimism.

She went inside to arrange them, thought she had a decent hand at it. Then looked around the empty cottage. The sad wanted to come back, but she shook her head.

Marco told her to have fun, and she'd already started. She could write. Maybe it was late in the day to begin, but it was her day, after all. Her time.

So she opened what she thought of as a writing Coke and settled in at her desk.

She wrote—maybe not a flood, but a decent stream—until hunger stirred. Grateful Marco had seen she had leftovers so she wouldn't have to dive right into cooking, she warmed up a meal. And thought of him flying over the ocean.

She hoped he drank champagne and watched movies on the smoothest air imaginable.

She did her dishes, then took her delayed walk along the bay in the long summer evening.

When she looked back at the cottage, glowing in the lights she'd left on, she felt wonder, and she felt comfort.

"Right again, Marco. I'll be fine. This is what I want. It's what I need. I miss you, but I'm happy. I'm going to work on staying that way."

She took her time walking back while the moon rose over hill and water.

The water of the bay held a stream of the moonlight, and the breeze murmured of promise. She heard an owl, maybe just wakened, call out.

"Who?" she responded. "Who am I exactly? I'm going to find out."

She went back inside, remembered belatedly to lock up. And pre-pared to spend the first night of her life completely on her own.

Or so she thought.

Sleeping, she didn't see the lights dancing outside her windows, keeping watch. Or the hawk perched on a branch nearby to guard Eian Kelly's daughter.

She woke once when the phone in her hand signaled a text from Marco.

Smooth flight and ur boy's back in Philly. Thanks to the best pal in the world 4 an awesome trip. Now go back 2 sleep and text me tomorrow.

Glad you're home, she texted back. Give everyone a kiss from me. Going back to sleep as ordered.

Nearly there already, she set the phone on the bedside table to dream of rainbows and dancing lights.

CHAPTER TEN

S he found a rhythm.

Always an early riser, Breen usually woke at dawn. Her reward: a misty bay, a shimmering eastern sky. Fueled with coffee, she wrote her daily blog in her pajamas—and considered it her warm-up for the book.

She changed into workout gear, got her body moving before she took a second cup of coffee and whatever came easiest to hand for her morning walk by the bay.

She learned to recognize the birds, the whooper swans, the kestrels and reed buntings, and looked forward to watching them glide and soar while the mists thinned over the water.

She wrote in the quiet, just the breeze and the birds, and was always astonished how the day slid by.

A late afternoon or evening walk with the magpies and wildflowers in the woods. She kept her phone handy for photos, and once marveled at herself for framing a shot of a doe and her fawn who looked at her with more curiosity than alarm.

In a matter of days she realized being alone didn't mean being lonely. She missed Marco, but found the challenge, and the freedom, of being truly on her own satisfying.

She could handle making a meal—especially if it happened to be frozen pizza. She had scores of books to choose from, and hours and hours to write, to walk, to consider what she wanted to do with the rest of her life.

On the last, she made a list.

I'll keep writing, whether it's the blog or a book or just stories for myself. I won't give it up.

I'll find a job I actually like, and one I'm good at.

I'll buy a house. A small house, but with room enough for me and Marco, and a little office for writing. Must have a yard.

I'll plant a garden.

I'll get a dog.

I'll keep trying to find my father, and when I do, I'll find a way to forgive him for leaving.

I'll figure out how to talk to my mother, and find a way to forgive her for . . . everything.

One day, she imagined, she'd start crossing things off that list. When she did, she might add more—big things, small things. But for now, the list encompassed what she most wanted, and that was enough.

At the end of her first week, she drove into the village for supplies, and reminded herself she had to get out and about at least now and again. After a week of near silence, she found it jarring to see all the cars, the people—and admitted she was working herself into becoming a hermit.

To counteract it, she walked through the village, browsed the shops, and by taking the time came across a music store—with an Irish harp in the front window.

It drew her inside, where a woman about her age with a short wedge of black hair sat behind a counter and played a dulcimer.

She stopped, smiled. "Good day to you."

"That was lovely. Please don't stop."

"Oh, just passing the time. Is there something I can help you with?"

"The harp in the window. It's beautiful."

"Ah, the Irish baby harp. It's a lovely piece. Would you like to see it?"

"Yes, thanks."

"And do you play then?" she asked as she came around the counter to walk to the display window.

"No. It's for a friend, a musician."

"Well now, a finer gift you couldn't find." She set it on a table in a room full of mandolins, banjos, accordions, flutes, drums.

Breen wondered how both she and Marco had missed the shop on their earlier visits. It was Marco heaven.

"It's beautiful," Breen said again, "the wood, the shape."

"Rosewood, it is." The woman trailed a finger over the strings and produced a sound, angel pure.

"Was it made in Ireland?"

"Not only in Ireland, but right here. In the back. My father made it."

"Your father?"

"Sure, he builds instruments, repairs them. Oh, not all of these," she said with a smile as she gestured around. "But quite a few of what we have now. You said you don't play, but would you care to sit and get a feel for it?"

"I . . . Yes, actually, I think I would."

"Here then, have a chair, won't you? I'm Bess, by the way."

"I'm Breen. I appreciate this."

Breen sat, and Bess brought her the harp, showed her how to hold it on her knee.

Breen had a flash, clear as glass. Her hands on the strings of a harp, her father's over hers, guiding.

"My father had a harp like this," she murmured.

"Did he now?"

"I remember how he started to teach me . . ."

She put her fingers on the strings, closed her eyes to cast her mind back. And played a melody.

"'The Foggy Dew.'" Bess clapped. "And you remember very well indeed."

She didn't know why or how she'd forgotten.

"I—I want to buy it."

"For yourself?" Bess asked with a smile. "Or your friend?"

"For my friend. And I wonder if your father has a minute."

"Sure he does. I'll just go fetch him. Play more if you like. I'll just be a moment."

She would play more, Breen thought, but not here. At the cottage, alone, where she could let the emotions out—all the joy and the pain—with no one to see.

But she ran her fingers over the wood, remembering so well how her father told her it wasn't just the playing but the caring. An instrument was a garden, needed love, needed tending.

The man who came out had silver shot through the black of his hair. He wore a brown carpenter's apron over a tall, robust frame.

"Well now, it's pleased I am to see my darling there go to someone who knows what she's about. You hold her with love."

As my father taught me, Breen thought.

"She's beautiful, and her notes are so pure. She'll be treasured."

"For that I thank you."

"I wondered . . . My father's a musician. He had a harp much like this when I was a little girl. He was from Galway. Eian Kelly."

The man fisted his hands on his hips. "You're Eian Kelly's girl, are you? Wonder I didn't see it right away. You've the look of him."

"You know him." Cradling the harp, she stood.

"That I did. I made him a fine box once upon a time."

"A box?"

Now he grinned. "An Irish accordion—squeeze box, you see. Custom work, as he had very specific wants in it. And the man could play like a fleet of angels or demons. Does he still?"

"I don't know, but I imagine he does. He and my mother . . ."

"Ah well, I'm sorry to hear it. I heard he went to America."

"Yes, but he came back here. I think here in Galway."

"I haven't seen him for . . . Oh, I can't count the years."

"He grew up on a farm in Galway. Would you know where?"

Sympathy covered his face. "I don't, and I'm sorry for that. I can ask around and about if that might help."

"It would, very much. I'll give you my number in case. I'm staying nearby for the summer."

When she walked out, carrying the harp in its case, she thought maybe, just maybe, he'd find someone who knew someone who knew.

She wanted to go back to the cottage, but pushed herself into the market for those supplies. Then made herself put everything away before she changed into hiking boots.

No writing, she thought, not when her mind was so crowded. A long walk into the peace of the woods might quiet it.

But when she stepped out, Seamus stood on the little patio with a big painted pot at his feet and a flood of flowers waiting to be planted.

"And how are you today, miss?"

"Glad to see you. What a beautiful pot. Are you going to plant flowers in it?"

"Well now, I thought you might like to do that yourself."

"Oh, I'd love to, but I wouldn't know where to begin."

He offered her gloves and a spade. "You start with earth and good intentions."

He showed her how to fill the bottom of the pot with broken crockery—for drainage—and how to mix soil and peat and rich compost in the barrow.

But he wouldn't pick the flowers for her.

"What if I choose the wrong ones?"

"There's no wrong to it. All of these are happy in this clime. And what's left, well, we'll find another spot for. There's always a spot waiting to be filled."

He gave her the names of the ones she chose—the Dragon Wing begonias, the lantana and lobelia, bells of Ireland, heliotrope and impatiens and sweet alyssum.

"It's a good eye you have, for the color and the heights, the textures."

As once her father's had over harp strings, Seamus's gloved hands covered hers as she placed a plant. "That's the way of it, there you are now. And we wish it good fortune, and a long, happy life in its new home."

"Can I add this? I love the color—such a pretty green."

"Creeping Jenny, she is, and you'll want her at the edge so she can flow right over and show off her skirts."

"It's like a rainbow. A really bold one."

"It is indeed, it is just that. You did fine and well. Now we'll water her up, though you'll have some rain tonight. You'll want to keep the soil moist, you see, but not wet. What you do? You stick your finger into the soil to test it."

When they'd finished the pot, he helped her choose spots for the leftovers. She dug in the dirt with a kind of giddy glee.

"I'm going to find a house and plant a garden one day. Like this one, where it all seems unplanned and beautiful."

"You'll do well with it." His voice, so soothing, sounded like a whisper in her heart. "It's all connected, you see, young Breen. The earth, the air, the water that falls from the sky, the sun that brings the light and warmth. And all that grows—the plants, the animals, the people. The bees that buzz, the birds that fly, all bound together.

"You'll talk to them now, to the flowers, sing them a tune now and again. They'll reward you for it."

She sat back on her heels, smiling at her grubby garden gloves. "I was feeling a little sad when I got home. Now I'm not."

"Gardens bring the joy."

"This one sure did." She, so often uncomfortable around strangers, felt as if she'd known him all her life.

Connections, she thought. All bound together.

"Seamus, have you always lived in the area?"

"I haven't, no. I'm here now, of course, but Galway's not my home."

Then he wouldn't know her father, she thought, so no point in asking.

"Now I'll be cleaning up this bit of a mess before I'm on my way."

"We'll clean it up." She stood. "That's part of it, isn't it?"

He shot her that crooked smile. "That it is."

With the patio swept, she offered him the gloves.

"Oh no, miss, those are yours now, and the little spade as well. Such things are handy for gardening."

"Thank you. Can I make you some tea?"

"Thank for you the asking, but my wife'll be putting on supper before long, so I'd best be on my way. I'll be back again in the week, or sooner if I'm needed. Enjoy the flowers, young Breen, as they enjoy you."

"I will."

And she'd start by taking a picture of her very first flowerpot.

She took a couple, then thought she'd like one of Seamus for her blog. But when she turned, he was already gone.

"He moves fast," she murmured.

She took her gloves and spade into the mudroom.

Instead of the walk—where she could admit she would have brooded through most if not all of it—she poured a glass of wine, sat at the little patio table.

And admired her work.

That evening, she followed—religiously—one of Marco's simple recipes for a one-skillet chicken, potato, and broccoli dish. It mostly worked.

She took a photo for the blog before she bundled in a sweater, poured another glass of wine, and took it all out to the patio again.

She'd remembered something about her father that, now that she'd settled, made her happy. She'd found the perfect Christmas gift for her best friend. She'd planted flowers in both a pot and the ground. She'd made a decent—okay, halfway decent meal.

Not to mention she'd written nearly two hours that morning before she'd ordered herself to get out of the cottage.

"A good day," she told the flowers. "Really, a damn good day." She toasted the garden, the woods, the bay. "Here's to many more. I've got this," she decided. "I think I've actually got this."

But that night she dreamed of a storm. It raged over the hills, swept over the fields. It churned the water into a dark morass. The trees whipped in its tossing wind.

Heart pounding, she ran through it while lightning flashed—blue fire—and thunder roared in warlike fury.

Still, it wasn't the storm that chased her, but something darker, something much more wicked. She could feel that dark clawing at her, fighting to get a pinching hold.

For her soul. It would take all she was, and drink it like wine.

You were made for this, it told her. *I am destiny.*

The sword on her belt banged against her thigh. She could use it. She would use it. To fight, or to end herself.

She would end herself before she lost herself again.

As her hand closed over it, she saw a light ahead. It glowed, and it grew. Like a door opening for her.

Like salvation.

In the light, another voice called her.

Come home, Breen Siobhan, daughter of the O'Ceallaigh, child of the Fey. It's time you came home. Time you awakened.

As the claws of the dark scraped at her back, she leaped into the light.

And woke, sheened with sweat, tangled in the sheets.

Because her first instinct was to call Marco, she reached for her phone. Then, very carefully, very deliberately, put it back on the nightstand. She wouldn't call her friend, thousands of miles away, to soothe her over a stupid nightmare.

She was fine. She was awake. No storm raged, and no one chased her.

Still, she picked up her tablet, wrote out everything she could remember.

Maybe she'd work it into her story. A nasty dream ought to be worth something in the light of day.

Because the light of day was some hours off, she left a lamp on low rather than risk the dark.

She hit routine, and happily. Writing about the music store—though she had to leave out seeing and buying the harp to keep it a surprise for Marco. She wrote about planting flowers, making a meal, and got her day off to a solid start.

When she stepped outside to grin at her flowerpot, she noted it had rained, just as Seamus had predicted. Maybe it had stormed, and her subconscious twisted reality into a weird, scary dream.

Either way, after her morning walk, she'd spend the rest of the damp, cool morning writing. Out of habit, she started toward the bay, still misty, still gray under the struggling sun.

A series of yips had her glancing toward the woods. If not for the barks, she might have taken it for a very small, odd-looking deer or really big rabbit.

But as it raced toward her, she saw a puppy—still odd-looking, with a purple cast to its tightly curled fur, and a hairless little whip of a tail.

"Look at you!" She crouched down to greet him and was rewarded with adoring puppy kisses and scrabbling paws. A good-size pup, he had a smooth face beneath a kind of curly topknot and above what she thought of as a cute beard. His eyes, a deep brown, shone with excitement.

"Oh, aren't you sweet! Look at those curls. Where'd you come from, cutie? Are you lost?"

He answered by racing in circles around her, leaping back to lick at her hands, her face.

"Yes, I'm glad to meet you, too. But you belong to someone, and someone takes good care of you. They'll wonder where you are."

She took out her phone to take a picture. After several blurred attempts, she managed one.

"I'm going to text this to Finola. Maybe she knows who you belong to."

As she started to, he raced away toward the woods.

"No, now wait. You'll get lost."

She tried whistling him back. He did stop, wagging that hairless whip of a tail.

Then he raced in circles again, stopped, eyeing her.

"Fine, I'll come to you."

She should probably take him inside, text Finola.

But when she got close, he dashed toward the woods again. Stopped again, looking back as if to say: *Come on! Let's go!*

Committed, she stuck her phone back in her pocket, and followed.

He must live nearby, she decided, as he showed no signs of being a stray. And, clearly, he knew where he wanted to go.

"Well, I wanted a walk, so I guess I get one this way."

He trotted ahead, doubled back or waited, always keeping her in sight. Not in the direction that led to the village, she noted, so he probably didn't come from there.

An outlying farm, maybe, or another cottage she'd yet to see.

Leaves and pine needles dripped on a path soft from the night's rain. And the air swelled with the scents of damp earth and green. Blankets of moss coated the bark on trees and branches snuggled in the shade while the weak sun slid through here and there to dapple the earth.

The pup chased a big, black squirrel up a tree, where it scolded him with outraged chitters.

Because she'd never walked this deep in this direction, Breen made sure to pay attention, to fix landmarks—a fallen branch, a small clearing half ringed with starry white flowers, a huddle of gray stones, one as high as her waist.

As she walked on, she thought the trees grew thicker, taller. The path narrowed, roughened as if few walked this way.

But the dog gave another happy yip, and she heard her first cuckoo call.

She could find her way back, Breen assured herself. A few twists and turns, sure, but she had her landmarks, and she had the cottage on her phone's GPS. She and her new friend were having an adventure.

She'd wanted to put a dog in her book, hadn't she? And now here he was.

She avoided the brambles encroaching on the path, and so did the pup. Though he sniffed occasionally as if interested, and once squatted to pee.

She considered trying to grab him up, but wasn't sure—at all— she could carry a big, wriggling pup all the way back to the cottage.

"We've come this far," she told him, "might as well see it through."

They walked by a bubbling little stream, and the pup leaped in to splash.

Webbed feet, she thought, meant some sort of water dog. Though too shallow for swimming, he scrambled up on rocks, down them again, stuck his nose in the water and enjoyed himself so much she took more pictures.

She'd share them with his owner, she decided. She felt certain the woods would open any minute to that farm or cottage.

He climbed out, shook wildly so the dense curls bounced. And with a wag of his skinny tail, trotted on.

Then she saw it and stopped in wonder and admiration.

Not the little farm or cottage, not an opening to the fretful sunlight.

The tree, enormous, had branches curving down, then up again like a giant's arching arms. Some so big, so deeply dipped, they skimmed the ground before bowing up again.

Its trunk, wide as her arm span, grew out of a mound of large gray stones. Or the stones grew from the trunk—she couldn't say which. Its leaves, larger than her hand, glowed a bold, bright green.

The dog sat in front of the wonder of it with what might have been a look of pride.

"Yes, I see where you brought me, and it's amazing. Just amazing. Sit right here so I can get a picture. I've never seen anything like it."

She framed it in, tried a different angle, then another while the dog waited patiently.

"Is that carving on the trunk?"

She moved closer, and the dog rose to paw at her legs and wag.

"It is carving! I think it's ogham—it looks like it. And what is that? Some symbols."

She had to climb on the rocks, balance a hand on one of the curved branches to keep her balance for a closer look.

She'd have sworn it all vibrated—the stone under her feet, the wood under her hand.

She'd have sworn she heard it hum.

"We're just excited, right?" she said to the dog. "We found a magic tree in the woods. I'm going to get some pictures of the carvings. I can google them later."

She spread her legs, planted her feet until she felt steady enough.

When the stacks of clouds smothered the sun, she used the flash. She took pictures of the leaves, thinking she could show them to Seamus. He might tell her what kind of tree this beauty was.

Then she crouched to study the base, the rocks.

"It's like they're one unit. I really can't tell where the rocks start and the tree ends, or the other way around."

She glanced back at the dog, who'd climbed onto the rocks behind her. "And I really don't know how we're going to get around it, as it's wider, by a long shot, than the path. Unless we climb and crawl our way. And I don't think that's the best idea."

He boosted himself onto the rock beside her.

"So let's go back to the cottage. I can text Finola. I'll get you a drink. I bet you could use one. Me, too."

She rubbed his curly head. Before she could work out how to get an arm around him to secure him while she climbed down, he let out another series of barks and ran forward.

"Oh, don't! Damn it!"

Muttering curses, calling herself an idiot, she crawled through after him. She swung her leg over one of the branches to sit, get her bearings.

And felt the world drop away.

PART II
DISCOVERY

Know thyself.
−Inscribed on the Temple of Apollo at Delphi

What we have to learn to do,
we learn by doing.
                                    −Aristotle

CHAPTER ELEVEN

She lay flat on her back on thick grass under a brilliantly blue sky. The few clouds that puffed across it were as white and fluffy as the black-faced sheep grazing only a few feet away.

The puppy braced his front paws on her chest and licked madly at her face.

Had she fallen—hit her head?

She'd been in the woods, hadn't she? The tree, and then . . .

She didn't know what the hell happened.

"Okay, okay." She pushed at the puppy, started to sit up.

Her head spun; her stomach turned over.

She lay back again, shut her eyes.

"I hit my head, I must have. A concussion maybe. I know it was gray and threatening rain before I fell. Jesus, how long have I been lying here?"

Slowly, an inch at a time, she braced on her elbow. Waiting, just breathing. But she could see the farm she'd imagined across a narrow dirt road. Big spotted cows grazed behind a stone fence, crops of some sort grew behind another.

The house—stone again, like the outbuildings—sat back from the road with smoke curling out of the chimneys.

"That must be home, right? I'm okay. I know my name, the date, where I am. Maybe a mild concussion."

Carefully, she reached back, looked for a lump on her head. "It doesn't hurt, and no bump. Just knocked the wind out of me. So, good."

She sat up, had to close her eyes again before she got shakily to her feet.

Her ears rang.

A little dizzy, she admitted, and a little queasy, but she couldn't lie there in a field with sheep. She just had to get across the road to the farmhouse, drink some water—God, she could use some water, and a ride back to the cottage.

She looked back to see how far she'd fallen, and saw the tree spread on the rise at the edge of the field.

No more than three feet, she judged, from those curved branches. How the hell did she knock herself silly dropping a couple feet, and onto thick grass?

But since she had, she walked carefully—staggered, really—to the stone fence. The dog climbed right over.

"Yeah, easy for you."

Under her current circumstances, she had to work at it. When she reached the road, she aimed in a diagonal line for the house.

An iron gate spanned the gap in the stone fence, so she fixed that as her goal.

She heard singing—a man's voice—and her gaze shifted over.

He sang as he walked behind a muscular horse, behind a plow that cut through rich brown earth.

He wore boots and trousers, with his hair spilling black beneath his cap.

She'd dreamed this once, she remembered. Maybe she dreamed again.

When he turned his head, when he saw her, he pulled the plow horse up.

For Breen the world went gray, all gray as she slid into a faint in the middle of the dirt road.

"Ah, Jesus! You stand, girl. You stand." He came on the run, calling out, "Aisling! Aisling, come help. There's a woman hurt out here."

He didn't bother with the gate, but vaulted over the stones to drop down beside Breen just as his sister burst out the front door.

"What woman? Where? Oh, dear gods, is she breathing?"

"She's fainted is all. I've got her."

"Bring her in. I'll have the gate. Bring her inside, poor thing."

Once she'd opened the gate, Aisling reached out to lay a hand on Breen's cheek, then pulled it back. "Harken, she looks like—"

"I see it now. Well then, Marg said she'd come, and so she has. But it's a hell of a welcome home."

"Lay her on the divan there," Aisling directed when he carried Breen inside. "I'll get a cool cloth, some water."

"I'll get them." He pulled off his cap, pushed at his thick mop of hair while he studied Breen. "If she comes around before, she's likely to be less frightened by another woman, I'm thinking. You'll check, won't you, if she's hurt or if she just came through too fast and unprepared?"

"Aye, aye, go on then."

She laid her hand on Breen's cheek again, moved to her brow, then her throat, her heart, looking in, feeling. Satisfied, she drew a throw over Breen's legs as Harken came back with a bowl and a cup.

"She's fine, fine and strong with it. Just unsteady is all, from coming through."

Taking the cloth from the bowl, she wrung it out, laid it over Breen's forehead. Then took one of Breen's hands in both of hers. Rubbed it.

"Come and wake now, Breen Siobhan O'Ceallaigh. Come slow and easy. Do you know what tea to brew, Harken?"

"Sure and I know what fecking tea to brew."

"Of course, aye, don't be so testy, and brew a cup. It'll help her steady up. Slow and easy now, and all's well."

Breen opened her eyes and stared into as perfect a face as she'd ever seen. Porcelain skin, a bow-shaped mouth in a gentle smile, eyes as blue as the sky, thickly lashed as dark as the ebony hair that spilled out of a messy topknot.

"There you are now. You'll have some water." She slid an arm under Breen's shoulders to lift her, then held a crockery cup to her lips.

"Thank you. I'm sorry. I was dizzy. I think I took a spill. There was a dog, a puppy . . ."

"This one here? The one looking at you with his heart in his eyes?"

"Yes. Is he yours?"

"No indeed. Not yours then?"

"No, he's . . . I'm sorry. I'm Breen Kelly."

"And it's lovely to meet you. I'm Aisling—Hannigan," she said after a slight hesitation. "And here's my brother Harken Byrne, who scooped you up from the road."

"Thank you. Thank you both."

He had the look of his sister, though his skin had a ruddier hue and his cheeks carried a scruff.

"It's nothing at all," Harken told her. "I've tea brewing up. It'll smooth it all out for you."

"I'm sorry to be so much trouble." Struggling with embarrassment, Breen pushed herself up. And when the room spun slowly, braced a hand on the cushion of the divan.

"A bit dizzy yet?" Aisling asked her.

"Just a little, not nearly as much. I was trying to get the dog back home. He took me through the woods, and all the way to that amazing tree."

Leaning back, she closed her eyes and didn't see the look brother and sister exchanged.

"I must've lost my balance."

"It happens, doesn't it now? I'll fetch the tea."

"I should get back," Breen said when Harken walked out of what Breen saw was a cozy living room with a hearth, a wooden floor, tables, chairs. "I don't know what to do about the puppy."

"I may have an idea about that, but here now, drink your tea first. It'll help. Your stomach's unsteady yet."

"You're right about that. Your farm's beautiful," she said as Harken came back with another cup.

"We tend it," he said. "It tends us."

"Thanks." Grateful, she took the tea. "You were plowing—with a horse."

"That I was. Starting, I was, the summer planting for the winter harvest."

"It was like a book or movie." Or a dream. "So charming. The tea's wonderful. What is it?"

"A ginger tea with some mint, and some this and that." Aisling smiled at her.

"It works." Relieved, she set down the cup. She not only felt like herself again, but energized. "Thanks so much, for everything."

"I wonder if you'd take a short walk with me." Aisling looked down at the curly dog. "I think I may know where he came from."

"Really? That would relieve my mind. He's so sweet, and I'd hate for him to get lost or hurt."

"No chance of it. I won't be long, Harken. The babies should sleep until I'm back."

"Not to worry. We'll all be fine. It's pleased I am to meet you, Breen."

"I'm lucky I met you." The kindness—it simply radiated from him—soothed her embarrassment. "Thanks again." She walked outside with Aisling and the puppy on her heels. "You have children?"

"I do, yes. Finian's near to three and Kavan's sixteen months now. And there's another growing strong." She laid a hand on her belly.

"Oh, congratulations."

"It best be a girl this time, I swear. I'm pining for a girl. My man's off with my other brother on . . . business. There's our cottage, you see there, where the bay curves into the land."

Breen shielded her eyes from the sun. "It's lovely."

She must have gotten turned around in the woods, she realized. She'd have sworn the bay would have been on her left.

"I'm staying in a cottage not far from here."

"Are you now?"

"Yes, for the summer. I love it there."

"We'll turn here. And I see the pup knows the way. I think we've solved the mystery of him."

They walked off the road and back into the woods along a smooth brown path flanked with shrubs smothered in blossoms of pure snowy white.

When the path curved, Breen stopped.

The cottage, stone walled, thatched roofed, sat snugly in the clearing. Flowers rivered around it, poured out of window boxes of gleaming copper. The door, painted a bold blue, stood open as if expecting visitors.

Something squeezed her heart, twisted it so violently Breen pressed a hand against it. Her throat closed, snapping off her air.

"It's all right now," Aisling said quietly as she slid an arm around Breen's waist. "Use your breath, and you'll be fine." Reaching up, she laid a hand over Breen's, pressed.

The pressure eased.

"Sorry. Just a really strong case of déjà vu. It's lovely, really lovely. Storybook time. Silly reaction."

"Not at all. We'll go in now, won't we? I'll wager Marg has the kettle on the hob."

She came to the doorway, stood in the shadows. Her hair formed a crown of fiery red. In a sweater the color of wild plums, stone-gray trousers, and scarred boots, she looked regal, even when the dog raced up to plant his forepaws on her legs. With her posture soldier straight, she reached down to gracefully glide a hand over the dog's head.

She knew that face, Breen thought. How could she not when it was like looking in a mirror, one that had aged a generation or two but remained perfectly clear?

"You're welcome here," she said. "You're so very welcome here."

Breen found her voice, and though it didn't tremble, it came out raw. "Who are you?"

"I'm Mairghread O'Ceallaigh. Kelly, you would say. I'm your grandmother. Will you come in? It's been a very long time."

"I'll leave you here."

Shaken, Breen turned to Aisling. "But—"

"She's waited for you, and you, I think, for her. I'll see you again."

"Thank you, Aisling, for bringing her."

"More than happy. She had a bit of a turn on coming through, but she's an O'Ceallaigh, after all. She's steadied up. Go on now, Breen, and talk to your nan."

Aisling gave her a quick rub on the back, then turned to walk back up the path.

"You've questions, so many. I'll answer whatever I can."

Isn't that what she wanted? To find answers. Bracing herself for them, Breen stepped forward.

"We'll have some tea, won't we? And you," Marg said to the dog, "I've a treat for you, then you'll be a good boy."

Marg stepped back; Breen stepped in.

Sunlight spilled through the open windows where sheer lace curtains fluttered. Two chairs, deeply cushioned in forest green, angled toward the stone hearth—unlit in the warmth of the day.

Candles and crystals and flowers decorated the stone mantel.

A small sofa, blue like the door, held plump pillows of intricate needlepoint and a throw of blues fading into greens.

"The kitchen's a family place," Marg said, and led the way back, through a stone arch, and into a room twice the size of the other.

A fire burned there, fragrant with peat, in a strange little stove where a copper kettle heated.

Open shelves and cupboards held bright blue dishes, white cups, gleaming glassware, little jars filled with color. On the gleaming wood counters sat more flowers, potted herbs, more jars.

Kitchen tools, skillets, pots, an apron all hung on pegs.

She knew this place, Breen thought. But how could she when she'd never been here?

Because her father had described it to her—that had to be the answer.

"I thought tea," Marg began, "but you're a bit pale, and it's a day, isn't it, for both of us. Why not wine? Will you sit, *mo stór*?"

But she stood. "Is my father here?"

"In you, in me, he is always. But not the way you're meaning. Please sit. I've a need to myself."

Breen sat at the little square of a table, clutched her hands together in her lap. Marg took something out of a jar, then tapped her finger in the air at the dog, who'd hopefully followed them in.

He sat, wiggled in anticipation. Whatever Marg gave him had him prancing off to sprawl in the corner and gnaw on it.

She poured a clear amber liquid out of a jug into stemless glasses, then set them on a painted tray with a plate of cookies.

"Shortbread biscuits. They were one of your favorites as a child."

And still were, Breen thought.

"How do you know that?" she demanded as Marg set the glasses, the plate on the table. "I've never met you before."

Marg took the tray back to the counter, sat. "My girl, I helped bring you into this world. It was my hands that drew you from your mother's womb. Yelling, you were, your little fists shaking and ready to fight, and a down of red hair on your head, already curling."

"You came to Philadelphia?"

"No, you were born here, just down the road at the farm."

"No, that's not right. I was born in Philadelphia. My mother said . . ." Had she? Breen wondered. Or had she herself simply assumed? "I thought—no, my birth certificate says I was born in Philadelphia."

"Such things are easy enough to fix as you please, aren't they now? Why would I lie to you about such a thing?"

"I don't know. Where's my father? Does he live nearby?"

Marg picked up her wine, sipped slowly. Then she set the glass down, met Breen's eyes. And because she saw grief, Breen knew before the words were spoken.

"No. No, he's not—"

"Do you think he wouldn't come back to you if he could? That he would leave you? You, the light and heart of his life? He loved you beyond measure, and you know that for truth. Your own heart knows."

"When?" Breen choked it out, then covered her face with her hand. "When?"

"You won't want the comfort of my arms now, for you only remember tiny bits as yet. One day, I hope we can comfort each other. He was my boy, my life, my only child."

Through a veil of tears, Breen saw sorrow, saw the depth of it.

"He came back, as it was his duty, as he was needed. He died a hero, understand that, fourteen years ago this past winter. Everyone in all the worlds owes him that honor and that debt."

"I don't understand. He wasn't a soldier."

"Oh, sure and he was much more than that." Pride joined grief. "If he could've had his own wish, he'd have been but a father, a husband, a son, a farmer, but he was called, and answered."

"Does my mother know?"

"I can't tell you." Marg picked up her wine again. "I would say she does, deep inside her, but it would be easier, wouldn't it, to believe he'd just left. She loved him," Marg said quickly. "Know that as well. When they met and made vows, made you, there was love between them, and deep, true."

Sense memory, Marco called it. Because she knew this place, the farm, the air. She knew it in her heart.

"If I was born here, when did they leave? Why did they leave?"

"There's a story here for another time, but I can say she was unhappy here, your mother, and grew . . . anxious for her own world. She wanted you in that world. And my Eian chose, as a man should, his wife and child."

"But he came back here?"

"Often, as often as he could." Taking a moment, Marg looked down at her wine, then lifted her gaze—eyes of misty blue. "I pined for you, I'll humble myself and say it. But he never brought you back, as your mother wanted you where you were. He hoped when you were older, and he could explain more to you, you'd come with him. But that wasn't to be."

"Why was she—and still is, really—so dead set against me visiting Ireland?

Marg glanced at Breen's untouched glass. "Would you rather tea after all?"

"No . . ." She picked up the glass, sipped. "It's good—it's so . . . fresh."

"My own making." Marg smiled, and Breen felt that the light went bright with it. "Dandelion wine it is. It's summer in a glass, I think."

"Yes. You never wrote or called or . . . He told me about you, about here. I just can't remember clearly."

"You will, in time."

A glass of wine at a kitchen table didn't bridge the gap of a lifetime.

"Why didn't you keep in touch with me? Why didn't you tell me when he died?"

"It was agreed it was best you forgot your time here, those first three years."

"Three years? I lived here until I was three?"

"Such a bright and happy child you were. Your mother . . . you mustn't blame her too harshly. I've wanted to myself, I'll admit it, but she was out of place here, and she feared for you. You were so gifted. And then, you were taken."

"Taken where? You mean . . . I was kidnapped?"

"Taken, yes, and she was terrified. We all were. We got you back, safe, unhurt, but your mother, it was too much for her."

Born on a farm in Ireland, kidnapped at three? How could that be part of her life?

"They never told me! It's not right they never told me, not any of this."

"She needed to close it off, to close it all off."

"You sent me money," Breen murmured. "My father, then you after . . . after he died."

"He did, and when he was gone, I did. It was all I could do for you until now, when you've chosen to come. If you chose to stay as you were, well, the money could soften your life. Your father put money away for you, and I sent it along as well after he died."

"She didn't tell me. She kept that from me, too."

"I know."

"How do you know?" Breen demanded. "Have you talked with her?"

"I haven't, no, as she wouldn't want to talk with me. There are ways to know and see."

"You're my grandmother—the only grandparent I have. She was estranged from her parents, and then they died years ago. Unless . . . Do I have a grandfather?"

"Another time for that."

Breen pushed up, wine in hand. "None of this makes sense, not really. I lived here, according to you, for the first three years of my life, but I don't remember."

"Don't you?" Marg said softly.

Sun streaming through lace curtains, the smell of baking. Music and laughter in that farmhouse.

And her father's hands guiding hers on the strings of a harp.

"I get blurry pictures sometimes, but they're mixed in with the stories Da used to tell me. And he's dead, and all this time, no one told me. I waited for him. I came looking for him. I was so angry with him."

Tears flowed now as much in anger as grief as she paced around the kitchen. "I have a grandmother who sent money—a hell of a lot of money—but never called, never wrote—and I'm a grown woman, so that's a bullshit excuse about what my mother wanted. You never said here I am, come visit me, or I'll come to you."

"It wasn't time."

"Time?" She whirled back. "It wasn't time for twenty-odd years, now suddenly it is?"

"Aye, now it is. You were unhappy, blocked from so much that you are. I kept my word to your mother, and now I'm keeping my word to my boy. For his last thoughts were of you. And dying, my boy . . ."

Grief poured into the air, so Breen sat again and pushed down her own anger. "I'm sorry. This is hard for you."

"I wanted a bevy of babies, and had only the one. Oh, but such a one. A comet he was. And as the flame of him was going out, his heart asked of mine to give your mother more time. He loved her, Breen, and never stopped. But his love for you was beyond even that. He asked of me to watch and wait, and if I saw you had a need to come through, even more than if you were needed—and you are—that I would see to it. So I have."

"How did you see to it? I didn't know about the money, and it was just, well, luck, that I found out. Then got pissed off enough to do something I wanted. I came to Ireland because I wanted to see and feel and know that part of my heritage. I wanted to see where my father grew up, and I hoped to find him. I didn't even know you existed when I decided to come to Ireland."

"Well, that's the thing, isn't it? You're not in Ireland now."

"Maybe you've had too much wine," Breen said carefully. "Because I'm sitting right here. I've been staying in a cottage maybe a mile away, in Galway, for two weeks."

"Aye, well, the cottage is in Ireland, that's true. But you came through."

"What? The looking glass?"

"And a fine story that is," her grandmother said easily. "We're fond of stories here. You wanted a dog." Marg looked back at the pup, who'd curled up for a nap. "I sent you a dog. Your father left his two with me when he left—and oh, you cried so hard for them. For me as well, but wept, inconsolable, for the dogs. They've passed now, gone onto the next, but they had good long lives first."

"Will . . . Will and Lute."

"So you remember," Marg said with a smile. "Eian named Will for the bard, and Lute as she liked to howl and did so musically."

"I . . ." She did remember. Both big, gray, shaggy. Wolfhounds, Irish wolfhounds. "Sometimes I'd ride on Will's back, like a pony. I shouldn't be able to remember that. I couldn't have been a year old."

"The heart remembers."

Because something in her started to jitter, Breen looked back at the sleeping pup. Safer territory. "So he is your dog? What's his name?"

"He's yours—a gift."

"I can't take him. I'm going back to Philadelphia at the end of the summer. And I have an apartment. I'm going to look for a house, but . . ."

"That's not a worry if you want him. You've wanted a dog. You've always had an affinity for animals and . . . living things. I wanted to give you something your heart wanted, and so there he is."

Not safer territory after all.

"Is it safe you're wanting?" Marg demanded. "Is it really what you're wanting when you wear the word for courage over the beat of your own heart?" She tapped a finger on Breen's tattoo. "Be brave, girl, and listen. You're blood of my blood, and I gave up the joy of you for reasons you'll learn as time goes. But the time for that is done, and the choices now will be in your hands."

"What choices?"

"So many, and some already made, as they brought you here. You came to the Welcoming Tree and went forward, not back, and so passed through the portal with Ireland and America and all the rest of that world on one side, and this world—your homeplace, Talamh—on the other."

Breen nudged her wine aside. "This area's called Tala? I haven't heard of it."

With some impatience Marg spelled it out. "Though you pronounce it well enough. It's a world, as real and solid as any other. But we are not of the others, nor they of us. Some worlds are very old, some very young. Some embrace violence, others embrace peace. Some, as the world you were reared in most of your life, wish for machines and technology to both build and destroy. But here, we have chosen to abjure such things and hold on to the magicks, their powers and their beauties."

Breen didn't doubt this woman was her grandmother. The resemblance was too strong, and the grief when Marg had spoken of her son unquestionably real.

But that didn't mean her grandmother wasn't a little bit crazy.

"You're actually talking about, what, a multiverse? That's comic-book stuff."

Marg slapped a hand on the table, made Breen jump. "Why are so many so arrogant they don't just believe they're all there is, but insist upon it?"

"Because science?"

"Bah. Science changes generation by generation—and more. Once in the realm of Earth the science said the world was flat—until they said it wasn't. Science changes, *mo stór*. Magick is constant."

"Science doesn't change so much as it finds new data and information to adjust its findings. I mean, gravity was gravity, right, long before the metaphorical apple fell on Newton's head. But . . . I understand things are different here, and I understand—to a point—why you didn't feel able to keep in contact with me. I'm grateful, so grateful, for the money you sent that helped me come here. I'm staying through the summer, and I'll come back and visit you. I . . . I'd like if you could take me—or show me—where my father's buried."

"You've gone there in dreams. You saw me as I saw you in the place where the Pious once walked. You heard the song of the stones and the murmur of prayers still spoken."

Panic dropped on her chest. "You can't know what I dream. I need to go."

Marg got to her feet, pinned Breen with a look.

"I am Mairghread O'Ceallaigh, once taoiseach of Talamh. I am of the Fey, a servant of the gods. I am Maiden, Mother, Crone. You come from me, child of my child, and in your blood lives all the gifts given."

The air changed. It . . . stirred. It rippled through Marg's hair, sent it swirling. Her eyes went dark and deep as she lifted her hands, palms up.

Dishes rattled on the shelves. The sleeping dog woke, sat up before he let out a howl that sounded like joy.

"Break the chains on the restrictions locked around you in the other. Listen and feel and see truth."

She swept out a hand, and the fire in the odd little stove roared as candles leaped to flame. "And here air whip, fire burn, here earth tremble, and water spill."

Now in her hand a fountain of water spurted up, shimmered in the light.

"All these elemental, all these linked to the magicks that form a world. Our world, and yours. You have come home, daughter of

Talamh, daughter of the Fey. You will know your birthright. And you will choose."

With a flick of her hand, the fountain of water vanished. Candles guttered out, and the air and all went still.

"You . . . put something in the wine."

With a roll of her eyes, Marg picked up her glass, drank deep. "Don't be foolish. You've lived with lies and deceptions too long. I'll give you neither. You are loved, Breen. Whatever your choices to come may be, you will always be loved. But you can't make true choices until you awaken."

Marg walked to her, put a hand on her cheek. "You need time yet. I'll walk with you some of the way, and the dog will guide you back to the cottage. When you're ready, I'll do as you ask and take you to the place we laid the one we love."

"I can find my way back. I can't take the dog. I don't even have the supplies to feed him and—"

"All you need for him is there. He'll be a companion for you, for now, we'll say. Do me this small favor and let him be with you for a day or two."

"Okay, fine. I really have to go. It's a long walk back."

"It is a journey, one I hope you'll make again."

"I'll visit you." She owed the woman that much. But before she did, she'd read up on delusions and hypnosis.

Marg led the way to the door, stepped out, then smiled.

"I see you have other guides waiting."

The falconer, Breen saw, with the glorious bird on her gloved arm. With a happy bark, the dog raced to them.

"I met her. I met her in Clare."

"Oh, long before that. You and Morena were friends as babies, as close as her grandmother and I have been all our lives."

"Was she in Clare to watch me?"

"Ah, child, so wary you are. She was there because she's headstrong and saw the chance to see you again. I'll leave Breen with you and Amish then," Marg called out. "You'll take her back safe, won't you, and not badger at her?"

"We'll see her back safe. I can't promise it all."

"Well, I suppose that has to do." Turning, Marg laid her hands on Breen's shoulders, kissed both her cheeks lightly. "Open yourself, *mo stór*, and see what's around you, and inside you."

She stepped back, and into the cottage.

And in the quiet alone, wept for what might have been, and what might be.

CHAPTER TWELVE

Because badgering was exactly what Breen had in mind, she walked down to Morena.

"Why did you tell me you worked for the falconry school?"

"But I didn't, did I?" Cocking a hip, Morena put her free hand on it. The gesture reeked of sarcasm. "You assumed that. You didn't remember me, and that cut a bit even though Marg and my grandmother both said you wouldn't. Not right off."

She lifted her arm so the hawk winged up. As she started walking, she turned. "Are you after staying or going?"

"I'm going."

"You promised you'd come back when you went away, but I stopped believing it, as you never tried."

"I'm not going to take flak for that. How am I suddenly in the wrong when I'm the only one I can see who didn't lie? And I was three, according to my grandmother, when I left Ireland for Philadelphia."

"You left Talamh."

"Oh God, not you, too!" Out of patience, Breen threw her hands in the air, turned a circle. "Is it something in the local water?"

"I could ask the same of where you've been, as I don't understand how you could forget who you are, where you came from. I'm still holding a grudge about that."

Morena's tone mirrored Breen's frustrated circle. "We played, you and I, in the woods around Marg's cottage, and in the dooryard of the farmhouse where you lived until your father left and turned it over to the O'Broins. We had tea parties and picnics and shared secrets whispering at night when we were supposed to be sleeping."

"I was three! I'm sorry I don't remember. But you're not helping by fostering my grandmother's delusions about this being some sort of Brigadoon."

As if waiting for an insult, Morena's eyes narrowed to slits. "What's a Brigadoon?"

"It's a fantasy story about a place that only exists for one day every hundred years."

"Oh, it sounds like a fine tale." Mollified by it, Morena reached down to pat the dog that trotted along with them. "But this isn't that, as we're here all the time."

"She put something in my wine."

"Ah, don't be a git. Why would she be doing that to her own kin?"

"It made me see her doing the impossible."

"Well now, there's not much impossible for the likes of Marg. She's as powerful a witch as I know."

As the crazy built around her, Breen considered pulling her own hair out. "Now you're all witches? Look, I get Ireland's got its folklore and its legends, but—"

"Ireland's on the other side, and I'm not a witch. I'm of the Sidhe."

"I can see you're a woman."

"Sidhe," Morena repeated. "I'm of the faerie clan."

"Faerie clan. Of course. I should've seen it right away."

Unfazed, Morena lifted a hand in a wave toward Harken as he led a spotted cow to what Breen assumed was a barn.

"It'll be easier on you going back through with me. Harken and Aisling said you took a turn coming through, and likely because you'd blocked it all out."

With the hawk circling above, Morena hopped the stone fence.

For the first time, Breen saw steps carved into the rise leading up to the tree.

"I fell. I lost my balance and fell, that's all."

"As you like."

Seven steps, Breen counted as she climbed them. Steps of rough stone with mica gleaming in the bright sunlight.

"I was going after the dog," she said in her defense. "And distracted because the tree's fascinating."

She gripped one of its curving branches, tried to climb up as gracefully, effortlessly as Morena.

She felt herself start to fall, as if the ground vanished under her feet. Then Morena gripped her hand.

The next thing she knew she stood on the path under a soaking rain.

"I don't understand how—"

"Because I'm thinking you don't want to." Temper, very visibly, began to rise and spew. "You don't want to take back what's yours by right, by blood, would rather close your eyes to it and pretend."

"I think I'm standing on firmer ground than somebody who claims to live in an alternate reality as a freaking faerie."

"Firmer ground, is it? You'd best hold on as we're about to see about that."

Before Breen could evade, Morena clamped an arm around her waist. They lifted off the ground.

"Oh God, oh my God."

"Hold on, I said. You're no bag of feathers."

With that Morena flew through the rain, several feet over the path. Tongue lolling, the dog raced under them. The hawk cried overhead as he soared.

Instinctively, Breen reached out to grip Morena's waist. Her hand brushed wings. Big, beautiful, luminous wings of violet edged in silver.

"I'm dreaming. This is all a dream."

"My arse." They dipped down, up again, to avoid branches. "There was a time you'd have given us a boost." Turning her head, Morena looked into Breen's shocked eyes.

"This isn't happening."

"I should drop you on your head and knock the sense back in you."

Instead, she burst out of the woods, skimmed over the wet grass and garden. She set Breen down on the back patio.

"I'm going in to dry off a bit."

The dog followed Morena inside as if they both belonged there. Amish landed on a nearby branch and folded his wings to wait.

Shivering now, Breen felt the rain soaking her to the skin. It felt real, but how could it be when she was obviously still in bed having a very long, very strange, very lucid dream?

She stepped inside. Morena, her jacket drying on a peg, offered the dog something out of a jar on the counter.

"He deserves one," she said. "I see my grandmother brought them for him, and there, a bowl for his food, one for his water. The sack there would be his food."

"Your grandmother."

"Aye, Marg would have asked her to see to it. You know my grandparents. They're Finola and Seamus Mac an Ghaill. McGill. My nan settled you and your friend into the cottage Marg made for you, and Grandda's been showing you how to garden again."

"Again."

"Even when we were babes you had a way with living things. Plants, animals, people." Morena wandered the kitchen as she spoke. "Not so fine a way now with people, I see, as you've yet to light the fire to warm me or offer me a drink before I take my leave."

Her ears rang. Spike in blood pressure, and no wonder, Breen thought—with she believed admirable calm. "You had wings."

"Had and have."

"Like . . . Tinker Bell."

"Oh, I know that story, and it's a grand one. But she would have been a pixie. One of the Sidhe for certain, but a pixie. They're very small."

"I'm not asleep," Breen said slowly. "I'm dripping on the kitchen floor, and I'm cold and I'm wet."

"Then light the bleeding fire."

"I'll light the bleeding fire." As if dreaming, she walked into the living room, where she'd set the logs for a fresh fire only that morn-ing.

A lifetime and world ago.

She set the starter under the log, reached for the matches.

"Really now, that's how you'd do it?" Morena, smelling of rain and forest, crouched beside her. "To light a fire is the first power of the Wise, and so a child must be taught, and carefully, of its powers, its dangers, its benefits."

"I don't know any other way to light a fire."

"That makes me sad for you," Morena replied as Breen struck the match.

Breen simply sat on the floor when the starter caught. "I can't think. I know this can't be real, but—"

"You know it is. I saw wine in the kitchen place, so I'm getting some for the both of us."

"Tell me how my father died."

"That's for Marg." Morena pushed to her feet. "It's not right that I would take what's hers to tell. I can say I know no man in any of the worlds was better than your da. I'm getting the wine."

The dog stretched across Breen's lap, and somehow she felt com-fort stroking his damp curls.

"What kind of dog is this?"

"He's an Irish water spaniel, and you can trust he has a strong heart and a true one or Marg wouldn't have chosen him for you."

"What's his name?"

"Well now, that's for you to choose, isn't it? But we all have called him Bollocks because as soon as he was weaned he could find trouble without looking."

Breen choked out a laugh. "Bollocks?"

"He earned that name, though Marg trained him well since we dubbed him. He'll sit when you tell him, and do his business in the out-of-doors, and he won't chew your boots, though he once had a taste for mine."

Morena sat, handed Breen a glass, then scrubbed a hand over the dog's head. "Didn't you, you scoundrel? She's pined for you, has Marg, all these years. That I can tell you. And I'll confess I went against her to go through to meet you that day in the woods by the castle."

"How did you get there? You flew," Breen answered herself. "On the wings."

"I've friends, and good ones, but I've never had one so tight in my heart as you. It may be we won't like each other so much now with the years that passed." She shrugged, drank. "But I wanted to see what you were about."

"I bought a gift for you."

Morena blinked at her. "A gift?"

"A thank-you. I thought you were with the school, then I thought you must've been trespassing because nobody knew you. Anyway."

"What was it, the gift?"

"I'll get it." She had to nudge the dog off her lap.

"Tell him to stay if you don't want him following after you."

"Stay," Breen said. "I'll be right back."

Everything in the cottage was the same. Normal. But she wondered, as she walked upstairs, if anything could or would be normal again.

She got the little gift bag, then stood a moment, staring at herself in the bedroom mirror.

She looked the same—not the same as she had before her life had changed in Philly, but the same as the woman who'd come to Ireland.

But she wasn't at all sure she was the same.

She went back down and handed Morena the gift bag before she sat again. "There's a card inside, too. I don't know if you can read."

"Of course I can read, don't be a git about it. We had poets and scholars in Talamh while those in this world were barely out of the caves."

The insult, clear on her face, faded as she took out the card and read. "That's lovely, that is. I'm told you're a writer yourself, and you do it well."

Then she opened the box, let out a gasp. "Ah, it's a hawk. It's a fine gift, a very fine gift. I thank you for it, and I feel I may not deserve it."

"Why?"

"I didn't lie, but didn't give you the truth."

"You gave me the hawk walk, and I'll never forget it. I didn't know, um, faeries had hawks."

"We have each other," Morena said as she fixed the pin to her shirt. "And it's time I took him home again. I see, now that I'm not so resentful, why Marg wants to give you time. I grew up knowing, and you were made to forget. I hate being sorry." She got to her feet. "Hate more having to say it, but it's sorry I am for giving you a fright in the way I brought you back."

"I don't understand any of this."

"I know it. I didn't want to know it, but I do. So I'll leave you be. Will I be welcomed back again?"

"Of course." Breen stood. "Yes, of course."

"That's enough then."

She went back into the kitchen to put on her jacket.

"How do . . . how do the wings come through the jacket?"

Morena shook her head. "Because I want them to, and they're mine, aren't they? Don't forget to feed the dog," she said.

Through the glass, Breen watched the hawk fly down, circle over Morena's head.

Then those luminous wings flowed out, and with the hawk, she flew through the rain and into the woods.

"I'm not crazy." Breen laid a hand on the dog's curly topknot when he leaned against her leg. "I'm not hallucinating. I know what's real."

She looked down to see him staring up at her. "It's too early for dinner, and I need to write this all down. I probably shouldn't give you another one of those cookie things, but what the hell, right? It's been a day."

Even as she took one out of the jar, he sat, eyes gleaming.

"Okay, can you shake hands? Is that stupid?" To test, she held out a hand. He offered his paw, making her laugh. She shook it, gave him the biscuit. "You're a good dog, Bollocks."

She put water in one of the bowls, then got out a Coke for herself to take into her office.

She tried to reconstruct everything from the moment she'd seen the dog in what she thought of as her secret journal. In writing it out she felt it again, the damp air, the light and shadows as Bollocks led her—no question he'd done just that—to the tree.

The Welcoming Tree.

To add to it, she uploaded pictures of the dog, of the tree.

And wished she'd pulled herself together enough to have taken some on . . . the other side. In (on?) Talamh.

The air, the light had changed. She could admit that now and document it. She wrote of the four people she'd met. Harken, Aisling, her grandmother, Morena.

It struck her all at once she'd been in the house where her father had lived, where she herself—according to her grandmother—had been born.

She sat back, sipped her Coke, stared at the rain outside. And noticed Bollocks had joined her and cozily curled on the bed.

"I probably shouldn't let you do that."

But he looked so comfortable, watched her so sweetly, she let it go.

Her father was gone. She didn't know how or why, but she had to accept that, too. He hadn't abandoned her, hadn't forgotten about her. He'd died.

Years ago, years and years, but her loss was as fresh as the moment. And something she didn't know what to do with. She had the picture of him in her bedroom, and memories that came and went. But she needed more.

She needed to see his grave, and she'd ask her grandmother for something of his, just some token she could hold on to.

"So I'm going back," she declared. "I guess I knew I would, but I need to work up to it."

She described how Marg had made the air swirl and the fire roar, even as she asked how such a thing could be possible. How could Morena sprout wings and fly? How could . . .

She sat back again, realizing what she wrote now ran along

the same themes and directions as the story she worked on every morning.

Not exact, no, not absolutely, but so close.

Because she'd always known. However fantastic, however opposed to the practical bent of her life, part of her had always known. The memories might be locked up inside, but they eked out, didn't they, bit by bit as she opened herself up to tell a story.

To do what she'd wanted to do.

> So, she wrote, it's not just a matter of finding out who I am—and I've made progress on that. But what I am. What am I? Daughter of Talamh, daughter of the Fey, one of the Wise. Wisewomen equal witches. I don't feel like a witch.

She shifted from the journal to a search on Irish water spaniels. The description fit Bollocks perfectly—and she found the nonshedding characteristic a nice bonus.

The breed boasted smart, energetic, affectionate dogs. Inquisitive, a bit of a clown. Loved water, naturally.

"In Irish folklore," she read, "you're supposed to be a descendent of the Dobhar-chú. And what the hell is that?"

She did another search. "Half dog, half otter or fish? Really? Oh, and a fierce predator of the oceans and rivers. You don't look so fierce."

He slid off the bed, stretched into a down-dog, and gave her a long, loving look.

"Getting hungry? Me, too. This took longer than I figured."

He followed her into the kitchen.

The handwritten note tied to the cloth sack told her how much to give him, how often. And that he wouldn't mind a bit if she added a raw egg or a bit of yogurt to the chunky kibble.

She chose the egg, as she had them on hand, and while he ate, scrambled some for herself with bits of Irish bacon, some cheese, tomatoes, broccoli.

She ate with the dog stretched over her feet, and tried to work out how to handle her daily blog. She couldn't leave out the dog—and didn't want to. She could say she got him from a neighbor. It was close enough to true.

She couldn't write about her father's death—not yet at least. And she wasn't ready to. She couldn't mention sitting in her grandmother's kitchen, or—Jesus—alternate worlds.

She'd figure it out, just as she'd figure out what to tell Marco.

She got up to deal with her dishes, and the dog stood, staring at her.

"You want to go out. Okay, do I just assume that because it's logical, or do I know because . . . I can read you. It feels like that. It doesn't matter, does it? Let's go out."

He danced when she grabbed her jacket, then shot out the door she opened like a bullet.

He tore around the yard as if he'd escaped from prison, then danced again until she walked toward him.

At that he streaked—a curly bolt of lightning—toward the bay. Barking like a mad thing, he leaped into the water and swam, head bobbing, eyes full of joy.

"Fierce predator of the seas," she said with a laugh.

Seabirds scattered, water splashed as he raced out, then in again.

Breen stood as the long-lived summer sun pushed against the western clouds to add just a glimmer to the sky. And realized she was absolutely, perfectly content.

She'd been happy enough in her solitude, but the dog—and yes, she'd always wanted one—added a shine.

Like the sun in a cloudy sky.

A change in routine didn't hurt a thing. So Breen told herself as she adjusted hers to feed the dog his breakfast, take her walk with him before sitting down to blog.

He'd slept at the foot of her bed, which she'd have to change. Probably.

She sent Marco a text to give him a heads-up. After all, he was her roommate, and would be her housemate. He deserved to know they had a dog.

She made sure to add the most adorable picture she could manage with the text.

He responded.

You what!! What kind of weird-ass-looking dog is that? And why's he so damn cute? Look what you do when I'm not around a couple weeks. Send more pictures.

She spent a happy few minutes texting back and forth before she settled down to—carefully—write the blog.

"Pictures of puppies never fail." She glanced over—and of course, Bollocks was curled up on the bed. "I'm going to work on my book for a couple hours, then we're going out. We're getting you a collar, a leash, some toys—and a dog bed."

He didn't mind the collar, but he didn't like the leash. While he didn't put up a fight when she clipped it on, he looked at her with sad, sad eyes.

"It's not that I don't trust you." She'd have sworn that's what he thought. "And we won't need it at the cottage. But we're going to walk around the village now, and we'll need it when we visit some sights I haven't gotten to yet."

He seemed less insulted by it when they walked, even preened when people stopped to admire him. He got to sniff at shoes, nuzzle kids, meet a couple of other dogs.

Breen told herself she was socializing him—as recommended—but she knew she was just showing him off.

She bought him chew toys, a bright red ball, and a small stuffed rabbit.

On the drive home, he sat in the back, a chew bone clamped in his teeth and his head out the window so his curls blew in the breeze.

Once home, she let him out for a run and a swim while she sat on the patio with her tablet. Since she hadn't found him a bed, she ordered one online. And a few more toys. And chew sticks, and a dog tag with his name and her cell phone number.

"God, if I ever have kids, I'll be a maniac."

Fresh from the bay, Bollocks raced up to her, so she tossed the red ball. He just cocked his head at her. "You're supposed to run after it, get it, bring it back to me so I can throw it for you again."

She could all but hear him thinking *What's the point?*, but he trotted to the ball, clamped it in his teeth, trotted back. She tossed it again.

After the first couple times, he seemed to get more into the spirit, gave serious chase.

"Okay, you've got it, and my arm's worn out." When she set the ball on the table signaling game over, he trotted toward the woods. He gave a bark, looked back at her.

"No, we're not going there. I'm not ready. I've got laundry to do, and I'm going to write more. And . . . I'm just not ready. Let's go in."

When he came back, she patted his head. "Maybe tomorrow."

But she had excuses at the ready the next day, and found it surprisingly easy to fill the time. Especially when she took a break from her novel to write a short story about the adventures of a magical dog named Bollocks.

She spent the day after that expanding the story as she realized it could be a book for middle schoolers. After all, she'd taught that age group, knew what they liked to read.

So she shifted happily between her novel, the children's book, and the new routine with the dog himself.

Then on a bold summer day where she took her work out to the patio, Bollocks raced toward the woods, his happy barks a clear signal.

She wasn't surprised to see her grandmother, and Finola with her, walk out of the woods.

CHAPTER THIRTEEN

They looked like ordinary women, Breen thought as she rose from the table. Maybe not ordinary, as both looked years younger than their ages. But they sure as hell didn't look—not from her perspective—like a witch and a faerie.

Marg carried a pouch, and Finola a basket.

The dog greeted them with mad joy and affection while Breen struggled with trepidation.

"What a fine day for being out and about," Finola said brightly. "And are you working here, darling? With us coming along and interrupting you."

"No, it's fine. It's fine." Breen closed her laptop. "I meant to come back sooner, but . . ."

"You're a busy one, aren't you, with the writing. And Seamus tells me you're adding gardening to that, and very well. Now you've this rascal on top of it all."

Finola took Breen's hand for a squeeze, a deliberate gesture of calming and comfort. "If it's all the same to you, why don't I just pop into the kitchen there, make us some tea to go with these sweet cakes I baked?"

"I—"

"It's not a bit of trouble." With her basket, Finola breezed right in, with the dog close behind.

With a little smile, Marg looked after her friend. "She knows I'm a bit unnerved, so she chatters to give me time to settle."

"That makes two of us—on the unnerved front. I really was coming back. I just needed to work up to it."

"I can't blame you for it. So much thrown at you at once. It's a lovely spot here. It makes you happy."

Easier, by far, to talk about that.

"It is, and it does. It's the first time in my life I've lived on my own, and done what I wanted to do. The first time—that I remember—I've had a dog, and he makes me happy, too. I want to thank you for giving him to me."

"Trapping you into it more like."

"He still makes me happy." And she needed to be grateful, and gracious. "Please, sit."

"You were working—writing."

"Yes. I think I'm not too bad at it, and hope I get better."

Marg sat, and in her slim pants and thin blue sweater, crossed her legs. "You show talent in the blogging."

"You read my blog?"

"In my way, yes. Your father had a way with words himself."

"He'd tell me stories. I couldn't get enough of them. I was coming back," Breen repeated. "And I wanted to ask if there was something of his, just some small thing, I could have to remember him by. I have a picture. A publican in Clare let me have it, one of him and his friends playing there. He was—his band—was very popular."

"Music was his first love, and an abiding one. I'd like very much to see the photograph before we go. As it happens, I've brought you something that meant a great deal to him."

Marg reached in her pouch, took out a smaller one tied with a white ribbon. "I have more of his things, of course, and you are welcome to choose whatever you like. But I know this he'd want you to have."

Breen opened the pouch, took out the gold ring. A claddagh and, she remembered, his wedding ring.

"He wore it always," Marg told her. "Even after there was no marriage between them."

Breen rubbed her fingers over the ring. "He loved her. He knew they weren't meant to stay together, but he loved her. They'd made me."

"It may be fate brought them together for only that."

"It means a great deal to me to have this." And shamed her because she'd meant to go back—but she hadn't.

"You're kinder to me than I deserve at this point."

"Ah, bollocks to that. I'm your nan, and have more than twenty years of spoiling to make up. Give me the chance to, won't you, Breen?"

Though Marg's voice stayed steady and calm, the plea shone in her eyes. "You've a good heart. Give me that chance."

"I have so many questions." But Breen reached over to take Marg's hand as she spoke.

"It will take time to answer them all."

"Then we'll take the time. I'm going to go get the picture. Next time I'm somewhere with a scanner, I'll make a copy for you."

She went inside where Finola fussed over a teapot and cups.

"You knew me when I was little."

"I did indeed. You and our darling Morena twined together like ivy. She lives with us now that our son and his woman—Morena's parents—are in the Capital."

"The Capital."

"Aye. Talamh isn't so big as this world, but it's more than you've seen as yet." She glanced up, looked at Breen with those strong, direct eyes. "Will you see it again, Breen?"

"Yes."

"That would make your nan very happy."

"I'm just going up to get a picture of my father to show my grandmother."

"I'll take the tea and cakes out then. She is a woman of great strength and power," Finola added. "One who has suffered deep losses, and still stands. She is my friend, as dear to me as a sister. Perhaps dearer, come to that. It's my great hope that you take after such as Marg."

She didn't know if she took after anyone, but since she only had one grandmother, she'd stop evading.

She brought the photo out to where Marg and Finola sat with the tea, and Bollocks sprawled under the table with one of his biscuits.

Breen stopped, staring down at the little squares of frosted cakes on the plate.

"The pink ones taste like roses."

"They were always your favorite." Smiling, Finola put two on a small plate. "I told you, didn't I, the girl always had a fondness for my sweet cakes. Morena favored the blue ones, and the taste of a summer sky."

Sitting, Breen offered the framed photo to Marg.

"Ah, look at my boy there, so handsome! And there's your own Flynn with him, Fi."

"And so it is! That's Morena's da there, with the pipe. And there's Kavan—he who was the best of friends with your da, Breen, and father to Harken and Aisling, and they you met, and Keegan as well. And there's Brian holding his *bodhrán* drum. And only my own Flynn with us still."

"They're . . . gone?"

"Brian long ago, and Kavan as well. It's good to see them young and alive and doing what they loved doing."

"I'll make copies, and bring them. Will you tell me how he died, my father?"

"When you come and I take you to where we laid him to rest, we'll talk of it. Can today not be for the sadness?" Marg asked her. "There are other questions buzzing in your mind. Pick one I can answer that doesn't bring grief to tea and cakes."

"All right. You're of the Wise—that's witches, right?"

"So I am. Once such as I am—and you are—were respected in the worlds. Until fears and greeds and envies and the like grew in those without powers. It's not such in Talamh, where our gifts and skills and knowledge are given to help and heal and defend."

"Okay, and you?" Breen turned to Finola. "Are one of the Sidhe?"

"We tend—the earth, the air, the growing things."

"Is that it? I mean, as far as your world? Witches and faeries?"

"Oh, other tribes she's meaning, Marg. We live, work, mate, defend, all as Fey, as people of Talamh, but we have other what you would think of as tribes. The Elfins—they tend as well, and prefer the forests and mountains to the fields and lowlands."

"Elves. Like . . ." Fascinated, Breen held her hand a couple of feet from the ground. "Elves."

"They're not the little ones with pointed ears the storybooks in your world would make them," Marg said. "Nor are the weres the thing of nightmares who transform under the full moons to attack and kill."

"Weres? Like werewolves?"

"A were has a spirit animal, and can become—at his will—a wolf, a hawk, a bear, a dog, a cat, and so on."

"The mers," Finola added, clearly enjoying herself as she nibbled on a cake. "Who live in, tend, and guard the waters. The trolls who mine."

"And with all these, there are abilities," Marg continued. "A troll may have the ability to communicate with animals, though this is more likely to be found in a witch, an elf, a faerie. A were might have dream visions. We have what the gods give us."

Fascinating, Breen decided. Not frightening now, not impossible now. Just fascinating. "What gods?"

"There are many. Even in your world you give them different names, purposes, lore."

"Did they make the tree? The Welcoming Tree?"

"This was an agreement between the realms of man and gods and Fey, and choices made more than a thousand years ago. The portals were a way to travel from world to world, but worlds change, and more choices had to be made."

"What kind of choices?"

"In this world such as we began to be persecuted and hunted and murdered."

"Witch trials." That was history, Breen thought. Solid and inarguable. "Burnings and hangings and drownings."

Marg nodded. "And most who suffered those fates had no power at all. I think a kind of madness came over the realm of men. We were to be feared and damned—then we were simply stories and superstitions. This world, as worlds will, pursued a different path. Machines became a kind of god, technology a kind of sorcery—and the true magicks faded to shadows. The Fey of Talamh chose to preserve what they are, choosing the magicks over this progress."

"But I went through, and you came through this way. My mother, you said, lived in Talamh. Is she Fey?"

"She's of this world." At ease now, Marg poured more tea.

"She came through willingly to ours for love of your father. No one can be brought in without their full consent—that is law. And all in Talamh are encouraged to go through, to explore, to spend time in another world. They may choose to stay in that world, and that is their right—but they must take the most sacred oath to never use their power to harm unless in defense of another. Even then, there must be a judgment. Some, like your mother, come to us and stay. Some find it's not their place, and leave."

"Wouldn't they tell people about everything?"

"Who would believe them?" Marg said with a smile. "You, who remember some, have seen some, still struggle to believe."

But believing wasn't as hard as it had been, maybe should have been.

"I lived my whole life—at least since I was three—in this world. In a place so different from where I'm sitting right now. And I was taught for so long that I wasn't just ordinary, but barely average."

Something flashed in Marg's eyes before she cast them down. "That was your mother's fear to blame. I can believe she was wrong, very wrong, but not slap at her for it. You are far from ordinary, in any world, *mo stór*. You are brighter, stronger than you may think. What's in you is sleeping. Let me help you wake, just a bit."

She stood, held out her hand. When Breen put hers in it, she led her to the garden. "The rosemary there, such a useful plant. Would you touch it, think of it, how it grows, how it basks in the sun, fills the air with its fragrance."

Seeing no harm, Breen brushed her fingers over the soft needles.

"Its roots spread through the earth. When the rain comes, it drinks. Think of it, what it needs, what it gives. Think of what you give it."

She thought of it, how it smelled—how her fingers smelled when she ran them over it. How it branched up toward the sun. How it—

"It grew!"

To her astonished eyes, Breen watched the branches reach up another inch.

"You did that."

The dangles at Marg's ears glinted as she shook her head. "Not I, no. This is in you. I may not tell you all, not at once, but I will not lie. This is in you, and more. It's all one, you see—linked together. Water, fire, earth, air, magicks. All in you as well."

"All connected, Seamus said," Breen murmured. "All bound together."

"So it is. And this is enough for one day. I want to ask something of you."

Breen turned, and Marg took her hands. "What do you want?"

"If you would come, stay a day or two with me."

"You'll take me to my father's grave."

"I will."

"I need to write."

"That won't work." Marg glanced at the laptop. "But there are other ways. I'll help you so you can do what you love and need. A day or two, my darling girl."

"All right. Tomorrow."

"I'm more than grateful. We'll leave her be now, won't we, Fi."

"And sure a lovely visit we've had." Finola gathered her basket and rose. "Bright blessings on you, child."

"Thanks . . . and on you."

"Tomorrow then. I'll watch for you."

Breen stood where she was as they crossed the lawn to the woods. Bollocks trotted over with them, then raced back to her.

"I guess I should pack something. What do I pack to spend a couple days in another world?"

She opted for an abbreviated morning routine. The blog, the novel, the children's book all got her attention even if she gave them all less time.

By midmorning, she hitched on her backpack and carried her nerves into the woods with Bollocks. She could feel his excitement in every step, and wondered if somehow he could feel her anxiety.

Either way, he led her, as before, through the shifting light and shadows while the pulse under her tattoo beat fast.

She thought of what her mother would say.

Don't be stupid, Breen. You're not equipped to handle any of this. Go back, book a flight, and come back where you belong. Follow the rules. Live a quiet life. If you reach too high, you'll only fall.

And hearing all of that inside her head pushed her forward, lengthened her stride until she reached the tree.

And there it is, she thought. Strange and glorious and terrifying. Every logical bone in her body insisted a tree—however fantastic—couldn't be a doorway to another world.

But she'd been there—and had the dog to prove it.

"'There are more things in heaven and earth,' right, Bollocks? So . . . here we go."

He took that as a command, scrambled right up the rocks and branches. Remembering the spill she took before, she followed with more caution.

When once again she felt herself falling, she gripped a branch. She hovered in a flood of light, in a kick of wind that tossed her hair, lifted her jacket. She had to fight the part of her—her mother's voice—that desperately wanted to jerk back.

Instead, she stepped forward.

Her head spun as two worlds seemed to revolve—the dense forest behind, the green fields ahead. But she stood on a sturdy ledge, catching her breath as Bollocks leaped down to chase the sheep.

"It's real. That's the first thing. It's all real. So, we have to see what happens next."

Her legs might have been a little shaky, but she managed the steps, crossed the field. With the dog beside her, she went over the stone fence to the dirt road.

She saw the man—Harken, his name was Harken—walking to one of the stone outbuildings. And Aisling hoeing in what appeared to be a vegetable garden while a pair of raven-haired boys sat on the grass nearby. The smaller one hooted as he banged two tin pails together. The older carefully built a tower out of wooden blocks.

An enormous gray wolfhound sat beside them, as watchful as a nanny.

Aisling saw her, leaned on her hoe, and waved. Then she worked her way out of the garden, scooped up the youngest boy. She took the other by the hand. With the pony-size dog beside them, they walked toward the road.

"So you've come back, and welcome to you."

"Yes, to visit my grandmother."

Breen walked to the stone fence so that she stood on one side, Aisling and her brood on the other.

"You've made her happy, that I can promise you. And here are my boys. Finian, say welcome to Mistress Kelly."

"Welcome."

"Thank you. Breen's fine." Though his was grubby with grass and dirt, Breen offered a hand to shake.

"And this hellion is our Kavan."

To Breen's surprise, Kavan let out a laugh, threw his arms out to her.

"He's a friendly sort, but none too clean at the moment."

"I don't mind."

When Aisling passed him over the fence, he immediately tangled his none-too-clean hands in Breen's hair, and babbled happily.

"He likes your hair, you see. Red's his favorite, isn't it now, my wild one? And last here is Mab. She's angel sweet, so not to worry."

Bollocks, forepaws planted on the fence, stretched up to lick at Mab's face while the big dog tolerated it with quiet dignity.

"We won't keep you, as I know Marg's waiting, but I hope you'll come see us while you're here. My man and my brother are due back anytime. They'll be pleased to meet you."

"I will."

"Come back to Ma now, my little man, as your new friend has to be on her way." Aisling took the boy, settled him on her hip.

"I have something for you and your brother."

"Do you?"

"Yes, my grandmother said . . ." Breen took off her backpack, unzipped it. She took out a framed photo. "Your father, with mine and other friends."

"Oh! Oh, would you look at that!" Aisling shifted the baby as she took the photo. "Look here, my lads, it's your grandda."

"How did he get in there?" Finian demanded.

"It's a likeness, you see. Like a drawing from when he was a young man. Oh, this is such a treasured gift, Breen. I'm out of words to say."

"You're welcome. I'll come see you before I . . . go back."

"See that you do, and give our best to Marg, won't you?"

"I will. You have beautiful sons."

Aisling's smile beamed with pleasure and pride. "I'm blessed with them. Now, if I can just have a girl—just the once. Come on, lads, let's take this fine gift safe inside."

As Aisling walked back to the house, Kavan grinned at Breen over his mother's shoulder. And she watched little wings, bold and red, flutter out as if to wave goodbye.

"That's something you don't see every day. Except maybe here."

She continued along the road, made the turn into the trees toward the cottage.

Once again, the doors and windows stood open to the day, and smoke trailed up from the chimney.

Marg gathered flowers from her thriving garden to lay in the basket on her arm.

"And so you're here. Aye, and you as well," she added when Bollocks raced to her. "Come in and welcome. I'll show you to your room right off, and hope it pleases you."

She's nervous, Breen realized, and knowing it calmed her own jitters.

"How did you fare coming through this time?"

"I didn't end up flat on my back and faint."

"Better then. Just this way," she said, gesturing. "My room's on the other side, so you'll have privacy. There's a bath chamber—not what you're used to. If you've questions, I'll show you how it all works."

"Okay."

She stepped into a room full of light, lace curtains fluttering back to frame views of the gardens and trees. The four-poster bed stood sturdy and draped with white, with a chest at its foot painted with dragons. Candles and flowers and raw crystals decorated the mantel over a hearth.

A pretty little desk and chair looked out of one of the windows.

"It's really charming." Wandering, she set her tote on the chest. "Really lovely. The cottage didn't look big enough to have a room like this."

It struck her, so she turned back. "Because it wasn't here before."

"It's here now, and will be always for you."

"I try—it's knee-jerk—to convince myself all this is some elaborate dream or, I don't know, nervous breakdown. But I know it's not. And standing here, being here, I don't want it to be."

"It's your home, whatever you choose in the end. It will always be home for you. I'll put on the kettle if you want to put your things away."

"It's not much, and it could wait, if we could—if you could take me to my father's grave. I have this."

She opened the backpack to take out another framed photo. "For you. And I have one for Finola. I saw Aisling on the road, and gave her one. I have another. I didn't know if the other friend, the one you said had died, too, had family who might want it."

"He does, and they would cherish such a gift. It's thoughtful of you, Breen."

Marg took the photo, pressed it to her heart. "I'll take you to his stone. It's a far walk, so we'll take the horses. I have my own Igraine, and we'll borrow one from Harken for you."

"I don't know how to ride. I've never actually ridden a horse."

Surprise flashed on Marg's face. "Oh, but you did indeed. You had your own pony, and called her Birdie. And you rode on your da's mount with him. Such things will come back, no doubt, but for today, we'll take Igraine and the cart."

"There really aren't any cars here?"

"No cars, no." Marg retrieved the basket of flowers before she led the way outside and across to a lean-to where a horse stood idly munching from a basket of hay. "Here's our Igraine. She's a fine, gentle thing, but she can move when moving's needed. We'll just hitch her up to the cart."

The horse from the dream, Breen realized. The sturdy-looking white with the black dappled hindquarters.

"Can I help you?"

"Best to watch and learn this time around."

Marg led the horse to a two-wheeled cart, where she stood, tail switching, while Marg fixed some sort of harness over the horse's chest and withers. It ran under the belly, along the flanks, and the way Marg managed it all told Breen she'd done it countless times before.

All the while, the horse stood patient.

"It's all padded, you see, the breast strap so it won't rub her. And you have this that controls her head, but you watch you don't put it so high it pushes her windpipe. You buckle it up with the traces. And you have the saddle—not like one for riding—and the braces. They're for stopping, the brakes."

Marg gave the horse a rub. "Then the girth, and that you need good and tight. And here the harness and the bit—there's my girl."

While Breen watched, fascinated, Marg strapped and buckled, checked all was as it should be. Then stepped back to lift the cart.

"Let me help."

"All right then, the shafts on either side have to go into the togs. The loops, you see? The leather loops."

She explained it all, step by step—a lot of steps—before they had cart and horse ready for the trip.

"All that," Breen marveled, "every time you want to go somewhere with a cart."

"It takes a bit of time, but why hurry through the day just to get to the next?"

As agile as a teenager, Marg climbed up to the seat, waited for Breen to do the same.

"In the back with you," Marg told Bollocks. He leaped in, then rested his head on the seat between them.

With a little click of her tongue, Marg sent the horse and cart forward.

Breen caught movement out of the corner of her eye, turned to see a cat, polished coin silver, wind around the side of the house.

"You have a cat."

"In a manner of speaking."

CHAPTER FOURTEEN

As an experience, Breen decided her first horse-before-the-cart ride might have rattled some bones and teeth, but the exhilaration outweighed that.

The quiet—just the roll of wheels, the mare's lively trot on the soft dirt—meant she could hear birdsong and the lowing of cows as they traveled.

She sat in sunlight, with a breeze smelling of grass wafting around her, and she could see other farms, other cottages—and a man with a thick walking stick who tipped his cap as they passed him on the road.

She saw children playing, clothes flapping on lines, horses actually frolicking in fields.

"Was that a fox?" Breen asked as she watched something red and sleek streak across the road.

"It was, aye. Have you never seen one?"

"Not really. There's a round tower over there. What's it for?"

"For remembering now. In the long ago, the Pious took to them for safety, as they were persecuted. Then again, they did some persecuting of their own in that time."

"That's the name you used before—for the place where you said my father's buried."

"A place it was—or was meant to be—for prayer and good works and contemplation. But there are always some, aren't there, who believe what they believe is the only. And will do whatever it takes to force that belief on all. For me, those who would kill and burn and enslave in the name of a god, well, they don't hear the god they claim to worship. Or the god is a false and cruel one."

She turned the horse and cart onto another road, steeper, and when they topped a rise, Breen saw it.

The spread of gray stone, the turrets, the battlements. And the high grass around it, with headstones, and sheep that grazed.

And there, on another slight rise, the stone circle.

"You dreamed this."

"I did. That place, and you, and the horse. Not the cart, you rode the horse, and wore a brown cloak with a hood. I can't get used to it," Breen murmured. "I don't know if I ever will."

"It's sanctified, this place, a holy place, as it was meant to be. Any blood once shed here, any sins committed, are long forgiven."

"Why is he here, instead of closer to where he lived?"

"He was taoiseach, and this is his honor. When my time comes, I will lie here as well."

"What does it mean, that word? Teesha?"

Marg spelled it out. "It means 'leader.' Our Eian was leader of the tribes, one and all. Chosen and choosing, as I was once as well."

"Are you, like, elected?"

"Chosen and choosing," Marg repeated. "As I chose to pass the sword and staff of the taoiseach to another when I had failed, when I had allowed myself to be used and deceived. I'll explain," she added, laying a hand on Breen's. "I promise you. Your father was but a babe when I abjured, and but sixteen years when he took up the sword and staff himself."

She stopped the horse. "Would you fetch the flowers for me?" she asked as the dog jumped out to investigate the sheep and the stones.

As she climbed down, Breen got the basket. Marg took them out, circled a finger in the air. Their stems pulled together as if with twine.

"I think with you here now, we'll put these in the ground so they grow and thrive."

"But they're cut flowers, not plants."

"Fresh they are, fresh enough for this."

She took Breen's hand, walked with her over and through the

grass to a stone carved with her father's name and the symbol of a sword crossed with a staff.

"He's really gone. Part of me didn't want to believe . . ."

"He's in you, as he's in me." Marg slid an arm around Breen's waist. "Never forget that. He's with the gods now. Only his ashes and our memory of him lie here."

"You . . . he was cremated?"

"In our tradition, the dead is placed in a boat, on a bed of flowers. The candles are lit, the songs are sung as the boat sails on the water. Then the fire takes it. The ashes come back through the air and into a stone jar, and the jar is placed in the earth. And the dead is one with the five."

"The four elements, and magick."

"Aye. Do you want me to leave you for some time?"

"No. No, he was yours, too."

"Then together, we'll give him the flowers."

"I don't know how to do what you're asking."

"Kneel with me. We hold the flowers together, just beneath the stone. Think with your heart now, open it.

"In this place of peace and rest," Marg said, "we offer our gift to one loved best. Flowers bright, grow day and night. For father, for son, from her, from me. As we will, so mote it be."

Breen felt something, a change in the air, in the ground beneath her. The stems of the bouquet simply slid into the earth. And they spread, wild with color, until they formed a blanket.

"It's . . . it's beautiful."

"You were part of it." Tears glittered in Marg's eyes, but didn't fall. Just gleamed like light over a misty blue sea. "It's in you, *mo stór*. If you choose, I'll teach you what you need to know. Now take your moments with him. You need them whether you think it or not. I have others I knew and cared for here, and will pay respects."

"All right."

Sitting, Breen brushed her hand through the blanket of flowers. She didn't believe she'd had any part in creating it, but she couldn't deny she'd felt something pull inside her, and open inside her.

But for now, she just wanted to be.

"I miss you so much." More keenly now, she realized, than she had even as a girl. "I should've tried to find you sooner. I should've broken away somehow, and tried. You'd have already been gone, but I'd have known. I'd have come here.

"It's beautiful, the old ruins, the hills, the fields. And so quiet. Peace and rest, she said, and that's true. I'm not sure what I believe about after death, but I hope that's what you have now. Peace and rest. There's so much I need to remember, but I never forgot one thing. I love you."

She got to her feet, blinked and swiped at tears.

The horse let out a sharp whinny, and rising up to paw the air, nearly overturned the cart. Without thinking Breen started running back to grab at the bridle, to try to steady her.

She heard a *whoosh*, like a strong wind sweeping the trees.

Struggling with the horse, she looked up.

A man dived out of the sky. His gold hair streamed back, his dark wings spread. She had only a moment to wonder at the strange beauty before she realized he came straight at her.

And the look in his eyes was as dark as his wings.

She ran, zigging, zagging over the uneven ground to avoid stones. Something grabbed her hair, yanked her back. When an arm clamped around her waist, she kicked, struggled, and pulled in her breath to scream.

"Nan! Run! Run and hide!"

The chuckle came close to her ear. "Hiding's done. Odran waits for you."

And she kicked the air as he lifted her off her feet with the ground spinning beneath her.

She heard a roar, thought it was her panicked heart beating in her head. Then it dived out of the sky, gleaming emerald and gold and impossible. Its long, sinuous body streaked through the air with the man on its back, black hair flying. The sunlight struck the sword raised in his hand.

What held her let her go, and as she fell, too stunned to scream, she saw him draw a sword of his own.

She hit the ground, lay dazed and dizzy, as the clash—blade against blade—shook it beneath her.

"Breen!" Marg dropped down beside her. "I've got you. Let me see where you're hurt."

"It's a dragon." Breathless, Breen wheezed out the words. "It's a dragon."

"And thank the gods for it."

The dragon turned, body curling, tail whipping. And its rider sliced his sword.

The winged body dropped like a stone. The head hit the dirt road with a muffled *thump*, then rolled into the high grass.

"Oh God, oh my God."

"There, it's all right now. You're safe. Bruised, but nothing's broken. Just sit, catch your breath. It's all over and done."

The dragon glided down, keen claws scoring the dirt road. It studied Breen out of eyes shades deeper than the gold scales as it lowered to its belly.

The man swung a leg over its wide back, then jumped down as easily as another might have jumped into a cool river on a hot day. He sheathed his bloody sword as he strode toward Marg.

He didn't look particularly pleased, but neither would she, Breen thought, if she'd just beheaded someone.

His hair flowed back, night dark, well over the collar of the leather duster that billowed out as he walked. His eyes, a dark, intense green, spared a glance at the severed head.

She knew that face, hard and handsome, from dreams.

"Odran didn't send his best." Then he shifted his gaze to Breen with the same look of mild disdain. "Her?"

"I'm grateful to you, Keegan, so don't be a git and spoil it. My girl's had a shock and a spill, and I'm keen aware it would've been worse if you hadn't come when you did. Breen, this is Keegan O'Broin."

"You have a dragon."

"We have each other. Can you stand?"

She wasn't altogether sure, but when he held out a hand, she decided she'd feel less idiotic on her feet than sitting on the ground with the dog making worried whines and licking her face.

He hauled her up, then gave Bollocks a kinder look than he'd given her.

"And who's this then? One of Clancy's litter?"

"He is, and Breen's now."

"You failed at guarding." But he gave Bollocks a quick, careless rub. "You'll have to do better next time." He looked back at Marg. "So will she."

"The girl's had no time," Marg began.

"I'm standing right here, but I can walk over that way if you'd both like to talk behind my back awhile."

"Well, some spine anyway, so we'll see." Dismissing Breen again, he looked up. "Mahon shouldn't be far behind me, and he'll see you safely home. This one was likely an opportunist, as Odran wouldn't send such a poor swordsman. I'll take care of what's left of him."

"You've been gone more than a fortnight. Will you be staying for a time?"

"As long as I can. I've missed the homeplace. And here's Mahon now."

"Ah, Aisling and the children will be happy to have him home."

With wings the color of aged mahogany and hair of the same hue in dozens of braids, the faerie glided through the sky.

"Will you need help getting this one back in the cart?" Keegan asked Marg.

"Oh, for—" Insult completely overrode lingering fear and continuing wonder. "Bollocks!" Breen snapped, and started for the cart. Her ankle twinged, but she refused to limp.

"Bollocks?" Keegan repeated with a hint of humor.

"That would be the dog's name, and leave off poking at the girl, Keegan. What happened here is my fault. It's mine."

She walked after Breen before Mahon dropped lightly to his feet.

"You flew off like a gale and nearly sent me into a spin," Mahon complained. "And more, it looks as if I've missed the fun. A dark faerie, was he?"

"One of Odran's, as he had Marg's granddaughter a foot or two off the ground when I got to them. And her, kicking and screaming like a tot having a tantrum."

"The message Aisling sent said she'd come through."

"And nearly had herself taken off again. See them home safe, will you, Mahon, before you take yourself home."

"I will, of course."

Keegan stepped over, picked up the head by the hair, tossed it beside the body. "Cróga! *Lasair*," he said to the dragon.

With a rumbling roar, Cróga spewed fire. And the power of it turned the remains to blackened ash. At the sound, Breen looked back, and he realized by the way the color drained from her cheeks, he should have waited until they were out of sight.

Well, no help for it now.

"You might've been more delicate," Mahon commented, then strolled over to the cart. "My lady." Despite the formal term, he leaned in to kiss Marg's cheek. "I'm sorry you had trouble, and here, at a holy place. And I didn't know you had a sister."

"You're a one, Mahon. Breen's my granddaughter, as you well know. And, Breen, here's Mahon Hannigan."

"I've met your family." Because she could smell the smoke, Breen spoke carefully so her voice didn't shake. "Your children are adorable."

"And a handful with it. Are you well enough to travel, my lady?"

"I'm fine, thank you. I'm fine."

"I'll be seeing you safely home again, so not to worry."

His wings spread, and up he went. Breen forgot to be astonished.

After Marg clicked to the horse, after they'd gone beyond the stench of burning and smoke, Breen turned to her. "I need answers."

"You do, aye, you do. This, what happened, it's my fault."

"Before we get to that, I want to get this out so I can stop thinking about it. That man was riding a dragon."

"Such creatures are lore and legend in your world, but a part of this one. I asked none come near for a while, as I thought you . . . You had so much coming at you, and I thought . . . I was wrong. I've been wrong, and you might have paid dearly for it."

"He's Aisling and Harken's brother? The dragon rider."

"He is. And the taoiseach of Talamh."

"Him? Well, why the hell not? Now, why would some dark faerie try to drag me off against my will, and who the hell is Odran?"

"I believed you were still hidden from Odran, that there was time still to prepare you, to explain, and to teach. I can't say whether the one Keegan killed was sent, or if he was a scout or spy who got lucky, you could say, before he got unlucky."

"That doesn't answer either question."

"He would have wanted to take you. There would surely be a grand reward for it. He would have been one of Odran's. Your grandfather."

"My— Why would my grandfather, one you failed to mention, want me scared witless and hauled off by . . . He's the one who took me when I was a child."

Her face tight, Marg urged the horse to quicken her gait. "The fault's mine there as well. We're a peaceful world. You have to work to have peace, and there are times you have to fight for it. There are those who live for, who thrive on destroying, on taking, on the ruling of others against their will. Odran is such a one."

Any world, Breen thought, magicks or not, was the same.

"Why does he want me?"

"You're his blood as you are mine. And you're so much more than you know, *mo stór*."

Before she could speak again, Breen saw the dragon glide overhead before it, and its rider, veered off toward the west.

"Where's he going?"

"He would take the ash of the dark to the Bitter Caves, bury them deep, and salt the ground." Marg drove the cart a moment in silence. "We'll soon be home. Can you wait for the rest?"

She wanted to protest, but noted Marg looked as pale as she felt. "I've waited this long."

She looked up, watching Mahon soar. "If Keegan is taoiseach, who is Mahon?"

"His oldest friend, and a brother to him even before he and

Aisling took vows. A good man, is Mahon, and one you can trust, who stands as Keegan's right hand."

"He's . . . of the Sidhe, and Aisling—you said—was of the Wise. So the different . . . tribes, I guess it would be, can intermarry."

"Of course. A heart loves who it loves. Harken pines for Morena, and always has. But he's a bit slow on such matters, and she's more than a bit stubborn, so they circle each other yet."

Marg turned onto the path toward the cottage. "When I have Igraine settled, I want to look you over again, or I could call on Aisling, as healing is her greatest strength."

"I'm not hurt. Probably some bruises, and my left ankle's sore, that's all."

"We'll have a look, and we'll have some wine, and I'll tell you what you need to know."

"All of it," Breen insisted. "Not what you think I need to know."

"All of it."

When she pulled up, Mahon dropped down to help Marg out of the cart. "I'll see to the horse and cart."

"Ah, Mahon, I know you're wanting home."

"And I'll have it soon enough." He gave her another kiss, gave the dog a rub. "You're very welcome in Talamh, my lady Breen."

"Thank you."

Because her ankle had stiffened up on the drive in, she had to fight not to hobble to the door.

"Sit there, by the fire." Marg flicked her fingers to have it going from dying embers to low flame. "Let's put that foot up now, and get the boot off."

"I just twisted it when I fell. My ass actually took the brunt of it."

Marg frowned over it. "A bit bruised, a bit swollen. Healing's not my greatest strength, but I can tend to this."

Sitting on the low table, Marg propped Breen's foot in her lap.

"It just needs ice and elevation."

Marg said, "Hmmm," and gently ran her fingers over the ankle, slow circles, the lightest touch. "When you learned to walk, you only wanted to run. Bruises and scrapes, scrapes and bruises. You'd just pop back up again and go."

"I like to run. I ran track in school. For a while."

The fingers felt so soothing, so cool and soothing, Breen's eyes drooped.

"Now just sit, and I'll get us some wine, and you some balm to finish off the healing."

When Marg got up, Breen opened her eyes again. Not only was the stiffness and ache gone, so were the bruises, the swelling.

"Is it some sort of spell?"

"Oh, no indeed. A skill, you could say, though if it had been serious, I'd have wanted Aisling or one of the other healers. You have the skill. I remember once Morena burned her fingers on the stove. You healed them with kisses."

"How . . . how did I know?"

"Your heart knew. Now here you are." She brought in the wine, a plate of cookies, and a biscuit for the dog. On the tray sat a little blue jar.

"Just some balm. Lotions, potions, balms, salves, spells, and such, those are my strengths."

"It feels fine now."

"This will keep it that way. You called me Nan." With that same gentle, circular touch, Marg applied the balm. "You called me Nan, and told me to run and hide."

"You didn't hide."

"You thought to shield me. Would I do less for you?"

She gave the biscuit to the dog, who stretched out in front of the fire to gnaw at it.

"Do you always leave the door open?"

"Not always, no, but I like the air. Would you have it closed?"

"No, it's nice, the breeze, the fire."

The welcome, she thought. Because an open door meant welcome.

Marg sat, picked up her wine. She turned the cup in her hands before drinking. "I'll tell the tale my way, but it'll be the truth. The whole of it. And what questions you have, I'll answer."

She drank again.

"When the taoiseach before me died—and he had a long life, and held the peace—I joined the others at the lake. This is how we choose and are chosen. The sword is given back to the lake. Going into the lake is the first choice we make. So I went in. Eighteen years was I, and with no ambitions to lead. I wanted to be—a good witch, you'd say, and when I found my heart mate, a good mother to our many children. These were my desires when I went into the water. But there, in its depths where others looked, only I could see the sword. So I chose again, to take it up, to accept my destiny."

"Like, in a way, the Lady of the Lake, the Arthurian legend."

"Legends come from somewhere, don't they? So I took up my duties as well, practiced my craft, and the odd politics of leadership. There were men who wished to share that station with me, but none I wanted in return. Until I saw Odran."

Sitting back, she looked into the fire, into the past. "Ah, gods, he was handsome, with hair like sunlight, eyes gray as a storm cloud. Tall and well-built, so charming. He romanced me, long looks, sweet words, thrilling touches. I thought he was of the Wise. I thought he was of Talamh."

"He wasn't? Isn't?"

Marg shook her head. "I was blind to what he was. I was young and full of love and lust for him. I'll never know if that was from me, or his powers to mold my feelings. So I bedded him. He wasn't my first, but he was what I wanted—or so I believed."

The cat came in. It took a long look at Marg, then walked back toward the kitchen.

"We took our vows, first at the Capital, then again at the farm where my family worked the land for generations. And as was my deepest wish, we made a child. So attentive was Odran while I carried our son. He worked the land with my father, brought flowers to my mother. Then Eian was born. The joy lasted weeks more, for you see he wanted the baby plump with my milk—witch's milk—and growing in power."

"Why? What for?"

"To take it, into himself. To drain it, bit by bit, a child that carried his blood, and mine. The taoiseach. One night I woke from a dream—a dream of storms and blood. I felt not well, and dizzy and weak, for he'd dosed me in the tea he kindly brought while I was nursing my babe. And I saw him, saw him for what he was, saw the dark and the purpose as he held the baby—sleeping as well, and too deep. Drawing that innocent power in, draining the child we'd made."

"He—he was killing the baby? His own son?"

Marg shook her head. "Not killing, but taking, draining slowly. The power, the soul. Drinking it in, you could say. And, aye, death would have come in time when my sweet babe had no more to give.

"And I found my wrath, and my strength with it. I stopped him, a curse from a mother's torn heart. I cast him out of the house, out of the world—I believed forever. But you see he was more than I knew, even then, and my worry for the baby dimmed my sight. For he came back, with his dark and his demons, and the long peace ended."

For a moment, Marg laid her head back, closed her eyes.

"We waged war, more than a year. People died, good men and women who fought those forces. My own father, my own brothers fell in that year. And within the next my mother died with a bitter and broken heart. Never did she forgive me."

"How was any of that your fault?"

"I was taoiseach. Did I protect the world I'd sworn to? No. I gave in to my own desires and wants. And so, when we sent him back, and into the dark, when we honored the dead and began to build a new peace, I gave the sword back to the lake for another to be chosen."

"Not my father. He would've been too young."

"No, there was another, and she did well for her time. Then it was Eian's time. Only a mother knows, I think, the feeling of great pride laced with great fear. I felt that the morning Eian came out of the lake with the sword held firm in his hand. But he held the peace, my boy. And he met your mother when he took one of the journeys. All here are encouraged to see other worlds, to learn, to understand we are not the only. So, as I told you, he brought her here, willing, and they took vows, and they made you."

A man came in, a man with silver hair, and walked to Marg, poured wine in her glass. "You need more wine, and a meal come to that."

"I'll eat when I've told her the rest. She's not as safe as I believed."

"I saw you." Breen pushed to her feet. "I saw you."

"Only because I wanted you to." He topped off her wine. "In hopes to stir what needed stirring."

"You were spying on me?"

"Sedric is my dear friend and companion. I sent him to you, to watch. There were signs, Breen, I couldn't ignore. Beyond the deep unhappiness I felt from you, there were signs the time had come. Sedric would never harm you."

"I thought I was going crazy."

"But things stirred," he said with a slow smile, and strolled out of the room.

Something in the smile, the movements . . . "He's—he's the cat!"

"A were he is, and of the Wise as well from his mother. I'm as devoted to him as he is to me—and to you, always to you. No doubt he has the arrogance of his spirit animal, but he would give his life for mine, and for yours."

It fell into place for her, bit by magickal bit. "It wasn't just luck I found out about the money."

"You needed your independence. You needed to choose, and you did. Do you regret it?"

"No, but I'm not sure what to do with it."

Marg leaned forward, took Breen's hand. "You'll know when you fully wake. I only ask that you let me show you, teach you, so you'll be strong."

She remembered, she could see it. "He came in the night. I was just . . . I was just a baby really. He said . . . he said, he would teach me to fly, like the faeries, like the dragons. He looked like a little boy, but he wasn't."

"We had protection around you, and still he slid through, a snake slithering through the dark."

"He put me in a glass cage, a box, and I couldn't get out. I cried for my da, for my mother, for you."

"And we heard you. He didn't think we could—he thought his power so strong, but it crumbled against what you have in you, as well as your father's love, and mine, your mother's tears."

"He said you couldn't hear me, would never hear me. At first he tried to be soothing, but I wouldn't stop calling and crying, and he got angry. I remember. I can hear it, see it."

"If it's what you want, take my hand, look into the fire with me now. Our memories will join. I will see what you saw, and you what I saw. These answers are there, if you want them. But understand, you will feel it all, as if it were happening now."

It frightened her, the very idea of reliving it, but she reached out and took Marg's hand.

"Look into the fire, into the flame, the heart of the heat. Through the smoke and flickers of light and into what was. I am with you, and you with me."

She knew fear, and the fear screamed and raged inside her. Just a little girl, beating fists on a wall she couldn't see. Beyond it, the world swirled a pale green, like the waters of a lake. Deep, deep. The sun barely reached down to offer a murky light.

"Let me out. Da!"

"I am your father now, and mother, and all." The voice, nowhere, everywhere, filled her cage. "Be still, be quiet, and I will give you sweets. You will be as a princess with golden toys and sugared plums."

Tears spilled. Her hands hurt from pounding. "I want my da! I want my mama! I want Nan! I don't like you!"

"Stop your blubbering, or you will know pain."

Something pinched her, hard, on the arm. She squealed in shock, fell down to curl up and weep and weep.

"Good girls get treats. Bad girls get pinches and slaps. Be good, and grow. As you grow, what's in you grows. What's in you is mine!

When it's ripe, I'll take it. When I take it, you'll live in a palace in the sky."

Even through her fear she heard the lie. She called for her father, her mother, her grandmother. And as she called, something built inside her.

What she'd known of power until then had given her little things, shown her the pretty and the fun. Butterflies that fluttered to her hand, birds landing on her shoulder to sing.

But this, this growing thing, was hard and sharp, like the knives she wasn't allowed to touch.

And she, who had never known the ugly, screamed out her truth. "I hate you! My da will come and fight you! He'll hurt you for hurting me."

Not a pinch now but a slap, hard and sharp like the knives. No one had ever struck her, and the shock of it, the insult of it, carved through the fear and found the rage.

Cheek stinging, the raw red mark on it like a burn, Breen got to her feet. Her fists clenched at her sides. Her eyes went dark, dark as night, as what had built inside her erupted.

"You're not supposed to hit!" Screaming it, she threw out her hands—and what was in her.

Something howled, as if in pain, as the glass shattered.

Water rushed over her, sent her tumbling. She kicked, slapped out with her hands, but she couldn't find the way out. She knew to hold her breath in the water—Da had taught her to swim—but she couldn't, she couldn't.

Hands gripped her, and panicked, she pushed, struggled, started to scream. She swallowed water, choked, then her head broke the surface.

"I've got you, *mo stór*. Nan's got you. Hold on to me, hold on to Nan."

She coughed up water, clung as Marg dragged them toward the bank of what was a curving river.

"Fi! Help me."

Finola, pale pink wings spread, reached down, took Marg's hand.

She pulled them to the bank, swirled off a cloak to wrap a shivering Breen.

"There now, poor little mite. You're safe now."

"She's not." With sweeps of her hands, Marg dried and warmed her granddaughter. "Take her back, Finola, to where she will be. Take her to her mother. They need me here. Eian and the others need me with them."

"I'll come back."

"No, please. Stay with Breen and Jennifer. Stay with them."

Still drenched from the river, Marg crouched, held Breen to her. "Go with Finola now, my baby. Your mother's waiting for you."

"You come! And Da."

"Soon. Take her, Fi. I'm needed."

"I'll keep her safe." Gathering the child, Finola lifted into the air.

Wrapped in the cloak, held close in the faerie's arms, Breen looked back. She saw her first glimpse of war, the terrible light and dark of it. And the screams rose up until she pressed her hands to her ears, and Finola swept her away.

CHAPTER FIFTEEN

Looking into the fire, Breen saw what her grandmother had seen. The carnage, the brutality. Blood soaked the ground; it spilled into the river to run red.

She saw Finola fly toward a towering waterfall, carrying the child she'd been. And when the faerie flew through it, when Marg knew the child was away, she gathered herself.

The dragon came at her call, an emerald and sapphire flash through the haze. She mounted, took up her sword, her wand. Merging her mind with the dragon's, she flew into battle.

A dozen gargoyles, black teeth snapping, charged through the thick woods and fog toward a line of Fey. She shot out with her wand, torching them even as she sliced and hacked with the sword at winged demons.

Shrieks and screams echoed; drumbeats boomed.

She knew some who fought in the air, on the ground, were enslaved or bewitched, taken from her world and others to build Odran's army. With their minds trapped, they killed and died for him.

She broke spells and chains when she could, ended lives when she couldn't.

The air thundered; the ground cracked. More dark poured out of it to meet sword, claw, power, and flame.

The thunder of war rolled its violence across the land.

She led a trio of dragon riders to the waterfall. "Hold the line! None get through but our own."

She rode through the smoke-choked air, higher, higher still, until she found the fresh. There, she pulled Eian into her mind, her heart, her blood, until she saw him with his chosen forces waging fury on Odran's guards.

She rode the wind, trusting those left behind to hold back the dark while she flew to its source.

Atop the stone island, across the Dark Sea from the high, raw cliffs, stood the fortress Odran's greed and power had built.

Its black walls gleamed like glass, and glittering crystals crusted its turrets like spikes.

Eian and his dragon riders battled Odran's bat-winged demons while below more soldiers of Talamh cut bloody swaths through gargoyles, demon dogs, the bewitched, and the damned.

Power stung the air, the clash of black to white burning it so that it smoked and trembled.

Wild with rage, she flew into it, spinning her dragon so its tail cut through knife-edged wings to send bodies tumbling into the fury of the sea below.

She fought side by side with her son, her hair streaming back, her power burning like a fever. She worked with him to draw those cursed guards away, lure them just enough away while Feys scaled the fortress.

With wing, with claw, with power, with rope, they climbed.

Her eyes met Eian's. Together they threw power that whirled and spread blinding white, then coalesced into white fire that burst through the barred doors of the black castle.

The Fey flooded in.

"He'll flee," Marg called out.

"Aye. He'll try."

On his bloodred dragon, Eian flew toward the breach, and Marg after him.

Inside, they met the chaos of war among the ruins of jewels and treasures stolen or conjured in blood for Odran's pleasures.

Slaves, collared like livestock, ran screaming or huddled in fear.

They fought their way to the keep, through the stench of smoke and blood and the ooze of slayed demons.

He knows where to find him, Marg thought. He can feel Odran while I cannot. It's blood calling to blood.

"He wants you to find him." Terrified for her son, she screamed it out. "It's a trap."

Eian, eyes storm gray, hair a flame, lifted his sword high. "It's only a trap if you're the prey."

On his dragon, his bold hair streaming behind, Eian streaked over the smoldering bodies of demons and into the keep. The stench of death, burning flesh, boiling blood fouled the air.

Eyes stinging from the smoke, Marg guarded Eian's flank, slashing, shooting fiery white light. Inside, gold columns, silver tiles glittered behind the haze of war. Wounded, facing death and defeat, Odran's forces scattered on wing and scale and claw. Eian's troops pursued, driving demons into the ground, sending them flaming over the high cliffs.

There would be, could be, no surrender, Marg knew. The evil spawned here must be crushed. Any who escaped, wormed their way back into other worlds, would carry the tale of Eian O'Ceallaigh and his soldiers of Talamh.

And would tremble as they spoke his name.

So it must be.

The keep, a maze of curves and plundered riches, echoed with the clash of swords, the shrieks and merciless spurts of flame. Desperate to keep her son in sight, Marg fought her way through even as the knife-edge of a black wing scored down her arm before she turned it to ash.

There, in the throne room, he sat, wildly handsome and still on a towering throne adorned with the skulls and bones of those he'd slain in his relentless search for power.

His golden hair fell shining to his shoulders under a crown of clear crystal and brilliant jewels. He wore gold, trews and tunic, belted with more jewels.

And sat smiling the smile that had seduced a young woman reaching for love to shine over her own powers.

Even now, she thought, even now he radiated sexuality and charm, almost irresistible through the stink of blood and death.

"Ah, my beloved and my son." His voice, deep, drugging, dangerous, seemed to stroke like a lover's fingers. "Come now, come. Sit by my right and left hands as has always been meant."

"Stand," Eian demanded, and leaped off his dragon, sword in hand. "Stand or meet your death on your arse."

"Such harsh words, such a price already paid in the blood of your people. And all for a whining brat you chose to make with a weak, powerless woman from a world beneath your rank. And all because I wished a bit of private time with my granddaughter—such as she is."

"She is more than you." Marg stayed mounted, every sense tuned for the trap. "Stronger and brighter."

"Do you think so, beloved?" Odran spoke mildly. "She is my blood. She is mine by right, and so is whatever pitiful power she holds."

"She will never be yours."

Odran spared Eian a glance. "The day will come when I drink every drop of what she is."

"Stand," Eian ordered again. His eyes, storm gray with power, stared from a face streaked with blood and soot.

"Your creatures bleed and burn as those who can slink back to their hells. Your palace of lies crumbles around you. The day has come for you to pay for what you did to my mother, to me, to my child. Draw your sword, Odran the Damned, and meet me like a man."

Slowly, deliberately, Odran stood. "But I am not a man. I am a god."

He threw out his arms. The gale he called blew Eian off his feet, nearly unseated Marg. For a moment, only a moment, she spun wild and without control.

"I am not the prey," Eian told her. "Be ready."

She saw the quick shock on Odran's face as Eian lunged toward him. A moment was enough for demons, dozens of them, to crawl through the gold walls and silver floors.

As she cried out for her son to mount again, dozens more Talamh forces raged into the throne room.

Then a sword was in Odran's hand, obsidian dark against Eian's silver. The clash shook the columns, sent spiderwebs of cracks along the floor.

"Lead them out!" Eian shouted. "Get everyone out." And, pushing a hand into the air, he sent the roof of the keep spiraling up with a thunderous roar.

Faeries poured through to slash at the demons and swoop up any Talamh forces that couldn't take to the air on their own. Though her heart banged in her throat, Marg did as her son ordered.

She led others out through the maze, casting light ahead to clear the path.

She saw only snatches of the battle as she struggled to meld her thoughts with Eian's. Odran's eyes, she saw them, darker than the smoke and alive with raging hate.

When she had the troops safely away, the wounded carried off to home, she whirled her dragon back.

Before she reached the keep it imploded. The sheer violence of it stormed against her, through her.

Still, she fought to drive the dragon forward.

Then she saw him—her son, her boy—rising up above the smoking rubble. Bloody, smeared with ash, but alive.

He dived toward her.

"The waterfall!" he shouted. "Get through, get everyone through. The moment all are safe, we block the portal. I need you to help me close it."

"I'm with you. You're hurt. You're bleeding."

"So are you." Across the air, he reached out, touched her hand. "I couldn't risk letting you see what was in my mind. He might have seen, seen just enough to defend."

"You are taoiseach. And Odran?"

"I don't know, not for certain. He would have buried us both in that cursed place rather than see me live. Now he's buried there. Gods will he stays buried."

"But he didn't." Marg spoke to Breen now. "Years passed, and we came to believe him gone. We blocked the portal into that world, and still, he slithered through. But you were safe. Your father made certain of it, for as long as he could."

"By taking me out of the world he loved."

"We cast spells for your protection, and some to dull memories so the heartbreak wouldn't be so keen. His dearest friend lost his life in that battle. Kavan, father to Keegan, Aisling, and Harken. And so he gave Kavan's widow and his children the farm. It would be in the best of hands, and they would be secure in a home. He would have given up the sword and staff, but after the Battle of the Black Castle, the people pleaded with him to retain them. So when he took you and your mother through the portal to the world she knew, and became yours, he remained taoiseach. He came back often, as often as he could, and kept the peace for as long as he could."

"How did he come back? He lived . . . There were never out-of-town gigs, were there? He never traveled for his music—for that first and abiding love."

"Know this." Once again, Marg took Breen's hand. "He loved you beyond measure. He loved Talamh. And so he gave up something he loved to be your father, to serve his people."

"He was a warrior. I saw as if I'd been there, because you were. I saw him. I never knew that part of him."

A warrior, Breen thought. A leader. A hero.

"There was no need for you to know. Now there is."

"And I broke the glass of the cage. I did that."

"You did, aye, you did, a child of only three."

"How?"

"It was in you, but until that moment, it was soft, it was sweet, and it was innocent. In that moment, when it was needed, you woke full and strong."

"I don't know what that means. I don't know what's in me. I

saw—but I still . . . Demons, like in books and movies. Gargoyles, alive and vicious. They exist."

"There are worlds where they exist," Marg confirmed. "He brought them into what he claimed as his."

"You were . . . terrifying and magnificent. You rode a dragon, you had a sword and a wand. A magic wand?"

"So you could call it. An extension of power. I am of the Wise, as you are."

"And my father was. My mother wasn't—isn't."

"No. She is what she wished, what she needed you to be. Human. Only human."

"I need to—" Rising, Breen circled the pretty, cozy room with its simmering fire and sparkling crystals. "What am I then? Half human, half something else? And Odran, my grandfather? He called himself a god. So he's crazy as well as evil?"

"He is many things. And while mad for power, he is not mad. A god he is."

"Wait a minute, wait a minute." She had to sit again. "A god? What, like Thor?"

Marg smiled at her, but the smile was weary. "Legends and lore, as I said, root in truth."

"But that's . . . I was going to say impossible, but all of this is. But it's not. If Odran's a god, my father was—"

"A demi-god. Born of the Wise and the gods. And you, *mo stór*, are of the Wise, the Sidhe, the gods, and the human. There is no one in this world or the world where you were reared like you."

"What does that make me? A freak?"

"A treasure."

"Mairghread." Sedric stepped out. "It's enough for now. She has enough for now. You need food and rest."

Breen saw it as truth. Her grandmother looked pale and exhausted. She had to bite back at the questions that sprang up, desperate for answers.

"It's a lot. I need to think. I know you're not lying to me because I saw. I've seen. But I can't balance it."

"There's bread and cheese while the stew finishes," Sedric announced. "You'll eat some."

Imperious, he turned and walked away.

"Is he your familiar? That's the term, isn't it?"

"He is my mate. I will never pledge again, but if I could do so, I would pledge to Sedric."

"Oh. So you're . . . oh."

Marg's face relaxed again, with some humor. "Such matters don't stop in youth, my girl. He fought that day. He bled for you. He would give his life for yours if needs be. Because he is mine, I am his. And so, you are his."

So they ate bread and cheese in the warm kitchen with the door open to the air and the oncoming evening.

And when questions, so many more questions, nagged at Breen, the steady stare in Sedric's eyes made her hold them back.

"I haven't unpacked. I didn't bring much, but I should take care of that. And you said there was a way I could write. I start early."

"I'll show you." Sedric rose, then brought Marg's hand to his lips. "Rest awhile. You've had a trying day. Tomorrow's soon enough for more."

"Don't fuss."

"If fussing I did, you'd be abed with a potion for a full night's sleep. Come, girl, I'll show you what you need."

"Tomorrow's soon enough," Breen told Marg. "We're all tired."

"Well done," Sedric said as he led her back to her room. "There's nothing she wouldn't do for you, and some she must do troubles her heart."

"You knew my father."

"Knew, admired, respected, loved. He was a son to me."

A son to him, Breen thought.

"You've been with my grandmother a long time."

"As long as she would have me. I remember you as a bright, charming child with a strong will. It appears your time in the world of Earth dulled that will. But no matter," he said lightly. "You have only to use it to shine it up again. For now, what you need for your work is here."

He gestured to the desk. On it she saw a tall stack of paper, and a pen. She walked over, lifted the pen—silver with a small red crystal on the top of the cap.

"A fountain pen?"

"More than that. Remember where you are. Your devices, as they're called, won't operate here. But this pen, conjured only for you, will never run out of ink. It will transfer your thoughts to the page, and in the manner you use for this blog you write, and the other stories and communications. It's a very fine gift of storytelling you have, and this pen, these papers will assist you."

"I'm not sure I know how to write that way. And for the blog, I include photographs."

"You simply describe the image you wish to use, and it will be done. We have people who live on the other side of the portal. They'll take what you write, and transcribe it to your device."

"People from here live in Ireland?"

"And beyond. They must take a sacred oath, and live by it if they choose to dwell outside Talamh. For now, know that we revere story-tellers here, and that you're free to continue, in this way, while you visit."

He stepped back. "We'll have our meal when you're ready, but I ask you not to take too long. Marg will feel better with a good bowl of stew."

"Ten minutes."

With a nod, he stepped out, closed the door.

Alone, she shook her head at the stack of paper, at the pen in her hand.

"I guess it could've been a fricking quill."

She considered the blog delayed for a day, maybe two, then, curious, uncapped the pen. Still standing, she put the tip on the top paper.

"If it was . . ."

She saw the words, and the rest of the thought appear on the page as if typed in her chosen font.

If it was good enough for Jane Austen. Oh my God! How is this— Stop!

She lifted the pen with a jerk.

Too much, she decided. It was all just too much for one day.

She capped the pen, set it down with great care.

She hadn't brought much, so put everything in the wardrobe that smelled of cedar and lavender before opening the door to the bathroom—water closet, she thought.

That about described it, she supposed. A big copper tub dominated the small room. She studied the tiny toilet with a pull chain with some anxiety. On a table, a large pitcher sat beside a bowl. The water in the pitcher was warm—very warm—when she dipped a finger in.

The impossibility no longer baffled her.

Shelves held a pair of fluffy white towels, crystal bottles filled with liquids, oils, tiny beads that smelled of herbs and flowers, and a cake of soap in a dish.

Iron sconces held candles as fragrant as the soap.

Maybe it lacked a shower, and maybe she remained dubious about the toilet, but she couldn't deny the charm.

Fingers mentally crossed, she tried the toilet, pulled the chain. She heard no expected *whoosh* or creaky flush, but when she stood the bowl was empty and sparkling clean.

"Okay, we'll call that practical magicks."

She used the bowl and pitcher to wash up, then used the iron-framed wall mirror to study her face.

"Might as well say it. You're not in Kansas anymore."

She went out, followed the scent of cooking into the kitchen.

The table held three place settings—crockery bowls, bread plates, white cloth napkins rolled into copper rings. Sedric stood at the little stove; Marg sliced brown bread on a board.

The easy domesticity told Breen they'd been together—not as witch and familiar, but as a couple—for, as she'd thought, a long time.

"It smells wonderful."

"Sedric's a fine cook." Marg carried the bread and a crock of butter to the table. "I can promise you won't go hungry. The bread I baked this morning before you arrived, as I'm a good cook myself. And the butter comes from the farm. The dinner wine is of Finola and Seamus's making, and you won't find better even in the Capital."

"I'm not a very good cook," she said, and sat when Marg did. "I'm trying to get better at it, as there's no easy takeout near the cottage, and Marco's not here to put something together. He's a really good cook."

"He's a good friend to you. Finola was particularly taken with him."

"She has an eye for handsome lads." Sedric set the pot on the table, then began to ladle stew into the bowls.

"She does that. I'm told he's musical, as you are."

"Oh, I'm not like Marco. He's what you'd call a natural. My father called him that, and taught us to play—the piano, the violin, the flute. But when—when he had to leave, Marco took more lessons. I . . . didn't."

Because it wasn't a conversation she wanted to have, she sampled the stew. "Oh, it's just wonderful. You grow your own vegetables."

"The soil is for growing. You have a talent there as well."

"I think I do. It's something I want to learn more about. We live in an apartment, so there really isn't anywhere to plant, and before . . . There wasn't time with my job and all the rest for a real hobby or interest."

"Your time is yours now," Sedric commented.

"I'm getting used to that. I want to ask—and if you don't want to answer or talk about it now, it can wait, but you've given me a lot of money. For me, it's a fortune. Where did it come from?"

"Well now, money is easy enough to come by. We have no currency here, but—"

"No currency? None?"

"And no need. We barter and trade, and tribes, communities, take care of those who fall into the hard times. Others may appeal to the taoiseach and his council for help—a death, a sickness, or some other misfortune that causes them troubles."

She had to say it again. "No money?"

"It's metal or paper or some other form that has no real value above what a people ascribe to it." Sedric shrugged, buttered some bread.

"But you gave me money."

"In the world you've lived in you require it for safety, security, for food, a roof, a bed. I am your grandmother. Your father and I agreed to see to your needs. We have things of value here that can be sold outside. So it was done."

"Thank you. Having the money changed my life, it gave me a freedom I didn't have before. It sounds shallow sitting here, saying that, but it's true."

"Every world has its own rules and laws and cultures."

"Sedric told me you have people who live outside."

"Of course. Some may find a life outside more suitable, or happier. All are free to choose. Some from the outside choose Talamh; some from Talamh choose the outside."

"When they choose to leave, they take an oath? You were explaining before."

"Most sacred," Marg agreed. "The most sacred of all is to cause no harm, to take no life except to defend life, not with magicks or without. Even then, if it's done to protect or defend life, it must be judged. The taking of a life, the causing of harm in any other circumstance is punished by a stripping of power and banishment."

"Banished to where?"

Sedric laid a hand on Marg's and answered. "There is a world where the single portal opens only from the outside. Those who break the oath and are judged to have done so are taken there, where they must live without magicks."

A kind of prison, Breen realized. "How do you know if they broke the oath?"

"We have Watchers, and their gift is empathy. They know, and must tell the council. We are people of the land, we are artists and craftsmen, storytellers, but we are also a world of laws. Most are not unlike the laws you know. To take a life, to take what is not yours or not given freely, to force another to lie with you, to neglect a child or animal. All of these acts cause harm, and our first law is to cause no harm."

The answers had more questions buzzing in her brain, but a glance from Sedric had her holding them back.

Enough, she thought again, for one day.

"I want to thank you for the paper, and the pen. I'm looking forward to trying to write with them."

"I hope you'll enjoy them, and work well. But also take time from the work to see more of Talamh. To let me teach you, to help you wake."

"To wake what I had that broke the glass when I was little."

"That and more."

"I'd like to see more, and learn more. I could start with you showing me how you deal with dishes. I've figured out there's no running water."

"We have a fine well, but you'll do no dishes tonight. Tonight you're a guest as well as family. You enjoy your walks, and it's a lovely evening for a walk."

"All right. If I wanted to use the tub later, how do I fill it?"

Marg smiled. "The pitcher will fill it, and the water will stay warm until you're done."

"Saves on plumbing bills." She needed the walk, she realized. Needed the air, the evening, the quiet to organize her thoughts, and reconcile them with what she'd come to know.

"Thank you for dinner. Everything was, well, perfect."

She hesitated, then went with instinct. She leaned down, kissed Marg's cheek. "Thank you, Nan."

When Breen went out, Marg pressed a hand to her heart. "There's so much, Sedric, so much left to give her, so much left to ask of her."

"One world struggles with the other inside her yet."

"And may always. Go, watch over her. Odran may have spies closer than we know. I'll see to the dishes."

He rose, bent down, kissed her lips gently.

As a man, he turned away. As a cat, he slipped out the door.

CHAPTER SIXTEEN

Breen spotted the cat slinking along in the grass on the side of the road, sinuously silver among the green. And realized almost immediately she wouldn't have seen him unless he'd wanted her to.

While she wasn't sure exactly what she thought of Sedric yet, clearly her grandmother trusted him—and just as clearly, they loved each other.

Breen would tolerate him. She was, kinship aside, a guest here. A visitor.

Stranger in a strange land, she thought.

The sun set fire to the western sky. Automatically she reached for the phone still in her pocket, tapped for the camera. It took her a minute, staring at the blank screen, to remember.

"Devices won't work here," she muttered. "No technology."

She stuck the phone away again, and ignored the cat. She imagined he snickered.

Instead, she enjoyed the long, slow setting of the sun, the spread of that fire over the waters of the bay, the lingering flames of it against the distant hills.

What lay behind the hills? she wondered. More of this—fields and farms, water and woods? Magickal people who tilled and planted, cooked stew, made music?

Because she heard music, something light and bright carried on the evening air. A fiddle, maybe a harp, a flute, all blending, lively and quick.

Like another kind of dream, she thought. The perfect music for a late summer evening with sheep and cattle huddled in the fields, the air smelling of grass and peat smoke.

And a were-cat keeping pace with her like a feline bodyguard.

A lot of good a cat would do her if some maniac faerie swooped down to try to grab her again.

Remembering it, she looked up, and just froze.

The dragon, riderless, glided over the dusky sky like a golden ship over the sea. Nothing, nothing she'd seen or would see in this fantastic place could be as magnificent, as glorious as that silent, gilded flight.

Awestruck, she followed that flight, and saw in that dusky sky two moons. Both pale yet as a single star woke to shine, and both half-moons—one waxing, one waning.

"But . . . there are two moons."

"As there always have been."

Ready to run, scream, fight, she spun around.

She hadn't seen him as dusk crept in, leaning back against the stone post of the gate. All in black, he blended into the oncoming night. He probably meant to.

The taoiseach, the leader, the rider of the gold-and-emerald dragon.

"How do the tides work with two of them?"

"They come in, go out, come in, go out. I'll see to her, Sedric," he called to the cat. "Unless she plans on wandering about half the night."

"I just wanted a walk before . . ." Explaining herself, she thought. She had to stop feeling obliged, always, to explain herself. "I don't want to be seen to."

"Want and need are different things, aren't they now? And Marg won't worry if she knows you're not alone."

That stopped her from arguing. "I haven't really thanked you for what you did today."

"Thanks aren't necessary, but you're welcome in any case."

She searched for something polite to say, and glanced toward the farmhouse, with all its windows lit like sunshine. "Sounds like a party."

He glanced back toward the music, the voices. "It is that, a welcoming home sort of thing. You and Marg and Sedric were invited, as was most of the bloody valley, but Marg felt you might want something a bit less . . . lively for your first night. Still, if you want to go in, you'll be welcome."

"No, it would be awkward yet. I don't really know anyone—or enough of . . . anything."

"Well, you'll need to learn, won't you?"

Though his voice struck her as another kind of music—what she still thought of as an Irish lilt—her hackles rose.

"I've learned enough to know I have some sort of crazed god for a grandfather who'd like to suck me dry of what I don't even know I have. And up until five damn minutes ago, I didn't even believe in gods."

He looked genuinely curious. "Why not?"

"Because they're supposed to be myths. Like worlds with two moons where dragons fly overhead and my grandmother's lover turns into a cat. Now I've got a pen that writes down my thoughts, a pitcher that never runs out of hot water. I can't use my stupid phone, but I looked into the fire with Nan and saw my father waging war. I saw it as if I'd been there."

He watched her as she spoke, still leaning back against the post, his hands casually in his pockets.

And a sword at his side.

"You were there, at least for the start of it. I was too young, though I begged my father to take me with him when they went after you."

And he'd died, Breen remembered. He'd died in that horrible place protecting her. "I'm sorry. I'm sorry you lost your father, sorry he died helping to save me."

"Wasn't a fault of yours, was it, as you were hardly more than a baby. And you fought, didn't you? A child of three pitting her power against the god's. There are songs and stories of the young one breaking down the god's walls with her will."

The idea of that burned the back of her throat. "I don't know how I did it."

"You'll have to remember." He said it as if nothing could be simpler. And kept watching her. "You stopped your practice and training far too soon, but that can be mended now that you're here."

Instinctively, she took a step back. "I'm not here. I'm visiting."

He pushed off the post. "This is your world as much as it's mine. Will you give it nothing?"

"What am I supposed to give?" she tossed back. "I'm trying to adjust, and it's huge for me. I'm just starting to figure out what I want to do with my life, then *bam*, I find out that most of my life, if not a lie, was full of half-truths."

"Want and need, again, are different matters. You need to hone your gifts, and there Marg will show you. You need to train, and there, bad luck for us both, you'll have me for instructor."

"Training for what?"

"To fight, of course, to protect yourself and others. To stand for Talamh."

"Fight? Like with one of those?" Appalled, she pointed at the sword at his side. "I'm not a soldier."

"You'll learn unless you expect to be rescued at every turn." Now that musical voice turned just a little snide. "Is that how you see things in your world? A woman such as yourself just cowers and screams?"

"I took a self-defense class," she began, then let her temper rise. "You know what, I don't have to explain myself to you, or anyone. All my life I've had people like you criticizing, bullying, making me feel less. And I'm done with it. I'm done standing back and apologizing."

"That's fine then. You'll need to step up instead. He'll try for you, believe that, Breen Siobhan, and I'll give my life to stop him. So will every man and woman in this world. You are the daughter of Eian O'Ceallaigh, the taoiseach before me, the one who, when mine fell, stood as a father to me. In his name, I'm pledged to protect you. But by all the gods, you'll learn to fight."

She did step back again, but not in fear this time. "You loved him. My father."

"Aye, he was a great man and a good one. Much of what I am, I am because he taught me. And so in turn I'll teach you. He would expect no less of me. Or of you."

"I don't know what he'd expect of me."

"You do, aye, you do, or will when you stop pretending otherwise. But for now, I'll see you home. I want my own bed."

"I can see myself back."

"You don't have to speak to me. I like the quiet when I can get it. But I'll see you safe to Marg's cottage, as she'd wish it."

"One question, then we'll have that quiet. Did I know you? Before, when I lived here before?"

"Sure you knew me, and I you, though you were well beneath my notice as a girl child."

He smiled, really smiled, and everything about him radiated charm. "You were after calling birds and butterflies and the like and whispering secrets with Morena. I was more interested in wooden swords and battles to come, and searching for the dragon that would be mine.

"One day," he added, "that's not this one, I'll tell you of another time we met, and how that sealed my blood destiny. Now the quiet."

She didn't speak as he walked beside her with those two half-moons bright in a star-washed sky.

She had plenty to think about, and she would. But for that, she wanted not just quiet but alone.

So she said nothing as he waited halfway down the path until she went inside the cottage. The fire burned low, and the quiet soothed.

Still, she glanced out the window, saw him walking back down the path.

She'd try out the tub, she decided, then the pen, then the bed. And with all of them, she'd think about her first day in Talamh. And what tomorrow might bring.

She slept deep and dreamless, as if cocooned. Part of that, she imagined, came from a long, hot, fragrant bath, then a full hour of writing with the magick fountain pen.

And not enough, she thought, could possibly be said about the entertainment of filling a huge copper tub with a bottomless pitcher.

Since she couldn't put that in her blog, she decided it was just as well she'd written the blog before her bath. And that she'd filled it with her thoughts on finding self—and learning to live with what was found, descriptions of the pretty, misty morning she'd enjoyed with Bollocks rather than actual activities and events.

Those went into her personal journal.

Pleased her night work left her clear to work on her book, she thought of coffee.

Obviously with no coffee machine—that was off the menu—but she thought she could handle brewing up some strong tea to get her brain cells working.

As she made her way to the kitchen, she wondered if she'd have to figure out how to light a fire in the stove, then found the kitchen warm, the stove hot.

Either someone rose earlier than she, or the fire was like the pen, and just never ran out.

In the dim dawn light, she studied the jars. No tea bags—of course—but loose tea. Since they had no labels, she calculated the process could take awhile, so opened the door for Bollocks.

"I'll come out as soon as I figure out how to make tea."

When he ran out, she walked over, took one of the jars, sniffed the contents. Floral, she decided, light and sweet, and not an eye-opener.

She went down the line—herbal, woodsy, kind of lemony, spicy.

She tried another, decided it smelled very like the Irish breakfast tea she'd bought (in bags). Of course, she couldn't be sure, and it might be something that would turn her into a toad.

It wouldn't surprise her at this point.

But it seemed careless to keep something that would turn someone into a toad on a kitchen shelf with herbs and spices.

Willing to risk it, she used what she thought had to be a tea strainer, poured hot water from the kettle on the stove over it and into a mug.

She studied the dark brown—nearly black—liquid. Sniffed it. Risked a tiny sip. It tasted like tea—brutally strong—and since it didn't turn her into anything, she considered the entire process a success.

In her pajama pants and T-shirt and bare feet, she walked out into the morning.

Not so different, she decided, from a morning at her cottage. The view of woods and garden rather than bay and garden, but that same soft air, the thin mists, the wild green of it all.

She'd walk the dog over to the bay here later, she thought, then heard splashing. Walking beyond the flowers, the herbs—a thriving vegetable patch toward the trees—she saw the busy little stream—and Bollocks making the most of it.

"Good enough then."

She turned to take in her grandmother's cottage from this new vantage point.

She spotted a stone well—simply picture-perfect—a tree with orange-red berries, and another with what she thought were tiny green apples.

Sea glass, crystal, polished half bottles hung from branches, and when she touched them, had music tinkling into the air.

Something white and gold and druggingly fragrant smothered some sort of trellis. Honeysuckle, she realized, and near it something else climbing with pink and purple blooms.

As for the cottage, it fit the nook of land as if it had grown there—maybe it had.

She thought it all beautiful and, despite the lack of coffee, idyllic.

She found the dog's bowls, his feed—added a brown egg. Because he carried the wet of the stream with him, she set his bowls outside.

"Let me know when you want in—and don't go wandering too far."

She gave his topknot a rub, then went back in.

In the quiet, sleeping house, she sat down at her desk, picked up the pen.

The dog broke her spell when he rushed in to drop his head on her lap and give her a long, adoring look.

"Hi. Either you let yourself in or someone else is up."

"Up we are and have been." Marg stood in the doorway.

She wore trousers again, mannish and forest green, with a sweater the color of top cream.

"You were deep into your work, so I didn't want to disturb. Bollocks had another idea on that."

"That's all right. I was about to stop." Because, she realized, she was starving. "I wasn't sure I could write this way, but it rolled pretty well."

"I'm happy to hear it. How about some tea now, and a bite to eat?"

"That would be great. I made tea early this morning," she said as she rose. "Or I think I did. From that jar."

Marg nodded. "A strong energy tea that one, and good for the morning."

"I tried to guess what was in the jars—by scent mostly. I think I hit the chamomile, and something with lavender, and some sort of mint."

"I'll teach you if you like, though your nose is right on it. Sit, and I'll make us some nice jasmine tea—a good, light choice for a pretty day."

"Jasmine—that's it. I couldn't get it, but I thought I recognized the scent. I don't want you to have to cook for me. If I get the lay of the land, I can make a sandwich."

"You poke about as you please, but it gives me pleasure to cook for you—and I suspect you had nothing but the tea to break your fast."

She got a squat cobalt blue teapot. "Tell me about your book, won't you?"

"Which? I actually have two. Or one novel, and one book for middle schoolers—kids from about ten to thirteen."

"A children's book? Ah, you loved being read to as a child. Like a sea sponge you'd soak it all up, then tell them yourself, often changing some parts as you liked."

"Did I?"

"Oh, aye. What are you writing for children?"

"Bollocks's adventures. Actually, I finished it, or I think I have. I don't know that it's any good, but I had fun with it. It's just practice. I don't expect to get it, or anything, published. I'm a rank amateur."

Marg turned from her work. She wore little silver triangles in her ears, and inside each was a trio of dark green stones.

"That's your mother talking in your head, and it makes me sad to hear you say it."

"Maybe. Maybe, but it's easier to write a story than send that story off and face rejection."

"And if you don't send it off, see what's what, it's already rejected, isn't it?" She looked over from whatever she cooked in a skillet on the stove. "You chose to carry courage on your wrist, so use it."

"Marco said the same thing, basically."

"A sensible lad he is then, I'd say."

"I haven't let him read it—or anyone. It's like Schrödinger's cat. As long as it's in the box, it's alive. If I opened the box, would you read it and be honest? It doesn't help if anyone says it's good to spare my feelings."

"I promised not to lie to you, and that holds on this as well." She slid something from skillet to plate, set it in front of Breen.

Toasted brown bread topped with Irish—Talamhish, she corrected—bacon and an egg, sunny-side up, dashed with herbs.

"I remember this. You used to make this for me. I called it Dragon's Eye."

"A half slice of toast back then, and a favorite of yours. More's coming through." Marg sat with her tea. "Will you let me show you, teach you? We can begin with something as simple as the teas and how to use them, how to blend them together for other uses."

"I'd like—yes, I'd like that. And we could start there, but . . ."

"Tell me what you want, child. If it's in my power, I want to give it to you."

"Morena said something to me. She said that fire—like lighting a fire or candle—is the first thing learned."

"It often is. It's this you want to know again?"

"I think, it's so tangible, so inarguable." So fascinating, Breen admitted to herself. "What I've already seen and felt, it's still almost like a dream. But if I felt this, from me, I couldn't close that back in the box. And you won't lie and tell me it was from me if it was from you."

"I won't, no. Nor will I about your story if you let me read it."

"It's on my laptop. I'll print it out, and bring it to you next time."

"Oh, we won't have to wait for that, if I have your permission. I can see to that."

"All right. God, I'm nervous."

"Eat your food, drink your tea, then we'll begin. Nerves aren't shameful. Not acting because of them is."

She felt them, those nerves, prickling along her skin, rushing through her blood as she sat in the quiet kitchen, the dog sleeping over her feet.

The candle stood between her and Marg, creamy white and slim.

"I often make my own candles, those I use for ceremonies, spells, healings—for the craft, I'm saying, rather than for lighting the dark. This one is of my making, a skill I'll teach you as well, if you like."

"It wouldn't just be forming wax, the kind you mean."

"There's more than that, a purpose, and the purpose goes into the making. This I made for celebrations, and I see this as that."

"If I can't do it—"

"Ah, put your mother out of your head." After holding up a hand, Marg took a breath. "I'll not say a hard word about the woman who brought you into the world, but you must set aside the doubts, the doubts of self, she put into you. Be open, *mo stór*, to what you are, what you have. This is the first lesson. Once open, you reach, once you reach, you hold."

"Okay." Breen played her fingers over her tattoo. "Be open."

"How would you put out the flame of a candle?"

"I'd blow it out."

Marg beamed as if she'd solved some complex equation. "And so to bring the flame, a simple way to learn, is to draw in the breath. With purpose. Opening, letting the power rise up. Focus, for what will become natural takes focus to learn. To ignite."

She tried, over and over, but the wick remained cold and clean.

"I'm sorry."

"You only disappoint yourself. The fire's in you. Call it, draw it up, feel it tingle inside you, just a ripple now, quiet kindling. Use it, see the purpose—the wick. See it flame. Draw your breath and spark the fire."

She felt it, a rising, a heat, and before she could think it was simply the power of suggestion, the wick sparked, and with a little snap, flamed.

"I— You—"

"No, I promise you, I did not." Marg blew out the candle. "Again. Bring the wick to light."

She trembled—fear, excitement, and what she realized was a gnawing hunger for more. Three times she lit the flame.

"You still learn quickly. You have so much in you."

"What am I, Nan?"

"My granddaughter, my blood, my treasure. You are a child of the Fey, a daughter of the Wise, from your father, from me and mine. And from mine long ago, there is Sidhe in you. You have human from your mother. And you carry the blood and power of gods."

Marg folded her hands on the table, gripped them tight. "For this he wants you more than even he wanted your father. Your father had all you have but the human, and Odran wants the power you have, and the human you have. You are a bridge, Breen, between worlds, worlds closed to him. For now."

"You mean my world? My mother's world?"

"He'd use you to take it, piece by piece, heart by heart. Destroy, enslave, corrupt, as he has with lesser worlds. You're the bridge he seeks to travel, and the bridge we need to stop him."

"Because I'm human, or part of me is?"

"You're unique. There is no one known with your heritage. I can't see. I've tried, others have tried. I only know that Odran seeks to use you, what you are, to destroy Talamh and the world you were reared in. I only know we must use all we are to stop him."

"I can't— I managed after an hour to light a single candle."

"It begins with one flame." Marg held up a finger, then spread both her hands. "You have a choice. If you go back to the outside, and remain there, he can't reach you."

"Is that absolute?"

After hesitating, Marg shook her head. "It is as sure as anything can be. He has yet to breach the barrier."

"But he can come here?"

"Can and surely will when he feels ready. We'll fight him. We've driven him off before, and will again. As long as we do, the other side is safe, and you in it."

"But he keeps coming. How do you kill a god?" She let out a breath. "With another god. Is that what you think? You think I can kill him?"

"I can't see; I can't say."

"My father tried to stop him. He killed my father. I—I want children one day. I've always wanted children. But if I have a child, that child would be like me—and . . . It would never stop."

"I can teach you what I know. Others can teach you what they know. And if, in the end, you decide to go back, to remain, we will do all in our power to keep the barrier strong."

"I'm sitting here at this table in a postcard cottage in a picturesque countryside, and you're telling me two worlds—hell, maybe more—depend on what I do?"

Sorrow, again sorrow, covered Marg's face. "It's a terrible weight to carry. I promised not to lie to you. I felt I could no longer evade—so close to the lie—now that the spark is again lit in you. The awakening will come, and soon, I think. You are what you are, Breen Siobhan. What you do is for you to say."

"I need some air. I'm going to take the dog and get some air. I feel like I'm living in my book. Maybe I am."

"Wear this, if you will." Rising, Marg took a round red stone on a chain. "I gave this to you after you were taken, for protection. I didn't know until you'd gone your mother had left it behind."

"It's beautiful. What is it?"

"We call this crystal a dragon's heart."

Breen lifted the thin chain over her head. "I'm not as pissed off at my mother, so that's something. More, after all this, I'm not having a major anxiety attack. Maybe because it doesn't seem real."

She walked to the door, opened it for the dog, who leaped up to dash out. "But it does. It does seem real, and I have to work it through in my head."

"May I begin to read your children's book while you're out walking? I can make it come if you allow it."

"Fine." Learning she was a crap writer was currently the least of her worries. Still, she hesitated. "I can see this wasn't easy for you to tell me. I think you love me."

Everything in Marg's face softened. "More than anything in all the worlds."

Because she believed it, Breen nodded. "I'll be back. I just want to walk, to let Bollocks swim in the bay. If you could think of something else to teach me—simple—I don't think I'm up for more than simple. I'll be about an hour."

"I'll wait for you."

And had, Marg thought, more than twenty long years.

CHAPTER SEVENTEEN

Wind blew in from the sea and swept clouds, gray at the edges, east, over a wide roll of fields and the rocky promontories above them.

At least, she assumed east. For all she knew the sun rose in the north here. Some sort of grain grew in the field, swaying gold over the green. She spotted movement along the tower of rocks, and thought goats until she clearly saw two-legged creatures, wearing caps and long vests.

As she wondered over that, a group of kids she estimated as about the same age she'd once taught came into sight around a turn of the road. Pushing, elbowing, but in joking ways.

She counted five of them—two girls, three boys. One of the girls—dark skin, hair a mass of blue-tipped black braids—held up a hand.

When she dropped it sharply, she and two of the boys raced off in a blur of speed—impossible speed—while the other girl sprouted rainbow wings and bulleted through the air and the third boy dropped to all fours and became, in front of her eyes, a young horse that galloped after them.

"That's something you don't see every day, unless you're here." She glanced down to see what Bollocks thought of it, but he'd already run to and into the water.

She followed him down and, because her head ached, sat on the sandy shale and closed her eyes.

It soothed, the brisk wind, the lap of the water, the splashes and yips of the puppy.

She'd accepted the impossible as truth, Breen thought, and now she had to decide what to do about it.

She heard a cry, looked up to see a hawk circling.

And Morena sat down beside her.

"Showing off for you, he is."

"He's entitled to show off. He's so beautiful."

"We saw you wandering down this way, but you seemed well inside your own head."

"I guess I was. I saw kids, five of them. If I have it straight, one was a faerie, one a were-horse. The other three were fast, ridiculously fast."

"Elves. I saw them myself. They're fast friends, that lot. You'll usually see another girl with them, but she's on a day of punishment for using a spell to do her chores."

"So, one of the Wise?"

"Not so wise to think she could get away with not doing her chores proper as she was told to."

Rules, Breen thought, and discipline for children. "So using magick to do the dishes, for instance, isn't allowed."

"We'll say it's situational. It's discouraged, especially in the young ones, to take the short way. You have to learn how to milk a goat, plant a carrot, wash your linens, and all of it. Otherwise, you'll end up lazy and fat, won't you? Magicks are a serious business, not that they can't and shouldn't be fun along with it. But they're not a convenience. If only that, you stop honoring what you have."

Simple, Breen decided. And in its way, pure.

"I don't know what to do with what I have. I lit a candle today. It took an hour of Nan's coaching, but I lit it with an indrawn breath."

"That's fine, and it won't take so long the next time around."

"I don't know what to do with it. I saw men climbing those rocky cliffs back there like goats."

"Trolls," Morena said easily. "Likely coming out from the caves they're mining to have their midday meal in the sun."

"Trolls, of course. I should have thought of that. Kids with wings and speed and hooves."

"Don't children run about on a fine summer day in the outside? There's no schooling—or not the formal sort—in the summertime, so why not run about?"

"You have schools?"

"Sure and we have schools! Do you think we want to be ignorant?"

"No. Schools, kids running, people sitting in the sun for their lunch break, it's all normal. Does the sun come up in the east here?"

"Where else would it come up?"

"Normal. But you have two moons."

"Some worlds have one, others two or seven. Astronomers are always finding something new in the skies, aren't they?"

"You have astronomers. Don't give me that look. I'm trying to balance out the normal with the fantastic. Nan told me what I am, all I am, and why Odran wants me."

In the way of friends, Morena rubbed a hand on Breen's thigh. "It was for her to tell, and as she did, she believes you have the need to know, and the spine to carry it. But it's so much, I understand that."

"I remembered being taken, and with Nan, I saw it all again, in the fire. What she saw, too."

"I was so frightened, all those years ago." Drawing her knees to her chest, Morena looked over them to the water. "The alarm sounded in the night. I'd never heard it before, but I knew to be afraid. They bundled me and my brothers off with the other children, and I heard from those who stayed back to tend us and shield us you'd been taken. It seemed like days, days and days, but it was only a few hours when my mother brought you back."

"She sang to me. She took me through the portal in the waterfall, and sang to me."

"There was blood on you—your own blood from your hands. It was Aisling who tended them before anyone else could. And I don't know if it will trouble or help you to know that in your eyes, on your face I saw such power, such rage, such might. It faded as the women all fussed and soothed and gave you a quieting potion to drink. You were just my friend again—my heart sister—who'd been brought home safe again."

"It must have been some potion, because I've spent most of my life trying to be quiet."

"And now?"

"I don't know." Idly, Breen picked up a piece of shale, tossed it. "I do know I liked what I felt when I lit the candle. I liked that it felt strong, and it felt like me. I need time to think about it all, but I also need to learn more."

"There's no better teacher on the ways of the Wise than Marg."

"That's what Keegan said."

"So you've talked with Keegan, have you?"

"Briefly. He was outside the farmhouse last night when I went out to walk."

"Oh, you should've come in." Now Morena gave Breen a little shove. "It was fine craic. So many want to meet you or see you again. We're a friendly sort."

"He doesn't strike me as especially friendly."

"Oh, well, that's Keegan. He's a broody one, but he's the world on his shoulders, after all. He's good company when he's not brooding, and as fair a taoiseach as any have been before."

Sliding her gaze over, Breen studied Morena's face. "Are the two of you . . ."

"What?"

"Involved?"

"Sure, we're involved as any— Oh!" Her face went bright with humor. "You mean are we mating? Gods no. He's next to a brother to me. Not that he isn't a fine example of a man, and I've heard he's more than fine in bed. Besides, I bed with Harken now and again, and though it's not forbidden, I'd find it awkward to bed brothers."

While Breen tried to think of a response, Bollocks dragged a piece of driftwood over, wagged hopefully.

Morena hopped up, threw it into the water. Delirious with joy, the dog leaped in after it.

"I'll tell you this," Morena went on. "You'll want Keegan to train you in hand-to-hand and sword work, as there's none better I know. It was your father who took up his training—and Harken's and Aisling's after their father fell—so it's no wonder."

Bollocks dragged the wood out again; Morena threw it.

"I could work with you some, show you the raw basics, but I'm a poor teacher, I think. I lack patience."

"You know how to use a sword?"

"Sure I know how. Being a peaceful people isn't the same as being a defenseless one."

There were dragons in the sky, three of them. A herd? A flock? She'd have to look it up, but for now Breen thought of family, as there were two large and one small. Like parents and child.

"Have you ever ridden one?" Breen asked.

"I have, and it's wonderful. I've not bonded with one, but I've ridden Harken's."

"Harken has a dragon?"

"They have each other, that's the bonding. He'd take you up if you wanted."

"I think I'll stick with feet on the ground for now. I should get back. Nan— There's someone in the water."

Afraid someone was drowning, she started to rush forward, but Morena put a hand on her arm.

"It's just Ala. She's a bit shy, and you'll frighten her."

Morena waved, and after a moment an arm waved back. The bobbing head with its streaming blond hair vanished under the surface. A shimmering tail of greens and golds and hints of red broke the surface, then vanished.

"A mermaid," Breen managed. "A shy mermaid."

"She's but ten, I think, and curious, but a bit shy with it. She'll likely come back if you bring the pup again."

So saying, she lifted her arm. The hawk soared down to land on it.

"You're not wearing a glove."

"I wore one when we met again, as you'd expect it. But Amish would never hurt me. We'll walk with you to the road, then I have to get home myself. I've chores of my own."

"I'm going back to my cottage tomorrow," Breen told her. "I think I need a couple days there, to think all this through. But I'll come back."

"I know you will. Give Marg and Sedric my greeting."

"I will. Ah, give mine to your grandparents."

"And so I will. Light the fire, Breen," Morena added as she veered off.

Breen spent the rest of the day learning about teas, about plants and roots and herbs. How to identify, how to harvest and dry and prepare and blend.

She found it fascinating as well as practical.

"You learn quickly."

"I know how to study. I studied my brains out for a degree I didn't want. This is interesting and fun—and it feels productive. And, well, natural."

She fed the pup, helped feed the horse, and tried not to make any major mistakes as she helped prepare dinner on a rainy evening.

"It's a lack of confidence you have more than a lack of skill."

"I think it's both." But she could smell the potatoes she'd helped quarter and coat in oil and herbs roasting. So she thought she'd done okay there.

And they tasted just fine, she decided, as did the fish Sedric caught only that afternoon and the peas she'd helped shell.

Breen waited until they'd finished the meal before she brought up what she thought might be a difficult topic.

"I need to go back tomorrow," she began. "I need time, and I need my own space. I'm not saying this well. I'd never lived on my own before the cottage, and I need to."

"Independence is a valuable thing."

"I didn't know how important it was to me," she told Marg, "until I had it. Honestly, I didn't know how much I enjoyed solitude until I had that. I know I'd close myself off too much, so I need to be careful there. Marco, well, he'd never let me, but he's not here. So I wondered if, after a couple of days, I—we—could work out . . . Not a schedule, that's so rigid. I don't want to be rigid."

At a loss, she picked up her wine, stared into it. Set it down again.

"Breen, tell us what you want."

"I would if I knew. For now, I think I'd like to try living in the cottage, but coming here. If I could come here after I write in the morning, and you could teach me more. I could go back in the evening. Maybe stay here with you on the weekends. I don't know if you even have weekends."

"I understand your meaning."

"I know it'll take longer to learn or practice or train, but—"

"Balance is what you seek, and it's a wise choice."

"I don't know if I can do or be what you hope for, but if I could take the time, this way, before I'm supposed to go back to Philadelphia, I think I could make a more, well, informed decision."

With a nod, Marg rose, patted Breen's shoulder. "Wait."

"I've upset her," Breen murmured. "I knew I would. I'm not—"

"You're mistaken." Sedric sipped his wine. "She doesn't want impulse or obligation in you—such things weaken with time. Myself, I'd have thought less of you if you'd let either lead you in this."

Marg came back, set a large book on the table. Carved on the dark brown leather cover was a dragon.

"The dragon, always your favorite. And he guards the magicks inside. I made this for you, began it the night you were born."

"It's beautiful." Breen opened the cover, saw her name, the date of her birth, in beautiful handwriting on thick parchment.

She turned a page.

"The first part you'd call recipes—such as we practiced today."

"The illustrations are wonderful. You drew them?"

"Some I did, and some Sedric drew, as he's a fine hand at it."

Breen looked at him. "A were-artist?"

That brought on the slow smile. "You could say."

"Drawings help you identify the ingredients," Marg went on, "the plants and roots and so on. From teas to potions, lotions, balms.

And on to crystals and stones and their meanings, uses. And then to spells, from the casting of a circle and beyond.

"It's yours, to take, to keep. I hope to study and learn, but yours nonetheless. I would ask you not to attempt any spell or ceremony without my guidance."

"You can rest easy on that one. Thank you. I will study it. And . . ."

It wasn't impulse so much as yearning that had her looking at the candle on the counter. She drew in her breath, set it to flame. "I'll learn."

In the morning, she walked the road with her book in her backpack and her dog at her side. She heard hoofbeats coming fast, stepped over to the side. A good thing, she decided, as the horse thundered its way toward her.

When Keegan pulled it up, her first thought was of course, just of course he'd have a huge gleaming black horse—probably a stallion.

And she'd seen the horse before, as she'd seen the rider.

In dreams.

He looked down at her, lifted an eyebrow. "Leaving, are you?"

"I'm coming back in a couple of days."

"Are you now?"

"I said I was. Look, I get you're king around here, but you're not in charge of me."

"I'm no king. We have no king."

Because the idea clearly irritated him, she shrugged. "Whatever you call it. I've had other people running my life for twenty-six years. It's my turn."

Now he cocked his head. "And whose fault would it be you let others run your life?"

"People like you can't understand people like me."

He swung off the horse, studied her with curiosity. "Who are people like me and people like you?"

How did he see himself? she wondered. She knew how she saw him.

Tall, strong, gloriously handsome, and absolutely sure of himself.

"People like you are born confident. They take charge, command respect, maybe some healthy fear. People like me are taught and expected to follow rules, to keep expectations low, rock no boats, make no waves."

"Well, rules matter in a civilized world, don't they? But a low expectation doesn't risk failure or success, so what's the point of that? If you rock no boat, you never end up in the water to see where the waves might take you."

"That's all very true and literal."

The horse turned his head, nuzzled her shoulder. Without thinking, she stroked his cheek. "You need to go. He's thirsty and wants his carrot."

The minute she said it—knew it—she stepped back in shock.

Keegan merely nodded, his eyes on her face. "Aye, he does, as we've had a good, strong ride."

He bent down, gave Bollocks a rub, then swung back onto the horse.

"Safe journeys, Breen Siobhan."

When he rode off, she let out a breath. "The horse is Merlin, after Arthur's sorcerer. I know that as well as I know my own name. Let's go, Bollocks. I have a lot of studying to do."

Something about the quiet alone soothed her like a warm bath, so she spent two days soaking in it. She wrote, she studied, tended the garden with only the dog for company.

She lit candles—the new way—and after considerable effort sent the fire crackling in the hearth.

"I'm a witch," she told Bollocks as she sat with him in front of that fire with the echoes of power still vibrating inside her. "And it doesn't feel surprising anymore."

She stroked the head he laid on her knee, gave his beard a gentle tug. "Just like having a dog doesn't feel surprising now, though what I'm going to do with you if I go back to Philadelphia, I don't know."

If, she realized—and that did surprise. She'd said, and thought, if, not when.

"Of course I'll go back—I have to go back. Marco and Sally and Derrick are there, and my mother, everything I know is there. This is just . . ."

A bridge? she wondered.

Like she was.

"No point thinking about it now. We'll reward ourselves for a good day of work with a walk before it gets too dark."

One moon, she thought as the dog raced straight for the bay. Nearly three-quarters full and hazed by clouds.

Tomorrow, after her morning writing, she'd leave her solitude behind for a world with two moons.

And even that didn't seem so shocking anymore.

She left at noon with the dog leading the way. She wore the red stone around her neck, added her father's ring to the chain. She'd pulled on a light hoodie the color of the forest with a T-shirt and jeans.

When they reached the tree, Bollocks didn't hesitate. With a happy bark, he climbed up and through. Breen followed, and stepped into the wonder of a thin, soft drizzle the sun turned into a double rainbow.

It arched over the farm, a curve of shimmering colors. As she made her way down the steps, a dragon, red as the stone around her neck, soared under it.

Solitude, she thought, yes, she prized it. But this? She'd been given a priceless treasure in this.

The dog leaped over the fence, raced across the road and over the farm fence to run mad circles around the wolfhound.

Beyond them, in a paddock, she saw Harken and Mahon at the head of a chestnut horse. A mare—obviously, Breen concluded—as Keegan held the bridle of his horse while the black stallion mounted her.

Both horses, all three of the men gleamed with sweat.

She'd never seen anything like it, found it powerful, sensual, and a little frightening as she stood on the grassy shoulder of the dirt road, watching.

The dog's barks alerted Harken. When he glanced her way, he called out, "Good morning to you, Breen! We're helping start a life here. You're welcome to take a part."

She thought: No. But she did climb over the fence to walk closer. And could feel, as she did, the lust, the pleasure, the ferocity from both animals in the mating.

It stirred in her own belly, heated in her own blood, and drew her to the paddock fence.

"Our pretty Eryn's in season," Mahon told her. He'd tied back his braids, much as Marco often did. "Merlin's more than happy to have a go."

"I can see that. You have to, ah, help? I assumed it was something they'd handle themselves."

"That they can." Harken shifted his grip, used his free hand to run soothing strokes down the mare's neck. "We wanted to breed these two particularly, you see, and controlling the matter keeps either from suffering any hurts along the way."

It took control, she could see that in the way Keegan's muscles rippled with effort under his shirt, wet with sweat and rain.

Then she felt it, actually felt it, that shock of coming, of peaking, so she had to grip a hand on the fence as the horses let out trumpeting cries.

"Hold now, hold," Keegan murmured to the stallion. "Give the lady another moment there. She'll be giving you a fine foal by the next summer solstice."

"How . . ." Because her voice felt thick, sounded breathless, Breen cleared her throat. "How can you be sure it took?"

He spared her a glance then. "The signs said this day, this hour, and each were given half an apple charmed for fertility before the mating. Easy now."

He turned his attention back to the horses as the stallion released, planted his forelegs back on the ground. When Keegan unhooked the straps he'd used for control, the horse tossed his head, lifted up his forelegs to paw the air before taking what Breen considered a victory gallop around the paddock.

"Proud of himself, he is."

Keegan swiped his hands on his trousers, smearing them with blood.

"Your hands."

He shrugged. "Merlin can be overeager at such times. If you've come for training, I'll need an hour first."

"No." Definitely no. "I'm on my way to see my grandmother."

"Aisling would be happy to see you if you've the time." Mahon continued to soothe the mare.

"I'll try to go by." She stepped back. "This was . . . interesting."

Harken grinned after her. "I'll wager she wasn't expecting to see such a performance."

"She needs to start training."

"Ah, give her some room." Harken swatted Keegan on the shoulder. "She's brought herself back, hasn't she now? Not all would."

"Coming through isn't enough, by far, and it won't be bits of kitchen magicks that break Odran for once and all."

"Patience, *mo dheartháir.*"

"Bugger patience." But he said it with some humor. "I use up a lifetime's worth every bloody time I'm stuck in the Capital. But I'll leave her to Marg for now."

The door of the cottage stood open and, considering that invitation enough, Bollocks went straight in.

Breen heard her grandmother's voice greeting him.

A little less sure, Breen tapped a knuckle on the open door before she stepped inside.

"Come in, come in! Oh, aye, I have a biscuit for you, my lad."

Breen walked in, saw Marg getting a biscuit out of a jar while the kettle steamed on the stove.

"It's pleased I am to see you," she said as she tapped a finger in the air to signal the dog to sit. "I've just come down for a cup of tea, and now I'll have company with it."

"I hope today's all right to come."

"You're welcome any and all days. Sit, won't you? I have biscuits for us as well."

"I've been reading the book you made for me. I thought, if you have time, you could show me how to do something from it. Something simple," she added. "I've been practicing the fire. I lit one last night—in the fireplace, I mean."

"That's grand."

"It took awhile," she admitted, "but then it felt natural. Is that right?"

"Right enough." After squeezing a hand on Breen's shoulder, Marg set a plate of cookies on the table.

"I need to ask. I saw Keegan when I left the other day, and he said I needed to train. To train to fight, and use a sword."

Marg only sighed. "The boy has more patience than once he did, and still barely enough to fill a thimble."

"So that's not a no. I couldn't use a sword to— I mean, even if I learned how to use one, which is doubtful, I couldn't use it to whack at somebody."

"There's time enough to worry about such matters, but I'll ask you to think what you might do if someone came in the door there with an eye to taking your life, or mine."

"I—the first thought is run."

"Not a bad thought, that one." Smiling, Marg set the tea out. "But if running isn't enough, would you simply stand and do nothing?"

Breen let out a sigh. "In our schools, I had to take my children— they're just children—through drills. What they had to do if someone came in to hurt them. Hide. Lock the doors and hide. Run, if that doesn't work. And it would be for me—as the one who has to look out for them—to fight if there's no other way. I never had to put that to the test. But I believe, I do, that I'd have done whatever I could to protect them."

"For this you train?"

"Yes. Yes, as a teacher you do."

"This isn't so very different. A sword wouldn't be your only weapon. You have a strong weapon inside you—to use as a weapon only to protect."

"I want to learn more about that."

"So we will. First, I've done some reading myself. Your book."

"Oh."

"You gave me leave to read it, and so I did." She looked down at the dog, smiled. "Oh, she's got you, my man, down to the bone. You have skill with words, *mo stór*, and that's a magick as well. Twice I read it through, and I laughed, and I thrilled to our boy's adventures. So brave and true in the story, just as he is, and sweet of heart even when foolish."

Marg reached over, patted Breen's hand. "That's the truth I promised you, not just a nan's sentiment. Now, did you send it away to the people who make books?"

"No, I . . ." When Marg's eyebrows rose up, Breen nodded. "You're right, they can only say yes if they read it. I've done the research on how to submit, so I'll do it tonight. I'll just do it."

"There now, a next step taken. So we'll take another ourselves. Bring your tea."

"Where are we going?"

"Out to where I do more than make teas and kitchen magicks." Marg rose. "We could say we're off to school."

"Like Hogwarts?"

"Oh, and sure those are some fine stories. But no, for this, it's only you and only me."

CHAPTER EIGHTEEN

They went out, then along a path deeper into the woods, beyond the lean-to where the horse dozed to where the stream curved under a small, arching stone bridge.

Another stone building stood, one half the size of the cottage. Unlike at the cottage, the thick door, covered with carvings, remained closed. Still, flowers spilled out of window boxes on either side of the door.

They crossed the bridge while a delighted Bollocks splashed into the stream.

Marg sent him an indulgent look. "He'll be fine out here."

"It's like a workshop?"

"So it is, as it's work we do inside. Give me your hand, child." And she pressed Breen's hand to the door under her own. "Now the door will open for you as well."

It did, just like that, opened without a sound.

The sun eked in enough for Breen to make out worktables, shelves full of jars, dried herbs and plants hanging from lines. A couple of wooden chairs and stools.

"Light the fire." Marg tapped her chest. "From here."

Like a test, Breen thought, and had to push through nerves as she stepped over to the hearth. She'd practiced, she reminded herself. Last night, again this morning.

So she closed her eyes, visualized the fire, and calmed her mind until she felt heat. And drew that heat up, from belly to heart, from heart to mind.

Just a flicker, weak at first, but she pulled more, opened her eyes. The peat caught, simmered, shimmered, then burned full.

"Well done. Well done indeed. Now the candles. Above you."

Breen looked up and saw more than a dozen candles in an iron ring. "They're farther away than I've done."

"Distance is no matter. Light the candles."

She drew in breath, drew up the heat, and the candles flamed.

"There, you see, you've learned by doing what's already known to you."

"It's seductive."

"Aye, and no harm there as long as you hold your purpose and your promises."

Now that candlelight, the crackling fire joined the quiet sunlight, she saw the room with its beamed ceiling and rough planked floor arranged into sections. Hanging herbs and flowers, bowls and jars of roots, powders, pale or bold liquids held one area; jars and bowls of crystals and stones, others in freestanding hunks or spears took up another. Dozens of candles, white, black, every color she could name, grouped together on shelves.

A third made a home for tools—pots, more bowls and jars yet to be filled, paddles and spoons, wands, knives with straight or curved blades. A doorless sort of cubby held various fabrics and yarns and ribbons. A book, not unlike the one Marg had given her, stood atop it.

The air smelled dreamily of the herbs—potted and thriving—on the wide sill in front of the window that faced the curving stream.

"Are those cauldrons?"

"They are. Did you study the list of tools in your book?"

"Yes. Cauldrons, bowls, bells, candles, wands, the ritual knives— athames—brooms, goblets, swords."

"It's time you learned to use them. Today, we'll make charms for calm minds, calm hearts, fertility, safe journeys, good fortune, and protection."

Herbs and crystals, ribbons and cloths—and, above all, Breen learned, intention. It seemed very basic, but she learned quickly the wrong crystal, the wrong herbs in a charm could draw evil rather than repel it, could cause a sleepless night instead of a restful one.

"Now keep this, of your own making."

Breen took the small purple pouch she'd sewn and filled. "For protection," she remembered. "I already have this." She touched the gemstone she wore.

"And now a charm bag as well. Do you remember what you filled it with?"

"Yes, I think. Betony and sage, a piece of amber, one of malachite, another of tourmaline—black tourmaline," she corrected. "A little shell and a broom straw. And I chanted: By my will, repel all ill. With this charm, protect from harm."

With a simple nod, Marg gave approval. "Well done. Very well done."

"What will you do with the others?"

"Give or trade as needs be. A young were I know is hoping for a child. I'll gift her the fertility charm. But for now, we purify our tools, and put it all away."

"I don't suppose you could teach me a spell first."

Marg laughed. "*Mo stór*, and so I have. A charm is but a spell in a pouch."

"A spell in a pouch." Finding that delightful, she slid it into her pocket. "We didn't do any love spells. I'd think they'd be popular."

"A charm or spell to draw another's attention, to encourage another to look and see—these are common. But a true love spell? These are forbidden, as to bind a heart to you with magick removes choice."

"I get that. Do they actually work?"

"Sometimes all too well, and always, always with a hard price. A woman might forsake her family, a man might strike down a rival. The bespelled might turn on the bespeller in a fit of jealousy, all twisted from magicks. A heart can go mad with love, after all."

She could believe it even without personal experience.

"It's so much about healing, protecting, bringing comfort—everything you've taught me so far. When I was little, I wanted to be a vet—an animal doctor. Not just because I loved animals, but because they need someone to take care of them."

"You have healing in you. I can help bring some out, but Aisling is stronger there."

They put away cloth and crystals and candles. Breen watched as Marg bathed the scissors and needles they'd used in water drawn in moonlight, how she wiped them dry with a white cloth.

"Now, you'll take some air, clear your mind. You might walk to see Morena, or Aisling. Then I can show you how to make a wand."

"You make them?"

"I could give you one, and will, but the making of your own imbues it with your self, your heart, your power. You'll choose the wood, the stones, the carvings. Your wand is an extension of the magicks inside you."

"I'm not very crafty," she began as they walked outside. "Arts and crafty, I mean. Sewing those pouches was pretty much the top of my skill level."

"And you did well there, didn't you? Ah, we have company, it seems."

She recognized the black stallion, unless he had a twin. Standing beside him outside the cabin was a smaller horse. She recognized the type from her young teen's love affair with horses as a buckskin.

"That would be Keegan's Merlin, the black beauty there."

"Yes, I saw him impregnate a mare this morning. She seemed agreeable."

"Ah, so he's mated with Mahon's Eryn then. That's a fine thing. The handsome gelding is one of Harken's. He's called Boy—from Good Boy, as he is one. If the pair of them are inside with Sedric, we won't find a crumb of those biscuits left."

Inside, Keegan sat by the fire with Sedric—and Bollocks. The two men each had a tall mug—a tankard, Breen supposed.

"And here they are," Sedric announced. "I've plied Keegan with a mug of ale to keep him from interrupting your work."

"And fine work it was. I'm told your Merlin did his job of work just this morning."

"He did at that, and successfully."

"It took. That's grand then."

"Isn't it too early to know?"

Keegan glanced at Breen. "Harken says she's carrying, and he'd know." He rose then, polished off the ale. "I brought Boy, as she has to learn to ride, and Harken says he'd suit her for it."

"A riding lesson," Marg said before Breen could object, "a patient and gentle one, would be a fine way for Breen to get some air after being closed up in the workshop."

"I'd rather walk."

"Walking won't take you as far as a good horse." Keegan cocked his head at her. "Sure you're not afraid to sit one?"

"Since I haven't sat on one, that I remember, I don't know."

"Best find out then. It's good ale, thanks." He started out, stopped to kiss Marg's cheek, then continued on.

"You loved riding as a child," Marg told her. "It's in you."

"Maybe." As she stepped out, she had to remind herself she liked horses. What she didn't like was the idea of getting thrown, or losing control and having a horse run off with her bouncing all over the saddle.

"He knows his job," Keegan told her. "But you'll make him anxious if you get up on him all quivering."

"I'm not quivering." Maybe a little—inside. But she stepped up.

"You'll want to mount from his other side, unless you want to ride facing his arse."

Great start, she thought, and went around to the other side of the horse. "There's no horn on the saddle. You know, something to grab on to."

"You're not in your Wild West with the lasso. I've been there," he added. "It's a vast place, it is, and I see the purpose of those big, heavy saddles there, but that's a different world. You'll have a rein in each hand. You'll pull the left to go left, right to go right, both to stop. Put your foot in the stirrup and swing your other leg over."

"Give her a leg up, as a gentleman would," Marg called from the doorway, but Breen swung her leg over and managed to plant herself.

"Other foot in. Aye, that's the right length for you. A rein in each hand. Hold them like this."

He showed her, and because he seemed patient enough, she concentrated on relaxing.

Keegan swung on the leather duster, then mounted Merlin, turned him around. "Left rein, smooth and easy to turn him."

"Just a walk now, Keegan, till the girl finds her seat. And have her back by the evening meal."

"She'll be fine, don't fret. Heels down, knees in."

She was riding a horse, Breen thought, and it was . . . okay.

When they got to the road, she turned him again—to the right this time. It didn't seem so hard, at least not at this pace, this easy *clip-clop* under a sky that had gone pale blue, and through air that had warmed since the rain ended.

She glanced down to see Bollocks trotting along beside her.

"The dog's with us. Is that all right?"

"The horses don't mind dogs; the dog doesn't mind horses."

He made her stop, then start again. Made her stop, then get the horse to back up, then go forward. He turned off the road onto a trail that wound through woods where the light went soft and the air cooled.

She saw something come out of an enormous tree before racing away in a blur.

"Elves—some young ones—playing."

"But . . . was he in the tree?"

"Of."

A bear ran across the trail, then stopped to give them a good look. Breen's throat slammed shut so her scream came out as a gurgle. And the bear raced off into the trees.

"That—"

"A were, and a young one. They're just having a lark in the woods. You'll need to get used to seeing such things."

"How do you know if it's a were or an actual bear that wants to eat you?"

"Bears, those that are the animal only, are more interested in berries than in you. But if you cross paths with one and he takes a dislike to you, you'll know quick enough."

He turned to her, as at ease on the stallion as another might have been in a BarcaLounger. "That's why you learn the sword, the arrow, how to ride at a gallop as well as magicks. It's survival and it's duty."

"I made charms today."

"Charms, is it? Well then, that'll send Odran packing in a hurry."

"Don't be dismissive. I've had dismissive all my life, and I'm done with it. The point is, I'm here and I'm learning. And right now I'm sitting on a goddamn horse."

Boy saw his chance, swung his head over to grab some tasty-looking leaves. While her stomach pitched in panic, Breen let out a squeal as she slid in the saddle.

Keegan grabbed her arm to right her. "Control him, as he'll take any opportunity to eat. He thinks he's a light one on his back. Show him he's wrong. You've the reins. Use them."

"You could've warned me he'd do that." But she muttered it as she fought Boy's head back.

As they walked and wound on, she did her best to read the horse, to anticipate. And, though her heart hammered as the trail began to follow the rise and fall of hills, she didn't squeal again.

When the trees thinned, they crossed a field where sheep scattered. Taking it as a cue, Bollocks chased them. She saw another farm, another dirt road, more cottages, most with clothes flapping on lines.

People worked the fields, the gardens, the livestock, pausing to raise a hand as they rode by.

Now and again Keegan paused to exchange some words, to introduce her—and politely.

She met a dozen, including a little girl who shyly offered her a daisy, and smiled when Breen tucked it in her hair.

That gesture earned Breen her first approving look from Keegan.

"You knew everyone's name," Breen commented as they rode on. "Do you know everyone here?"

"I was born in the valley," he said simply. "They need to get a look at you, those who haven't. Eian O'Ceallaigh's daughter. And you at them, and more of Talamh than Marg's cottage."

Boy took an interest in a hedgerow. She pulled him back, muttered, "Don't embarrass me. Is that a lake?"

She saw it in the distance, the way the sun struck the odd and eerie water of green.

The same color, she realized, as the river where Odran had once caged her.

"Lough na Fírinne. It means truth. And there all who choose dive in when the time comes for a new taoiseach."

"For the sword."

"Aye, for Cosantoir."

She glanced at the one at his side. "Nan told me. You were just a boy."

"I made my choice. You're doing well enough. We'll trot now before Merlin's bored into sleep."

"I'm not ready to—"

"You're ready enough. Heels down, knees in. Match Boy's gait. He's got a smooth one."

He nudged Merlin into a trot, and since Boy followed the leader, left her no choice. Her butt slapped the saddle; her teeth snapped together.

"Match his gait," Keegan repeated. "Sit up straight, and lift and lower with him or your arse will be black and blue."

She figured it already was. "I don't know how to—"

But she did. Whether it was muscle memory, self-defense, or blind luck, she began to move with the quick, lively trot.

"Better," Keegan judged. "Now turn him onto the road coming up on the right of you."

Turn and trot?

And the damn road started rising again. But she held on, almost relaxed into it while they passed the black-faced sheep and spotted cows, the wide fields, the sweeps of waving grains.

It all smoothed out, so it took her a moment to realize the horse went faster.

"A nice, easy lope is all. Gods' sake, woman, sit up straight. You've a spine in there, so use it."

The speed worried her, more than a bit, but her ass didn't want to bang and slap against the leather.

She didn't realize until he told her to go back to a trot, then a walk, that they'd somehow circled around. She saw the farm, the bay, Aisling's cottage.

She'd survived.

"Your seat needs improvement, and your hands are heavy yet, but you did well enough. You'll do better tomorrow."

"Tomorrow?"

"And tomorrow you'll learn how to saddle your own mount," he added as they walked the horses down Marg's path. "You dismount as you mounted, just in reverse."

The ground looked entirely too far away, but she didn't want his smirk. The minute she started to bring her leg over, the twinges pinged—everywhere. She bit back a moan, stiffened her knees as they quivered. And handed him the reins.

"Thanks for the lesson," she said with her voice as stiff as her back.

"You did well enough," he said again, then just turned Merlin, one hand holding Boy's reins, and took them both in a fast trot up the path.

She waited until he was out of sight, then limped to the open door of the cottage.

That night, Breen followed Marg's instructions and soaked in a hot bath laced with healing potion. Then she slathered every inch she could reach with balm. Propped in bed, the fire snapping, the dog sleeping, she wrote her blog.

She wrote of taking her first riding lesson—and though her instructor was more than a hard-ass and her muscles wept, she intended to go back for more.

Somehow, she thought, she had to figure a way to get pictures. Her blog followers expected them. But that was a problem for another day.

Over the next few days she learned how to cast a circle, how to make ritual candles, how to float a feather. She learned how to saddle a horse, how to groom one, and experienced her first gallop.

She solved the blog photo dilemma by asking Morena to bring Boy through the portal.

She made her wand. Under Marg's supervision, she chose wood from a chestnut tree and a clear, polished crystal that pulled in and shot out light. She cleansed and imbued the crystal under the light of the moons. She chose a carving of a dragon, one that rode up the shaft of the wand toward the light, and marveled, though she could feel it—feel it inside—when the image in her head carved itself bold red into the chestnut.

When her first week of learning—a word she much preferred to training—passed, she took her first solo ride.

Following Marg's directions, she walked Boy past the farm where Harken, Aisling's oldest boy, Finian, and a man she didn't recognize worked with the wolfhound and a lively border collie to herd some sheep into a pen.

Because she had an uneasy feeling those sheep might end up in lamb stew, she kept riding. More sheep dotted the hillsides, and overhead a pair of hawks circled. As she watched, one dived—so fast it blurred into a golden brown streak.

In the high grass, something let out a high, short scream.

Imagining a rabbit, thinking of the hard world of predator and prey, she rode on.

Then, the beauty astonished.

If Marg's cottage was a song, Finola's was an opera. Flowers flooded their way around the cottage with winding stone paths forming bridges. Wild and wonderful, they carpeted the ground, swam around shrubs and trees all pregnant with more blooms.

Here and there hung pretty little bird feeders, and birdbaths of copper shaped like open flowers.

A hummingbird, bright as a jewel, drank from the bold orange trumpet of a lily. Butterflies simply swarmed.

The scents—strong, subtle, sweet, spicy—all tangled together into a sumptuous drug.

The stones of the cottage itself glowed a rosy pink, with boxes at every window spilling with more flowers and trailing greenery. The door, a soft, dreamy blue, formed an arch.

Dazzled, she secured the horse as she'd been taught, then just wandered the paths. As she did, she heard voices. She followed them around the side of the cottage, through an arbor alive with white roses.

The sea of flowers continued, flowed into a fanciful herb garden where the plants formed rings, then the vegetable garden where Finola, a wide-brimmed straw hat over her hair, pulled a carrot for the basket on her arm.

Beyond her spread an orchard. Morena flew up, plucking what Breen clearly saw were lemons for her own basket. Then she flew down to where Seamus harvested—those had to be oranges—from the low branches of another tree.

How did they grow lemons and oranges in this climate?

Breen just shook her head and admitted she'd gone beyond the time for asking how.

Finola straightened, pushed a hand at the small of her back, and spotted Breen.

"Well, good day to you, Breen."

"This is the most beautiful home I've ever seen."

"Ah, now listen to you." But the pleasure showed as she walked to the end of the garden and along a path to Breen. "And how's it all going with you, darling?"

"I'm learning. I've wanted to come sooner, but there's been a lot of learning. I wanted to see you especially, to thank you for taking care of me all those years ago, for getting me away and to the farm."

"Sure and anyone would do the same."

"But it wasn't anyone. It was you. Anyway, I just wanted to thank you, and don't want to interrupt your work. I— You have lemons and oranges."

"We do, aye, we do, and peaches and plums, apples and pears, and we're growing bananas now from the funniest-looking trees."

"Bananas."

"It's my Seamus who's babied it along from a cutting Morena brought him back from a visit to the other side. Morena and my boys, myself, we're handy in the garden, but Seamus, well, he—"

"Has a magic touch?"

Finola laughed. "Oh, he does that for certain."

Morena flew down with her basket of lemons. "I see you have Boy out front. Riding on your own, are you now?"

"Keegan and Mahon had to go somewhere for the day, so I made a break for it."

"Why don't you get your Blue, Morena, and take a ride with your friend? Stop back on your way around and there'll be lemonade."

"Lemonade?" Breen repeated.

"I'll jar some up for you to take to Marg, as she's fond of it."

"I wouldn't mind a ride, or the company."

"I'll bring Blue around front." Instead of taking the paths, Morena took wing and flew over the flowers.

"She's been wanting to give you room," Finola said, "your time with Marg, and the lessons with Keegan. There's no better horseman I know—other than Harken—can match Keegan."

"He's got a hard way as a teacher, but I can't say it doesn't work."

"You have some fun with Morena now, won't you? And come back for that lemonade."

"I will."

She went back to the front and mounted. She let Boy crop at the grass on the verge of the road while she scanned the flowers, tried to see how many she could identify by name.

Morena rode around the other side of the cottage. She sat a pale gray horse with three white socks. He had eyes of crystal blue.

"I see where he gets his name."

"He's a lovely one, my Blue, but fierce when needs be. He's sired five colts."

"He's a stallion?"

"How could we geld such a one?" Her voice shined with love as she rubbed Blue's neck. "Where are you wanting to ride?"

"I'd like to see the lake. I can't pronounce the name."

"You're meaning Lough na Fírinne. All right then. Blue will want a gallop, as I haven't had him out for a day or two."

"I'm told I have a poor seat and heavy hands, but I can gallop. Sort of."

"Keegan's words." With some humor, Morena rolled her eyes. "A hard taskmaster he is, but he rides like a god. Still, don't let him bully you."

She had Blue going from a standstill to a gallop. Used to working her way through the gaits, Breen had to hold on when Boy followed suit.

Still a little terrifying, Breen admitted as they all but flew down the road. But exhilarating, too. Hardly more than a week before she'd never sat on a horse—or not that she remembered—and now she galloped along almost like she knew what she was doing.

She felt Boy's pleasure in the run, in the company, and had to agree with him.

Morena slowed to an easy trot, tossed over a smile. "You've learned well, whatever Keegan has to say."

"I spent the first three nights after the lessons soaking in the tub and moaning. I can mostly yoga it out now."

"And the other lessons?"

Thrilled her, Breen thought. Simply thrilled her.

"I made my wand. I know Nan's pleased with my progress, but I'm not there yet. I can tell she's waiting for something from me, of me. I don't know what it is."

"You'll know when you know. Where's the pup?"

"He opted to stay with Marg. I think I saw your hawk. He was with a friend, then he dived down. I'm pretty sure he killed a rabbit."

"He's a hunter, that's his blood. His friend was likely a female he's been flirting with, so he'd share the meal with her."

She gestured ahead to the lake, and Breen saw a family of swans gliding over it.

"The swans guard the lake."

"From what?"

"Any with dark intent. They say in the long ago, the lake was formed by the tears of the goddess Finnguala—my grandmother was named for her. She, the daughter of Lir of the Tuatha Dé Danann, was cursed by her stepmother, Aoife, and doomed to live for nine hundred years as a swan."

"Harsh."

"It was indeed," Morena agreed as they walked the horses along the banks.

They moved through reeds and cattails. Dragonflies, iridescent as faerie wings, darted to and from the water.

"What happened to her? To the goddess?"

"Well, so she wandered year by year, and they say in her despair wept Lough na Fírinne."

Morena lifted her hand, and a dragonfly, blue as her stallion's eyes, landed in her palm.

"When she wed Lairgren, and the curse broke at last, she came here again to swim, to remember the injustice. And so she crafted the sword, for protection of the true, and the staff, for justice and judgment so none could be condemned as she had been."

The dragonfly shot away.

"She cast them into the lake so that the leader worthy would find them, would wield them—taking them up with free will to serve as well as lead, to guard the world as her swans guard the lake."

"Do you believe that?"

"Why wouldn't I? For there 'tis, isn't it? And from it, generations of taoisigh have taken up sword."

"It's beautiful—the story and the lake. The water looks opaque. How does anyone see in it to find the sword?"

"That's the thing. When you're in it, it's clear as glass. You can see for yourself if you want to have a swim."

"That's allowed?"

"Sure and why wouldn't it be? If you had dark purposes, the swans would run you out again. Fierce creatures, swans, for all their graceful beauty."

"Maybe some other time. My grandmother, then my father, both went into that lake as hardly more than children and came out leaders. I wanted to see it. Did you go in?"

"I did, of course, with all the others. I thought, I'll be finding that sword, and Marg will give me the staff when I stand before her. And I'll be the strongest, wisest, bravest taoiseach Talamh has ever known."

Shaking back her hair, she laughed. "Lack of confidence I've never had."

"I admire that, so much. The confidence to believe you can do and be strong and smart, and—I don't know—worthy."

"You're all of that, and always have been." Shifting in the saddle, Morena looked at her. "You mustn't let others take that away from you."

"You'd like Marco. He says the same. Different words, same meaning."

"So you choose your friends wisely."

"Yes. Yes, I do. How did you feel when you didn't find the sword, and Keegan did? Were you disappointed?"

"Ah, gods no. In the water, I saw Keegan, the sword in his hand, and through the water I could see him looking at it as though it weighed a thousand stone. Then I thought, No, no not at all. No, that was a weight I'd not want to carry.

"But he did, and he has, and he will until the time comes for the next. And, please the gods, that won't be until I have grandchildren leaping into the water."

CHAPTER NINETEEN

Because Marg asked, Breen visited Aisling for lessons on healing. Take away the weaving loom, the crossed swords over the mantel, and she found Hannigan cottage not so different from any home with a couple of active children and an enormous dog.

Chaotic, noisy, with scattered toys and considerable roughhousing.

"You've no more manners than the pigs in the sty. Pick up your mess, then out with you. With your hands," she warned her oldest son, "as that's how you got them all out."

"You're so busy." Breen could smell bread baking, saw wool on the spindle of an actual spinning wheel. "It's all right if you don't have time for this right now."

"It would be a relief for me, and that's the truth." Aisling shoved at the dark mop of hair bundled on top of her head. "A bit of the quiet, and a body over the age of three to converse with in it."

She made tea—someone always made tea—as the boys dragged their feet in the cleanup. The youngest toddled over to show Breen a little wooden top.

Obliging, she hunkered down to make it spin.

"Mahon and Keegan came back last evening, and wouldn't you know, Mahon had to wrestle the boys, toss them about, turning them inside and out again with excitement. So they were late to their beds, which never stops them from being up with the sun."

She smiled over at Breen. "So a bit of quiet time and another woman are welcome. Put the top away now, there's my good lad.

And put your caps on. Kavan, you help your brother brush the pony, and see you both wash at the well before you come back in."

When she opened the door, Bollocks raced out. The wolfhound stood by the door until the boys ran outside, then followed at a dignified pace.

"There's no better nursemaid than Mab, that's the truth of it. Sit now, won't you, Breen. I'll just get this bread out and on the cooling rack, then we'll have our tea."

"How are you feeling?"

Aisling sent her a puzzled glance, then it cleared with a smile. "Oh, you're meaning the baby. More than fine. Not to tempt the gods, but I had an easy time with both boys, and this one seems to be the same. I lose my taste for ale, but I don't mind it. And I get uncommonly randy—and Mahon doesn't mind that."

She put the bread on a cooling rack, took off the apron she wore, then sat with the tea. "And how is it all going with you?"

"I've seen and I've done things I'd have thought impossible a month ago. And I feel things, I don't know, stirring inside me. As if there's more to come."

"Marg's pleased with you."

"I hope so."

"It means all the worlds to her you come. Every day, you come, and not just to learn your craft, but to see and spend time with her. Not all in your place would."

"I haven't figured out my place yet. Did you always know yours?"

Lifting her tea, Aisling looked around. Bread cooling on the rack, the kettle sputtering on the hob, a wooden box of jumbled toys. The spinning wheel by the window and a basket of darning waiting by a chair.

"I thought once I would move to the Capital. Not a farmwife would I be, oh no. I would sit on the council, I would, dispensing my wisdom, and dine with the scholars and artists and the rest. Then, well, Mahon convinced me otherwise, and I'd have it no other way. We don't always end as we think when we start."

"Your home's happy."

"It is, and thank you, for that's what I want more than all there is. It's my mother who heads the council, and Keegan who stands as taoiseach while Harken and I tend the homeplace. It feels we're all where we're meant. As are you. Whether you stay or go, here's where you're meant now. Now, as for healing. This is more innate than learned, though what's held in can be opened with learning."

"Nan says you're the strongest healer she knows."

"It's good of her to say so. Any of the Fey may find this gift in them. Opening to another's pain or illness or distress can be a hard choice. You feel some of that pain and distress as you work to heal it, and that person may be a stranger, even an enemy. But once you accept the gift, you can't deny it."

"It's an oath? Like doctors take in my world."

"Very like, aye. I'm told, like Harken, you connect with animals."

"I always thought it was . . . I don't know what. But yes, and it's stronger since I've come here."

"What are we all, but animals, after all? Flesh and blood and bone, hearts and muscles. How do you know what your dog feels or needs or wants?"

Breen glanced toward the window. She heard Bollocks barking, and knew, just knew, he was barking with absolute joy.

"I don't know, exactly."

"You think of him, look into him. It's harder, believe me, not to look and see than it is to look and see. And you open without thought. Ah, here's a sweet little dog, or a fine-looking horse, or a poor bird with a broken wing. And you think, and care, and wonder. And open."

Aisling took her hand. "Will you let me look?"

"At me? Or . . . in me." Nerves popped. "I . . . that's part of it?"

"It can be."

"Okay. All right. Do I have to do anything?"

"Nothing at all."

And nothing changed as Aisling kept Breen's hand clasped in hers. The kettle still sputtered, the dog still barked.

"You're a healthy one, and that's a fine thing. Fit as well, you are. Strong—stronger than most will think, and isn't that grand? You have worries, of course, but so many come from thinking you're not good enough or clever. I'll say that's bollocks, but you have to learn that yourself. But we're connected now, not just hand to hand. What do you see in me?"

"You're beautiful."

Aisling laughed. "And didn't I do just a bit of a glamour this morning, as Marg said you'd come. Vanity isn't such a bad thing, is it?"

"I'd like to learn that one. I know you love your family. I can see that without magicks. And you must be clever because there's a spinning wheel over there, and a loom there. You must be a good mother because your kids are happy and healthy and really charming. And—"

She jolted; her mouth dropped open. "The baby moved! I felt the baby move. How—"

"We're connected, and I opened to you to help you see and feel."

"It feels amazing. It makes you so happy. And . . ."

"What?"

"A little smug."

Aisling laughed again. "Aye, it does. You're a good one, empathic, and that's helpful. Not all healers are empaths, not all empaths are healers. Having both makes each the stronger. Why not see what we have here?"

Aisling rose, went to her darning basket. She came back with a needle. She pricked her finger, held it out as she took Breen's hand in her free one again.

"See the blood, just a drop. The skin broken. Feel the little sting. Just a tiny bit of a thing. Let yourself feel that, just as you did the life stirring in me. Feel it, imagine closing that tiny bit of a wound. Open to it, and it's the light—the shine and the warmth of it—that heals what hurts."

She didn't know if she felt or just imagined the slight sting in her own finger. But she pressed her thumb against it, and Aisling smiled.

"Well done."

"But I didn't—"

"You did, with a bit of help guiding you." Aisling wiped the drop of blood away, then held out her finger to show the unbroken skin. "A small thing, aye, a first step."

Over Breen's appalled objections, Aisling burned her finger on the stove, nicked her arm with a kitchen knife. And worked with Breen to heal the small wounds.

"You've a talent for it," Aisling told her, "just as Marg said. More serious injuries take more, but you'll build to that, and learn to combine what you have with the right potions, balms, other treatments. Now I think you could use another cup of tea."

As she rose to make it, Keegan came through the door with a swirl of his duster.

"Morena said she was here. That's good then, I've time to start on her training."

"She has a name, as I'll remind you." Aisling spoke tartly as she continued making tea. "Breen and I have been working on her healing skills. She's done very well indeed."

"Well then, she'll find them handy when dealing with the bruises she'll have after training." He turned to Breen. "Basic hand-to-hand for today, so we'll see what you're made of."

If she could have glued her butt to the chair, she would have. "I don't intend to fight anyone."

"It's not about bloody intent. Are you going to do nothing but kick and squeal if Odran sends one of his creatures after you? Will you sit and shiver next time he puts you in a cage? Why should any risk protecting you if you won't work to protect yourself?"

"Out with you! Take your rude self outside. She'll be along soon enough." Aisling fisted her hands on her hips. "Out of my kitchen before I give you a bruise of your own."

Keegan only shrugged, but he left.

"I'll apologize for the boneheaded brother the fates have given me. Keegan does tend to be abrupt."

"That's a word we could use."

With a smile Aisling offered Breen the tea. "Oh sure, I've used many others when dealing with him over these years—all, in my opinion, well earned, as taoiseach or no, he's my idjit brother. But . . ." She sat again. "He's also got the right of it. You must learn, as he said, for your sake and that of others. There's not a one in this world who wouldn't give their life to protect you."

"I don't want—"

"It's not what you want, it's what is." Reaching out, Aisling took Breen's hand, and her eyes—so clear and blue—looked deeply into Breen's. "I remember when you were taken as a child. I remember the battle drums. I remember how many we sent to the gods who lost their lives to help bring you home safe. My father was one of them."

"I'm so sorry." Guilt strangled her. "I'm so sorry."

"It's not for you to be sorry." In comfort, in strength, Aisling's fingers tightened. "You were a child. And you fought, you fought with all that's in you. The shield around you won't last forever, and the fact of it is, it's already been breached once. Keegan was there, and so you sit here now.

"He's a man who strains for patience, and uses it up, I'll tell you, in dealing with the council, the judgments, the politics, the weight of his rank. His approach on this is boneheaded, as I said. But that doesn't make him wrong."

Sitting in the kitchen that smelled of fresh bread and tea, Breen remembered the battle she'd seen through Marg's eyes, and all the people who'd risked their lives for her.

"All right. He's going to be really unhappy when I'm not any good at it."

"That's yet to be seen. And there's no one better to teach you in this than Keegan. He was trained by our father, and then yours, and he'll give you—in his way—what they gave him."

As Breen saw it, she had two choices. Say no and deal with the guilt—and feel like a coward. Or go out and take her lumps— probably literal lumps.

She'd rather have bruises on her body than on her still-shaky ego.

She went out to see Keegan galloping bareback around the paddock on a dark brown horse with both boys—the younger in front of him, the older behind.

While her first reaction was he rode too fast, she couldn't deny the absolute glee on both boys' faces.

He spotted her, and slowed down. When he pulled the horse to a stop, he got pleas for more from front and back.

"Later," he said. "Off you go, Fin."

With obvious reluctance, Finian climbed down onto the paddock fence. Keegan swung off, plucked the younger off the horse, gave him a quick, high toss.

"Go on and pester your mother." He gave them each a rub on the head before plunking Kavan over the fence, then swinging over it himself.

He looked strong, she thought, and pondered those lumps.

"Make a fist."

She knew that one because Marco had shown her—thumb out, not in.

He gripped her balled hand, then annoyed the crap out of her by gripping her biceps with the other.

"You're no weakling, but there'll be times you'll come up against the bigger, the stronger. You need to learn how to use what you have to defend, to use what they have—that strength and size—against them."

"I took a course. I know SING."

He just stared at her. "A tune isn't going to stop a fist aimed at your face."

"No, not that. Solar plexus, instep, nose, groin. S-I-N-G."

Head cocked now, he gave a slight nod. "All right then, show me."

"Well, if I were in a parking garage, for instance, and you were a mugger or a rapist who came up behind me."

She turned her back. Keegan swept her legs out from under her.

Astonishment came first—no one had ever knocked her down. Resentment followed fast. "You said to show you."

"I'm still waiting for that, and wondering why you'd turn your back on an enemy."

She got to her feet. "To demonstrate."

"And what if I'm coming at you, face-to-face?"

When he lunged forward, she stumbled back. And he knocked her down again.

"The tune might be more useful," he commented, and pulled her up.

She punched his solar plexus—met a solid wall—and ended up on her ass again.

"You've got more muscle than that."

"I didn't see any point in hurting you." Before, she thought. She got up, punched again with feeling. But when she tried to bring the heel of her foot down on his instep, he sidestepped, and flattened her again.

She had to admit the process had worked better in class.

"Your singing may have some merit, but not if you lack speed and power. Try again."

She punched, hard enough to make her hand sting, then skipped the middle steps and brought her knee up. Though part of her wanted to, she didn't follow through.

He grinned at her. "Now there's potential. And what if—"

He spun her around, clamped an arm around her throat. She jabbed back with her elbow, as taught, but missed the instep as he had his legs spread.

"Stop struggling. Go limp. Use your wiles a bit. You're a woman—weaker. Make who has you believe you're weaker. Go limp."

She was weaker, and the reality of his far superior strength frightened more than a little.

He could hurt her, and she couldn't stop him.

She sagged.

"In your mind, think the next steps. The one who's attacked you thinks he's won. Now the elbow. Aye, not bad—harder the next time—and his grip loosens. Use it."

She slid down, managed to turn and bring her knee up again.

"Not so pitiful. What if I just—"

He rammed a fist toward her face, stopping just shy of her nose.

Shaking his head, he stared into her shocked eyes. "You'd be done, and likely out as well. You'll block."

He yanked up her arm so it knocked his fist away. "Firm! And strike back. Fast!"

She spent an hour, a great deal of it on the ground, before he left her with faint praise.

"You'll do better tomorrow."

She had to call the dog, had to keep her voice away from the whine inside her. She'd thought learning to ride a painful experience, but it was nothing compared to the throbs, twinges, stings, aches she experienced now. She waited until she'd made the turn onto Marg's path, until she was sure she was out of anyone's sight, before she sat on the ground, brought her knees up, lowered her head to them.

Bollocks licked at her, letting out the canine versions of the whine she'd held in.

She'd never experienced physical violence, had never had anyone deliberately cause her physical pain. Or known the terrible desire to cause it in someone else.

Was this the price of power—of self?

She thought of her life before, so ordinary, so uneventful. So, yes, confining, but still . . .

She lifted her head, wiped at her eyes. "Freedom costs," she told the dog. "I don't know how much I'm willing to pay."

But she sat and used what Aisling had taught her to soothe the bruises.

For himself, Keegan walked into his sister's house and poured a whiskey.

Aisling eyed him as she chopped cabbage for a supper of colcannon. "A bit on the early side for that, I'd say."

"Not from where I'm standing."

"How'd she do then? I found I couldn't watch you knock her down another time without wanting to come out and box your ears until they rang."

"She's strong, and she's quick when she doesn't think so damn much. The woman's in her bloody head more than she's out of it." He tossed back whiskey. "She learns, I'll give her that."

He tugged up his shirt to study the storm cloud of bruises on his ribs.

"Caught you more than once. Here, let me see."

"No, I'll see to it." He dropped his shirt. "She regrets, and it holds back what she has. She could've bruised my balls more than once, but holds back, regrets the harm done before she does harm."

"Don't we all, at the bottom of it?"

Though he wanted to disagree, he couldn't. Not when he lived with regrets every bloody day of his life.

And still.

"Regrets need to be set aside to keep worlds safe and whole. But that's a lock in her I don't know she'll open. And inside with them she keeps doubts close—like a woman might a favored jewel."

"She needs time."

"So do we all. That doesn't mean we'll get it."

When he stepped over to stare out the window, she stopped her kitchen work to go to him. Slipped an arm around him.

"It's not all of it on her shoulders, Keegan. It's for all of us. All the Fey, and all those with us."

"I know it, but I swore to Eian, I swore to him I'd protect her, I'd help her become. I don't know how to keep my promise any other way but this."

He felt the warmth over his ribs, sighed. "I told you I'd see to it."

"Now it's done." Because she loved him, she kissed his cheek for good measure. "Are you having supper here?"

He shook his head. "I thank you for it, but no. Harken and I will make do, and I need to send a falcon to Ma. If I can keep her and the rest up-to-date, I don't need to go back to the Capital for now. I feel I'm needed here more than there."

"Send love with the bird," she told him, and went back to chopping.

Since she'd managed to soothe her body, Breen soothed her mind and heart FaceTiming Marco.

"Look at you! Girl, look at that face. I miss that face."

"We FaceTimed last week."

"I still miss that face."

"I miss yours, too. Busy night at Sally's?"

"Wall-to-wall. DesDamona's got a new act, and it slays. I'm gonna crash after we talk. Everybody's missing you and reading your blog. Now tell me everything you're not writing in the blog."

If only she could. "It's pretty much all there. Writing, walking, hanging out with Bollocks, learning to ride."

"Can't believe you got yourself up on a horse."

"I really like it."

"Dogs and horses. We're gonna have to start looking at farms or something if you keep this up. Something going on," he decided, narrowing his tired eyes. "I know that face. You tell me what's going on."

"I'm still figuring it out, Marco. There's an awful lot of figuring out."

"You're not getting out enough. How come I don't hear about you sitting in pubs, singing a tune, flirting with some hot Irish guy?"

"Flirting's not on the schedule right now, especially with my wing-man thousands of miles away. How about you? Any new man?"

"I've taken a couple for a dip. Just no sparkage. I'm in a slump there, girl. Come on now, Breen, who knows you like me? I can see something's going on. You homesick, honey?"

"I miss you, and Sally and Derrick. Maybe a part of me thought I'd hear from my mother, but I haven't. And I'm okay with it. I don't like being okay with it."

"More than that."

She needed to give him something because he did know her. Since she couldn't give him Talamh, she grabbed something else. "I guess I'm feeling anxious, and I don't want to write about it in the blog, and get people who follow it going on about it."

"What now?"

"You know that children's book I wrote?"

"About the dog, sure. I'm going to keep nagging until you send it to me."

"What I did was . . . I queried an agent."

"You did what now?"

He popped up from where he'd been sitting so all she saw for a moment was his lean torso in a white tank top. "Well, for Christ's sake, you don't tell me this so I can send all kinds of vibes out?"

"I figured if I ever get a response it'll just be don't ever darken our door again."

"Stop that." He wagged a finger at her. "You send me a copy right now."

"In the morning. If I email you a copy now, you'll stay up and read it because you love me, and you won't get any sleep. I'll send it tomorrow. I promise."

"I'm proud of you, girl. You wrote a book, and that's something else. And you talked to an agent."

"I haven't actually talked to her yet."

"Same thing."

"Well, close. Now take my mind off it, because it gives me the jitters. Tell me what everyone's doing, how everyone is. Give me all the dish."

Since he always had dish, they talked for almost another half hour before she closed her tablet.

And she did feel soothed.

She loved the time she spent with her grandmother. The more Breen came to know her, the more she found someone she admired. She learned more than the careful casting of spells, the joys and responsibilities of power. She learned of her heritage, of the part of her so long locked away as if it were something shameful.

The next day she walked with Marg beyond the workshop, into the screen of trees, to cast her first circle outside.

"How do you do it?" Breen asked her. "How do you shed the anger, the resentment toward my mother?"

"By remembering she once loved my son. By knowing all that

lives in a mother's heart. By understanding my world was never truly hers." Marg set the tools she'd brought on the stone dolmen she used as an altar. "And still, truth be told, I have to work at it more often than not."

"I've tried—maybe not very hard, but some. I can't get over the lies. Not just the money, Nan, although without it, I don't see how I'd ever have come to Ireland, and then here. All the time wasted—"

"Not wasted, no. Never wasted. Every day is a gift, every day you learn. How do we know you would have found what you've found here if not for the life you led in the other?"

"She made me feel less. That's the bottom of it. She always made me feel less than what I am."

To soothe, to cherish, Marg laid a hand on Breen's cheek. "Now that you found more, you respect it more than you might have."

"But I wonder if I have so many doubts about myself, about what I can do, should do, because she told me—not just in words, but in looks, in actions—that I was less. And I believed her, and settled for less."

"You have a chance and a choice to be what you are." Firm now, Marg put her other hand on Breen's cheek to cup her face. "Take it, build on all that came before, reach for what comes next. If you fail, well, greatness rises from first failures. Now, *mo stór*." She stepped back. "Clear your mind and cast your circle."

As she'd been taught, Breen used the broom to sweep out negativity, making a determined effort to sweep her own out with it.

At the east point of the circle, she placed a yellow candle and incense, at the south, a red candle and a dragon's heart stone. Then at the west a blue candle and a shell, before she placed a green candle and a small bundle of herbs at the north.

As Marg watched, Breen walked the circle three times.

"This circle of protection I cast as a shield from evil future and past. With love and light this ring I form and add my vow to do no harm."

On her last circle, she drew up her light, loin to belly, belly to heart, heart to crown, and set the candles flaming—air, fire, water, earth.

The nerves didn't come, not this time, as that light held strong inside her. She lifted the athame from the altar, turned east.

"I call on the gods of the rising sun who grant me power to hear my call from this place, at this hour. I am your servant. I am your child."

She repeated the call to the south, to the west, to the north.

As she spoke, the air stirred; the candles flamed higher.

And she felt the stir, felt the flame, inside her.

She went to the altar to perform the simple spell Marg had chosen for her, one to bestow clarity.

She added the herbs, the crystals to the cauldron on the altar, poured the water from the cup over them. Tapping her wand three times on the cauldron, she lit a fire beneath it before anointing her third eye with oil.

"Rise, smoke, rise and bring the vision to my eyes. To my heart grant the sight; to my mind bring the light. Through the mists let me see. As you will, so mote it be."

The smoke spiraled up, thin and white.

Through it, she heard an echo, dull at first, as if the fog smothered sound. As it cleared, she knew the crash of sea against rocks. And as it cleared, she saw the cliffs, the stony island, the rubble of black stones above that crashing sea.

She saw the ritual on those cliffs. The circle—painfully different from what she'd cast. A ring of black candles with bloodred flames, the ring of demons inside it. In the center stood a slab of altar, gleaming black.

Bound to it, the boy fought. His screams pierced the smoke, tore through Breen as the figure in a black cape and hood stepped to the altar.

Chanting, garbled and thick in a language she didn't know, pounded like drumbeats.

The hooded figure lifted one hand to the sky, and it began to boil. With the other he lifted a long, curved knife. When he drew it across the boy's throat, lightning exploded, bombs of violent light. Thunder rolled, rolled as he caught a stream of blood in a gold chalice.

She saw the face of her grandfather as he lifted the chalice high, as lightning struck it. As, bathed in its light, he drank deep.

With the vision faded, mercifully faded, Breen dropped to her knees. Only then did Marg come to her.

"You must finish. You must offer your thanks, and close the circle. I'll help you, but you must finish. Then I'll give you a potion—you're so pale—and you'll tell me."

"It was him. It was Odran."

"Aye, so I thought it might be."

CHAPTER TWENTY

Because it was closer, Marg sat Breen down in front of the fire in her workshop. She added a potion to wine, and found herself grateful she'd done so for both of them as Breen finished her tale.

"Lightning struck the chalice, and the flash . . . It was dark, but it still illuminated. Then Odran drank, he drank— Oh, that poor boy, Nan. He couldn't have been more than twelve. After he drank, the demons, they . . . they devoured him. They just fell on his body and—"

She shuddered, drank more wine.

"It was horrible, beyond horrible. It had to be from years ago because Odran looked so young."

"He is any age he wishes, at any time. I can't tell you when, only that he would have a purpose for blood sacrifice. There is no greater crime, no greater sin."

As she spoke, Marg paced, unable, as yet, to find her own calm.

"For this, so it is written, the gods cast him out of their realm. You said the black castle was in ruin."

"Yes, yes, that's right. So it had to be after he took me."

"After, aye." Marg sat again, then took Breen's hand as she studied her face. "Your color's better. I'm proud of you, Breen, for finishing after so brutal a vision. This was not the spell we wrote."

"I know. I don't know where it came from."

"From you. You asked for vision, asked to see. There's a purpose in this as well. It may not be clear, but there's a purpose. I'll ask Sedric to tell Keegan you won't be training today."

"No. Believe me, I'd rather have a root canal, but if I skip today, he'll just make it twice as hard on me tomorrow."

With a smile, Marg squeezed her hand. "There. You've come to know him, so that's some clarity as well. But he'd take my word you're unwell."

"I can still see . . ." She breathed it out. "Getting knocked down will give me something else to think about. I'd rather get it over with than worry about what he'd pile on me tomorrow. He brought out swords yesterday. They won't draw blood, but they sure as hell bruise. I'll go."

She rose. "I don't suppose we could do a spell so I have the skill to knock him on his ass for a change."

"Best not tamper with that. Would you like me to come with you?"

"It's humiliating enough without an audience, thanks." She bent over, kissed Marg's cheek. "I'll see you tomorrow afternoon."

"You have the tea for restful sleep."

"Yeah."

"Drink some before bed, and what do you place under your pillow?"

"Rosemary and amethyst or black tourmaline."

"You learn well."

She wished she could learn to fight nearly as well, Breen thought as she started her walk to the farm. Actually, she didn't, and that was probably at least part of the problem.

She could easily go the rest of her life without wanting to punch somebody, much less whack at them with a sword.

Except . . .

She thought of the boy, struggling, screaming.

Wouldn't she have tried to protect him, by whatever means?

She looked over the fields as Bollocks raced up the road, then back again. Everything so green, so lush, so peaceful, with the blue water of the bay curving in.

It actually hurt, physically hurt, she realized, to know such evil existed when the world offered such simple beauty.

The poor boy. Had he come from this world, hers, another? Impossible to know. But she knew he'd been terrified and still he'd tried to fight. Right up until the end, he'd tried.

She could hardly do less.

She saw the hawk before she saw Morena. Amish glided down to land on one of the stone pillars flanking the farm gate. Bollocks—growing so fast!—raced up to plant his forepaws on the pillar and bark.

"He's far too dignified to play with you," Morena called out. Her hair, free of her usual braid, waved sunnily to the small of her back.

She beat Breen to the gate, crouched down to rub the dog, who plopped down to show his belly. "But I'm not." Amusing them both, she gave Bollocks a quick wrestle before looking up at Breen. "Ready to take on Keegan, are you then?"

"I'm never ready for it."

"Ah now, Harken tells me you're improving."

"How would he know?"

"Sure and he's watched a time or two, from a discreet distance."

"God. Mortifying." But she opened the gate.

"I'll see for myself."

"No, it's bad enough. He knocks me down regularly, and adds insult to injury. Apparently, I've got feet buried in a bog, the balance of a one-legged drunk, and the hands of a three-fingered tinker."

"All the more reason you need someone cheering you on." Morena tossed an arm around Breen's shoulders. She smelled of the garden—sweet, spicy, earthy all at once.

"I'll wager you're better than you think."

"You'd lose that bet. Oh, Christ, he's got the damn swords out. My arm was like rubber after yesterday."

"Rubber's the thing that bounces, isn't it? You'll bounce then. And there's himself, looking all fierce and steely eyed."

Keegan turned his head, grinned at her. "And here's herself, come to torture my brother again."

"He doesn't seem to mind it." She hefted a sword with a style Breen envied. "You've bespelled them."

"I have, of course. I don't want to hack something off her, do I?"

Morena ran the blade over her palm, nodded. "But you don't mind her feeling the sting."

"Feel nothing, learn nothing. Harken's in the stables. One of the horses is off her feed."

"I'll look in on him later." She handed back the sword. "I mean to watch for a bit."

"See you keep clear."

He turned to Breen, tossed her the sword. It hit the ground as she jumped back.

And Keegan cast his eyes to the sky. "And this is what the gods give me to work with. Pick up the sword. I trust you remember which end is which."

"You stick them with the pointy end."

He actually smiled. "I read that story. Arya was but a child and learned fast and well. You're a woman grown. Come now, stick me with the pointy end."

She tried. He blocked without moving his body an inch, and she felt the sting in her belly as he stabbed her.

"Try again."

This time the sting in her shoulder told her she'd have lost an arm.

"Balance your weight," Morena called out from her perch on the paddock fence.

Keegan's duster hung over the rail beside her.

"Quiet, you." He pointed the sword at Morena, then turned back to Breen. "Again."

"Feck it all, Keegan, she's just beginning. Ease up a bit."

"Just beginning and dead twice over. Again."

So it went. Mortal wound after mortal wound until her whole body felt the stings.

"Bloody bully! Put your shoulder into it, Breen. Block the bastard."

She tried. Sweat dripped into her eyes, ran down her aching back, but she tried. She managed to block a blow that might have decapitated her, felt the slap of blade to blade scream up her arm.

"I need to—"

"Block!" He snarled it at her. "If you can do nothing else, block."

But her sword slid weakly down his, and he killed her again.

Standing hard against her, not winded in the least while her breath whistled, he gripped her wrist.

"Hold the damn sword, you've muscle enough. And use your feet, for fuck's sake, and your head before you lose it. I mean to kill you, that's all you need to know. I want your death." He slapped her sword with his, again and again. "Fight to take mine."

He drove her back, back until she had to use both hands to hold the sword. "Strike out!"

She swung, and his block had the sword spinning out of her sweaty hands. Her legs wobbled, and he finished her off with a shove.

"You're not training but badgering and bullying." Incensed, Morena stomped over to retrieve Breen's sword. "It's no fair fight, and you know it."

He rounded on Morena so they stood—both armed and toe to toe. And both spewing temper.

"There's no fair fight in battle, and you know it. Do you want her alive or dead? For dead she'll be if this is the best she has. For she's useless with a sword and nearly as bad with her fists."

He wrenched the sword from Morena, tossed it down beside Breen. "Pick it up, get on your feet, and try again."

"I'm not useless."

"Prove it then, if you've the belly for it. Take up the sword. Fight, or die."

She hurt, everywhere, but that was nothing compared to the rage that flooded into her.

She was not useless.

"Die then," he said, and strode toward her, sword poised for the killing blow.

She threw her hand out, threw the rage with it. And the rage had heat, a burning that seared through her, boiled out of her.

It shot him into the air and back a solid ten feet before he struck the paddock fence, snapping wood as the force sent him tumbling through.

For a moment, Morena froze, eyes wide. "Stop. Stop now, Breen," she said before she raced to Keegan.

He sat up, waved her off. And looked over at Breen with a kind of dark satisfaction. "Well then, somebody's waking up at last."

Breen pressed her shaking hand to the ground. It vibrated still inside her, that shocking spurt of power.

"I didn't mean . . ."

"You should." Keegan got to his feet. "You should mean whatever it takes to send the enemy down rather than yourself."

"Your nose is bleeding."

Carelessly he swiped a hand under it. "As it has before, will again. Pick up the sword, get up."

"She's shaken yet, Keegan. Gods, so am I. Let her be."

"It's still in her. I can see it." Crouching by Breen, he gripped her chin. "Just as you feel it. You'll use it. We'll work to focus it, to channel it, to control it, so it comes and goes at your will."

His eyes—so intense—glowed into Breen's. And in them she saw pleasure and approval.

"This is what you wanted," she realized.

"Aye, it's what's needed. Morena, go hold Harken off, as he's racing out of the stables as if they were on fire. And have him do the same with Aisling and Mahon. Tell them all we're fine here.

"On your feet." He gripped Breen's arm, pulled her up. "As now true training begins."

Appalled, at him, herself, at everything, she tried to shake him off. "You did that on purpose, goaded me, slapped at me."

"And it took far too long for results. You're a slow burn, Breen Siobhan, but you've hellfire when it finally lights. Now we'll use it."

"I don't want . . ." Not true, she realized as he simply stood, the iron grip on her arm, and waited. However terrifying, she did want whatever had exploded in her, out of her. Because it had been glorious, too.

"I didn't do it on purpose. I didn't control it, and I could've done worse than a nosebleed."

"All true enough, and so I'll help you. I'll help you," he repeated, and for the first time his words didn't bite or sting. "I've some in me, as I'm of the Wise, but I've no god's blood, so you've more. Your father had the same, and when my own died, he took up my training, and he stood for me as a father would."

Pausing, he looked around, the fields, the paddocks, the house of sturdy stone. "This farm is yours by birthright."

"No. I'd never—"

He flicked her a baleful glance. "I didn't say, and wouldn't, you'll have it back again. Eian gave it to my family because he knew we would tend it as he would, and so we have. But what I do with you, I do for him. I do for Talamh. I do for the light.

"Will you do less? Will you be less?"

"I don't know what I'll do. I don't know what I'll be. But it won't be less. I'm never going back to less."

"Then pick up your sword. The day's wasting."

She picked up the sword. "Don't piss me off like that again."

He only grinned. "I've defenses of my own. I haven't given you a taste yet."

He gave her a few, and though she didn't like the flavor, she learned, at least a little. When an enemy had the power to spin the wind, you spin with it, use the momentum to gather speed, and strike back. When you fall down, get the hell up before you're impaled.

She didn't have to like the lessons to learn them.

"I have to stop. I have to go. It's nearly dusk."

"Battles don't stop when the sun sleeps."

Did he never get tired? she wondered.

"I need to go back through. I don't want to walk nearly a mile through the woods in the dark."

"Pixies will light your way if you ask, but you have the means for it yourself."

"I didn't think to stash a flashlight on the other side." Which wasn't a bad idea. "And I'm not stumbling through the woods with a candle or lantern."

"Bring your light."

"What light?"

The sharp slide of his sword into its sheath sounded of impatience. "Give me your hand."

"Why?"

"Ah, women." He grabbed it, turned it palm up. "You know how to bring fire."

"Yes, but—"

"Fire's not only flame, and even that can be cold as well as hot—as you will. Fire is light. As you can bring the fire, you can bring the light. Draw it up. The roots are in you; draw, from the roots, the light, cool and bright. Draw it up, see it, a sphere, a ball, a globe, in the palm of your hand."

There was amber in his eyes, she realized. Like light. Flecks of light in the sea of green.

"I've never—"

"Focus on the light, within, without. See it, feel it, know it. Cool in your hand, white, pure, a globe formed from your light, by your will."

It flickered. She nearly lost her focus in surprised joy, but his fingers tightened on her wrist.

"Hold it, strengthen it. Bring it."

And she did. She held a ball of white light in her hand with his wrapped on her wrist. She looked up at him, the light shining in her hand, in her heart, in her eyes.

"It's beautiful."

"Enough to light your way."

He released her wrist, stepped back. "Your focus is slow and apt to fracture. You'll be working on that. Come back tomorrow."

He took her sword, swept his duster off the rail, then started toward the house.

"Thank you."

Turning, he just stared at her a moment, a man with a sword at his side, another in his hand with the quieting sunlight washed over him.

"You're welcome then."

She called her dog, wound her way toward the gate while she admired the light in her hand.

Morena caught up with her. "I was going to light you home, as it grows darker in the woods as dusk comes."

"Exactly. Look what I did!"

"Very pretty. I'll have a walk with you, else Harken will pull me into the evening milking."

"Walk to the cottage and have a glass of wine with me to celebrate my surviving another day."

"I'll take the wine, and happily. But you did more than survive this day."

"Scared the crap out of myself."

Bollocks bounded up the steps and through the tree ahead of them. In the woods on the other side, the light glowed.

"And me as well. You looked so fierce and furious, and the crack of power set my ears ringing. Jaysus, he flew, didn't he?" Laughing, Morena tossed her hand, scattered pretty sparks of light. "A bird in a gale, he was. I love him like a brother, and for a moment I feared for him. But since he got no more than his nose bloodied, I'll say he well deserved the flight."

"It scared me," Breen repeated. "It just shot out of me."

"He meant it to. Oh, maybe the force of it took him by surprise, else he'd have blocked it at least a bit. He was hard on you, I know, and I didn't like it. But I see his methods and his means now. You'll have some bruises, I'll wager."

"That's a bet you'd win, but I'm getting pretty good at healing them."

"So Aisling said." Waving both hands, Morena scattered more light.

"Show-off. I guess I don't have to wonder how you'll light your own way home."

"You won't, though I'm after going back to the farm after the wine." She tossed her miles of luxurious hair. "And settling in bed with Harken."

"Show-off," Breen repeated, and made Morena laugh.

"Is there no one wishing for you in their bed back in Philadelphia?"

"No. Not for quite awhile now."

"You've got good looks, a good brain and heart. I think the men in Philadelphia must be gits, one and all."

"I was different there. I'm different here."

"There are plenty who'd be happy to give you a roll if you want one. We should have a ceilidh, so you can look over your choices."

"I think with writing, lessons with Nan, with Aisling, with Keegan—and recovering from lessons with Keegan—I don't have much time for a roll."

"Ah, sure and there's always time for that." With a shake of her head, Morena scattered more light as they came to the edge of the woods. "If you think otherwise, I have to say the men, or women if you like, in your Philadelphia aren't very skilled in the matter."

"You may be right, at least the men I ended up with." As they crossed to the cottage, she looked down at the light in her hand. "He didn't tell me how to put it out."

"Will it away," Morena said easily.

"Will it away."

It took a moment, but Breen watched the ball dim, shrink, then vanish. "Hah! Wine! You pour that, I'll feed the dog."

"A good bargain."

Breen glanced back as they went inside. "I'm not attracted to women, sexually."

"As I'm not either, I wasn't after planning to seduce you."

On a laugh, Breen shook her head. "But it occurs to me I didn't have any close girl friends—women friends—in Philadelphia."

"Something wrong with them as well?"

"No, it was me." A strange and lowering admission, she realized. "I had Marco, always. And Sally and Derrick and the people who worked at Sally's."

"Sally's a girl's name."

"For Salvador in this case. And it occurs to me, the three people I'm closest to in Philadelphia are gay men."

"Happy friends make a happier life."

"They're pretty happy, but I meant . . . They're all attracted to men. Sally and Derrick are married."

"Ah, aye, that's one of the meanings of the word on this side. In Talamh, gay is just happy. And there's no special word for what you mean as love and sex, well, they're just love and sex."

"That's so . . . sensible."

Breen filled the dog's bowls while Morena poured wine.

"It's nice, reconnecting with you. It's nice having a glass of wine with another woman at the end of the day."

"It is," Morena agreed. "So we'll have two."

They had two, and after the wine, after Morena left, Breen practiced bringing the light, letting it go.

When she took Bollocks for his last walk of the night, she stood on the shale by the bay while he splashed. And, curious, she tossed the light over the water, watched it fly, then pulled it back.

She bobbled it the first few times, but she got better. With the light in her hand, she looked up at the moon.

She stood in Ireland now, she thought, and still she held light and power in her hand.

No, she would never be less again.

In Talamh, in a sky with two moons, Keegan rode his dragon. He'd intended to take to his bed and read until the day washed out of him. But he could sense—no matter how he tried to block—Harken and Morena pleasuring each other. And the two of them, he had reason to know, could go on till dawn if the mood was on them.

So he left them to it, flew toward the Capital. Not for politics or meetings or judgments—his mother had those well in hand for the moment.

He needed a woman, and knew where to find her.

To avoid questions, conversations, he had Cróga hover over a balcony of the castle keep. He dropped down lightly. Cróga would take himself off, and come again when needed for the flight home.

Through the billow of the thin curtains he saw her sitting at her grooming table. She drew a brush, slowly, through her long flaxen hair.

She wore white, as she often did, as thin as the curtains.

Shana, whose father served on the council, whose brother had fought by his side, met his eyes in her mirror as he parted the curtains.

"Good evening, Taoiseach. We weren't expecting you back." Born and raised in the Capital, she had the accent of the east and the city. And the posh manners of both. "Your mother will be pleased to see you."

She rose and the light from the low fire simmered through the thin white gown, as they both knew she intended.

"I didn't come to see my mother."

"Me then." She smiled, slow, her eyes tawny as a cat's. "I'm honored. Will you have wine?"

"I will, and thank you."

She moved like a dancer. Her Elfin blood meant she could move quickly, but she took her time now so he could look his fill.

"And how do things go in the west?" She poured ruby wine into two glass goblets.

"Well enough. The peace holds still."

"We're grateful. But I meant with Mairghread's granddaughter. I'm told you're training her personally."

"I am, as Marg is teaching her the craft. She needs it."

She handed him a glass. "I'm told she has great beauty. The fiery hair of her grandmother, the storm-cloud eyes of her grandsire."

"She has beauty enough." He reached out, pulling a lock of hair that waved to Shana's waist through his fingers. It, like her skin, smelled of the jasmine that bloomed in the night.

"But not the sort that draws my eye."

A lie, one he hated to admit. He could still see the way she'd looked up at him, the globe of light in her hand, the joy and power alive on her face.

"But you think of her." Pouting, Shana ran her fingers down the laces of his shirt.

"I have to think of her." He tipped her face up. "But I've come to you."

"Expecting me to open my arms and my bed to you. I might have been sharing them with another."

"Happily you're not."

She laughed, sipped some wine before setting it aside. "Happily. I'll always open them to you, Keegan, but a woman wants a bit of wooing first."

"I've flown through the night for you, Shana. If that's not wooing enough." Knowing her, appreciating her, he flicked his wrist, and offered her a white rose.

"Ah now, is there a woman who could resist you?" She brushed the flower over her cheek as she looked up at him under her lashes. "I never have found the way, have I?"

She laid a hand on his cheek in turn. "So take off your sword, your boots, and the rest of it, and come into my arms, come into my bed. We'll leave the west behind."

He could take off his sword, and did. He could take off his boots and the rest. But he could never leave the west behind.

Because he knew her he accepted she'd never understand the why of it.

So he went into her arms, into her bed, and gave himself over to silken, perfumed skin, to the warm lips, the skilled hands of a woman who knew his needs and his body as he knew hers.

He closed off his mind, just for now, just for now, to everything else. Here were generous breasts to fill his hands, his mouth. Here a woman's sighs and gasps to stir his blood. Her pulse quickened for him; her hair fell like fragrant curtains around him as she mounted him.

"I've missed you, Taoiseach." Her head fell back with a moan as she took him in. "I've missed this."

Her hips rocked, slow, torturous pleasure. He gripped them as he matched her pace, but lightly so as not to mark that soft white skin.

He watched her face, the stunning beauty of it, saw in her eyes when she went into herself. He let her ride, closed his eyes to center himself on only this, only her, to block out the images that wanted to intrude.

When she came, he rose up to her. He wrapped around her, driving himself to the end.

When she whispered his name, he cursed himself for wanting someone else.

He stayed with her another hour. He brought her wine, listened to her sleepy gossip, and stroked her hair until he felt her drift into sleep.

He rose quietly to dress again, felt some regret for leaving a warm, naked woman in a soft featherbed. And guilt—which sat poorly in him—for thinking of another woman.

"Won't you stay?" She murmured it as she rose on an elbow. Her hair spilled over her breast as she reached out a hand. "Sleep with me, wake with me."

"I have duties."

"You have duties here as well."

"I don't forget them." Whether it was guilt or regret, he couldn't say, but he conjured another rose for her, laid it beside her. "I'll come back when I can."

She gave him the tart look that always appealed to him. "I may be otherwise occupied."

He took her hand, kissed it. "Then it's a fine thing you're on the third floor so I can toss who occupies it off your balcony. Sleep now."

He stepped back through the curtains. He'd already called the dragon in his mind, so Cróga circled the courtyard. When he glided down, Keegan stepped onto the balcony wall, swung onto his back.

Shana walked to the doors, parted the curtains, and watched him fly away.

One day, she thought, he would not fly away from her. One day he would not go back to the west, with its endless fields and sheep.

One day he would stay.

PART III
CHOICE

The difficulty in life is the choice.
                    −George Moore

To believe only possibilities is not faith,
but mere philosophy.
                    −Sir Thomas Browne

CHAPTER TWENTY-ONE

With Bollocks on one of his sniffing, wandering, racing back and forth routines, Breen walked through the woods toward the portal.

The bright, beautiful morning had lured her out to the patio to write in the garden with warm bay breezes and strong sunlight that turned the colors of everything vivid.

She'd nearly blown off her daily visit to Talamh and her grandmother for the simple luxury of basking in what promised to be a stellar afternoon.

But she'd promised, so that was that.

Still, she loved the learning and hoped to do more spell-casting. She'd even written her own, her first. A little twist on an illumination spell that conjured seven balls of light and floated them.

With Marg's approval, she could try it out.

She didn't want to spend her last two hours or so in Talamh swinging a damn sword or punching and kicking. She'd work with Keegan, but she wanted to spend that time on magicks. That focus he kept pushing on her.

Focus and control, she thought. She just had to convince him that training her in that area made more sense than slapping bespelled swords together.

As always, Bollocks bounded through the portal ahead of her. And if the kids or dogs were outside at the farm, she knew he'd race straight there.

Or, if he caught sight of them, he'd run around for a while with what she thought of as the Gang of Six—the group of kids from different tribes who raced the roads and roamed the woods.

The dark-skinned elf, Mina—definitely the leader—often approached Breen with questions about the other side. A child couldn't go unaccompanied through the portals until they'd turned sixteen, but Mina already had plans to see everything she could see.

Bright, curious kids—and still kids, Breen thought, whether they flew or slid into trees or turned into a horse.

If they, or Aisling's boys, were out and about, Bollocks would make his way to the cottage after a playdate.

She climbed onto the thick, curving branches, over the sturdy rocks. Out of sunlight and into chilly fog and dripping skies.

With sincere regrets for the change in the weather, she pulled up the hood of her jacket, zipped it. She took care maneuvering down the slope, then headed across the soaked grass.

The blanketing fog obscured the farm, and she could barely see the outline of the stone wall or the road beyond it. Definitely an indoor day, she decided as she climbed over the wall.

And one near a fire, as the damp turned the air raw.

She called for the dog, and stuck to the side of the road. No cars, of course, but someone could come galloping along, and with the fog swirling she could barely see two feet ahead.

She conjured a ball of light, thrilled with how quickly it formed in her hand. Mostly it bounced off the shifting curtains of fog, but it helped a little.

Those curtains blocked out sound as well as sight and added, for her, an appealing eeriness to what had become a familiar walk.

Like being inside a cloud, she thought, alone and quiet. And with a fire and a warm drink at the end of it.

She tossed the ball, caught it, to amuse herself, and sang, as it seemed to fit, "The Long and Winding Road."

"It's a lovely voice you have."

The woman stepped out of the fog as if part of it. She wore a long gray cloak with the hood up and over her gray hair. When Breen jolted, nearly bobbled the ball of light, she smiled.

"Ah, I've startled you. I'm sorry for that. Such a mist we have this day. You'd be the daughter of he who was taoiseach, granddaughter of Mairghread. Breen, isn't it? I'm Yseult, and pleased to meet you, even on such a day."

"Yes, I'm Breen."

The woman carried a basket with the feathery tops of carrots spilling out. Her eyes, gray as her hair, held that easy smile.

"Do you live nearby?"

"Oh, a ways yet to go. I bartered some of my wares for the carrots at the O'Broin farm—what was yours once. I've never had the knack of growing them."

"I'm just on my way to see my grandmother."

"I'm sure she's happy to have you near after all this time." In the chilly air, Yseult drew her cloak tighter. "Might I walk with you, make use of your pretty light in all this gloom? I'd like to stop by and give greetings to my old friend."

"Of course. You know my grandmother?" Breen began as they started to walk.

"Ah sure, everyone knows Mairghread, and we came up together you could say. And I knew your father since he was a babe in nappies. You've the look of them, the O'Ceallaighs. But for the eyes. Those you have from your sire and his before him."

"Yes, so I'm told."

"You spent many the year on the outside." She wagged a finger at the ball. "Learning the craft from your da then?"

"No. I've only started to learn since coming here."

"Well now, that's a pity, isn't it? Your sire had great power, from the O'Ceallaighs and from the god. Much he could have taught you. The power's in you as well, and the blood of the god."

"My grandmother's teaching me."

"To conjure little balls of light."

Breen glanced over at the dismissive tone. The smile, that easy smile remained, a contrast. The eyes, she saw, weren't gray, but nearly black.

Dark and deep.

"Light's the core, the heart, the foundation."

"Do you think so? When light is so easily snuffed out?" She plucked the ball from Breen's hand, closed hers around it. When she reopened her hand, the light had vanished.

"Such a weak glow really, and easily killed. Black will always smother white, my girl. Dark will always defeat light. Learn this lesson well, for so it will always be."

Not gray, Breen realized when her head spun a little. As she watched color flow into the hair under the hood. Red. Not a bright, fiery red, but deep, dark red. Like heart blood. The cloak turned black.

Whatever was in the basket began to slither and hiss.

"Who are you?"

"Yseult, as I said. One who knows your grandmother well. I am the dark to her light. I am one who helped Odran send your father, that weak excuse for a son, to his death. Come, come watch, child, while I do the same to the woman who bore him. Then I'll take you to your grandsire. He waits to cloak you in robes of gold and show you the true power in your blood."

Dizzy, sick, Breen stumbled back. The beauty of Yseult's face, a face that had been pleasant, even ordinary, grew to terrifying.

She glowed, a dark light, while the snakes—two-headed snakes—in a basket—not of straw, but gold—began to slither over the sides.

"No. I'm not going anywhere with you. You're not getting near my grandmother."

The smile flashed, brilliant in its confidence. "So young, so foolish, so weak. Will you make another pretty ball of light to stop me?"

When she gripped Breen's arm, the heat scorching through her skin nearly buckled her knees. Even as she jerked back, one of the snakes struck. That pain dropped her.

Still she struggled to draw up the light, the power, to find a shield, a weapon.

It snapped from her fingertips, struck Yseult's cloak. Smoked.

Eyebrows arching, Yseult stepped back. Then the smile returned.

"So you have a bit more than I thought. But not enough, little flower. Not enough."

Breen crossed her hands in the air. This time the little bolts of light fell harmlessly to the ground.

"You want more. I can feel your need. I can give you more. Your grandsire can give you more than your feeble mind can imagine."

"I don't want anything from you, from him."

"But you'll have it. And we'll take it."

As Yseult stepped forward, Breen prepared to fight with whatever she had left. And the dragon roared through the fog.

He swung his tail to encircle Breen as Keegan leaped off his back.

With the sword already in his hand, he charged Yseult. She up-ended the basket, sending the snakes streaking toward him as she whirled into the fog.

"She'll be your death, Taoiseach," she called out. "And take her place in the black tower while Odran rules for all time."

"I will be yours."

The snakes screamed as he shot them with light. When they turned to ash, the fog swirled away. Yseult was gone.

Keegan sheathed his sword. "I will be yours," he repeated, and turned to Breen. He signaled his dragon to uncurl his tail, then shook his head.

"And how do you expect to fight sitting on your arse?"

He took one step toward her, then his expression changed from temper to shock.

He rushed to kneel beside her. "Did they strike? Are you bitten?"

"My arm."

Roughly, he shoved up her sleeve, cursed. Helpless, mired in the searing pain, she screamed.

"I'm sorry, truly. No, no, stay awake!" As her head lolled, he gripped her chin hard enough to bruise. "You have to stay awake. We need to burn the poison out before it takes you into the Sleep, and there's no time to get you to Aisling. We do this together."

"I don't know how. I'm so tired."

"Look at me. Join with me. Light with me, fire with me, power with me, two into one. See the dark moving in your blood, cleanse with white fire until there is none. Say this with me."

Everything blurred, her eyes, her mind, her ears. "What?"

"Stay awake, gods damn it. Look at me. My eyes are your eyes, my mind is your mind, my will is your will. Speak the words with me and call the fire.

"Join with me," he repeated, and she mumbled with him.

When they finished the first incantation, the pain leaped back, sent her into gasping moans.

"I know there's pain. Use it. You're already stronger. We say it again now. We hold together now. Three times, it takes. So twice more."

Not pain, she thought. This was beyond pain. She'd been lit on fire from the inside out. When she screamed, when she sobbed, he waited.

"Once more, just once more, and it's done. I promise you." His grip on her hand tightened. "I'm here with you. Once more."

She had to catch her breath, had to bear down knowing that unspeakable pain would rip through her a third time.

She kept her eyes fixed on his, gold lights swimming in the green. "Join with me," she said, and wept, unashamed, through the rest.

"There now, there, brave one, let me have a look. Don't close your eyes, don't sleep, not yet."

Gently, so gently, he brushed her hair back from her damp face. "Ah, she burned you for good measure, the whore bitch. This I can fix for you, and it won't hurt so much. Look here, do you see where the bites were, the red heat, the swelling? It's gone. The poison's burned away. There's only the brand she put on you. Leave that to me."

She let her head fall back, didn't even have the strength to wonder that it rested against a dragon's leg.

"Where are we? This isn't the road by the farm, by the cottage."

"She lured you away."

"I hear . . . the waterfall."

"Aye. Odran can't come through, but she comes and goes as she pleases it seems. She meant to take you through the portal here with her dark magicks."

"I . . ." She sighed, beyond relief as her arm cooled, as the pain, even the hint of it vanished.

"There now, that's done." He brushed his hand lightly over her cheek. "You did well. You did the hard and you did it well." Then he sat back on his haunches. "Now what the bloody hell were you thinking, going off with such as Yseult?"

"I didn't know who she was, and I was just walking to Nan's. She asked if she could walk with me to visit Nan. She said they were friends—or implied it—then everything changed. She took the light. I had a ball of light, and she took it, crushed it."

He held her hand still, and she wouldn't forget that. He held her hand because hers trembled.

"Why would you have a ball of light on a clear afternoon?"

"There was fog, and it was raining and foggy, and—"

"As it was here, when I came?"

"Yes, like that."

"Her witchery is all it was."

"There wasn't fog?"

"An illusion, for you."

"But . . . how did she get me here? We only walked for a few minutes. And how did you find me? How did you know?"

"She entranced you. You were singing. I could hear you sing, but you were nowhere to be seen. She's powerful, is Yseult, and planned it well."

He glanced over, gauged the distance to the waterfall, to the portal.

"But not well enough. I saw your light, heard your voice. And after they were both gone, I followed the light in here." He tapped a finger just above her heart.

Then he rose, took a skin from the saddle. "Just water. You need it after the purifying. Marg will have something to set you full to right, so don't sleep until you are."

"I feel . . . sort of drunk."

"That's not surprising, is it? It's the first either of us have worked that spell."

Water streamed like magic down her throat. Before she almost choked. "You never did that before? How did you know it would work?"

"It did, didn't it? Now on your feet." He took the skin, then simply wrapped an arm around her to haul her up. Tightened it when she swayed.

"Dizzy," she managed, and dropped her head on his shoulder. "I need a second. I don't think I can walk yet."

"You won't be walking."

Though still limp when he swung her up, she went rigid when she ended up in the saddle.

"Oh no, I don't think—"

He swung up behind her. "I won't let you fall."

Then the dragon simply lifted into the air and, like the falcon, wove through the trees as he climbed.

The wind rushed through her hair, over her face.

"You— There aren't any reins."

"We know where we're going. The saddle, it's for the rider's comfort, and for carrying supplies."

She wanted to just close her eyes until she could feel her feet on the ground again. But something else inside her wanted more. So she looked out at the sky—blue and white and gold. And down, at hills and fields, streams and cottages. Green and green, brown and gold again, the blue bay, the white froth. The sudden rise of an iridescent tail.

She'd thought she'd begun to understand magicks, even feel them. But until that moment, she hadn't known.

She reached back, gripped Keegan's hand.

"I said I wouldn't let you fall, and we're nearly there."

"No, no, no. Not that. It's . . . it's all so amazing. It's wonderful. It's all so beautiful."

Enchanted, she took her hand back, lightly stroked it over the dragon's back. "He feels almost polished, like jewels. He protected me."

"It's his nature. It's his heart."

She saw the farm below and found herself regretting her first flight—maybe her only—had been so short.

"I'm grateful, to both of you. I'd be dead if you hadn't come."

"They don't want you dead. Yet."

With that, they landed, and Marg raced over behind a whining Bollocks.

"Where was she? What happened?"

"Yseult happened." Keegan jumped down, then reached up and lifted Breen from the saddle. "She'll do," he told the dog, who pawed at his legs to try to reach Breen.

Instead of putting her down, he swung her up again to carry her toward the house.

"I can walk now."

"Not well, I'd wager. Sleep snakes she had, and Breen was bitten."

"How long?"

"Get her inside." Aisling hurried over. "We'll purify."

"Already done."

"You?"

"Both of us." He paused, and his voice filled with frustration. "I can't get her inside if you're in the way, can I now?"

"Let me see." Aisling reached up, put a hand on Breen's heart, one on her head. "She's clear. She's clear, Marg, not to worry. Well done, Keegan."

"She'll need the after potion. My poor girl."

"Mahon, my love, take the children out back. Breen needs the quiet. Harken, the after potion, if you please."

"Yseult," Keegan said to the men.

Mahon cursed, earning wide eyes from his sons, and a hard look from his wife. Keegan carried her in, dumped her on the settee, where Bollocks planted his paws on her chest and lapped madly at her face.

"I need Mahon to scout with me—as we were about to do before this came about."

"See that Mab's with the children then. Go on now, Bollocks." Aisling gave him a nudge and a rub. "Leave her to us for a bit now. Go on with the boys."

"Go outside." To reassure him, Breen kissed his nose. "I'm okay."

Keegan nodded, took another look at Breen. "We'll train tomorrow, and harder. This wasn't a random scout on his luck, but planned. Odran knows you're here. He knows you've awakened. We'll train harder."

Harken walked in with a cup as Keegan walked out.

"Drink this now," Aisling ordered. "Every drop. Then we'll have some stew for you, I think. It empties you out, the purifying."

"Yeah. I feel hollow everywhere."

"I should've known." Sitting beside her, Marg took her hand, pressed it to her cheek. "I should've expected, prepared."

"It's not your fault. You've been preparing me. Keegan's been preparing me. I hate that he's right. I have to work harder. I was weak, and stupid. I was," she insisted when Marg protested. "I won't be next time."

"You'll have some food," Aisling declared. "And you'll tell us, from start to end. And we'll see what needs doing. She's your blood, Marg, and neither weak nor stupid. But Yseult's a wily one, and potent with her bloody snakes. So we'll hear it, then we'll see what's needed."

When she'd finished, and felt herself again, Harken stepped away from the window where he'd kept an eye on the children. He cupped Breen's face in his hands and kissed her lightly on the lips.

"Trapped in a bespelled fog with a powerful black witch, branded by her, and bitten by a sleep snake, and still there was enough light and fight in you to guide Keegan to you. You're your father's daughter."

She hadn't thought of it that way, but only of failure.

"I hope so. I don't understand the Sleep thing. Keegan said they didn't want me dead."

"'Tisn't death," Aisling told her, "but it mirrors it."

"You know the tale of the Sleeping Beauty?" Harken asked. "Well, it wouldn't be a kiss to bring you back. One bitten by a creature such as that will fall into a dark, deep sleep, wakened only by the will of the one who commands the snake."

"We'd have broken the spell." Marg reached out and took Breen's hand. "But it's difficult and it's dangerous for all. It's good you and Keegan killed the poison before it reached your heart and your head."

"She was going to take me through the portal in the waterfall. How would she get me through?"

"I haven't heard of her back in Talamh since we shuttered it. It must have taken her years to work a spell. She's from here," Marg added. "So that would help her. There are other portals, of course, all closely guarded. Still scouts slip through, as did the one Keegan killed when we visited Eian's grave."

"She came alone," Harken pointed out. "If she went through the waterfall, she couldn't bring soldiers with her, that tells me. I'll be taking myself off there, seeing if I can shore up whatever chink she managed."

"Don't go alone. Don't," Aisling insisted.

"What little faith you have in me."

"I'd say the same to any, you blockhead. Go with two others to make three."

"The witch rides with a faerie and a were," Breen said. "An elf and a troll will come through the green wood. And with wood, stone, light, and magicks, the five close the door again."

Breen slumped back, stared at the faces around her. "What was that! I could see it. You and Morena and a man who becomes a bear. A woman who comes out of a tree, a troll with a stone axe."

"A vision." And Marg smiled at her.

"I don't have visions. I mean, I have dreams, and they can be lucid. And I get flashes like anyone, but—"

"Not like anyone at all."

"Likely it is when you joined power with Keegan it gave you a bit of a boost. Would you like more tea?" Aisling added.

"No, no, I'm fine. It was like being there, watching, but through a curtain, a thin curtain."

"The curtain will lift with time," Marg told her. "Now I think you need some rest. You've had a trying time of it."

"Not rest. Practice. I need to learn more, and get better at what I learn."

"All right then." With a nod, Marg rose. "We'll practice."

When they'd gone, Aisling put a hand on Harken's arm. "What does she feel? You looked, I'm sure, out of concern, to be sure—as I needed to be about her body—that her mind was clean and clear. But you saw what you saw."

"I did." He strapped on the sword he rarely wore. "And while clean and clear it was, she's caught between fear and fascination just as she's caught between Talamh and the world she's known. Her loves, her loyalties, her needs, her doubts, they tangle inside her like vines."

He put on his cap, his jacket. "There's naught for us to do about it, Aisling. She'll make her choices when she makes them."

"I could bash your head for your patience alone."

"And it would still be what it will be." He kissed her cheek. "Now I need to saddle a horse and go fetch Morena, and I think it must be Sean she saw in her vision. If Mahon and Keegan aren't back, stay for supper."

"Cook it, you mean."

"Well, of course," he agreed in his cheerful way. "But I enjoy the company and the children as well as the food."

She gave him a swat as he walked to the door. "And when will you finally ask Morena to wed you so she'll cook your supper?"

"She's a terrible cook, as you know very well. And I'll be asking her when she is ready to say yes, and not before."

"Why not give her a bit of a push?" Aisling wondered when he shut the door. Then she sighed, said, "Blessed be, brother," and walked back to the window to look out on her children.

She'd kill for them. She'd die for them, she thought as she folded her hands over the life growing inside her. Now she could only hope Breen would fight for them, and all the children in all the worlds.

CHAPTER TWENTY-TWO

She worked and practiced until moonrise. She ate, and gratefully, the roast beef and vegetables Sedric prepared. Though Marg urged her to stay, Breen insisted on going back to her cottage.

She wanted the space, the quiet, and she wanted to sit down and write out every detail about what had happened.

Writing it down would help her remember those details so, hopefully, she wouldn't make the same mistakes again.

When she settled into bed with Bollocks curled in front of the fire she could now light with a thought—progress!—she started to put rosemary under her pillow.

Then, thinking of the vision in the farmhouse kitchen, she set it aside. Maybe it was time to welcome dreams, whatever they might hold.

So she dreamed again of the black castle with its walls like glass, of the stony island on which it rose, and the raging sea below the sheer cliffs.

The god stood on a wide balcony on the topmost tower. His black cloak swirled as he threw dark bolts of light at the sky and sent it to boiling.

His eyes gleamed with rage, his face a mask of fury.

From that boiling sky rain, sharp as arrow tips, fell. On the ground below and on the cliffs, those who served him screamed and scattered and sought cover from the lethal storm.

Some the arrows pierced and burned through like acid. Some the whirling wind lifted up and tossed into the thrashing sea.

Buildings that had begun to rise again from the rubble on the cliffs toppled and crashed.

And still, Odran's wrath did not abate.

Yseult stepped out. The gale whipped at her bloodred hair, at the gown of the same color. In the dream, Breen could read the fear in her eyes no matter how she tried to hide it.

"My king, my liege, my all."

He spun around, clamped his hand around her throat, and lifted her off her feet. She didn't resist. Though the fear spiked, she didn't resist.

"You failed! You were to bring her to me. Why should I not hurl you into the sea? Why should I not see your body break on the rocks?"

Instead, he threw her onto the floor of the balcony. Breen saw pain mix with the fear, but Yseult gathered herself to kneel at Odran's feet.

"All the power I own is yours to command. I would hurl myself onto the rocks if you command it. She has more than we believed, more rising up in her than we knew. But my king, my lord, this knowledge is to your benefit."

"It would benefit if you fulfilled your duty."

"More has awakened in her. When you have her, you won't have to wait, not long, to drink her powers. She will become much sooner than we believed. And when you drink her dry, on that glorious day, no door will be locked to you, no world will be barred against you."

She bowed her head. "My king, my liege, my all, I am loyal only to you. I have forsaken all oaths but my oath to you. With the black magicks, I joined with you, with the blood of seven virgins, I helped you restore your castle. And I will fulfill my oath to help you rebuild your glorious city, to help you take your throne above all gods, above all worlds, and crush to dust any who go against you."

She lifted her head. "I beg you, Odran the Incomparable, not to take my life in anger. If you must have my death, let it be taken in cold blood, with cold mind, and on the altar of sacrifice so my death will serve you beyond my life."

He studied Yseult, gray eyes—like Breen's father's, like her own— calculating. "You would go to the altar willing, witch?"

"My life is yours to use, to take, to do with as you wish. As it has been since I took my vows to you in blood and smoke."

"Rise." He flicked a hand at her, turned. The killing rain ceased, and the wind died. He stood, his gold hair shining to his shoulders. "It's not your loyalty I doubt, but your skill. You disappoint me, Yseult."

"I have no deeper regret."

"Send a slave with wine—a comely one. And see the mess below put to order again."

"As you wish."

She slipped back inside.

Odran stepped to the wall, gazed out across the sea.

For a moment, one terrible moment, it seemed his eyes locked with Breen's. She saw something in his—quick surprise, dark satisfaction.

And woke shivering as if dipped in ice.

She grabbed her tablet, wrote it all down.

And put the rosemary under her pillow.

In the morning she managed to write a blog, focused on the garden. Everything bright and cheerful and full of pretty pictures.

She started back on her book and made a little progress because she introduced an evil witch who wore a magickal pendant of two-headed snakes.

Later, she'd bring in the live ones, but she wasn't ready for that yet. In any case, she couldn't keep her head in the story, not when it wanted to go back to the dream, or the fog, or the intensity in Keegan's eyes when he'd helped her heal.

He'd felt the pain, too, she realized. That scorching, inhuman pain. And still, he hadn't pulled away.

"*Misneach*," she murmured, laying a hand over her wrist. He had courage.

Some time on her own, she thought. She needed that to contemplate whether she had more than the word over her pulse.

To let her mind clear, she decided to shut down early and take care of some household chores she'd neglected.

She started some laundry before driving to the market in the village. That reminded her she'd gotten so used to how life worked in Talamh, the Irish village seemed like the other world.

With laundry done, groceries put away, the garden weeded, she checked her email before leaving for her afternoon with the Fey.

"Oh my God."

She read the email, pushed up. She walked around and around the room in a way that had Bollocks racing in and out.

She read it again, standing up.

"Oh my God! Stop, stop, stop. Don't get so excited. It's just the next step. Oh, hell with that! I'm so excited."

When Bollocks jumped up to lean on her, she grabbed his front paws and danced. "The agent wants to see the whole manuscript. She didn't say don't ever contact me again, you pitiful excuse for a writer. No, no, she said she loved the first chapter and synopsis I sent her, and wants to see the rest!"

She had to walk outside, breathe, dance with the dog again.

Then she made herself sit down, write a response she read over three times to make certain it was professional.

"Okay, here goes!"

She attached the manuscript to the email, then just sat.

"Hit send, for God's sake! Just hit send."

She looked at the dog, who'd laid his head lovingly on her thigh. "I wish you could do it. But you can't. So . . ."

She hit send and then breathed again. "Okay, we've got to get out of here or I'll sit and obsess about this all day."

She obsessed about it on the walk, then firmly locked it in the back of her mind. If she thought about it, she'd end up telling someone about it. She didn't want to tell anyone, not yet.

Not even Marco.

She went straight to her grandmother's. She didn't bring up the dream, not yet, because it would distract from the work she wanted to do.

She had to get better, faster.

She spent two hours spell-casting, even the one she'd written herself.

After she'd cleaned the cauldron and tools, set the crystals out for charging, she sat with Marg over cups of tea and the biscuits Sedric put on a plate warm from the oven.

"These smell amazing."

"Lemon biscuits," Sedric told her. "Finola sent fresh lemons."

"Taste amazing, too." She studied the cookie. "I've never baked cookies."

"How can that be?" Marg demanded. "They're baked for Yule—for Christmas—this is tradition. And for the jar for children."

"My mother doesn't bake, and she didn't approve of me eating sugar. We'd sneak off to the bakery sometimes," she remembered. "Da would take me to the bakery. I used to wonder why he so often let her have her way. I understand that better now."

She thought of her excitement and joy on reading an email from an agent. Of the magicks she'd practiced in the afternoon.

Of the dream of storms and dark gods.

"He lived in two worlds, and felt guilty for it. He couldn't give her, or me, all of himself, because he owed a duty to Talamh. And because he had to protect me."

She got up to take the papers she'd folded into the pocket of her jacket.

"I had a dream last night—or a vision. I wrote it all out. I think it's clearer if you read it instead of me trying to tell it."

She sat again. "Please," she said to Sedric. "You can read it with Nan. I understand what you are to each other. I don't remember, but I feel these aren't the first lemon cookies—biscuits—you've made for me."

"You always favored them."

He sat beside Marg, a hand on her shoulder, as they read what Breen had written.

When they'd finished, Marg folded her hands over the pages. "She's wily, is Yseult, offering herself in sacrifice. She would know when his mind cooled, he'd understand he needs her skill and power. But in the end, they'll betray each other for more. It's their nature. She betrayed her people, her vows, as he did. There is no loyalty in either."

"She was afraid of him. I felt it."

"As she should be. And she overrates herself. That and her thirst for the more will be her undoing. As it was his," Marg added. "They are much the same creature."

"He saw me, in that moment before I woke. How could he?"

"You're connected by blood. You opened yourself, seeking to see, and so gave him a moment to see in return. But the power was yours, the control was yours. You need to take care to keep it."

"He wants you." Sedric spoke now, choosing his words carefully. "For what you are, the mix of you that offers him the unique and powerful, even more than your father."

"Because of my mother—human and from outside. I know you said I was the only one, but there have to be others who—"

"There is no other with the blood of the outside, the blood of the Fey—both the Wise and the Sidhe—and the blood of the gods. You are the only," Sedric told her, "in all the known worlds. And you are the only with his blood in you. You offer him the way to rule or destroy Talamh, the world of your mother. And with those, more still."

"By draining me. Like a transfusion."

"Your power, your light, your life."

"He will never have you. *Mo stór*, from the moment of your birth we've protected you. We will never stop."

"My father, Keegan's father, how many others died to protect me? You brought me here, gave me the means to find you, so I'd learn how to protect myself."

"You've done well," Marg began.

"With the magicks, pretty well. Because I like it. With the rest? Not so much, really, because I don't like it. That has to change."

And would, she promised herself. Starting now.

Keegan brought the swords to the near field he'd designated as training ground. He saw her walking up the road from Marg's cottage.

One thing could be said about Breen, he thought. She was prompt, always.

Clumsy with a sword she was, and he feared she would ever be. Pitifully easy to fell in a physical battle. But she was reliably timely.

She'd tied her hair back in a horse's tail, but there was simply too much of it to fully contain. She wore the pants that molded her legs and hips, and would provide ease of movement, and an open jacket though the day was warm and bright.

Why, he wondered, when the woman moved with true athletic grace in a walk did her feet turn into leaden clumps whenever they sparred?

A mystery, he thought. She had many of them.

The dog reached him first, as ever thrilled with a rub before he raced off to devil the sheep and horses.

Keegan started to speak, but Breen took papers from the pocket of her jacket and thrust them out to him.

"Read this first."

With that, she strode off to watch the horses in the paddock.

She'd written down the dream in a way that brought him into it so he smelled the burning flesh and hides of Odran's supplicants and slaves.

The sulfur on the wind, the turbulent crash of the sea.

The fact he could all but taste Yseult's fear brought him deep satisfaction.

Refolding the papers, he walked to her.

"You let him see you."

"Not on purpose."

"You had the reins," he said.

Unlike her grandmother, she thought, Keegan wouldn't soften things. She'd let him read her dream because she needed the hard from him.

"I understand that now, but I didn't. And I thought—I believed I understood what he wanted from me and why. But I didn't, not really. Not enough. I do now. And I understand, after I was born, my father was more obstacle than prize to him. So he killed him. My father died to protect me. Yours, too. So many others. I understood that in my head, but it didn't reach my gut until now. It's a lot to take in, in one summer, so I think I'm entitled."

She took the papers back and put them into her pocket. "Sedric said I was unique. God, I used to long to be special in some way. In any way. Now if that's what I am, it's not all bright and shiny. It's a burden, and a responsibility."

She turned to him. "I'm pretty good at responsibility, and doing things I don't really want to do because they're expected of me. That ought to be a decent foundation for all of this."

She took off her jacket, hung it over the fence, and stood in a black T-shirt that showed off strong arms.

"So, you have to push me harder. With fighting—defense, offense. And teach me how to focus and channel what else I have. It can't just come when I'm pissed off. That didn't help me with Yseult yesterday."

"You were bitten."

"Before that."

He disliked making excuses for anyone, but in this, he felt, she earned them. "She bespelled the fog. Like a drug."

"Then I should've recognized that, and had some way to fight back."

He nodded. "Aye, you should. You do. You don't wield it well."

"It's your job to teach me how to wield it well." She marched back, picked up her sword. "Do your damn job."

He tried, and failed to turn his smile into a sneer as he went back for his own sword. "And so now it's myself who's lacking."

"I've been a crap teacher, so it's easy to recognize another."

He cocked his head, considered he was thought of as one of the best trainers in Talamh. But not, apparently, when it came to her. So he'd try another way.

"When you walk, you walk with confidence, with grace. You have strength in your body, good limbs. Then you pick up a sword and you're clumsy, awkward."

"It doesn't feel natural. It doesn't feel like me."

"It's not you, but must be an extension of you or you defeat yourself, not an enemy. You had training in dance."

"Well, I had ballet lessons, but only until I was about eleven."

"Why did you stop?"

"I was . . . my mother said I'd never be more than average at best, and she couldn't afford the time or the money as a single parent."

He thought of his own mother, who would never have demeaned any of her children so. Who would have lowered anyone who had done so.

Sympathy rose up, but he shrugged. "By eleven, what you learned is in your muscles. So use it. Can you . . ." He twirled a finger in the air.

"What? Pirouette? What's the point?"

"I'm your teacher. If you argue, it wastes time. Show me." He twirled his finger again.

She already felt stupid, but started to lay down the sword and obey.

"No, with the sword."

She'd probably trip and impale herself, but she set, rose up, spun.

"Your body knows. Do it again. Good. You know more steps. Show me."

She dug them up—a little jeté, an arabesque, even a couple of fouetté turns. Boots were not ballet shoes, after all.

"So, today, combat is a dance." And now he set. "We'll dance."

He worked her hard, but this time she considered the bruises and twinges badges of honor. And once, she surprised him—and herself— by incorporating a pirouette with a sword strike, then a kick that got through and landed—without much impact—on his belly.

"You let your body think," he told her. "It's better. But now." He punched power at her enough to have her stumble back. "What do you do?"

"I don't—"

"Block!" He punched out again.

"Stop. I don't know what's not enough, what's too much."

"Block," he insisted, and shot a shock wave from her toes to the crown of her head.

It wasn't answer so much as reaction this time. She threw up her hand, and their powers met and clashed. Light flashed between them, crackling, raining sparks. It singed the air.

"Now push. You hold it. It comes from you. It is you. Push."

It built. Flowing up through her, flowing out of her, hotter, stronger. And he met and matched until her body trembled from the effort of holding force against force.

"There's a sword in my hand," he called out over the clashing powers. "I mean to kill you with it. Take it away from me."

"How? I'm pretty damn busy here."

"Take it or die." With his free hand he swung the sword in the air.

She set it on fire, hilt and all. The warring powers fell away as the sword clattered to the ground. Harken, who'd come in from the fields to watch, started to rush forward. Then stopped when Breen leaped over to grab Keegan's wrist.

"Oh Jesus, oh God." The outline of the hilt had seared into his flesh. Even as her stomach pitched, she laid hers over it.

"I'm sorry, so sorry. I—"

Before he could snatch his hand away, she gasped, went bone white. She felt the burn scorch her palm.

"Stop. Not so fast, not so deep. Look at me. Look." He cupped her chin, gently this time, to lift her gaze to his. "Ease back now. Slowly back. The light heals, but not in a flash. It goes slowly or you risk too much, take too much."

Staring into his eyes, she nodded. At first she only sensed the difference, then she felt it. The cooling, the relief, the release.

"Let me see," she murmured, and turned his palm up. "It's okay now. I set the sword on fire."

"And a fine way to disarm an opponent that is. But it's a good sword, so put the fire out."

Not so different from lighting a fire in the hearth, she thought, and put it out the same way.

"I need a break."

"You said to work you hard," he reminded her. "We have time left before you go back."

"I need a break," she repeated. "Five damn minutes. I hurt you, and that's the second time. Maybe it doesn't matter to you, in your macho, I'm-the-big-taoiseach world, but it does to me. What if I'd set you on fire? I can't do this until I learn how to control it."

Because she wanted that five damn minutes, she sat on the ground. Keegan crouched in front of her.

She'd done well, he thought, better than he'd believed she could. And there, he'd misjudged.

"I didn't think you could do it, so the fault was mine as much as yours."

"You hold back because you know how, so I end up with some bruises, but that's all."

"It doesn't give me pleasure to put marks on you."

"Could've fooled me. Not the point," she added. "I can't do this if I'm afraid of what I have. If I'm afraid I'll do something that can't be fixed or healed."

"I'm not so easy to kill. But sure we can work around this." With a shrug he sat, cross-legged. "I can train you to be more than competent with the sword, with your body."

She offered a dour look. "Is 'competent' your version of 'average'?"

"You were average at best before today. You've improved on that, and will improve more, as I am not what you said. Not a crap teacher. You must have these skills, but they aren't your true weapons. That's in you, and you know this, so you fear it. You should, for what you have, as I do, is great. If the worlds were as we wish, the light would be only for joy and beauty, for healing and help. But the worlds are not what we wish. So we use the light to protect and shield, to fight the dark, even kill.

"They would snuff us out like the light of a candle. Should we let them?"

"No. I saw—in another vision—I saw what he did. A boy, just a boy, strapped to an altar. I saw what he did. We can't let them. But you don't give a child a weapon and let them use it. That's what I am with this still. I'm a child with a weapon."

"Bugger that." He snapped it out. "You've let too many tell you you're not able or ready. That's a flaw in you." He rose, then gripped her hand and hauled her up. "But we can work around this worry and fear for now."

"How?"

"Another enemy. An opponent you won't fret about harming."

"I don't want to hurt anyone."

"Wait."

He held out his hands then drew them up, drew them down. Again and again. In the wind he called, his hair blew. Breen felt the ground beneath her feet shake.

"So here I stir the earth and air. Five drops of water they will share. Now this image I form from one who sought to harm. Come, fire, flash to bind the spell until the wraith returns to hell."

He shot out his fingers, and yes, fire flashed. Smoke followed. And when it cleared a man stood, sword in hand.

"Where did he come from? You can't just make a person."

"It's a wraith. Real enough, but not living. I gave him the face of an enemy to . . . inspire you."

"An enemy? I don't . . . It's the one who attacked me at my father's grave. You killed him."

"Do you have ears? He's an image, a wraith, not a living thing. But he can move, as he did. He can fight. He'll fade at sunset if you don't destroy him first, but he'll make a worthy training tool for you, I'm thinking.

"Do you fear hurting him?"

"No. But—"

"Then fight."

Keegan snapped his fingers. The wraith leaped.

It killed her three times before she so much as began to find any defense.

Then it got an arm around her, wings spread, lifted her off the ground. She forgot it wasn't real and, in her ripe fear, struck out. Her power hit the wraith like an axe. As it turned to smoke, she fell, breathless, onto the grass.

"There you have it." Keegan hauled her back up again. "Again."

With a flick of Keegan's fingers, the wraith formed again.

"How did you do that? You didn't use a spell."

"It's already conjured. Again."

"I want you to teach me how to do that."

"Later."

In response, she sliced a hand through the air, turned the wraith back to smoke. "Now."

Keegan's eyebrows shot up. "Well now, there's some spine there. Kill it twice more—in combat—and you'll have the edge. I'll show you how to close the spell."

"And tomorrow, you'll show me how to bring a wraith."

"Fair enough."

He watched her fight. She'd never be brilliant with a sword, but she'd do well enough. Aye, well enough there. And now that she held back nothing, she showed a confidence she'd lacked, a grace that suited her. She was very nearly formidable in her odd and interesting way.

The focus, the control, well, they'd work on it, wouldn't they? And for Talamh, for the Fey, and in honor of her father, he'd take her to formidable and beyond.

CHAPTER TWENTY-THREE

For three days Breen worked from dawn till moonrise, starting her writing day earlier and earlier to give her more time in Talamh.

Staying at her grandmother's might have been an easier choice, but she opted for the harder, for the time away and alone. For time in both worlds.

Her father had made that choice, too, and now she knew just how wrenching that had been for him. He'd given up so much for her, and still he'd honored his duties to the Fey.

She wouldn't do less. She wouldn't be less.

And if she kept rosemary and an additional charm bag under her pillow to avoid the dreams and visions, she considered it simple practicality.

Without some decent sleep, she couldn't do the work she'd chosen.

So she was dead asleep at eleven forty-five when her phone rang. She fumbled for it, thought: Marco.

"Yeah, hi."

"Breen Kelly?"

Not Marco. Now, heart hammering, she fumbled for the light. Someone was hurt; something was wrong.

"Yes."

"This is Carlee Maybrook with the Sylvan Literary Agency. I hope I'm not disturbing your evening."

"No. No. Hello." She didn't have a clue what to say next. "It's nice of you to call."

"I just got out of a meeting, and wanted to contact you right away. I, and the Sylvan Agency, would very much like to represent you."

"Sorry, what?" Her stomach flipped; her skin began to tingle. "You would?"

"I loved *Bollocks's Magic Adventures*, and I'm confident I can place it with the right publisher. I'm hoping you'll tell me you've got more coming. You've got a series, Breen, and the target age group for this book loves series."

She heard about every other word through the buzzing in her ears as Bollocks, woken by her voice, got up, stretched, then walked over to plant his paws on the side of the bed and stare lovingly.

"I— You'd be my agent?"

"That's the plan on my end. I'm happy to send you a client list, answer any questions you have."

Questions? She should have a list of questions, but she could barely remember her own name.

"Can I just say yes, and thank you?"

That got a laugh. "Fine with me. I'm going to email you a contract. Read it over. Call or email me with any questions or concerns. When and if you're satisfied, sign it and send it back, and we'll get started. I'd love to see anything else you're working on."

"I started another with Bollocks, but it's only the opening of a first draft because . . . I've been writing an adult novel, a fantasy. It's not—"

"Can you send me the first couple chapters of the novel?"

Could a heart explode? Was it physically possible?

"You want to see it? Really?"

"Yes, I do. You're very talented, Breen. Your writing's fresh and fun, and Bollocks is a gem."

"Yes," Breen murmured, stroking his head. "He is."

"I want to help you build your career. I'm going to get ahead of myself for a minute. I'm confident I can pitch and sell your YA as a series with an initial three-book deal. If your adult novel shows the same fresh voice and sense of story and world-building, I'll work hard to put it in the hands of the right publisher."

"Thank you. I never really expected to get this far."

"Oh, I promise you, we're just beginning. I'll lay all this out for you in a cover letter so you have it in writing, and attach the contract. You contact me, anytime, with any questions. And send me those chapters."

"I will."

"Have a lovely evening, and we'll talk soon."

"Yes. Thank you. Bye."

She stared at the phone. "I'm not dreaming. That happened. That happened." She slid out of bed to hug the joyful dog. "Look what you've given me!" Overwhelmed, she pressed her face into the dog's curls. "You are a gem. My magic gem. My lucky charm. Who can sleep now? Let's go down, get you a treat, and send those chapters. I have to call Marco!"

She jumped up. "No, no, I might jinx it. Tell no one. It's just you and me for now, my canine muse."

She did read the contract, and in her blissful haze found every word thrilling. As she composed a cover letter she drank a glass of wine as much to help her sleep as to celebrate. She sent back the signed contract and, with a tangle of trepidation and hope, sent the first two chapters of her novel.

She'd make a trip to the village to send the hard copy of the contract, but for now, she took the rest of her wine and the dog outside.

The cool night air on her face, and her whole future rolling out in front of her like the sea.

She took the flickers of light dancing in the dark as fireflies at first, then realized they were pixies. Did they come every night after she slept? she wondered. Were they part of her guard, her protection?

She stood here, and only a mile away others danced in the dark, or slept in their beds, or rocked a fretful baby.

Two worlds, both somehow hers. How would she ever balance them?

"I have to find a way. But I'm not going to find it tonight. Come on, Bollocks. Let's try to get some sleep."

Since she only managed four hours, and it showed, she tried her first glamour—not for vanity, but to ward off questions and concerns.

She lived in the world of one moon for the morning, in the world where any magick stayed below the surface, then made her way to the land of the Fey.

"You seem distracted."

With Marg, Breen stood in the circle she'd cast. She'd brought the fire under the cauldron, selected the ingredients. And with Sedric's help—as she could barely draw stick figures—had sketched the image of the athame she would create for herself.

Some tools, Marg told her, could and should be passed on or gifted. Others should come from the one who would use it.

"Did I make a mistake?"

"Not at all, but I can see your mind go somewhere. You said you didn't dream."

"I didn't. But I didn't sleep long. I got caught up writing."

Not a lie, she thought, as she'd written the cover letter and a brief synopsis to go with the two chapters.

"You ask much of yourself."

"I do?"

"My darling girl." Gently, Marg rubbed a hand along Breen's arm. "You have your stories, and this is work. You ask me to push you harder, and I have. You ask Keegan to train you harder, and he does. I know this, as Morena spends time watching your training."

"She's my cheerleader."

"And she tells me you've improved there, but at a cost. You should take a day for joy."

"This gives me joy, what you've taught me gives me joy. I can't claim joy from my sessions with Keegan, but I'm getting some satisfaction from them. I destroyed two wraith demons yesterday. One at a time, but I got them."

She hesitated, then spoke her mind. "That part of it—the

fighting—it still feels surreal. Like a hard, physical game I don't especially like playing. But this, what I do with you? It's as natural as breathing to me."

"Then breathe, *mo stór*, and do the spell."

A complex one, Marg had warned her, requiring precision and concentration.

Pushing everything else aside, she quieted her mind, opened her heart. It did come naturally now, like the rain, like the sun. And she prized it.

"First the silver mined from the deep by trolls who go where dragons sleep." She slid seven balls of it into the cauldron. "And out of seven will form one.

"For light and strength crystals charged by the moons, and for wisdom three stone runes. Now mix and merge in my cauldron. A feather from a dove, the symbol of peace, and for beauty heather from the heath. Bubble and swirl what I have begun."

She stepped back to pick up her grandmother's athame.

She felt out of herself, beyond herself, and yet more centered in herself than she could remember.

"Rise smoke, rise white to carry my words into the light. A single drop of my blood to bind this spell, and three times I ring the bell. And last this image I desire I cast into the blessed fire. Burn bright in the light, and so my spell is done.

"What comes I will use faithfully. As I will, so mote it be."

She circled the cauldron three times, then extinguished the fire.

"You glow." Tears, ripe with pride and love, thickened Marg's voice. "From the power, but, aye, from the joy. Take what's yours, child of my child, child of the Fey, blood of my blood. And know you have proved yourself this day."

Breen reached into the cauldron, drew out the knife. The ogham script—COURAGE—ran down the blade, and on the hilt, in the center circle of the fivefold symbol, a single dragon's heart stone glinted red.

"It's beautiful. I never thought about a knife being beautiful, but it is. It feels like mine."

"As it is."

Still riding on the spell, Breen turned the knife in her hand. "Nan, there's a dragon carved on the back of the blade. We didn't sketch that. Did you add it?"

"I didn't, no." Laying a hand on Breen's wrist, Marg studied the dragon in flight. "A gift from the gods. You did very well. Come, close the circle. You'll have a meal before you go to Keegan."

Then Marg hugged her, held her. Breen felt not only centered but loved.

From the sublime to the painful, Breen thought as she walked to the farm. She paused, one hand on Bollocks's head, to look up, watch the hawk soar.

She could feel Bollocks vibrate under her hand, could hear him think: Don't stop. Let's go. Dogs, kids, fun.

"Go ahead." She gave him a rub. "I'll catch up."

A pair of dragons glided overhead, one burnished silver, the other spring-leaf green. Both carried riders. She found she could envy them the flight even while being grateful her feet stayed on the ground.

As she watched, Morena walked down to meet her.

"They're so incredibly beautiful."

"And brave with it. Scouting now. It looks like Deaglan and Bria Mac Aodha—you'd say Magee. Twins they are. You wouldn't have seen them about before, as they live nearer the Capital than here. And how did it go with your nan today?" she asked as they started walking.

"It was amazing, especially the last part. I made an athame." She drew it out of the sheath on her belt. "I was going to leave it in the workshop, but Nan said I should carry it with me for a day. Sort of a bonding."

"Of course. You conjured this?"

"About an hour ago. I'm still feeling a little rush."

Morena shook her head when Breen offered it. "For the day, it should only know your hand. It's brilliant, that's the truth. What's more is most don't succeed in this level of alchemy until they've had years of study and practice."

She gave Breen an assessing look. "You should be very proud, as no doubt Marg is."

"I'm more just really happy. I've had an amazing day. Now you can come watch me be taken down several pegs."

"I wouldn't be sure of the pegs, as you're holding your own well enough. But I can't watch today. For one I saw Keegan saddling horses, so I'd say you're riding somewhere. And for another I promised Harken I'd help him shear the next round of sheep. Gods help me. Never give a promise to a man when you're still all soft and warm and tingly under him."

"I'll keep that in mind, should I ever have the opportunity again."

Morena elbowed her. "I told you before, you could all but have your pick."

"By the time Keegan's done with me every day, I don't have the energy for tingly. Good luck with the sheep."

"Ha!"

They split off, Morena toward the fields, Breen toward the stables. She didn't get far before Keegan walked the two horses in her direction.

"You need more riding practice."

"Hello to you, too, and I'm happy to take a ride." She greeted her usual gelding with a rub as Bollocks joined them. "I've missed riding."

"We'll see if you say the same after today." He held out a sword belt. "You have to learn to fight and defend on horseback as well."

"Oh." The anticipated pleasure took a dive, but she started to strap on the sword.

"What's this?" He tapped the sheath.

"The reason you can't possibly spoil my day. I made my athame this afternoon."

At the crook of his finger, she took it out. Like Morena, he didn't touch it but took her wrist to turn it, study all sides.

"You did the spell yourself?"

"Not the sketch. I can't draw worth crap, so Sedric did most of that, but the rest, yeah. Except the dragon. That wasn't on the sketch, but it's on the blade."

"Then it's meant to be." He shifted his gaze from it to her face. "It's good work, more than good. You chose your symbols well."

He mounted, waited for her to sheath her knife and do the same.

"If you don't have anywhere really specific, could we ride to the ruins—the Pious? My father's grave. I haven't been back since that first day."

"It's as good a ride as any."

"If we're going to work with a wraith, I'd like to try to conjure one myself. I feel like I'm on a streak."

"We'll see about it."

"I saw the dragons and riders," she continued as they walked the horses to the road. "Morena said they were scouts."

"So they were." He'd had a talk with them before they'd headed east. He'd have to do the same himself, and Mahon with him, before much longer.

That not only took Aisling's man, the father of the children, away, and while she carried another, but left the work of the farm solid on her and Harken's shoulders.

It troubled him, and always did. Always would.

"Morena's helping Harken shear sheep. Do you—"

"Less talk, more riding." Merlin leaped into a gallop.

She rolled her eyes, but followed.

A lot different from bumping along in a cart behind a plodding horse, she thought. While speed held its thrill, he gave her no time to enjoy the scenery, and she worried Bollocks would fall too far behind.

"We have to slow down. The dog's following, and we're too fast for him."

"Tell him where we're going."

"I don't remember how to get there."

"Bloody hell, woman." He slowed, but only to a canter. "Put the image of the place in his mind. He's been there with Marg, he'll find his way."

"I don't know how you expect me to do so much at once." She put the dog and his welfare first, slowed to a walk. When he caught up, she brought her memory of the graveyard, the big stone ruin, the field of sheep, all she could bring back into her mind, then pushed it toward Bollocks.

He wagged that skinny whip of a tail, and trotted off in his happy way ahead of her.

"It might be too far for him to walk. I should've stopped at Nan's, left him with her."

"Gods, woman, he's descended from demon dogs. There's no need to coddle him. And there, you see, he's cutting time and distance by leaving the road. No fool is he. Now use your knees, take the reins in one hand, and draw your sword."

When Keegan drew his, she came perilously close to one of her old panic attacks. "No, wait."

"An enemy doesn't wait, but looks for weakness. And that's what you're showing. Defend!"

He killed her before she unsheathed her sword.

"Reins with your left, sword in your right. Again."

She got the sword free, but dropped the reins. Keegan had them back in her hand with a flick of his.

"I want to learn how to do that. How did you toss them back up?"

"I willed it. Stop talking and defend. Use your knees to guide the horse."

She tried, even managed a weak block, but the strike skewed her balance, and nearly dumped her off the horse. But she felt the push of air, like a shove of a hand, right her again.

She wanted to ask how he'd done it, but she couldn't catch her breath. And he killed her again.

She sat, winded, under a pretty summer sky, trying to shake her hair out of her eyes while Keegan scowled at her.

"Pitiful. Your seat, your sword arm, your focus. Your horse is a weapon as well, but you don't use him. Ah well, we've given the dog a bit of a lead, so we'll go on."

Sheathing his sword, he turned his horse, then left her in his dust.

She started to complain. She'd only learned to ride—at all—a few weeks before. And she'd first picked up a sword after that.

But it reminded her time was running out. The summer wouldn't last forever.

Incensed, she stretched her mount into a gallop. She'd never have caught the stallion, but Keegan slowed his pace just enough.

See how you like it, she thought.

She gathered the reins, drew her sword.

"Defend!" she shouted.

Later, she'd admit she caught him completely off guard, and still his sword all but leapt into his hand. With the reins in her hand she punched out—but with power.

It knocked his sword back just enough for her to follow through with her own.

He had a hell of a grin for a dead man, she thought, and wanted to curse him for it as he made her want to grin back.

She liked the power of being pissed off.

"Much less pitiful," he told her.

Far from mollified, she shot her sword home, and rode ahead.

"You've gone beyond the turn!" he called out, and she heard the laughter in his voice.

"Bollocks, bugger it, bloody hell," she muttered. And with her exit spoiled, turned her horse around and followed him.

She died three more times on the journey, once to the cheerful applause of a towheaded toddler bouncing on his mother's hip.

It touched her to see the dog lying beside the garden she'd helped plant over her father's grave. He sat up as they approached, but stayed beside it.

"I'll take the horses to the stream. They'll want water, and you'll want some moments alone with your father."

First the grin, now simple kindness. Any hope of rebuilding her temper faded.

"Thanks." She dismounted, handed him the reins.

"This area's well patrolled now, so you should have no worries."

"All right."

"But don't be pitiful. Come with me then." He snapped his fingers at the dog. "And you'll have yourself a swim."

So he left her by the grave with the flowers blooming, a lovely carpet spread in front of the stone.

For a moment she stood in the light breeze gathering herself, and her thoughts.

"I know more of what you did and why. A lot more. I'm learning from Nan, and I won't give up that part of me ever again. The part you gave to me. I wish I could talk to you, really talk to you the way we used to. I understand why you didn't tell me, but now that I know . . ."

Crouching down, she traced her fingers over his name.

"You had your heart in two worlds. I think—no, I know it's the same for me now. And duty, on both sides."

Straightening, she looked up, the stones in the grass, the hills rising. She could hear the wind whisper through the grass, rumble through the ruin where the Pious had once walked.

She heard sheep bleating, and Bollocks's happy bark.

"You would never have left here if not for me. Your heart was never on the other side, but I was. God, I don't want to let you down. I'm going to try with all I am not to let you down.

"I love you," she whispered. "I miss you. I'm not the only one," she said as she looked over toward the stream where Keegan stood, his back to her while the horses drank.

She walked through the grass, around the graves, past the ruin that made her spine tingle.

She glanced toward the old building, toward the opening. A wide one, she noted, and imagined the two thick doors that had once closed it off.

Closed what walked there in.

Something still walked there—she felt that in her bones.

She kept her distance as she made her way to Keegan.

"I'll take the horses now. You'll want some moments, too."

He said nothing at first, just looked at her in that way he had. Straight on and searching. "I do, aye. Thanks for that."

He handed her the reins. "There's a buck, a big one, twelve-pointer, through the trees there toward the south a bit. He might move enough for you to spot him. He's a beauty."

He knew that tingle in the spine near the ruin, as he'd felt it many times before. As he knew the whispers that sounded through the archways, along the curve of stairs.

He knew the pulse, like a thick heartbeat, in the air.

And sometimes, some trembling times, through that pulse came the screams of the tortured, and the unanswered pleas for mercy.

Another day he might have gone in, taken Breen with him. To see what she felt, what she heard.

But not this day.

He saw though the sky held clear, clouds and gray gathered up in the north. There'd be a storm that night.

He wouldn't mind it.

He sighed as he looked down at Eian's grave.

"She's doing better than I believed she would. A ways to go, for certain, but she's doing better. Better yet when she remembers she has a spine and a spirit. I remember her mother, but I think the one who reared her on the other side became a different sort. I'm sorry for that—for you, for Breen, but that's what we have, isn't it?

"Gods, Eian, I'd give a limb for your counsel. The bloody politics could make a sane man mad as a hatter. Thank those gods for my mother and her cool and clever head. I'll need to take your daughter to the Capital when she's ready. And what they'll make of her I couldn't say."

He glanced over to where she stood, as he had, with her back to the graveyard.

"She's full of twists, your daughter. It seems to me the power in her's ripe one minute, green the next. But I can tell you she doesn't stop. Once she's stepped to the line, she keeps going, so there's that."

As Breen had, he crouched, traced a finger over Eian's name.

"I can't fail you—my greatest fear in the world is failing you. I give you my oath, taoiseach to taoiseach, man to man, Fey to Fey,

THE AWAKENING   331

I'll give my life to protect her. And not only because she's the key in the lock, but because she's yours."

Rising, Keegan slid his hands into his pockets before he said the rest. "She's beautiful. I've tried not to notice, but I've eyes in my head, after all. When that spirit flashes, she's more beautiful than any I've known. So, well, there you have it.

"Be at peace."

He walked back to Breen.

"I saw the buck," she said without turning around. "He's magnificent. It made me wonder how you know it's a buck or a were in deer form."

"Fey recognizes Fey, and none would nock an arrow till they looked. Those from outside who live among us only hunt with a Fey beside them. This is the law."

"And you make the laws."

"The council makes the laws, and the taoiseach is part of the council. The law such as this has held for a thousand years, and will hold a thousand more. But we're not here to talk politics and policy. We're here to train. The field across the road will suit."

When he took the reins to lead the horses, she fell into step with him. "If I don't know the laws, I might break one."

When he turned his head, she thought she saw amusement rather than impatience. Maybe.

"Do you intend to kill someone who is not an enemy of the light? Or take what's not yours? Cause deliberate harm to someone or their property? Force yourself on another? Will you misuse an animal?"

"None of those are in my current plans. Is that it?"

He used stones to weigh the reins, leaving the horses free to crop at the grass on the side of the road. "There are laws within the tribes recognized by all. The casting of a spell, the use of magicks to cause harm, to steal, and so on."

"What are the punishments?"

"They should befit the offense."

"But how do you decide?"

He didn't sigh or curse, as he might have liked to do. Because she'd been in the right. She needed to know.

"For most minor issues—squabbles between neighbors, craftspeople, lovers—I would hear them, or my mother who stands for me would hear them, and judge."

"And for serious issues? For rape or murder?"

"We're a peaceful people." He looked out across the fields and saw a young boy and his dog herding sheep. "Such offenses are rare. So rare I have never held a hearing or made a judgment on them. And I thank the gods for it, for the punishment is banishment. If my judgment is guilty, they're sent to the world of dark. Some say death is kinder. They may be right."

"Did my father ever banish anyone?"

Impatience eked through. "Why don't you know this?"

"Because no one tells me." She kept her eyes on his. "Will you?"

Keegan gestured to the wall, then sat himself. He watched the boy and the dog and the sheep. The breeze carried the boy's song, sweet and clear.

"This is who we are." He nodded toward the boy. "Tending the land, the animals, each other. Honoring our gifts and embracing the light. But there are some who harbor darkness within. After you were taken, after you were brought home again, we learned Odran had help. Yseult and three others. Two tried to hide in plain sight—you know this meaning?"

"Yes."

"When their complicity was discovered, they were held while your father and those he chose pursued the others. Yseult and the third fled. She escaped, but the third Eian hunted down."

"He—he killed him?"

Keegan looked at her, cocked his head as he heard the horror in her voice clear as bells.

"I have no doubt the temptation for that was great. But he was taoiseach, and he held the law. It's said the man—Ultan was his name, and you'll find no one who carries that name since—surrendered. It may be—it surely is—that no one would have faulted the taoiseach if he'd ended Ultan's life, but Eian O'Ceal-laigh held the law."

How odd and wonderful, Breen realized, to sit here on a stone wall in sunlight and summer breezes with a man who carried a sword as others did a briefcase. To hear his voice, often so abrupt, slide into the music of storytelling.

And the story he told was hers. Hers and her father's.

"What did he do—my father?"

"He brought Ultan back, and to the Capital, where they held the trial for the three captured. Because my father was killed, and these three were complicit, my mother took us to the trial, to show how justice and the laws worked."

Widowed, Breen thought, with three young children. Grieving, surely grieving. "It must've been hard for her. Painfully hard for her."

"She's strong, my mother. And wise with it. It helped to see the taoiseach in the Chair of Justice, to hear the words, to watch the laws work.

"Two begged," he continued, "and wept, and claimed they'd been bespelled. But there are ways to find the truth of that, and these were lies. Ultan, a believer in the radical wing of the Pious, remained defiant. Odran was a god, and as a god, was the true ruler, the true law. And the child—you—his to do with as he wished. You were an aberration, the mix of many, neither pure nor natural."

"Is that how they think? The Pious?"

"It's how many of them came to think." He looked back at the ruin. "And those who didn't believe as they believed they killed, tortured, enslaved, all in the name of the gods—whichever god suited them. It's a bloody and shameful mark on our history, and most are gone, have been gone for hundreds of years. A story for another day."

"All right. Did my mother go to the trial?"

"Eian brought her, and you, to the Capital for safety, but she remained secluded with you in her chambers."

"Not like your mother," Breen murmured.

"I know no one like my mother but herself." He smiled a little as he said it, and Breen saw love.

"And so the trial lasted a full week, for the crimes and the punishment were dire. We had rooms there in the castle as well. One day your father brought you to where we stayed. I think to get you out a bit, but also to show us what our father had died for."

"How old were you?"

"Old enough to note how you clung to Eian. But you went to my mother when she held out her arms. You went to her, and you stroked her hair as if to comfort. And I remember that well, for you did give her comfort."

"I don't remember. Some things come back to me in flashes and blurs. But I don't remember any of this."

"We do," he said simply. "On the day of judgment, your father said, for all to hear, that the three had brought dark to Talamh. They had conspired with a fallen and condemned god to steal the most precious of all things: a child. Conspired to bring harm, even death, to a child when we are bound, in every way, to do all in our power to keep our children safe, to tend them in all ways, to teach them the right and the wrong, and to give them love and joy.

"By this most grievous sin of all sins, they had caused the death of good men and women and left families grieving. He looked at me when he said this, not with anger, but sorrow."

He paused a moment. "I remember that look. In it, I saw our grief was his grief, and more, sorrow for the judgment he was duty bound to give. So the three were banished, and when the taoiseach brought down his staff to seal the judgment, to end the trial, not a sound was made, not a word spoken."

The shepherd boy crested the hill and moved out of sight.

"I had thought I would feel triumph. My father had been avenged, and I would feel triumph. Instead, I felt a kind of relief, and I thought, as I looked at Eian, how hard it all was to lead, to be the one to judge. And while the judgment was right and just, I learned that day there is often no joy in the right or the just. How I would never want to sit in that chair or hold the staff."

"And now you do."

"The irony has never been lost on me." He rose. "Now you know, as best I can tell it."

"I appreciate it." She pushed off the wall. "You helped me see him, here." She looked back at the grave. "I get little flashes of him in Talamh. Carrying me over a field at the farm, playing music by the fire. But most of what I remember of him is on the other side."

"You're welcome. Now."

He started to conjure a wraith.

"Wait." Not even a damn minute to settle her emotions. "I want to conjure one."

He continued to form a gargoyle demon with teeth and claws like razors.

"Kill this one first."

CHAPTER TWENTY-FOUR

With time ticking down, Breen poured all her energy into honing her skills, learning the craft, focusing her power. Day after exhausting day.

She spent a few pleasant hours on a rainy day in Marg's workshop making charms, brewing potions and balms. The fire simmered, gold and red, the air swirled with fragrance, and her power beat like a pulse—natural and steady.

She assumed, due to the downpour, Keegan would either cancel her session or move it indoors.

Instead, she found him waiting, drenched and hatless, in the usual spot.

"You're late."

"It's raining."

"Is it? Send your dog over to Aisling's. The children would enjoy the visit."

She looked at Bollocks, who gave her hand a lick, then trotted off.

"How did you tell him?"

"I thought it."

"Good." He turned away, and carefully conjured three wraiths.

"Three at once? I can't—"

He shot a finger out to silence her. "Stop talking. They'll stay as they are as you learn. For one power, for another sword, for the third fists and feet. You choose. Choose wisely."

Resigned—though she'd hoped for the day off and a visit with Morena and her grandparents—she picked up her sword.

She had a woman, on the plump side with a pleasant face, a demon dog, and—she thought—an elf.

Since the dog worried her most, she blasted it with power as she charged the elf, took him out with the sword. But when she turned to punch out at the woman, she turned into a bear, one with long, keen claws and sharp teeth.

"Well, shit!" She punched, aiming for midbody to avoid the teeth and claws. And, like hitting a brick wall, you didn't bother the brick, but your hand hurt like fire.

"Not wisely."

Her hair, a wild, wet mess, fell in her face. Disgusted, defensive, she shoved it back. "I went after the biggest threat first, and the elf almost simultaneously because he'd be fast. That's sensible. And she looked like an aging milkmaid."

"Do you believe things are always as they appear?" He knocked his knuckles lightly on Breen's head. "You're of the Fey, but you didn't look."

"I don't know how."

"Bollocks. You knew the elf."

"I guessed . . . Or sensed."

"Knew. Now."

He dissolved the wraiths, conjured three more. All looked ordinary. Two women this time, one with gray hair and a basket of apples, one young with a white apron over a pink dress, and a man with a charming smile and thick golden-brown hair.

"Look. See. Act."

"I—"

"Quickly."

The snap in his voice jolted her, and maybe the jolt shook something loose, but she looked, saw, acted.

"Witch." She hit the old woman with power. "Were." Then took out the massive buck the man became with the sword before whirling into a kick that struck the young woman in the torso. "Faerie."

"Good."

He dissolved, then conjured, again and again. He seemed to have an endless supply.

"Good." He dissolved the last trio. "Tomorrow one will move."

Winded, dripping, she bent over to brace her hands on her knees. "Just one?"

"For now."

She'd worry about that tomorrow. Besides, arguing with Keegan wasted breath she currently couldn't spare.

"All right."

She started to put the sword down, but he picked his up. "Now, I move."

Soaked to the skin, she stared at him. "Wouldn't you like some ale by the fire?"

"I would, and will have some. When we're finished. Defend."

She blocked. Mostly, she knew, because he didn't come hard. Just as she knew that little courtesy wouldn't last.

She tried to sneak in a power hit on the side, but he blocked her, then flicked her with a shock.

Since it would've been a mortal wound, she stepped back to acknowledge it.

"I've been fighting in this stupid rain for nearly an hour already," she complained. "And you come in fresh."

"So might an enemy."

She fought. She'd never actually beaten him. Oh, she'd gotten some strikes in, when he wasn't really trying, or like when they'd been on horseback and she'd taken him by surprise.

But for the most part, her goal with him was to stay alive and on her feet as long as possible.

It would be sweet, really sweet to take him down. With skill, with cunning, with power.

She started with cunning, feigning more fatigue than she felt. Gradually, he pulled back. Blocking weakly, breathing harder than she needed to, she searched for an opening.

She struck out with power and sword at once, and knew she'd

rocked his balance. When she reared back for the killing blow, he punched back, but she blocked.

And was so thrilled, she spun too quickly, slid on the muddy ground. Cursing, she fell into him.

They both went down.

He gripped her so he hit first. Before she could think to be grateful he'd taken the worst of the fall, he rolled her over, and had his sword at her throat.

"Once again, you're dead."

"And wet, and muddy. I slipped."

"Do you think battles only happen on bright days and dry ground?"

"I've never been in a battle. I didn't used to have enemies."

"Things change." He removed his sword, but not his body. And took his sweet time considering her. "You pretended to flag so I'd hold back a bit."

"It was working until I slipped."

"You slipped because you didn't remember your feet. But it was a good ploy."

"I'm still dead. And wet and muddy."

"You're better than you were. You could hardly have gotten worse, but still better is better."

"And somehow you think that's a compliment."

"Compliments are for ballrooms and trysts in moonslight. But one I can give you? You may not have the skill or mind of a warrior, but you have the body of one. You have strength and endurance. You had both when we began, and now you have more."

And hair the rain had turned to long, wet, red ropes. Eyes gray as the broody sky and lips full as a joyful heart.

Beautiful. Not the breathtaking beauty of a Shana, but a more interesting one to his mind. A face, he thought, made to study and remember.

He studied her now, as she looked steadily back at him. Steady or not, heat rose into her cheeks—a redhead's curse, flushing them like garden roses.

She felt him, he thought, and felt that shimmering heat as well. She wondered just as he did.

"Am I alive again?" she murmured.

"You appear to be."

He started to lower his head, got a breath away from the taste of those full lips. And the shock ran along his ribs.

Now those full lips curved. "Now you're dead, wet, and muddy."

"Clever," he muttered as frustration and admiration warred. "A woman should always use her wiles, as they're a keener weapon than most blades."

"You'd be the first to ever claim I had any to use."

"You have them right enough." He rolled off her, stood, then gripped her arm to haul her up. "The rain brings the dark early. We had some enemy scouts try to break the line in the south."

"Oh."

It made it real again. All too real.

"There's no worry. We held them back, sent them back, shored it up. But I'll walk you back over nonetheless. Marg would expect it," he said before she could argue. "As would my mother. So you'll give me an ale by the fire as my reward."

"I don't have any ale."

Sincerely baffled, he stared at her. "That's a sad and pitiful thing."

"I have wine."

"That will have to do. Call your dog."

She looked over, and through the rain and gloom, saw the lights glowing in Aisling's cottage. "I've never called him from so far."

"Distance means nothing. Connection is all."

She reached out to the dog, mind to mind, heart to heart.

Time to go home, Bollocks. Come on back, boy.

She felt the click—connection. In less than a minute, she heard the familiar happy bark.

"He loves you." As he watched the dog race through the rain, Keegan shoved his dripping hair back. "He'll always hear you, always come to you."

He bounded up to greet her with licks and wags, then generously did the same with Keegan before they started for the road.

"There was a time I'd never have been caught in the rain without an umbrella—always prepared." She shook her head. "It was cloudy when I left this morning, and probably rained on the other side, but I didn't even think to grab an umbrella."

"The wet won't melt you."

When Bollocks leaped over the wall, Keegan gripped Breen by the waist and lifted her over. "The story of the evil witch with the green face."

"*The Wizard of Oz.*"

"Aye, that. The water from the pail wouldn't have melted her, but it was a good story nonetheless. Mind your feet on the steps."

"Do you have a favorite book?"

"Why a favorite when there are so many, and I haven't read all of them?" He swirled his hand and brought globes of light to the gloom of the woods.

Unsure of herself, she dug for small talk. "Let's try this. You've traveled in this world."

"I have."

"What did you like about it?"

"I liked the mountains and the vast open in your Montana, and the forests and the tall white mountains in the farther west. Here, in Ireland, I like the familiar green and quiet of the hills."

"What about things?"

"Things?" In his fluid way, he reached down for a stick, then threw it for the dog to chase. "Ah, all the books. And the music, so much to hear. I like some of the television. And pizza. This is brilliant. I had the best of that in the land of Italy, I think, and there they have art that opens the heart or twists it."

Here in the woods, the rain came as a little patter. She liked listening to his voice weave through it.

"I'm a fan of pizza myself, but of all the food in the world, that's it?"

"Ice cream, in the cone. And burritos." He shrugged. "There's much good food in this world, and many things of value. You've built great cities that have their own kind of beauty, but such noise. A constant din. You have great art, but many who covet it, and want to close it in for only themselves. And people who have kindness and generosity, who love their children, help their neighbors. But so many with such anger and greed and envy. Some with hate boiling like poison in the blood. Those who strike with violence for no cause, wars, so many at once. Rulers who clutch power, but not for the common good. None of that is our way."

"No, it's not. But some from Talamh choose to live here."

"They do. I have a cousin who lives in Paris in France. He has a bakery there, and is happy. He has a family, and has made his life there. So."

They came out of the woods. "His choice was right for him."

She led him into the house. "I just need to feed the dog."

"Check first." After taking off his dripping duster, he hung it on a peg. Then in a gentleman's gesture she hadn't expected, held out a hand for her jacket.

"He was with my sister, the children."

"Right." She looked at Bollocks, saw he'd eaten and well. "A treat then, for being such a good dog. I'll get that and the wine if you light the fire."

He lit it from where he stood and followed her into the kitchen.

"Marg did well here." He glanced around, with interest and attention. "This is a pleasant cottage, with good views and protection."

"The pixies come at night."

"Aye. You're protected here, but they watch. They'd get word to me or Marg if you needed us."

He tapped on the stove. "Do you cook on this?"

"Not really." She sighed as she gave Bollocks his biscuit. "And when I do, poorly. I was going to work on learning to cook this summer, but . . ."

"Things change."

She got out the wine, the glasses, poured. "They really do." Then she frowned at him. "Why are you dry? Even your hair."

He stepped to her, put his hands on her shoulders, and, watching her, ran them—very deliberately—down her sides, along her hips.

She felt the warmth from his hands on several levels.

"Better?"

"Um."

The phone she'd left on the charger on the counter rang. Blowing out a quiet breath, she turned away. "Sorry." She saw her agent's— her agent!—name on the display. "I really have to take this."

With another shrug he wandered into the living room and the fire to drink his wine.

He would never list phones, especially the ones people carried around in their hands, as a thing he liked. Or the smell and sound of cars. He couldn't understand why people would choose to fly in a machine, closed in. Or live in boxes stacked on top of each other.

How did anyone find any peace in their mind?

A cottage like this he could understand. It offered room, and quiet and comfort. Did she know, he wondered, that much in it had been crafted in Talamh and sent through?

He drank more wine. And when he decided she'd made him wait long enough, walked back.

She sat at the table, her head lowered to it, weeping, with the dog's head in her lap.

She might as well have stabbed him in the heart.

"No, no, there now." He nudged the dog away as he crouched down to stroke her hair. "What is it? You had hard news."

With tears streaming, she lifted her head, shook it.

At a loss, he lifted her off the chair, carried her in to the fire. "Tell me now what hurts you, and we'll find a way to fix it."

Still weeping, she pressed her face to his shoulder. "My book. I sold my book."

"Well then, don't worry. We'll get it back for you."

"No, I mean. I wrote a story and someone bought it who'll make it a book. And people will read it."

He tipped her chin up. "Is this what you want?"

"More than anything."

"Ah then." He brushed a tear away. "Full heart tears. Sit then, shed them if you must. I'll fetch your wine."

When he came back, she sat, hands clutched in her lap.

"I shouldn't have told you."

"Why?"

"I told myself, if it ever actually happened, I'd tell Marco first. My best friend, my whole life my best friend. And I'll tell him face-to-face."

"This is the one who came with you, and lived with you in Philadelphia."

"Yes. I should've told him first."

"Well, he'll be the first of this side you'll tell. It would be a pity if you didn't tell Marg so she can have the pride and joy for you. And he'll still be the first in this world you share this with."

"Yes." She knuckled a tear away. "He would be. He's the one who pushed me to write when I wanted to but didn't believe I could. And now."

She pressed a hand to her mouth. "I sold a book. Three, actually, but I haven't written the other two."

Curious—and relieved the weeping ended—he sat on the arm of the sofa. "How do you sell what you don't have?"

"You make a promise—a vow. And I—" She took a deep gulp of wine. "Hell, I might as well blab it all. I'm writing another book—for adults. The one I sold is for children. My agent—she's the one who sold the book. She represents me. She asked to see some of what I've written on it, and she likes it. It's not finished, only maybe half done, but she likes it."

She hopped up, whirled around the room. "Everything in my life has changed. Everything. This time last year I was stuck. Or I thought I was. So unhappy. So dull."

"Dull?"

"Dull," she confirmed. "Believe me. Now I'm—" She flung out a hand and lit every candle in the room. "Magick! I'm a witch. I'm a writer. And by this time next year, I'll be a published writer, and no one can ever take that away from me. No one can say it doesn't matter."

Baffled, he frowned at her. "Why would they?"

"You don't know my mother. Everything's changed. I've changed." She glowed, like the candles, as she whirled again. "Let's have pizza!"

He wasn't sure how he found his voice through what she stirred in him. "You have pizza?"

"It won't be like what you had in Italy, but it's pizza. Let's have pizza and more wine."

She rushed into the kitchen and started to yank open the freezer.

And found herself whirled around, her back against the refrigerator with Keegan's hands tense on her hips.

As the moment, the meaning shot through her, she said, "Oh."

"Quickly." His body pressed, not so lightly, against hers. "Yes or no."

"Yes or—"

His mouth came down on hers, hard and hungry. Every cell in her body erupted, a chain reaction of pleasure and panic and passion so long repressed.

He pulled back, but kept his hands on her. "I heard yes."

"I didn't exactly . . . Yes." She dragged his mouth back to hers. "You heard yes."

He swept her, literally and figuratively, off her feet. "Show me your room, put it in your head."

"Oh, it's . . ." She gestured vaguely as she mentally went up the stairs, made the turn.

No one had ever carried her to bed. No one had ever kissed her senseless in the kitchen. No one had ever looked at her as if the want for her might set the air on fire.

She started to tell him she wasn't very good at this, and rusty on top of it. But she stopped herself, let herself ride the moment.

Oh yes, yes, yes. She'd changed.

He'd find out for himself, but she'd have the moment. Hoping for the best, she pressed her lips to the side of his throat to taste his skin, to breathe in his scent.

He smelled of rain and leather, of green grass and rich earth.

Of Talamh, she realized. He smelled of magick.

When he turned into the bedroom, he glanced toward the fire. It leapt into flame as he set her on her feet by the side of the bed.

"You're an orderly soul," he noted. "All in its place."

The candles on the mantel, the nightstands, the tables sprang to life.

"I guess I am."

"I appreciate order." The window opened a few inches, and the breeze, the night, flowed in.

"You won't be cold," he told her, then ran his hands down her sides, up again over her breasts, up through her hair, down her back.

Waves of pleasure swamped her so it took a moment to realize she now stood naked.

"Not a warrior." He took the hand she instinctively lifted to cover herself. "But a warrior's body. One I want. One you'll give me."

His free hand glided over her breast, rough palm over tender flesh. "Do you wish fast or slow, *mo bandia*?"

"I don't care." As long as he kept touching her. "I don't care," she repeated, and chained her arms around his neck, fused her mouth to his.

She willed his clothes away, heard his laugh when his sword clattered to the floor. "You forgot the boots," he told her, and took care of them himself as he laid her back on the bed.

"My first magickal undressing." She ran her hands over his back, over iron muscles. A warrior's body, she thought. A warrior. A man who wanted her.

Then she thought no more as his hands moved over her.

He found soft skin, firm muscles, lovely curves, fascinating angles. He felt her pulse beat in hammer strikes as he learned her body. So easy, he realized, to discover what pleased her, what excited.

He'd wondered and wondered how she would feel under his hands, how her body would move under his, and now he knew and wanted hours of her, days of her, nights of her.

How avid her mouth in seeking his; how greedy her hands as they roamed him.

He knew her breath would catch an instant before it caught. Her quiet moan sounded in his mind before she loosed it. When his fingers, his lips made her tremble, he lingered there until tremble became shudder.

She gave herself so willingly, without pretense or guile. Showed him, so openly, she wanted him, with hands that grew more demanding, with hips that pressed her center to his until he wanted nothing but to give her all and more.

So long since she'd been touched, and never, never like this. Rough hands destroying her, and still somehow making her feel precious. The scruff of beard on his face scoring over her skin lit impossible little fires inside her.

She'd forgotten any shyness and self-doubts in the glorious, craving thirst for more.

Nothing about him was smooth or pampered or polished. And everything about him excited. When his hand skimmed over her center, the glorious shock whipped through her, ripped through her until her body quaked.

She cried out on the unbearable release, and still he didn't stop. Helpless, she wrapped her arms around him, held on, held on.

Let go.

"God. God. Keegan. Wait."

"You're strong," he murmured. His voice, thick, breathless, had her opening dazed eyes. "Take more. Take me."

He slipped inside her, slowly, almost gently at first.

She saw lights whirl around the room, saw them reflected in his eyes.

"Strong," he said again. "Soft. And, gods, the heat of you."

He began to move, and she came again, a flash of orgasm that arched her body, had her hand flying up to grip his shoulder.

"Don't stop. Don't stop."

"All the gods couldn't stop me. Ride with me now. Ride with me."

She rode, a hard gallop now, reckless and desperate and thrilling. The light pulsed, faster, still faster as the bed rocked under the flurry of speed.

They blurred, everything blurred but him as for one brilliant moment his face, so close to hers, came into sharp focus.

And all the lights spun into one, in the room, in her, in him.

As his body collapsed on hers, he buried his face in her hair. She'd gone beyond soft, like wax melted in the sun, and still her heartbeat echoed the thunder of his.

In the room, now quiet, he heard the crackle of the fire, the easy music of the wind, and Breen's long, long sigh.

"I'm heavy," he mumbled, with no intention of moving yet. "But you're strong."

He felt her hands in his hair, felt her fingers run along his tribal braid. "I wasn't expecting this."

"Then you weren't paying attention, were you? This is a flaw you should fix."

She sighed again. "I didn't think you liked me, especially. Considering how often you kill me, or insult me, or curse me."

"I don't like you on the training field because I'm to train you, so I kill, insult, and curse because you need it." He lifted his head, looked down at her, at the riot of fire curls spread over the pillow. "I like you otherwise."

"I guess that's fair, because I don't like you on the training field either, where you're a bully. But I like you otherwise."

She glanced toward the fire, where Bollocks curled on his bed, sleeping.

"Bollocks slept through it."

"A wise dog, as this was no business of his."

She smiled, looked back at Keegan. "I'm not used to this."

"To what?"

"Lying under a world leader, to start with."

"You lie under a man who wants you. Why should the rest matter?"

"I could also say I'm not used to being naked with someone so . . . built. Fit," she qualified. "Hard-bodied."

She amused him, allured him. The combination struck him as unique as she herself. "Did you choose soft, weak men for lovers?"

"Comparatively." To please herself, she pressed a hand to his chest. Yes indeed, hard-bodied. "This has been a strange and wonderful day. A red-letter day."

"I'm fond of red, it seems." He wound a lock of her hair around his finger, unwound it. "So then, can there still be pizza?"

She laughed, then hugged him in such a free and friendly way his heart tipped.

"Absolutely, because I'm starving."

CHAPTER TWENTY-FIVE

Though he hadn't intended to, Keegan stayed through the night. When you stayed and slept after mating, you added import and risk, but he stayed.

And in the morning, before the sun broke the night, they mated again. After, there was coffee—something he had only on his rare visits to the other side.

She scrambled eggs, piled them on toast, and he found it more than good enough, breaking their fast outside at the table in the weak sunlight with the dog splashing happily in the bay.

He had no complaints when he went back to his world and his duties, and she remained—for the morning—in hers.

Still, he continued hard on her in training—her life could depend on it after all. And he resisted going to her bed the next two nights, telling himself to keep some distance, and using the need to join the night patrol as a reason.

The third night he cast a circle. He worked a spell he'd devised to see through the portal, through the locks he had helped make. Odran's scouts and spies continued to push through cracks, and some, he knew, had slipped through.

If he could see through to the black castle, if he could link just enough to read the plots and plans in the black god's mind, he could better defend Talamh, and all in it.

But though the power of the spell was great, so great it all but burned in his blood, he could see only shifting shadows in the dark, only hear mutters and murmurs, and once the horrible cry of the tortured and damned.

It weighed on him as he unwound the spell, as he closed the circle.

If he couldn't penetrate the dark, if this remained out of his reach, he'd have to risk more spies of his own.

And not all came back.

He called his dragon, intending to fly out over the water and let the remnants of the spell still echoing inside him quiet.

Instead, he flew through the portal, then high over the trees to the cottage, to Breen.

Enough distance, he thought. He'd burn off the spell and his failure inside her, and sleep.

Only a single light burned in the window, one below her bedchamber, when he landed. He told himself to leave her be, to let her sleep. But he walked through the fluttering pixies and opened the locks and the door with a wave of his hand.

He stepped through, glanced back at Cróga. "Go rest where you will, *mo dhearthái*. I'll make my own way back."

The minute he closed the door, he felt her.

Sleeping yes, but with visions that brought fear and pain.

Tossing light ahead of him, he raced for the stairs and up. He found her shuddering in bed, her eyes wide and glazed. The dog stood on the bed beside her, and whined in distress as he licked her face.

"I've got her now, friend. I've got her. But bloody hell, she has to go through it. Visions come for reasons."

He knelt on the bed beside her, smoothed back her hair. "But you're not alone now, *mo bandia*." He reached for her hand so she'd find comfort when she came through it.

And found himself ripped into the vision with her.

The world, his world, the heartbreaking green of hills and fields burnt to black, with the smoke rising so thick it blocked the sun and sky.

Gray, all gray, and the stench of it like death.

Lightning, black as pitch, ripped through the smoke to turn the house of the farm entrusted to him, to his family, to smoldering rubble.

Through the blasts and roars, he heard the screams of the dying, the keening wails of the grieving. Bodies—men, women, children, animals—littered the ground with pools of their blood seeping into the scorched earth.

It ripped his heart, ripped it into pieces that would never, never be mended.

He drew his sword, pulled up his power, a power now so fueled by rage and grief, the steel in his hand pulsed red. He sliced through a demon dog who'd stopped to feast on what had been a young faerie.

Pushing himself through the smoke, he cut down a dozen with blade and fire and rage. And still they came. He fought his way to his sister's house, where even the flicker of hope died. Nothing remained but a tumble of blackened stone.

He stood, a man of power, a man of duty, and screamed out in fury that would never cool, in grief that would never rest.

Still, he could feel dim flashes of light as others fought with what they had left in them. He called his dragon, but already knew Cróga would never come to him again.

The severed bond, another grief, another fury.

Cróga was gone, as the farm was gone.

Without horse or dragon, he'd never reach the Capital, and his mother, in time to launch a defense. Even if the Capital still existed.

He pushed his way back. If Marg lived, if he could find Breen, they could join power and find a way, there had to be a way, to save what was left.

He nearly stumbled over an old couple, elves, grievously wounded, curled in each other's arms.

He tried to heal the woman first, but even as he spread his light through her, her eyes dimmed and died. When he turned to the man, the old elf shook his head.

"No. My life mate has gone to the gods. I choose to go with her. They came so fast, and the dark with them. Go, go and fight, Taoiseach. Save us."

He ran, sword slashing, power sweeping.

And hope flickered again. Though the gardens had withered black, Mairghread's cottage stood.

"Breen!" He shouted for her as he ran toward the cottage, and she stumbled out of the smoke.

Blood coated her hands, streaked her face.

"No!" She threw power at him, weakly, so weakly. "I saw you fall, I saw you die. It's just another trick. You, Nan, Morena, everyone's dead. They killed Bollocks. They killed everything."

"It's not a trick. I'm here."

As he started toward her, Odran dropped down at her back. He wrapped his arms around her, smiled at Keegan.

"You've lost, boy. This world is mine now. She is mine now."

"She will never be. Talamh will never be. Move away from him, Breen." He couldn't lash out, not with power, not with sword, or he'd harm her as well.

"I couldn't stop them."

Odran spoke close to her ear. "You're not enough. You'll never be enough."

"I wasn't enough," she said dully. "I've never been enough."

"Lies." All of this a lie, Keegan realized. Spun into visions by the dark god. "Go back to your hell. Your illusion's done."

"Soon it will be truth."

"Wake," Keegan ordered, and though enough of Odran seeped into the vision to singe along his skin, he reached out to grip Breen's hand. "Come with me, and wake."

He dragged her back, dragged both of them back.

"Dead, everyone dead."

When her head lolled, he shook her.

"No, a deception, an illusion. Cast it aside."

"He struck you down while I watched. Your blood on my hands. I wasn't strong enough to stop it."

"Lies. I'm here, aren't I?" He shook her again. "Look!"

When she did, the shuddering started. "Is this real? Are you real?"

"Aye, this is real, as I am. The rest was lies."

"They came so fast, so many. The screams, the fires, the smoke. I couldn't stop it. I wasn't enough."

"More lies. You let him see your weakness, and he used it to wind the vision. Mine as well," he admitted. "As when I joined you there, I believed. Here now, you've frightened the dog."

"Bollocks." She shifted to wrap her arms around the dog and weep. "He killed him. He just flicked his fingers and set Bollocks on fire. I couldn't save him. I couldn't save anyone."

"Stop." Keegan pulled her back. "He wants you weak, afraid, full of doubt. Will you give him what he wants so readily?"

"It felt real, all of it. What if it was a vision of what's coming?"

He didn't know, couldn't know, but gave her what she needed.

"It wasn't, and when I saw through the lies, his power broke. But you're bringing it with you now, and you mustn't. You need a potion. Where do you keep them?"

"No. I need to see."

She pushed away, ran to the window, flung it open.

"And do you see? The moon, the pixies, the shadow of the hills, how the trees move and whisper in the night?"

She nodded, and when he stepped behind her, turned her, she leaned against him. "He said everyone would die unless I went with him. He said he'd make me a queen, and I could choose the world I wanted to rule."

"More lies." He stroked her hair, but thought of the pixies who'd sent no warning.

"He found a way to close it in. I didn't feel any of his darkness until I came inside. He found a way, so we'll find a way to counter."

"I didn't use a charm or rosemary. I thought if I had a vision, a dream, something, I might learn something."

Brave of her, he thought. Maybe foolish as well, but brave. "And sure you did, and I did as well. He fears you."

She'd have laughed at that if she had a laugh left in her. "That's not what I learned."

"Then, once more, you don't pay attention, do you now? He used his powers to try to make you feel weak, then blame yourself for it.

He does this because he knows you're strong, but you have doubts. Your mother did much the same near the whole of your life because she fears you."

"She—what?"

"Think." So she'd look at him, see the truth as he believed it, he snapped her back. "She fears what you are, what you have. Her fears of you may come from fears for you—I don't know what's in her heart. But she does the same, makes you feel weak, feel less than you are and could be so you forget the power she fears, so it's buried so deep you can't find it, use it. He does this to weaken you, to damage your spirit."

After he let her go, to settle himself, he paced a moment. "If you won't have a potion, will you have wine?"

She shook her head.

"Well, I will." He put in his mind where she'd gotten the bottle, the glasses, and because he didn't want to leave her alone, brought a glass of wine to his hand.

"I could use some water."

He cocked an eyebrow at her. Coddling wouldn't help her. "See it, will it, bring it."

She sighed, closed her eyes. No point in telling him her head throbbed like a bad tooth. He'd just tell her to fix it.

When she opened her eyes again, she held a glass. An empty one.

"I got it half right."

She assumed she must have looked as bad as she felt, because he lifted a hand, tipped it down, and filled the glass with water.

"Just water?"

"Only water."

He paced, drank wine while she sat and sipped water.

"Not through the protection," he muttered. "Not through the pixies or the charms. Through you."

He stopped, studied her. "So it was only here, inside, as you were inside. Aye, this is how it's done. You said he felt you, perhaps saw you when you had the vision of the black castle. And sure, oh, aye, he devised this spell—Yseult—and he's been waiting for you to open enough to let him in with it."

"How do I stop it? Do I just use charms to block dreams and visions?"

"You could, but no." More canniness, more calculation needed here, he thought. "You'll leave a window open when you sleep, and when you're alone here altogether. It won't stop the visions, but there'll be a warning. As for the rest, denying him the control of them, I've some ideas on it. I'll work on it."

"We'll work on it, please."

"All right then." He nodded. "You've a right on it. But now, you're weary, so back to bed with you."

She didn't argue, not with her head throbbing and her body hollowed out.

When he took off his sword, she wanted to weep again. In relief. "You're staying."

"Not for mating. For sleep." Then he stopped, stared at her. "Are you thinking I'd leave you alone after you've had such a time of it?"

Avoiding the simple yes that popped into her head, she climbed into bed. "I'm too tired to think at all."

"Then sleep." The minute her head hit the pillow, he put her under. "For quiet rest," he began, and started to soothe her mind. "Ah, bugger it, why didn't you tell me you have pain?"

He soothed the headache, then sat to take off his boots. "She's a puzzle to me, friend," he said to the dog, who watched and waited. "Women are often puzzles to a man, but she's more puzzling than most to my way of thinking."

He didn't undress, but lay back to consider the ceiling and think how best to help her control her visions.

By the fire, the dog circled his bed three times, as they were wont, then settled down to sleep.

A long time passed before Keegan found his own.

They worked on a nightly spell to help Breen recognize and fight off illusionary dreams. Rain or shine, night or day, she left a window open.

She didn't think it was the curse of self-doubt telling her she'd reached her pinnacle in sword-fighting skill. She felt she'd qualify as solidly above average under most circumstances in that area. But if it ever came to actual combat, she knew she'd have to stretch high to reach the average mark.

She didn't think it was wishful thinking she'd improved—vastly—in spell-casting and other magicks, or in focus and control.

And she came to realize she had more skill in bed than either of her two previous lovers had given her credit for. Then again, neither of them had been Keegan. Undoubtedly having an exceptional bed partner made a difference.

Confidence in her writing went up, went down, but the joy of it never abated.

When she shut down after a productive morning, she sighed, content. She could see the end of the book—weeks off yet, but she could see it. And Bollocks's next adventure had started to take shape.

How lucky was she? she thought, to be able to bounce from one story to the other, from one world to the other. From one life, really, to the other.

When she started to get up, prepare for that other world, her tablet signaled a FaceTime.

Though it wasn't their usual time, she accepted the signal from Marco.

"Hey! You just caught me before I . . . went for a walk."

"I was hoping." He grinned at her. "Girl, you look fine!"

"I feel fine. It's really early for you." So early, she noted, he still wore the Spider-Man T-shirt he often slept in. "What're you doing up?"

"I couldn't wait. Breen, I think I found the house."

"The house?"

"You wanted something with some land so you could have a garden—and now you've got yourself a dog. I've been poking around at it—not real hard, but this one just sort of *boom*! It's got four bedrooms, so you could have a writing space, and maybe we could have like, a music room. A really nice kitchen, too, and that whole open-concept deal. It's not right in the city like now, but hey, a freaking acre.

"You still want a garden and all, right?"

She had to talk over the flutter in the back of her throat. "Yes."

"I can commute into work, no problemo. It's in a nice neighborhood, too—no Gayborhood, but there's only one of them. Not one of those Stepford developments or anything either. Derrick's cousin's bestie's a real estate lady, and she gave me the heads-up. It's not on the market yet. They had a deal, but it fell through, so they're juggling whatever, then tossing it back up in a few days.

"I'm gonna send you a link for the listing and pictures so you can see it, think about it, maybe talk to the money guy about it. You're going to be home in a week, so I thought, well, shit some bricks, this is like meant."

"A week." She knew that, in her head, but she hadn't said it out loud. She hadn't made it real.

"You take a look. Maybe I'm off the mark, but I think I bull's-eyed." Then he frowned. "You still want a house, right?"

"Yes. Yes, I want a house."

But where?

"Kinda ambushed you with it, I guess. I just got really juiced up. I know you've had one hell of a good time over there, but, girl, I miss you like a limb."

"I miss you, too." There, she could speak in absolute truth. "I really miss you, Marco. And Sally and Derrick, and everyone at Sally's."

"Don't you go falling in love over there."

Too late, she thought. She'd fallen in love with an entire world.

"But you should have yourself some hot Celtic sex."

"Actually . . ."

"What?" He lifted his arms, did some jazz hands. "Tell me, tell Marco all."

"When I get back." Some things, like hot sex and selling a book, needed the face-to-face.

"Just a tiny little detail. I know you, so it's just one guy. Is he gorgeous?"

"Yes, ridiculously."

"Oh, my heart and balls! Send me a picture."

"I don't have one."

"Jesus, girl, take one."

"We'll see." She had to stop talking or she'd say too much. "I need to take the dog out."

"You go on then. I'll send you that link. Seven days, my best girl."

"Seven days. I love you, Marco."

"Love you back, squared. Text soon."

She ended the call, then sat back.

Seven days.

She worked harder, studied longer, practiced obsessively. With Keegan and her grandmother she devised a spell to help her control her visions and dreams. Because it involved a potion, a charm, and an incantation, she worried about the complexity.

"You fight for the reins with a god, *mo stór*," Marg told her. "You need more than power and skill. You need faith, in the light and in yourself."

They sat, alone now, in Marg's workshop, and Breen thought how much she'd miss this, just this when she returned to Philadelphia. Just sitting with her grandmother on a quiet afternoon, doing what she thought of as elemental magicks.

She carefully mixed a potion for settling nerves while Marg finished a balm for aching joints. The air smelled of herbs and candle wax.

And peace, she thought. If peace had a fragrance, she found it here.

"I believe in the light. I've seen and done too much this summer not to."

"And yourself?"

"More than I did or ever thought I could. I know the reasons, even understand them, but I still regret and resent that I didn't know you until this summer. I didn't know myself, or Morena, Talamh, everything, everyone. I didn't know what my father was, what he did, what he did for me."

Marg sealed the lid on the balm, labeled it. "Now that you do?"

"I'm pulled in two directions, by two worlds."

With a nod, Marg rose. She set the balm on a shelf, then walked to the stove to brew tea. That, Breen knew, signaled the pause in work, the time for talk.

"You're of them both, have loyalties to both. This alone makes you unique. And troubled."

She wore a dress today, a long one in pale, pale blue with a white apron over it. With her glorious hair a curled crown, she looked like a picture in a history book. A woman out of time.

But she wasn't out of time, Breen thought. I am.

"And so," Marg continued, "will you speak with me now? The last days you've buried this trouble with work and training, but I feel it.

"You're mine," Marg said as she brought the tea to the worktable. "And I feel your troubled heart and mind."

"Nan." Breen shook her head, stared into her tea.

"The summer is ending. Soon the light changes, the spice of autumn wakes, and harvest begins. The wheel turns as it must."

"Whatever I do will hurt people I care about."

"Those who care for you will honor your choices."

Anxiety spiked in her voice and drenched her eyes. "I have to go back. I can't leave so much undone. If I'm from two worlds, I have to find the way to do what's right for both."

"But what is right for Breen?"

She would ask that, Breen realized. She would think that—and want that.

And that was love.

"I don't know yet. I have to figure it out, and there's so much . . . I sold my book. Bollocks's book."

"Oh!" Marg's face lit, and the tears that rushed to her eyes glittered with pride. "*Mo chroí!*" She reached over to grip Breen's hands. "This is the happiest of news. I'm so proud."

"You're part of it. You pushed that dog on me."

She let out a laugh, full of delight. "I did, aye, that I did, but this is yours. This comes from your heart and mind and skill, and your courage. When the time comes, we will have your book in the great library in the Capital, and I will have one here. Young Bollocks will be famed, far and wide. In two worlds."

"I want that. To write, to be read, to have my book—my books," she corrected, "in libraries and homes and schools. I want it more now than I did when I started. For that, I need the other world. I have people I love on the other side, Nan, and I can't cut them out of my life. I have to go, do what I left hanging. And I have to go to be sure."

She tightened her grip on her grandmother's hands. "But I promise you, I swear to you, I'll come back. To you, to my friends here, to Talamh. I'll come back for love and for duty."

"Your father swore the same to me, and kept his oath. I have no doubt you'll do the same."

"I will. I have two favors to ask you."

"What would I not give to the child of my child?"

"Will you keep Bollocks until I come back? I don't want to take him away from here. He's happy here, and free here. And, well, there are a lot of practical reasons why taking him with me wouldn't work."

"I will, of course. He'll miss you keenly. As I will. As all will."

A weight dropped off her shoulders. "Thank you. I just couldn't keep him in the apartment, in the city. Marco's been looking at houses . . . One of those things I left undone. Can you keep the cottage for me, for when I come back? I don't know exactly when, but—"

"My darling child, the cottage is yours. I made it for you. It will always be yours. Your dog, your cottage, and all of Talamh will wait until you make your choice. And I promise you I will never stand in the way of that choice."

She rose again. "I have a gift for you."

"You've already given me so much. You've made such a difference in my life."

"This is a gift for me as well."

She brought Breen a mirror, silver-backed with a dragon's heart stone in the center.

"A scrying mirror, your great-grandmother's. When you need me, wish to speak to me, to see me, you have only to look into the glass and call me."

Magickal FaceTime, she thought. "It's beautiful. I do need you, Nan." She stood, wrapped her arms around Marg. "And I won't let you down. I'll find a way."

"Now you must find a way to tell others who care for you as you've told me."

Breen only sighed. She didn't count on anyone else being as understanding as her grandmother.

She expected Aisling to come close—and was wrong.

"You will do what you will do," Aisling said briefly as she carried a pail of water from the well to the kitchen. "My father died so you would be free to do what you will do."

"Aisling—"

"The father of my children fights and flies to keep Talamh safe," she barreled on as she poured water into a pot. "And one day while you live on the other side where you get water from the turn of a knob and ride in the cars that foul the air, my children may be asked to do the same."

"I'm not going back for cars or water from the tap. I have obligations there, too."

"Is it life and death, your obligations there?" Aisling demanded. "Is it light or dark, slavery or freedom?"

"No. I'm not important there. I'll come back. I promised Nan, I'm promising you, but there are loose ends . . ."

She trailed off as Harken came in.

"She's leaving," Aisling snapped out, and began to ferociously peel a carrot.

"Ah well." He took off his cap, simply stood looking at Breen.

"I'm coming back. I swear it. But I have to—" The hell with it, she thought, and gripped his hand. "Read me, mind and heart. I'm not going because I want to leave, but because I need to try to do what's right. And I'm coming back to try to do what's right."

"It hurts you. Having love and duty pull so hard from both sides hurts." He glanced at his sister. "Mahon often feels this pull when he must leave his family for duty. I wish you safe journey, Breen Siobhan, and a safe return to us."

He touched his lips to her forehead. "Morena stopped outside to speak with the children. Keegan even now prepares for today's training. You must tell them both."

"I know. I will." She looked over at Aisling. "I'm sorry."

"She leaves most of her heart here," Harken said when Breen went out.

"Most of her heart isn't enough to stand against Odran."

He just went to her, wrapped his arms around her. Aisling stiffened, started to push him away, then leaned in.

"You can't open or close a lock without the key, Harken."

"She'll be the stronger for it when she comes back."

"If." Through the window Aisling watched Breen walk to Morena. "If she comes back."

CHAPTER TWENTY-SIX

Like swallowing medicine, Breen thought, get it all over with at once.

But she waited while Morena adjusted Kavan's arm so he could call the hawk to glove.

That magnificent flight, Breen thought, that majestic spread of wings as the hawk flew from high on a tree branch to the arm of a little boy.

Then tolerated, stoically, the boy's happy squeals.

"Sure and it's fine falconers you'll both make one day. We'll have another lesson next I come, but now Amish is after hunting."

"Da says if I learn well I could have a hawk for my next birthday."

Morena smiled at Finian. "If that's the way of it, I'll be pleased to help you train one. Go on now, Kavan, let him fly."

"Bye! Bye! Bye." Kavan lifted his arm as taught.

"Well done, well done indeed, the pair of you." She helped them remove the child-sized gloves she'd made for them. "Now put your gloves away, right and proper."

They ran toward the house. Finian's face still shone as they reached Breen. And Kavan, as always, lifted his arms. As Breen picked him up, she realized she'd miss them beyond imagining.

"Morena made us gloves of our own," Finian told her. "We flew the hawk. We took turns. I'm going to get a hawk for my birthday."

"When's your birthday?"

"On Samhain. Ma says I chose that day so my soul and my grand-da's could meet when the veil thinned. Come on, Kavan, we have to put the gloves away."

"Bye!" He shouted it as Breen set him down. "Bye. Bye."

"Fine boys they are," Morena commented. "I know Aisling pines for a girl, but she and Mahon make fine sons."

"They really do. You're so good with them."

"Ah, that's easy enough. And good practice as well for when I de-cide to let Harken plant one in me."

"Oh."

"I'm more about the babies, I'm thinking, than the whole hand-fasting business right now. And he'll be wanting both, of course. So, well, there's time yet to see how the wind blows me. And are you ready for today's training?"

"Do I have a choice?"

"Not in Keegan's mind, no. Still, you've been working at it like a mad thing the last few days, so either you've come to like it or you just want to bruise his fine arse."

"Well, I haven't come to like it—not the sword or the fist anyway. I've been . . . can you walk over with me? I need to talk to you."

"Sure and I planned to watch a bit—and throw insults at the man, in any case. What do you need to talk of?"

"We're friends. You were my first friend, and even if a lot of that's still blurry, I feel it."

"You're troubled, and I can feel that without Harken's gift."

"I have friends on the other side. I have one who's like a mother to me, who's given me kindness and understanding and support when my own didn't, or couldn't. I have Marco."

"The one my mother met. Handsome, she said, and with a good heart and charm."

"He's all that. He's been a constant in my life. A friend, a brother, a wailing wall, a cheerleader as long as I can remember. It's been hard not to share all this with him, not to tell him the truth. To know I can't tell him the truth."

"I know that." Sympathizing, Morena draped an arm over Breen's shoulders as they walked. "It was hard over the years when I visited the other side not to go to you. But real friendship doesn't always take the easy way, does it?"

"No, and I'm not taking the easy way now. Morena, I have to go back."

"Go back? Go back to . . . But you're needed here, and you're happy here. You awakened."

"Yes, yes, yes. But I have to go, there are so many reasons why I must. There are things I have to do and say and resolve. I can't just turn away from the people I care about and who care about me."

Her face blank, Morena lifted her arm away. "But you can with those here?"

"No. That's why I'll return. I need time first. I need to work out things I haven't. I need to see all of it again knowing Talamh exists, knowing everything I've learned."

"You spent most of your life there before coming here. You should know where you belong."

"I need time," she repeated. "I'll come back. For friendship, for all that calls to me here, for my grandmother, and for duty."

"When? When do you go?"

"I have three days. Two more," she corrected, "after today."

"And when will you return?"

"I don't know, not exactly. But I will."

"The last time you said this, more than twenty years went before you came."

"It won't this time. This time I make the choice, this time I'm not a child."

Morena looked out over the farm, then turned to face Breen. "You may not know as yet, but I do. This is your true home. So you will come back. Have a care, Breen, you don't take too long at it. You told Marg?"

"Yes. And Aisling, then Harken, as he came in while I was."

She nodded. "So you save Keegan for the last of us. Since you're my friend I'll wish you luck with that and mean it. But it's best I leave you alone to do it."

"All right."

"I'll see you before you go."

Breen started to speak again, but Morena turned and walked back toward Aisling's cottage.

So when Bollocks romped back to her, she continued to the training field, where Keegan sat methodically polishing one of the swords.

"You're late yet again, and sure took your bloody time of it. I've known women in more than one world who like to think a man has nothing better to do than wait for them. They're all in the way of being wrong."

"I don't think that and never have, but I had things to deal with today. I still do."

She sat on one of the mounting blocks he'd set down for brief rests—or as part of a brutal obstacle course he'd fashioned and whipped her through more than once.

"I had to talk to Nan, and . . . others. I guess I still have others I should talk to. I have to talk to you."

He looked up, into her face. She could see the shutter come down over his eyes as if he snapped them shut over a window.

"You're going back then."

"Yes, but—"

"In a matter of days now, two more after this, so that's mere hours."

"Yes," she said again, surprised he knew.

"Do you think I wouldn't know when the time you'd laid out before was up? Yet you've said nothing. Easier for you, I'm thinking, to let me—all of us—believe you meant to stay and see this through."

"No, not easier. Maybe easier for a while not to think about it at all, so I didn't. I just didn't. And when I did, I didn't say anything because I wasn't sure how."

"Now you've said it." He got to his feet. "So there's no point in it for me wasting my time on the training of you when you choose to go back across."

"Not fair." She sprang to her feet. "Not fair. Why did I think you'd be fair or listen to what I have to say?"

"You're leaving, so it's said. All in my world look to me now to hold the line against Odran, to keep that vision of death and destruction we shared from becoming. I lifted the sword from the lake as you told me I must."

"I—what? I never—I wasn't even here."

"You came, after I saw it through the water, when I thought no, not for me, no, I don't want it. I don't want to lead. But you came, and in the water spoke to me. So I lifted it, and all the burdens it holds. And you, who were born with the power to guard worlds, throw the burden aside."

"I'm not. I won't. I'll come back. You don't know who I was before I came here." Dragging her hands through her hair, she turned away. "You wouldn't like who I was. I don't like who I was. I have to go back as I am now."

"For what purpose?"

"To prove I can be who I am now. To prove I am what I want to be. To make the choice knowing what I know. Goddamn it, Keegan, you and everyone in Talamh travel outside, are encouraged to go, to spend time, to see and feel. Then make your choice. But I'm not allowed to do the same?"

"You lived there."

"Not me." She turned back, rapping a hand on her heart. "A woman who did everything she could not to be noticed. Who followed rules someone else set for her. A woman who believed her own father couldn't love her enough to stay. But that's not who's going back. I haven't spoken to my mother in months, and not once has she tried to contact me. But the woman who's going back is going to have one hell of a conversation with her."

"So you go back to show your mother you're strong?"

"That's part of it, yes. And what's wrong with that? Haven't you been training me to be strong? All these weeks, isn't that what you've done?"

Whirling around, she grabbed a sword. "She trained me to be weak." And slashed the air with it. Hot light sizzled and snapped from the blade. "I damn well will show her I'm not. I have people who love me, and I need to see them, I need to somehow tell them I'm not staying, that I'm coming back to Ireland. Since I can't tell them I'm coming back here. I can tell them I'm coming back to Ireland to finish my book, that'll work and isn't a complete lie."

She sighed, and put the sword down. "But it's enough of one it bothers me. And it's going to hurt them. Marco, my friend, and I were going to get a house. He found one, and it's exactly what I wanted before . . . before everything changed. I have to disappoint him because I can't do that until—I don't know when now."

"So you think of houses and your pride. Do you forget the vision, the screams and the smoke?"

Eyes hard, dark and hard, she lifted her face. "I'll never forget it."

"Do you understand Odran knows you've awakened? He will continue to push against the portals, to send his scouts and demons. He will do whatever he can to push into your dreams."

"I have the spell—"

"But no one to help should it fail."

"Then I'll have to be good enough."

"And if you're not, and he can use what you have, Talamh is lost. And when lost, so will your world be, as you are the bridge."

"I'll have to be good enough," she repeated. "Before I came here a handful of people—less—believed I was good enough, and I wasn't one of them."

It cut to the bone to realize he wasn't one of them either.

"It's harder to go than to stay. You won't understand that, but that's my choice. To go, to do what I need to do, then come back and give whatever I have to the Fey."

"Then I won't waste my time or my breath. And since there's no point in the training of you now, I'll spend both where they can be of more use."

"I still have today, and tomorrow, and—"

"It's not likely, is it, you'll be needing a sword in your Philadelphia." He sheathed his with a decisive snick, picked up hers. "So go, Breen Siobhan, and do what you feel you must, for it seems what's human in you burns stronger than what is Fey."

He walked away from her, and moments later she saw his dragon dive out of the sky. He mounted. Without a backward glance, they soared up to disappear into the clouds.

She didn't go to the farm again. As she doubted she'd be welcomed, she spent much of her remaining time with her grandmother, with Sedric. She visited Morena and her grandparents, watched the young Feys race the roads and woods.

On the evening before her departure, she left Bollocks with Marg.

He whined for her, and the plaintive sound of it stayed with her as she walked from the cottage, the gardens, and to the road.

She'd stretched her time until dusk, when the light softened to a pearl gray and the far hills stood cloaked in shadows.

A time, she knew, when Talamh fell quiet with the workday done, the evening meal finished. A time, she thought, for reading by the fire or conversations as the children slept. For music, and she heard that now as the lovely sad strains of a violin drifted from the farmhouse.

It sounded like tears. Nothing could have suited her mood more.

Lights shone in the windows of the house where she'd been born, and her father before her. Her heart wrenched as she walked past it with the mournful tune following her like a ghost.

Morena sat on the wall with the Welcoming Tree behind her, and stood as Breen approached.

"I thought to say a last goodbye."

Saying nothing at all, Breen walked to her, wrapped around her, held on.

"It hurts you to go. Anyone can see it, so the need to go must be fierce."

"It is. I can't explain it, but it is."

"You've explained well enough for me." With a last squeeze, Morena pulled back, glanced toward the farmhouse. "If not for all."

"Harken plays like an angel. A grieving one."

"Harken can play, and more than well, but that would be Keegan."

"Keegan? I didn't know he played at all."

"Your own father taught him, and Harken and Aisling as well. I suppose he didn't mention the matter when the two of you tucked up in bed."

She knew, Breen thought. Of course she did. Probably everyone knew. "No, he didn't. And he's too angry with me now to mention anything."

"He has worlds on his shoulders, in his heart and hands as well."

"I get that, I really do. It's why I can't be angry back when it would be a lot easier."

"You'll mend it all when you come back."

"I'll come back, but mending's something else." She tried a shrug and a smile. "I think I may be the only woman in history to be dumped in two worlds."

"Men are fragile creatures at the base of it."

"Are they?" Breen asked wistfully.

"Take my word on it. Now, you gave me a gift when you came, so I've one for you for your leaving."

She handed Breen a small wooden box etched with magical symbols.

"It's beautiful."

"Oh, well, the box is fine enough, but what's inside is the real gift."

As she opened it, Morena flicked on some faerie lights so Breen could clearly see what she held in the palm of her hand.

"It's Nan's cottage. It's a perfect miniature of Nan's cottage, with the garden in front, and the door open as she likes it."

"I first thought to make one of the cottage on the other side, where you've been living."

"You made this? It's incredible."

"I'm pleased you think so. I thought of the farm as well, as you've such ties there. But in the end, I thought for sentiment, it would be Marg's cottage for you to take on your journey."

"I couldn't love it more, or you for knowing what it would mean to me. Oh, Morena, I'm going to miss you."

"Don't miss me too long then. I'll be here when you return."

Carefully, Breen placed the miniature back in the velvet padding inside the box. "Look in on Nan and Bollocks for me."

"I will, of course."

"I have to go."

"I know it. Fair journey to you."

Breen walked across the field, up the short steps, then turned to look back where Morena still stood.

"I think I'm the only woman who has the best of best friends in two worlds."

Then, with the box pressed against her heart, she stepped from one world to another.

The entire day of travel passed like a dream. Loading the car, checking the cottage one last time, then the drive through a soft rain that made the green glow like drenched emeralds.

When she finally walked into the airport, the noise, the crowds, the movement hit as a hard culture shock that nearly woke her. But she focused on getting through, just getting through all the steps and stages. When she finally sat in the relative quiet of the lounge to wait for her flight, she stuck with water. She already felt outside her body, and her hands shook a little as she raised the glass.

As she boarded, she thought how she'd flown on a dragon once, and that was real. Then she answered Marco's cheerful text to try to ground herself to what was real now.

As the plane rose, she didn't look out the window. Couldn't bear to look at what she left behind. She didn't want a movie or a book, but tried to lose herself in writing for a time.

It helped, a little, and when the story slipped away from her, she used the bathroom to take the potion, do the spell, and with the charm in her pocket, slept the time away.

Steps and stages, she reminded herself when she landed, and pushed through all of them until she wheeled her luggage out into a world of sound and rush that made her ears buzz and her stomach pitch.

She might have turned then and there and rushed for some sort of escape, but there stood Marco, both hands waving in the air. Marco, grinning from ear to ear. Marco, grabbing her in a hug that lifted her off her feet.

"Here she is!"

"Here you are," she murmured, and, laughing and crying at once, pressed her face to his shoulder.

"Let me get a look at my best girl." He pulled her back, blinked. "Girl, you were buff when I left, but shit my pants, you are frigging ripped. What'd you do?"

"Am I? I worked out a lot."

Sword practice, combat training, riding, walking.

"Looks damn good on you. Where's that dog of yours? Where do we have to go to get him?"

"I couldn't bring him right now." And she began to cry in earnest. "I left him with . . . I'll explain."

"It's all right, baby, it's okay. Stupid apartment."

"I really want to get out of here, Marco."

"Sure you do. Here, I'll push this little mountain." He got behind the cart. "I borrowed my cousin's minivan—that's an embarrassment to my breed, but it works. You just wait at the curb, and I'll bring it around."

"Thanks."

"You must be worn out."

"I guess. Everything feels so strange. Except you." She gripped his arm as he wheeled the cart outside.

"My clock was off for days when I got back. You okay here?"

"Yeah, all good."

No, she thought as he jogged away. No, nothing's okay. The air smells wrong, the sky looks wrong. Too many people talking at once. Too many people and cars everywhere. The thunder of planes taking off, landing.

He pulled up in a cherry-red minivan, then hopped out to open the cargo doors. "You go on, sit and catch your breath. I'll load up."

"No, I'm good, and I need to move after the long flight."

By the time she slid into the passenger seat, her head throbbed.

"It's gonna feel weird driving on the right, I bet." He pulled away from the curb. "I got the night off, so I'm going to fix you a good dinner. I know how you are about getting everything in its place, but you can wait till tomorrow to unpack. Just chill."

"Maybe. I've got so much to tell you."

"And I want to hear every bit of it. Especially about the Irish hunk you hooked up with."

"That's over."

"Hey, maybe he'll come over to visit you."

She shook her head. "I had to go; he had to stay."

"Don't you forget about Sandy and Danny. Summer love can last."

At her blank look, he rolled his eyes. "*Grease*, Breen, it's the word."

And he made her laugh.

She did her best to shut out everything but him as they drove into the city. She knew all of this, she thought, all of this so familiar. And now as distant as the two moons.

They carted all the bags up to the apartment.

"I've got to get the van back. You just chill, and I'll be back again in a half hour. You chill, you hear?"

"Yes."

He gave her another hard hug. "Welcome the hell home, Breen."

When he left, she looked around. All this familiar, too.

But it wasn't home, not anymore. No matter how much of the person she'd been remained here, no matter how much of Marco, this would never be home to her again.

She unpacked, squeezing the gifts she'd brought into her little closet. On her dresser she placed the wooden box, the miniature, and the scrying mirror. And, feeling guilty, she tucked her wand, the crystals and potions she'd brought back, and the spell book away in drawers.

She hadn't risked bringing the athame, not on the plane, but had left that with her grandmother.

When she heard Marco come back, she stepped out of her room.

He fisted his hands on his hips. "You unpacked, didn't you?"

"I couldn't help it."

"Girl." He let out an exaggerated sigh. "You sit down. I'm getting us an adult beverage, then we're going to play some catch-up before I make us my famous chicken and rice."

"I missed your cooking."

"Came clear in your blog you weren't doing much of that your own self."

"I suck at it."

He poured them wine, sat with her. "Good thing you got me. Now you tell me everything."

"There's so much, I don't know where to start."

"Pick a spot."

"I left a lot out of the blog because it was too personal. And I didn't tell you when we talked or texted because that wasn't personal enough. I should start with my father."

"Jesus, did you find him?"

"He died, Marco, years ago. He would've come back but . . ."

"Oh, my baby girl." He rose to crouch down, gather her in. "I'm so sorry. Breen, I'm so sorry. I wish I'd been there with you. You shouldn't've gone through that alone."

"I wasn't. I found my grandmother. His mother."

He pulled back, eyes wide. "Where, how?"

"I . . . got lost one day, and I ended up at this farm, this beautiful farm. I was born there, Marco."

"You— What?"

"I never knew, but I was born there, not here. And they knew my father. My grandmother's cottage is nearby. I spent a lot of time with her. You'd like her. You'd really like her."

"Breen, it's like fate, right?"

"Yes." Just that simple, she thought. "It's like fate."

She told him what she could, blending Talamh into Ireland.

"So since she gave me the dog, I left him with her until . . ."

"Your dad never told you?"

"I think he sort of did, in the stories he told me. But I thought they were stories. And my mother, well, she quashed all of that."

"It's all just—" He put his hands to the sides of his head, made an exploding sound. "You could write a book."

"About that." She let out a breath. "You know the one I wrote about Bollocks?"

"Know it, read it, loved it."

"I'm working on a second one, and working on my adult novel. And I got an agent."

"You did not! I mean whoa, look at you! This is fan-fucking-tastic, girl."

"I can do better. She sold the Bollocks book, and two more to be written in a package deal."

He blinked. "You said what?"

"I have an editor. I have a publisher. Bollocks is going to be published next summer."

He set down his wine, then stood up, walked around the room.

As her heart sank, she began to babble. "I didn't want to tell you until I could tell you. I wanted—"

"Shut up. Shut up."

He plucked her out of her chair, swung her in two circles. Then pressed his face in her hair.

"I'm so proud of you. I'm so happy for you. So proud."

When he drew back to kiss her, she brushed tears from his cheeks. And now her heart filled and overflowed.

"You're the reason," she murmured.

"Breen, you're the reason."

She took his hand, rubbed it lightly over the tattoo on her wrist.

"You helped me find it. And tomorrow I'm going to use that courage and go talk to my mother."

"Used to dip in a toe, now you dive in. You want me to go with you?"

"No." She laid her head on his shoulder, and found, in what felt like a foreign world to her now, he was still home. "I'm going to handle it."

CHAPTER TWENTY-SEVEN

In the early hours of the morning, she used the scrying mirror.

Thinking of the thin apartment walls and Marco, she kept her conversation with Marg brief and her voice low. Still Bollocks heard her and, with a trio of joyful barks, wagged himself into view.

Then, wakeful, restless, she wrote, and since the world she weaved took her back to Talamh, she found her own joy. Long after the sun broke through her little bedroom window, she heard Marco stirring.

She put the work aside to go out, make coffee.

"Man, I missed having you start coffee in the morning." He gave her a one-armed hug as he drank. "You put a blog up already. Three thirty in the a-freaking-m."

"Time clock."

"Take a nap, girl."

"Maybe." But sleep wasn't on her mind.

"I head straight to Sally's after the music store. How about you meet me there? You've got big news to spread, and if you don't spread it soon, it's gonna bust right out of me."

"I will. I want to see Sally and Derrick, and everyone."

She'd need them after she confronted her mother.

"You're going over to your mom's."

"You read my mind."

He tapped her temple. "I know what goes on in there."

"She should be home by six if she's not on a business trip. I'll come into Sally's after I talk to her."

"I'll have a drink waiting. And if you need me, you text me. I gotta book. Got a lesson in about fifteen. Take that nap."

He rushed out as he always rushed out in the morning, because he always cut the time close.

She walked to the window.

She'd always loved this neighborhood and, looking out, she saw what she'd loved—the clever shops and restaurants, the delightful little bakery. She and Marco splurged on their orgasmically gooey sticky buns every Sunday.

She loved the brick-paved streets and the tiny slice of the river she could see if she squinted. She loved that she could go into any shop or restaurant on the block and someone would greet her by name.

They knew her here—even when she'd tried to disappear. Maybe because of that, she considered. Because it really was a neighbor-hood.

She considered going out for a walk, but realized it simply didn't appeal as it once had. No green fields flowing into green hills. No bay reflecting the mercurial sky.

No Bollocks to race ahead, chasing sheep or squirrel.

She told herself she simply hadn't adjusted yet—and couldn't.

Things to resolve, she thought. Until she did she'd stay caught between worlds, between loves, between obligations.

She'd go back to work, but first, she needed to make some calls.

After the workday, she took the bus out of habit. Because panic fluttered right under her collarbone, she slid a hand in her pocket to slide her fingers over the charm bag she'd made for strength of purpose.

She imagined driving the winding roads of Ireland, imagined riding the charming gelding over the fields, through the woods of Talamh.

It helped get her through the crowded bus ride in rush-hour traffic. She could almost ignore the horn blasts, or the tinny muffle of hip-hop leaking out of the earbuds of the passenger in front of her.

The air brakes thumped, the bus door squeaked open, closed. People squeezed off, squeezed on.

By the time she reached her stop, she wished she'd listened to Marco and taken that nap.

The walk helped clear her head. Even at this hour, her mother's neighborhood trended quiet. The narrow front lawns held their summer green, trees offered leafy shade. Maybe landscaping tended to be more regimented and manicured than she'd become used to, but it still offered color.

She wouldn't want this, of course. If and when the time came, she'd want—and need—more room. More solitude. And yes, more simplicity.

She turned up her mother's walkway. At the door she took one more steadying breath, then rang the bell.

When the door opened, Jennifer's face showed nothing, not a single tic of surprise. Which told Breen her mother had checked the security screen before answering.

"Breen. So you're back."

"Yes. I'd like to come in."

"Of course."

She'd changed her hair, more highlights for the summer, grown it out a bit into a sleek swing. She wore cropped pants and a sleeveless shirt, so she'd changed from her work clothes.

And she carried an evening cocktail—not wine but a G&T, which told Breen she'd had a difficult day at work.

She was about to have one at home.

"Have a seat." Jennifer gestured as she turned into the living room. "Would you like a drink?"

"No, I'm fine."

No changes in here, Breen noted. It remained perfect.

"I take it you enjoyed your extended vacation and assume you're ready to come back to reality. Under the circumstances, you'll have to make do with substitute teaching offers until—"

"I'm not going back to teaching."

Taking a slow sip, Jennifer studied Breen with disapproval so strong it should have snapped the glass in two. "A few million dollars may seem like a world of money to you, but it won't last long the way you've chosen to spend it. Trips to Europe, new wardrobe, no other income."

"I have other income. My writing."

It was small, it was petty, but the dismissive sound her mother made brought enormous satisfaction. Because she'd have to swallow it hard.

"I sold my first book. In fact, my publisher contracted me for three."

Jennifer only sighed, as an adult might over the fantasies of a child.

"Breen, scam artists who claim to be publishers troll the internet for people just like you."

"My agent's with the Sylvan Agency, one founded thirty-two years ago. My publisher is McNeal Day Publishing. You may have heard of them," she said—baldly—when she finally saw that tic of surprise. "If not, you can look them up.

"I'm having meetings next week in New York with my agent, my publisher, my editor, and so on. They actually believe I have talent. They believe I can build a career. So no, I won't be going back to a career I never wanted and had no real talent for."

"Writers rarely manage to make a livable wage."

"Aren't I lucky to have backup while I try to do just that? And it strikes me that in a normal relationship you'd be happy for me. Maybe even a little proud. But we've never had that, have we? A normal relationship."

"That's insulting nonsense. I've looked out for you, guided you, helped you avoid pitfalls your entire life. If you consider being coddled normal, that's a lack in you."

So much here, Breen realized, she'd never really seen. And so much not here she'd accepted.

No more.

"You looked out to make sure I didn't color outside the lines, dragged me away from what you considered pitfalls that I might have considered fun or opportunities. Well, I've colored outside the lines now, and I like it. I'm never going back to what I was, to what you made me believe I had to be. You need to accept that. Or not," she added. "Either way, I'm never going back."

"When the money runs out—"

"You know, I've learned life, a good one, isn't all about money. I hope to make a living doing what I love, and not depend on the generosity of others. But if I don't, I'll find another way. I've learned life, a good one, is about love, about standing up for yourself and others, about that generosity, giving back. I had a good basis for that, not from you, but from Sally and Marco and Derrick."

"Did they put food on the table, a roof over your head?"

Was there hurt? Breen wondered. Just a hint of hurt under her mother's outrage?

"No, and I owe you for that. That's why I'm here. I understand a little better why you always made me feel less. Because you knew I was more, and you feared that."

"Now you're being ridiculous, and you've climbed on a very high horse over the sale of one book."

"This isn't about the book, though that's a happy by-product of the rest. I might never have found the courage to write without the money. I might never have found the courage to go to Ireland. And if I hadn't gone to Ireland, I wouldn't have found Talamh."

"I don't know what you're talking about."

Not a tic of surprise now, but a leeching of color, every ounce of it from her face. Her body stiff, the hand on the glass visibly unsteady, Jennifer pushed to her feet.

"Now I have work to do."

"You know exactly what I'm talking about, where I'm talking about. I met my grandmother. I spent most of the summer getting to know her, my birthplace, my birthright."

"Eian's mother was, and undoubtedly is, unstable, which is exactly why I kept her away from you. Still, she's cagey enough to have pulled you into her fantasy world. You need to—"

"Don't tell me what I need." Incensed, Breen rose. "She never spoke ill of you. Not once. And the first thing you say about her—

someone you let me think didn't even exist—is she's unstable, a fraud. A fantasy world? You spent four years with the Fey."

"You're delusional. You need to go."

"Delusional?" Breen spun her hand, held a ball of cool white light. "This isn't delusion. It's not fantasy. It's power. The power you tried, all my life, to beat back."

"Stop! You will not bring that aberration into my house."

"Aberration?" The same word, she thought, Ultan had used during his trial. "Is that what it is to you? What I am to you?"

"I won't have it! Not in my home. This is the world we live in, do you understand? I told your father—"

"He's dead."

Anger, maybe fear with it, had brought high color to Jennifer's cheeks, and a wild glint to her eyes. Now her eyes went dull; her face gray.

The glass slid out of her hand to shatter on the floor.

"You didn't know. You really didn't know. And maybe Nan was right. You did love him. You did love each other."

"He left. He left a long time ago. I have to clean up this mess before it damages the floor."

"Now you stop." Sweeping her hand, Breen vanished the broken glass and spilled liquid.

"You will not bring that into my home, or you will not be welcome here."

"Is that what you told him? Is that the ultimatum you gave my father? He left his home for you."

"And constantly went back."

"He had obligations. He was taoiseach."

"Tribal bullshit!" When her voice broke, Jennifer whirled away. "We were his family."

"He had family there, too. A world to protect."

"He didn't protect you, did he? Stolen from your bed in the middle of the night."

"He did protect me. He fought for me. I came home safe."

"He chose them over me time and time again. A sword and a staff, what idiocy. He could have thrown them back in that cursed lake, but he wouldn't. He could have lived here, with me, with you, like a normal man, a normal husband and father."

"But he wasn't normal the way you mean it. Damn it, you tried to burn out the light in him just like you tried to burn it out in me."

"He'd be alive if I had."

Grief, yes, she could see some grief. But she couldn't let it soften her, not now.

"And very likely as miserable as I was for so much of my life. Odran put me in a cage, but so did you."

"How dare you say that to me. I kept you safe."

"Safe on your terms. Always on your terms. You kept me boxed. And when he left that last night, and didn't come back—because he died weeks after protecting me, you, his world, and this one—you made me think he abandoned me because I didn't matter to him."

"I never said that."

"In a thousand different ways, and you know it. You divorced him, and still he came back to this world time and time again. Because he loved us. Now he's gone, and we don't know how to comfort each other."

"If he'd loved us, he'd have given up the rest."

Black-and-white, Breen realized. How sad it had to be to live in a world of black-and-white.

"It's sad you believe that. It makes me sorry for you. Sorry you refuse to see, or are simply incapable of seeing the joy and beauty he fought for. But I see it, I know it. I've awakened. I'm of the Fey. You'll have to learn to deal with it."

"You won't bring the unnatural into this house."

"Understood. You know how to reach me if and when you want."

"You're staying here. You're not going back."

"Of course I'm going back. I'm my father's daughter," she added, and walked out.

And walked over a mile until she'd shaken off the worst of the anger and grief.

She started to call an Uber, then just wound her way to a bus stop. A moment after she sat on the bench, Sedric sat beside her.

"What—what are you doing here?"

"Marg said you were after speaking with your mother this evening. Knowing it would be a hard thing, we decided you might want a bit of looking after. So Marg conjured a temporary portal—just to keep an eye on you for the evening. But you looked to me as if you could use a bit of company. You walked a long way. I'm fond of long walks myself when I'm in the way of being upset."

"She . . . believes what I am, what my father was, what we have is unnatural. An aberration. And still, when I told her he was dead, I saw her face. She loved him. Nan was right. But she blamed him for not forsaking Talamh, for not pretending to be something he wasn't. I wasn't kind to her."

It surprised Breen when he put an arm around her. Surprised her more when she leaned her head on his shoulder. "I said hard things. I felt them. I needed to get them out of me. I had to come back for this. Not just this, but it was something I had to do."

"And now it's done so you'll be better for it."

She felt sick and sad, and shook her head. "Will I?"

"Sure and you will. When something's stuck in your craw, you can't feel strong and steady."

"I'm not there yet. I told her I sold a book, and she tried to make it seem like nothing. Even wrong somehow."

He turned his head, brushed a kiss over her hair.

"Doesn't matter," she muttered.

"Not a bit. Now tell me what Marco said when you told him of it."

"He cried a little. He was so happy for me."

"And there's what matters, isn't it? Here's the bus now. Should I ride home with you?"

"I'm going to Sally's."

"Ah, what a fine place that is. What good craic!"

"Do you want to come?"

Obviously touched, he smiled at her. "I might next time if I'm round and about, but I'll go home myself and tell your nan you're with friends."

"Thanks, Sedric." She got up, walked to the bus door. "I miss your lemon biscuits."

"You'll have some when you come home."

She got on the bus, took her seat. She started to lift her hand in a wave. And shouldn't have been surprised he'd vanished.

When she walked into Sally's, she expected to feel assaulted by the noise, the crowd, and found herself the opposite.

Here it was the familiar, the strange comfort of home.

While still too early for the first formal show and the real crowd, she recognized Larue onstage as Judy sweetly singing "Over the Rainbow."

She'd been there, Breen thought. She'd been over the rainbow.

She glanced around for Sally, for Derrick, and when she didn't see them, headed straight to the bar and Marco.

He set a flute of champagne in front of her.

"Champagne?"

"Sally said to pop open the good stuff for you to celebrate your book."

"My book?" she repeated with a deadeye stare.

Though he tried to look shamefaced, he couldn't pull it off. "I'm weak. I couldn't help myself. I'm putting an order in for loaded nachos 'cause I know damn well you didn't eat. Plenty of protein coming your way in a tasty package."

"Then you're forgiven, because I could eat."

She started to reach for her glass, but was spun around on the stool, gathered in, lifted up.

Sally, as Cher in the crowd-pleasing white jumpsuit and long black wig, scooped her up.

"Here she is, ladies and gentlemen, the world traveler, the bestselling author, the belle of any ball, Breen Siobhan Kelly!"

Laughing, she hugged back. "The book's not even published yet."

"I'm a never-miss fortune-teller, and I'm going to do 'Gypsies, Tramps & Thieves' just for you."

"I missed you and everything about you."

"Catch it, because it's coming right back at you."

"Hey, my turn." Derrick wrapped an arm around her before giving her a noisy kiss and a dozen white roses.

"Oh, they're gorgeous! Oh, thank you. I feel like a princess."

"You're ours."

Sally sat on the next stool, tossed back the long hair in a very Cher gesture, and winked at Derrick. "Honey, how about you put those beauties in some water so they stay fresh for our princess?"

"You got it."

"And, Marco, you put that order in—pour me a glass of that fine bubbly first, then scoot. Breen and I need a little girl talk."

Sally picked up his glass when he had. "Now, let's get this out of the way. How did it go with your mother?"

"I guess as well as could be expected."

"That bad?"

"Maybe worse. But." Breen lifted her glass in toast. "It's done. Besides, I'm with my real mother right now."

"Baby, you're going to make me cry, and this makeup's prime. Now, I'm going to say how sorry I am about your father. You were right there for me when I lost my daddy a couple years ago. I wish we could've been there for you."

"In a way you were. And as bad as it was—as it is—I know he loved me. He would've come back. He always loved me."

"And you met your grandma?"

"She's wonderful, Sally. You'd love her."

"I hope to meet her someday."

Breen sipped so she wouldn't sigh. "That would be amazing."

"And you got yourself that adorable dog—another I can't wait to meet—learned how to ride a horse, wrote a whole damn book and sold it. It's a good thing I wasn't in makeup when Marco told us. I blubbered some—proud, happy tears. Baby girl, you sure have been busy finding out what makes Breen tick."

"That's exactly right."

"Derrick and I read your blog every morning. We sit right there in bed with our coffee and our tablets and read, and damned if we didn't feel we were right there with you, seeing it all."

Sally wagged a red-tipped finger. "But you left something out."

"Something?" So many things.

"A certain Celtic god."

"A— What?" The fluttering panic below her collarbone again. Until Sally wiggled his eyebrows.

"Oh, you mean . . . That was just— He was only—" Now she did sigh. "Gorgeous."

Sally wiggled closer. "Paint me a picture."

So she did.

Over the next few days, Breen clung to routine. Writing early, breaking for a workout. And with the door locked, the shades drawn, conjuring a wraith to continue her training.

The next week, she boarded the train for New York.

She used the travel time to watch the world go by, and to think about that world. The homes and businesses, the farms and factories. All the people who lived here, worked here. She'd thought about it all before, of course, but had considered herself a small, unimportant cog in the wheel. Her day-to-day decisions didn't matter. Walk or take the bus, scramble eggs for dinner or order Chinese, buy new shoes or make do.

Nothing she did changed anything or made a real difference.

Now it did. Every decision she made—or didn't—mattered.

So she had to be sure she made the right choice.

Traveling to New York, and traveling alone, was an important personal choice, and one she couldn't have made six months before.

If she didn't have the courage for this, to take something so important to her, something she'd worked for and dreamed of, how would she find it to fight for a world, to use her gifts, her power to stand for the light against the dark?

Armed with her agent's detailed instructions, Breen transferred at

Penn Station to the subway going downtown. Everything struck her as huge, vast, and yet somehow too small to hold everyone at once.

Though Marco had selected her outfits for her two days of meetings, she worried she'd overdressed or underdressed, or just looked like what she was: a woman out of her depth.

She stood in the crowded subway car, clinging to her overnight bag and the lovely charcoal-gray computer bag Sally and Derrick had given her as a congratulations gift.

She saw a woman in a gorgeous head scarf jiggling an infant in a sling. A man in a business suit frowned as he read something on his phone. A woman in a red suit and high-top sneakers sat with an enormous shoulder bag on her lap and looked bored.

At every squealing stop, more piled on, some squeezed off. Shopping bags, briefcases, cell phones, earbuds. The smell of someone's burned coffee, someone else's too-heavy cologne.

To keep nerves at bay she concentrated on the next step.

She got off at her stop, wound her way through the tunnel with a flood of others. Grateful she'd packed reasonably light, she hauled her overnight up the stairs and into the sensory assault that was New York City.

She hadn't expected to like it, not even a little. But she found herself fascinated. It had such energy. She could feel it tingling along her skin, all but see it in shimmering colors as traffic pushed along the street, as people clipped—dodging and weaving—along the sidewalk.

She joined the cacophony of sound—blasting horns, so angry and impatient, a sea of voices in mixed languages and accents—and, under the bright blast of sun, began to walk.

She didn't care if she looked like a tourist as she gawked, as she craned her neck to look up at the towering buildings. Nobody paid any attention.

And that, she realized, was part of the beauty. No one paid any attention. No one knew her, noticed her, looked at her. She could slide into the flood of people. Not blend and fade away as she'd once done. But just be.

On impulse she stopped to buy a bouquet of stargazer lilies from a sidewalk cart, and took their scent with her on the short walk to the hotel Carlee recommended.

She'd wanted small and quiet, and when she stepped into the lobby, knew Carlee had delivered. Not big and bustling, not at all, but charming with its overstuffed sofas and polished marble floors.

Though too early to check in, she left her bags, assured of their security, and went back out to join the urban hike for the three and a half blocks to the agency.

Her agency.

She'd seen pictures of it on their website, but didn't feel the least bit silly standing outside the double town house with its creamy white bricks and dark wood doors to take a photo of her own.

With the lilies in the crook of her arm, she walked up to the door on the left—as instructed—pressed the buzzer. A moment later the door buzzed back at her, the lock thumped open.

She walked into what had been a dream.

As she waited in the contemporary casual reception, she worked on convincing herself this was reality. Then Carlee walked in with a broad smile and extended a hand to greet her.

"It's so good to meet you at last. How was your trip?"

"It was quick. And the hotel is exactly what I wanted, thank you for recommending it. Thank you for . . . everything."

She held out the flowers.

"Oh, they're beautiful. So sweet of you. Come on, let me take you up to my office. I'm so glad you could come in just a little early so we'd have time to talk before we meet Adrian for lunch."

She talked fast, moved fast, as she led Breen to a staircase and up in her low black heels, slim black pants, and starched white shirt.

She wore her streaky blond hair in a short, face-framing pixie cut. From their conversations, Breen knew she had two children, one in college, one in high school. But she moved like an energetic teenager.

Along the way, she stopped briefly in hallways—book-lined—in offices, poked into a conference room to introduce Breen to other agents, to assistants, a diverse group of men, women, races, ages.

By the time they reached Carlee's third-floor office, the names and faces blurred.

"And here's Lee, my keeper, assistant, and good right hand."

"So happy to meet you. I'm a big fan of your blog."

"Thank you."

Lee was tiny, Asian, and looked—maybe—sixteen.

"Lee screens queries and submissions. She put yours in front of me with orders to read it asap."

"Really big thank-you."

"I love Bollocks. What would you like to drink? Name it, we've probably got it."

"Oh. I—I'd love a Coke."

"You got it. Fizzy water, Carlee?"

"You know me. Would you put these beauties in a vase for me?"

"On it. Gorgeous," Lee added before she hurried out.

"Have a seat, Breen." Carlee went to her desk, opened a drawer. She brought an envelope back, handed it to Breen before she sat, curled up her legs. "Your on-signing payment came in. Accounting cut that for you this morning. I'm really happy to give it to you in person."

"It's real," Breen murmured.

"Bet your ass it's real. Now, we'll chitchat at lunch while you get to know Adrian. As I told you, I've known her for years. She's smart, dedicated, and insightful. I think she's a good fit for you. You'll have the opportunity to see McNeal Day Publishing and meet the people working on your books tomorrow."

Lee came back with glasses. "I'll give you a heads-up when you need to leave for lunch, in case you lose track of time."

"She knows I will," Carlee said as Lee walked out. "Now, put your first signing payment—the first of many—in your purse. And let's talk about the future."

CHAPTER TWENTY-EIGHT

That night after an exhilarating day, Breen slid into bed.

And in the strange bed in the strange city, she had the first vision dream since the one she'd shared with Keegan.

Back, she traveled back to the green wood with the green river, with the wide, wild waterfall tumbling.

She heard its thunder, and the birdsong ringing above it. She saw a deer pause in the green shadows to watch her, and a chipmunk race, chittering, up some mossy bark.

It all spoke of peace, of safety, of a quiet, secret beauty.

But she knew, even as it tried to lull her, she stood on the wrong side.

On Odran's side.

As she knew, as she watched, the deer grew fangs, and its placid eyes went oily black. Blood began to seep red through the moss while the chipmunk dived toward her, claws curled.

She swatted it away with a flick of power.

"I'm not afraid of illusions."

"What do you need to fear?"

Odran walked toward her, black robes swirling through the fog that began to crawl over the ground. "I'm your grandfather. We're blood."

"You're a monster." She held up a hand, pushing out power to stop him. He swatted it away as she had the chipmunk. But he smiled, and kept the small distance between them.

"You killed my father. Your own son."

"He left me no choice. I would have given him all the worlds, but he defied me. Attacked me. I made him for power, as he made you."

"He made me for love."

Now he laughed, an eerily charming sound. "Do you think so? How sweet! He left you because you weren't what he hoped when he mated with the human."

In control, she reminded herself. She would be and remain in control. "Lies."

"Why would I tell you lies, my child?"

He laid a hand on his heart, then held it out to her.

"Why would you choose to believe those on the other side when they spin their lies? They show you smiles and arms of welcome, but they wish only to use you."

"They've shown me the truth," she countered. "They've given me back what's mine."

"Have they?" As if in sorrow, he shook his head. "They awaken you, tell you soft, pretty lies to draw you in. To use what you are to destroy me. And then they would destroy you. You, of my blood, they will burn you in the ritual fire should you fail, should you succeed. How can they risk such as you? How can they risk your power?"

"They would never hurt me. They'd never turn against me."

"Haven't they already turned? You gave your body to their taoiseach, but he turned away, walked away—as did your father—when you were not as he wished. They only desire to hold what they have, and when your use is done, they will end you.

"But I?"

He'd moved closer, just a step, but she could feel his dark energy, deadly, damning, drugging.

"I will help make you the goddess you are, and give you your choice of worlds to rule. I will drape you in power like black silk. All I ask is for you to join your power with mine. To give me a few sips."

Closer still, close enough to touch her now if he reached out. She threw up her hands, pushed again. "No."

His face twisted all charm away. "Then I will drain you and leave you empty and mad. You'll be weak, lost, alone, as you've always been. Give or I take. Those are the choices."

She fisted her hands, drew her power in, and yanked herself out of the dream. As she did, she felt his fingers score over her cheek.

Breathless, she scrambled up, running a hand over her face as she wound a ball of light with the other.

No blood, she thought, but rushed into the bathroom to look in the mirror.

No mark, no blood, no scratches.

But she could feel the cold still, and the echo of pain with it.

"An illusion."

She went back to grab the bottle of water beside the bed, and drank half of it.

"But I controlled it. I held the reins."

Still, she wished she'd brought the scrying mirror, wished she could talk to her grandmother. Because, control or not, Odran's words hung heavy in her mind.

For the first time since kindergarten, Breen didn't spend September in a classroom. Twice, she woke, all but sleepwalked her way toward the shower to get ready for that classroom.

Her face in the mirror over the sink, her hair—bold red, not the dull brown of her classroom days—snapped her into reality.

And twice, she did a little dance in the bathroom.

The freedom hit, always, like that first sip of coffee in the morning, like a taste of fine wine, like the aftermath of really good sex.

Yes, she carried weighty responsibility, had hard decisions to make, but she didn't have to report to a job that didn't suit her, or one she didn't suit.

She believed an entire generation of middle schoolers would be better for it.

Freedom gave her time to write, time to spend with people she loved, time to think, and time to plan.

She waited, hoping to squeeze what she wanted to say to Marco between his arrival home from his day job and his date with a fitness instructor he'd been seeing for a couple of weeks.

But when he came home, he dropped down, then toed off his battered Nikes. "Let's order pizza."

"I thought you were going out with Mr. Hotness. Dinner, an art opening."

Marco held out a fist, thumb up, then turned it upside down.

"Oh. Why?"

"I'm not enough fun."

"Bollocks to that!" Insulted, Breen slapped her own fists to her hips. "You're awesome fun. You're almost too much fun."

"I work two jobs, horn in—his words—time for my own music, and I'm only up for going out, for partying, once, maybe twice a week. Anyway." He shrugged. "The art opening was my thing. He mostly wants to go clubbing, and I can get clubbed-out after working five, maybe six nights a week at Sally's."

"Well, he's shallow and stupid."

"Yeah." Marco grinned at that. "I knew that going in. I mostly just went for his body. I mean, holy shit, did you see his body?"

"I couldn't help it. It was right there. You don't want mine, but I'll take you to dinner and the art opening."

He looked at her, then patted his knee. Obliging him, she walked over to sit on his lap and have a snuggle.

"You're the best thing," he murmured. "My number-one thing. Let's stay home, eat pizza, and stream something we can binge-watch."

"No zombies or vampires."

"Chicken."

"Guilty. Want a beer?"

"You know, we could get married and just have sex with other people."

"Okay. In twenty years, if we're not married or committed to someone, it's a deal."

He snagged her pinky with his. "Done. Now go get me a beer, woman."

She got them both a beer, then sat beside him on the saggy sofa. "There's stuff I want to talk to you about anyway, since we have time."

"Yeah? Am I going to like it?"

"I'm hoping. So I told you all about Breen's New York Adventure."

"Next time, I'm going with you, and we're going to hit Broadway for a show."

"You're on. A lot of the things they talked to me about, and I didn't talk to you about yet, go outside the writing. I love the writing, Marco."

"Girl, it shows."

"And I really want to keep my focus on that, limit my distractions, especially since I'm just getting started. But I am just getting started, and it's going to be on me to do the bulk of promotion and all that. The social media, especially. Beyond the blog—which I also love writing—I need a good, up-to-date, easy-to-navigate web page. I need a social-media presence, like—God—Twitter. And you know I'd rather be eaten by a shark than go on Twitter. They talked about Instagram, maybe Facebook."

He tipped his beer at her. "What've I been telling you?"

"Yeah, yeah, all the things you've been telling me. I don't want to do them, Marco, but not doing them limits my chances of reaching readers and building a career."

"I'll help you."

Here goes, she thought, and sucked in a breath.

"I don't want you to help me. I want you to do it. I want to hire you as my social media manager or personal publicist or liaison to the internet—whatever the hell you want to call it."

"I'll set you up, Breen. I'm not taking your money for it."

"Now, wait and hear me out."

"Not taking your money," he said in a mutter.

"Listen. First, this is a real job. It's not like I can give you benefits or anything, but it's a real job. You'd have to coordinate with my publisher—so I don't have to. You may have to go to New York and meet with some of the publicity people. You'd have to design the website, then maintain it—so I don't have to. Then the whole social media thing. You'd go on all that as you; we don't want to be dishonest. But you'd be speaking for me, and promoting my book.

"There's more," she added. "I made notes because it's just a lot. A lot of things I don't want to do for more than one reason. I wouldn't be very good at it; it would take a lot of time I don't want to take. And if you won't do it, I'll have to hire somebody else. Somebody I don't know, who doesn't know me."

"I didn't say I wouldn't do it, Breen. I said I'm not taking your money to do it."

"Not finished." She shifted, gave him a long, hard stare. He gave one right back. "I hired an accountant."

"Wow. Where'd you get those fancy pants? When did that happen?"

"A couple days ago. I went in, met with Mr. Ellsworth—the broker? And he recommended a couple firms, so I met with people in both of them. I don't like the damn meetings, Marco, but I have to get things set up properly."

"Fuckin' A," he said, and tapped his bottle to hers.

"The on-signing payment's not huge, but it's substantial. Way more than I ever expected to make doing what I want to do. I used it—with their advice—to set up a business account, and both the broker and the accountant said it would be smart—from a business standpoint and a tax standpoint—to hire someone to do all this stuff I don't want to do. They both offered to help me find someone, but I said I had someone. It's a business expense, and one that benefits me. Everything I've said so far benefits me."

She drank some beer, and knew when he remained silent he was at least thinking.

"It benefits you, too—not just the salary we'd work out. You love working at Sally's, and this wouldn't have to change that. But you don't love working at the music store. I'm not asking you to work three jobs, but to work with me instead of the music store. That's just a stopgap for you, something to pay the bills. You like teaching, but the rest of it's just the bills. You could take students right here if you wanted to teach. Or go to them. Teach guitar and piano, violin, but here, or there."

She gripped his hand. "I don't want to hire somebody I don't know, somebody who doesn't understand me, and I have to explain everything to. You don't want to keep selling trumpets and sheet music, barely squeezing in time to write your own. We'd help each other, that's what we do. And we'd both win."

"It doesn't seem right."

"Because you're thinking of me as a friend and not a professional. I'm both now."

He tapped a finger at her. "That's a good one. You didn't used to be so good at winning an argument."

She sat where she was as he pushed up and paced. "Did I win this one?"

"How about this? I'll mock-up a website. If you like it, your publisher likes it, we'll go ahead with the whole thing."

She nodded, somber, sober, then set her beer down and rose to walk to him. "I've got only one thing to say."

"What's that?"

"Yay!" She grabbed him in a hug, bopped with it. "Oh God! Social media, internet weight, whooshed away! I can't tell you how relieved I am."

"Let's see if it works first."

"Oh, it's going to work. Just think, Marco, both of us will be able to quit jobs we don't want in the same year." She shut her eyes. "It's like fate."

And fate, she thought, was the next on her list to deal with.

Keegan dealt with his own fate as he rode into the Capital with Mahon. They'd spent more than two weeks on the journey as they'd crisscrossed Talamh, on horseback, on dragon or wing to check security. And had left small groups of soldiers along the way to ensure it, and to help where necessary with upcoming harvests, repairs, whatever was needed.

What he'd seen in the hills, in the valleys, on the coastlines, in the villages and the farms had been peace and bounty. But what he'd felt had been a low hum of anxiety.

Trouble brewed, and the air of Talamh carried its worry.

When he rode through the gates with Mahon, he saw the busy, bustling shops that bartered wares and crafts. The herbalists, the alchemists, the healers, and the weavers, and all who chose to offer their skills and services and chose to live and work in the shadow of the castle on the rise.

Music piped from the pubs. He smelled stew on the simmer, the spice of meat pies, the yeast of ale that spilled out of open windows and doorways under thatched roofs of buildings tucked too close together for what he considered comfort.

And aye, he knew some found comfort in just that.

The road, dry as the rain kept itself to the west, ran straight. And since it showed no muck from horses, dogs, livestock, he knew the committee that serviced the road remained vigilant.

A thatcher and his apprentice stopped their repairs to lift caps at him. A few stepped out of shops to do the same.

Around one of the five wells that serviced the Capital he saw a group of people with their pails and pitchers. A boy of about ten set his pail down to run to Keegan.

"Did you bring your dragon, Taoiseach?"

Bran was his name, Keegan thought, one of Morena's nephews. Keegan simply pointed up.

Bran's face went bright with delight as he saw Cróga glide overhead. Then the boy spread his wings to fly up for a closer look.

Roads veered off, right and left—to woodsmiths, blacksmiths, and stables, to homes, to dovecotes, coops for chickens, a second well, schools, one in each direction, before it climbed the rise.

The green climbed as well, gently at first, where some worked the gardens and would take what they needed for their labor. Sheep and cattle grazed, and beyond them wheat waved gold, waiting to be harvested and threshed at the mill.

Above all, the castle spread, in stone of a hundred shades of gray weathered by time and rain and sun. Its battlements marched, its towers and turrets speared into a sky of heartbreaking blue, where his dragon flew.

Atop the highest tower another dragon flew on a banner, red against the white field, with a sword in one claw, a staff in the other.

They didn't loom, Keegan thought, but watched, castle and dragon, over all who lived and worked below, over the whole of Talamh.

And so must he.

They rode through the next gate—a defense he hoped never to use—and over the stone bridge where the river wound below.

And here, a fountain for beauty and the flowers that ringed it. To the north, the deep woods for game, for ritual, for lovers' trysts and childhood games.

They circled around toward the stables, the falconry, and the wall that faced the cliffs down to the great sea.

A man he knew stood outside the stables, his cap in hand to show respect. "Word spread of your arrival. I'll see to your horses."

"With my thanks, Devlin, as this one's had us riding since dawn." Mahon dismounted. "And my arse feels it."

"And now you'll have ale," Keegan reminded him, and handed the reins to Devlin. "And how does your wife fare?" he asked. "She must be near her time."

"Her time came a week ago this day, and we have a daughter. Both are well, thank the gods."

"Bright blessings on your daughter, her mother, and you, Devlin. What have you named her?"

"She is Cara, Taoiseach, as she is dear to us."

"A fine name. Wait." Keegan dug into his saddlebag, took out the beryl he'd picked up when visiting the troll mines only the day before. "A gift for the new life you brought to Talamh."

"Thank you. She will come to treasure it."

Keegan hefted his saddlebag onto his shoulder. "Who would

think when we ran the fields and the woods that one day you'd have a daughter, and this one two sons and another child coming."

"Who would think," Mahon said with the ease of friendship, "that when we three and more went into the lake, this one would rise as taoiseach?"

"I'd rather the lady and the child," Devlin said with a grin.

"As would I," Mahon agreed.

Mahon took his own bag, then clapped Keegan's shoulder as they took the path to the castle. "I'm for that ale and a scrub. I expect you'll want the same. And while my woman's far to the west, you'll be wrapped in Shana's welcoming arms."

"I think no, I won't be. I've much else to do."

Mahon shot him a look. "Because you think of the redheaded witch?"

"Because I can't take time for distractions."

"We're too much friends for that."

Keegan paused while they were still far enough away from listening ears. "It strikes me I've ignored, more pretended not to know, Shana wants more from me than I'd ever give. Her father is a good man, and on the council. Perhaps he wishes for the same. It's time she looks to another for what she wants."

"She beds others, as do you," Mahon pointed out. "I took you as bedmates and no more."

"And so it was easy to pretend not to know. And it's not wrong, Mahon, there's too much to be done to have distractions. As you said, she beds others. Her nights won't be lonely."

Keegan chose a side door, hoping to avoid a flood of greetings. He knew the stairs and passages to take to avoid the main hall and public spaces where people might gather.

But he'd barely stepped into the blessed cool when his mother stepped up to greet them.

She wore blue, a soft, summery shade that suited her, and had her honey-toned hair braided up to show off ear dangles. With it she wore a pendant with a single, unframed clear crystal—one he knew his father had given her on the day of his birth.

"Welcome, travelers," she said, and held out her arms.

"I won't kiss you. We've only come off the road, and brought much of it with us."

"Nonsense." She moved right in, hugged Mahon, then her son. "And how is my daughter, how are my grandchildren?"

"More than well," Mahon told her. "And wondering when next you'll visit."

"Soon, I hope, as my heart's missing them. And your brother?" Tarryn arched her brows at Keegan.

"Also well."

"Then I'm pleased. Mahon, I've had a tankard sent to your chamber, and a tub's being filled in your bath."

"I have the most brilliant of mothers-in-law." He took her hand, kissed it. "And with your leave, I'll go make use of both. This one will ride the skin off your arse."

"So it ever was. I'll see you at the evening meal—a banquet and dance for welcome—and expect to hear stories about my boys."

"There's no lack of them."

He took the winding stone steps Keegan had aimed for, and Tarryn linked her arm with her son's. "I'll walk up with you. I'd like to speak to you in person rather than by falcon or through the glass."

"Is there trouble?"

"None yet. There are signs of trouble to come, but none yet."

She walked him to what they called the small hall, and he realized she'd sent out word to give him time to settle. People gave greetings, but no one approached as they took the stairs, walked by the tapestries that graced the stone walls, past the leaded glass windows.

And up, floor by floor, until they reached the tower chambers designated for the taoiseach.

"I wish you'd take this for your own."

"I'm not taoiseach."

She opened the door, stepped back so he'd go in first.

In the sitting room a fire burned low. A tray of fruit, cheeses, cold meats, bread sat on a table along with a tankard and a glass decanter of wine.

As he knew her preference, he poured her wine. "Will you have food?"

She shook her head, sat while he picked up the tankard and drank while pacing the room.

So restless, she thought.

She'd cleaned the room herself only that morning, brought in fresh flowers and herbs, freshened the linen. She'd made the new candles for the mantel—here and in the bedchamber—with him in mind.

Taoiseach or not, she would always be his mother, and would always try to find a way to ease that restless mind.

She'd yet to find it, but she'd always try.

"We have a full council meeting in the morning. You must attend."

"I know. That's why I'm here—or one of the reasons."

"Will you sit in the Chair of Justice after? People know you're here, Keegan, and will expect it."

"Aye."

"And will you dance tonight to the music that welcomes you?"

"With you, Ma." He glanced back with a smile. "Always."

"Only me?"

"I didn't come for the dancing. There are signs, as you said, and they show themselves all across Talamh." He sat then, leaning toward her, the tankard between his knees. "The world thrives, Ma, I see it, and yet I feel the storm coming. He would burn us to ash."

"You'll stop him. We'll stop him. I don't have faith in you only because you're my love, only because you're taoiseach. I have faith because I know the man I raised. And what of Eian's daughter?"

He sat back, shrugged. Oh, Tarryn thought, she knew that broody look. "She went back to her world."

"This is her world as well."

"She made her choice. We honor choice."

"Sure and we honor choice, as no one has the right to force will on another. But I have word, not just from you, but my other children, from Marg. She vowed to come back."

He looked at the fire, the red heart of the heat. But as he had since Breen left, resisted looking into it.

"Vows aren't always kept."

"You don't believe her then? You don't trust her?" Watching him, Tarryn sipped wine. "I'm told you shared her bed, more than once."

"That's a different matter."

"Is it now?" She smiled into her wine. Then the smile faded. "There was blood on the moons last night."

"I saw it."

"She's needed here, Keegan."

"As was made clear to her. What can I do about it?"

"That should be clear as well to you, if you weren't sulking. I know a sulk when I'm looking at one, boy of mine," she said before he could protest. "And it's clear you, Taoiseach, need to go over, remind her of her oath. And—not by force of will, but by persuasion and diplomacy—convince her to come back."

"And how many times have you told me my diplomacy is sorely lacking?"

"Countless. Do better this time. Maybe you could be adding just a touch of humility. Oh," she said quickly. "What was I thinking with that! I must be getting old and feebleminded."

"Ha." He drank more ale. "I've duties to see to here."

"You do, aye, you do. And when you have, you'll go speak with her, on the other side, and do your duty there. You've never failed to do your duty."

She set her empty glass aside, rose. And, bending to him, kissed his cheeks. "You never will fail. I'll leave you to your scrub."

CHAPTER TWENTY-NINE

Shana had many reasons for her friendship with Kiara. While true enough Kiara's cheerful chatter could sometimes wear, no one in the Capital gathered riper gossip. She also possessed a sweet nature and a sympathetic ear—and a genius for styling hair.

At the moment, she chattered away while patiently winding Shana's long, silvery hair into countless braids.

They'd bonded during their school years, as neither of them had enjoyed the classroom. Kiara used her skill with hair—much admired and sought after—and her love and unmatched patience with children to contribute to Talamh.

Shana gave her time to gardens—flowers and herbs—but paid close attention to council business, as she hoped to one day sit where her father now sat.

Kiara, for all her prattle, often passed along more detailed information than Shana's father shared.

The fact Shana's mother stood as Tarryn's closest friend and confidant sometimes meant little bits and bites from the taoiseach's mother and hand eked through.

Kiara's parents met when her father visited the world of Largus as a young man, and met Minga. Shana supposed Kiara got her romantic heart from the story of how the nonmagickal beauty from the desert province of Largus and the elf fell in love, and how Minga left her golden sands behind for Og and the green hills of Talamh.

Og had passed his Elfin blood and talents to his children—all five. Though Kiara couldn't claim her mother's great beauty—few could—she had the deep gold skin of her mother's world, and her mother's ebony hair and rich brown, long-lidded eyes.

Both friends appreciated the contrast, and how their dramatically different coloring added an extra shine.

They'd made a pact as girls never to compete for or fall in love with the same man. They'd kept it. So their friendship held strong.

"I mean to dance every dance tonight." With her nimble fingers, Kiara attached a tiny bell to the end of a braid. "Aiden O'Brian returned with the taoiseach, and it's time, I'm thinking, for him to stop pretending not to notice me."

"He pretends poorly."

"I have a new gown. I styled Daryn's hair, and his sisters', and tended Maeve's two children while she worked on her weaving. So Daryn made my gown. Wait until you see!"

"I'm wearing blue. Ice blue. Tell me you aren't after wearing blue."

"It's bronze. Daryn says it will make my skin glow. Blue looks so well on you, but everything does. Poor Loren Mac Niadh will sulk and stew, as the taoiseach has returned and will claim you for every dance."

"He may ask." She wasn't sure about the braids and the bells, but her mind had other things occupying it. "Hours he's been back, and hasn't taken one precious moment of his time for me."

"Ah well now, he's only just returned, and had meetings and such. And I heard his mother was closeted with him for a time."

"He finds time to come to my bed, doesn't he?"

"And beds no one else in the Capital these past two years or more. I would hear if he did, and I would tell you."

Shana reached back to squeeze Kiara's hand. "I know you would, even if I threw something at your head for it."

With a laugh, Kiara completed another braid. "I thought you might when I told you the whispers of him bedding Marg's granddaughter."

"People whisper of anything." With a snap, Shana set down the bottle of scent she'd toyed with. "You said as well he was training her like one of his warriors, and knocking her into the mud more often than not."

"Ywain—you know him, I think, he's Birgit's brother who lives in the west—said he'd seen that with his own eyes. And it's common knowledge in the west as well, they shared a bed as well as the training ground."

She began the final braid. "But what does it matter, as you've said yourself, who he tickles in the west, or the north or south, for that matter? As long as he comes to you in the east."

But Kiara knew her friend, felt the change, and began to soothe.

"She's gone now in any case, didn't I tell you? Gone back to her world. I'm thinking he bedded her to try to convince her to stay, as she's needed. Everyone says."

She swept the braids back, began to twist and coil.

"She has red hair, you said."

"Aye, the fire red, but no great beauty to go with it. It may be he'll think of her, Shana, but for the needs of Talamh. For his own? What man could look at you and think of another?"

She'd been wrong about the braids and bells, Shana thought. They formed a kind of crown, then fell in a waterfall down her back.

"It's time he pledged to me, Kiara."

Kiara lowered her head, pressed their cheeks together, gold against cream, black against silver. "Perhaps it will be tonight."

Shana wore the icy blue, the braids, the bells, and knew from the glances—admiration, envy—she looked beautiful. She'd learned beauty and sex could be weapons as well as gifts. And assets, she believed, for the taoiseach as his life mate.

She had a good brain for politics and policy, had been reared since birth on the art of diplomacy. And believed, with all her heart, she made the best choice for Keegan, and for Talamh, to stand by his side.

His mother had held that position, that honor, that right, long enough.

Still, she greeted Tarryn with a kiss, and another for Kiara's mother.

"You're radiant," Minga told her.

"Your daughter made me so." She gave her head a little shake to send the bells tinkling. "I thought I would be very late." Deliberately so, she thought as she turned back to Tarryn. "But I see Keegan is later yet."

"We aren't to wait for him, as you see." Resplendent in red, her honeyed hair a crown of coils, Tarryn gestured. People, already feasting, filled the banquet hall. "He's been delayed, but will join us when he can."

Loren walked to them. He wore silver matched with a doublet of blue, the exact shade of Shana's gown.

He'd bartered with Daryn to create it.

The witch, warrior, Shana's sometime lover, knew they made a perfect picture together as he kissed Shana's hand, offered her wine.

"You outshine every light in the room. Come, we have a seat for you."

"Go, sit with your friends, sit with the young," Tarryn said.

Tarryn watched them, the elf in cold, cold blue, the witch in silver, and thought how well they suited.

"A striking couple they make," she commented. "In every way. She'll turn to him, I think, when she fully understands Keegan will never choose her. And would never make her truly happy if he did."

"And yet her mind's set on him."

"Minds can change. Clouds are forming, Minga, and Talamh needs the sword and the courage to lift it, not the tinkle of bells."

"Ah, Tarryn, it's a party, after all."

"You're right in that, and I'm a bit too hard on her. I know you're fond of her, as I am. Come, let's sit with your family and enjoy what we have."

Shana had Loren, she knew. In the palm of her hand should she open it, in her bed whenever she wished it. She charmed him now as they sat with Kiara and others at a long table near enough to one of the fires that she could pull on its reflective glow.

She ate little, but spent the time flirting, smiling, and saw the appreciation in Loren's eyes.

Green eyes, but paler than Keegan's. He wore no warrior's braid in his deep brown hair, but would fight, of course, with power, with sword and bow.

He excelled with the bow, as she did. His build was good, but slighter than Keegan's. She knew both bodies very well.

As he preferred mixing potions, working his alchemy, Loren's hands remained soft. They didn't bring her the same thrill as Keegan's.

And when Keegan walked in, wearing unadorned black, her heart tripped up to her throat. She didn't see, and wouldn't have cared, that the light in Loren's eyes dimmed.

She lifted her wine, turned back to Loren with a light laugh, determined Keegan would come to her.

Instead, he wound his way through the hall, stopping here and there to speak with someone, to touch a shoulder, to kiss a cheek. To make a connection on his way to his mother.

There he greeted Minga and Og with easy warmth, as well as the three of their children who sat with them, and the others at the table before taking a seat with them.

She caught the few looks—how could she not—and the whispers behind hands. The taoiseach hadn't come to her, hadn't acknowledged her.

And that could not, would not, be borne.

So when the dancing began, she put her hand in Loren's and joined the line as his partner.

She took the steps, made the turns, well aware she shined in a dance. She danced with her father, with a were she knew pined for her, with half a dozen others before Keegan walked to her.

"You look beautiful, as always."

"Do I?" She tossed her head, gave him a sultry look under her lashes with their faerie dust carefully applied. "You seemed far too busy to notice."

"Busy I've been, but never too much to notice beauty."

"Not too busy, I hope, to take the air. I find it far too warm in here."

"For a few moments, of course."

He led her out and into the gardens, into the cool air that smelled of autumn, into moonlight that bathed the flowers in silver.

She turned to him, turned into him. "Oh, I've missed you." And gripping his face in her hands, closed her mouth over his. "Come, come with me now. Take me to your bed."

He'd never shared his bed with her, the taoiseach's bed, and they both knew she didn't ask only for sex.

He drew her back, gently. "I'm obliged here, Shana."

"You've danced—though not with me. You've had words with near to everyone in the hall, but not until now with me. More than an hour in the hall before you take my hand, so others laugh at me behind theirs."

"That's nonsense, and foolish."

"It's neither," she snapped back, and whirled away so the multitude of thin layers of her skirts whirled with her. "I would have you show those who titter at me what I am to you. Near the whole of the summer I waited, Keegan, and I'm done with it."

Hoping to calm her, he took her hand again. "I've never known you to care what others think, and I'm sorry to find you do. Sorry as well I've caused you distress."

"Then make it up to me."

Temper shifted to seduction quickly. Too quickly, he thought, noting the calculation.

"The wine flows," she murmured, with her hand stroking his cheek. "The music plays. You won't be missed if we take what we want now, what we need. And if they do, what of it? You're taoiseach."

"I am." And he knew she considered that a kind of status more than duty. "Aye, I am, and so I'm obliged to those who give their time to serve the wine, to play the music, to come tonight to have a moment, to have a word."

"Am I not one of Talamh? I want a moment. I want the words you've yet to give me. I want what you're obliged to give me."

Now he took both her hands—and held her at arm's length. "I'm obliged to give you my protection and the judgment I hold in staff and sword. I give you my affection and friendship freely, with no obligation."

"Affection? Friendship? You come to my bed whenever you will."

"And have been welcome there, and by your own words, and actions as well, with no obligation on my side or on yours. Now I see I've mistaken those words and actions, and am in the way of hurting you. That I regret, deeply."

"I don't want your regrets." She threw her arms around him again. "Come to bed, my bed then. Do your duty here if you must, then come to me."

He took her wrists, drew her arms away. "I'm sorry, more than I can say. I've cared for you, and do still. It will never be more, never be less, than that."

When she slapped him, he said nothing. He deserved that and more for not seeing what she held in her mind and her heart.

"You'd toss me aside then, as if I meant less than nothing to you. And for what? For some half-Talamhish witch who's gone? She left you, turned away from you. Just as her father did. Will you carry blind devotion for her as you did for him?"

"He never turned his back, not on me, not on my family, not on Talamh."

Though he spoke softly, his words bit. He meant them to. "Eian O'Ceallaigh gave his life for you, for me, my family, for every living thing in Talamh. And for his child hidden on the other side. Never, never disparage his name or his sacrifice to me."

"He's gone! She's gone! I'm here, ready to stand with you, to lie with you, to give you comfort, to give you sons. I love you."

"I can't give you back what you offer me. I'm sorry for it, but I can't give you what you want."

"So you hurt me, humiliate me, and you're sorry for it. Well then, Taoiseach, believe this. You will be. You'll regret turning me away like this. Others won't."

"I know it."

"Think of me with the one I choose. And regret."

She started to run back into the hall, but stopped herself. Willed back the tears, pushed back any signs of fury. She walked in, glided back to Loren.

Putting her mouth against his ear, she whispered, "The taoiseach wished to come to my bed, but I told him I had someone else in mind."

She nipped his earlobe before taking his hand. Though he didn't believe her, he went with her willingly.

The music and dancing continued after Keegan fulfilled his obligations. Weary, he sat in his rooms, ale in hand, and related the confrontation to Mahon.

"And you don't seem a bit surprised by any of this."

"Myself, aye. But Aisling, after but one meeting, claimed this is where Shana was headed, and I should never doubt her instincts. Last spring they met," he added, "when Shana rode to the west with her parents."

"She might've told me her bloody instincts."

"Would you have listened?"

He brooded into the fire, then shrugged. "Likely not, as I swear to you Shana was convincing. Not altogether true," he corrected. "As I'd begun to see, or feel in any case, she was looking for more from me, and I'd intended to step away. But I'd have done a better job of it, I'm thinking."

"Does it help if Aisling also said that while Shana might have strong feelings for you, she had stronger for the taoiseach?"

"And so I saw, or felt. How could she be reared in the Capital, where her father serves on the council, as dedicated as any could be, and not truly understand what it is to lead? Ah well, she'll have no lack of choices to fill the vacancy, you could say."

"And none have what she'd see as your status."

Keegan gave Mahon a long look. "You didn't like her at all, did you now?"

"Not true. Well," he qualified, "not altogether true. She's a charmer, and from all I've seen or heard, does her part, and is a good daughter to her parents as well. But as some do, she thinks more of how she looks or what trinkets she can barter for than things such as duty and the work it demands. So, in that, she'd never have suited such as yourself."

Mahon rose, stretched. "I'm for bed. Don't sit brooding too long."

"I can't. I need to break my fast down in the village, visit some of the shops and workshops and so on before I come back to sit in the Chair of Justice."

"Would you want company for the first part of it all?"

"Gods yes."

"Then I'll ride down with you. The Smiling Cat does a fine break-fast."

"Then there's where we'll have ours."

He spent the morning in the village, then the rest of the day hearing complaints, petty bickering, requests for help. Small things—and he could be grateful there—though not small, he knew, for those in-volved.

He listened to a man who claimed his neighbor's dog had howled through the night, and the neighbor who said he'd buried the dog, aged and well loved, two nights before the howling.

And the couple who reported they'd found one of their sheep burned black and gutted.

No small things these. He could and did replace the dog with a pup from a new litter, and the sheep out of the castle fields. But he knew the signs.

Dark crept closer.

The time he spent with soothsayers only confirmed what he knew. So he knew he could wait no longer.

At the edge of the deep woods, with the dark broken by starlight, he kissed his mother goodbye.

"I'll persuade her to come back, as she vowed she would."

"Tell your dragon to fly west."

"Why?"

"You'll want to bring her back there, where she'll have some of the familiar. The place, the people, Marg. Not here as yet, Keegan. It's jolt enough, isn't it?"

"All right then. You've a point."

"Mahon will bring your horse. I'll come myself, for Samhain if not before. It's past time I see the rest of my family. You've done well here, my dear love."

He handed her the staff. "Until I return."

"Until you return. Blessed be, Keegan."

"Blessed be, Ma."

Breen shut down her computer when she heard Marco come in. After a glance around the bedroom, she eased the door shut as she went out.

"How'd it go?" she asked him.

"My last day in retail. I can hope that's forever."

"No regrets?"

"I'm officially working for two people I care about more than anybody, you and Sally. Feels weird. Good weird. I'm going to take my fine self over to the coffee shop for my day job—that's you—so you can have the apartment for writing time."

"You don't have to do that. We can—"

"Better for both of us." He wandered to the front window. "And a hell of an easy commute."

"I hear regret. Marco, everyone loved your web page design. I know they had a few suggestions, but—"

"Good ones. I'm cool there, Breen. It's a way big step for me. And I'm going to miss the easy access to the instruments. I mean, I've got my keyboard and guitar here, but I'm not gonna be able to grab a sax or a banjo and see what I can do, you know?"

"Wait."

She dashed into the bedroom, took the harp in its case out of her closet. "I was going to give this to you for Christmas, but . . ." She didn't know where she'd be for Christmas. Even if she would be.

"But I can't wait," she continued. "And this seems like the perfect time."

"Whatcha got there?"

"Sit down, open the case, and find out."

When he did, he simply stared at the harp.

"As soon as I saw it, it said: *I'm Marco's.* There's a shop in the village. It's family owned and run. The father builds the instruments—some of them. This harp. He made an accordion for my dad."

Marco looked up then, his eyes glossy with tears. "I've got no words."

"You don't need them. I know you didn't love your job at the music store, but this is still a change, a big one. You're doing it for me."

He plucked strings, and the notes rang pure. "Listen to her—she's got such a voice. I've got a lot to learn. You gave me a push, Breen, and I figure I needed one. I'm never going to be a rock star or a hip-hop star, or any kind of star."

"You've got such a gift."

"Lots of people do." Even as he shrugged, his fingers found music in the strings. "I gotta earn a living. Doesn't mean I have to give up playing music, writing songs, but the way things were, I'd have kept spinning on in the music store to get the rent paid. Now I can do something I'm good at, have time to play for myself, and yeah, maybe try teaching some. Right here, like you said.

"I can do that," he said, his eyes still wet and on hers. "Because you're going back to Ireland."

"Marco, I—"

"Girl, who knows you better'n me?"

"Nobody," she murmured. "Just nobody."

"You've been thinking about going back since you got here. You don't talk about getting a house anymore. That was a big clue right there. And you're different since you came back. Not bad different. There's just . . . more to you. And some of the more, it's got its mind back there."

When she said nothing, he used the back of his hand to wipe his eyes. "Am I wrong?"

"No, you're not wrong. I'm sorry."

"Don't you be sorry. You got a granny there. Hell, you got a dog. Something clicked for you, man, I could hear it click when we got over there. Don't you be sorry, not to me."

"I need to finish what I started." What else could she tell him? "What I started there."

"Yeah." He trailed his finger, back and forth, over strings. "When you figure you're going?"

"I . . . I was looking at flights before you came. I thought next week."

"Next week?" His fingers stilled. "But you've only been back a couple weeks."

"It'll be a month, Marco. I should've told you sooner. I didn't know how, and there was so much I wanted to get done, settled, before I went back. I don't know how long I'll stay, not yet. It could be a few weeks or a few months or . . ."

"Forever?"

"I'm not thinking forever about anything. Finishing what I started, that's all I'm thinking about. When I have, I'll figure out the rest."

"I'm not going to tell you not to go, but I'm asking how much the guy you hooked up with over there has to do with this."

"Not that way," she said quickly. "Absolutely not that way. I'm not going back, not even a little bit of a fraction, because of a relationship—that kind."

"Okay, because sex—let me tell ya—can blur shit up. And if you think it's more than sex? Blurs shit up even more. People are dumbasses for love."

"Not blurred, I promise. I knew I was going back when I left, but I didn't tell you. I should have, but I didn't."

"Tell anybody else?"

"I promised my grandmother I'd come back and . . . but here? No, I haven't said anything yet."

"You need to face that up. I gotta change to head to Sally's. You oughta come, tell him and the rest of them."

"Okay."

He rose, pulled her to her feet for a hug. "The harp's the best present I ever got. And if going back makes you happy, I'll be happy, too. Might take me awhile to get there, but I will."

Keegan waited until midnight to cast the circle inside the deep dark of the woods. He wanted the power of the ending day, the new beginning of the next for what would be a long and complex ritual.

Reopening the portal on the other side would take less because of what he put into this. But, as his mother had asked, he would need to open it again not here, but in the west.

He'd need to be precise as well and so had to study his mark. Not just the country, not just the city, but her apartment. Like hitting the bull's-eye in a target he saw only in his mind.

Then, shifting it all yet again, to move the opening miles west of where he stood now.

He'd considered going to Marg to have her help him with the ritual, as the shared blood between her and Breen would simplify the matter.

But in the end, he was responsible. And if his hard words on her leaving had added to her staying away, he would have to find softer ones—somewhere—to persuade her back again.

So he cast the circle, spread the light through the dark. He called on the gods to bless his efforts in the name of that light. He drank the wine, poured the rest in the goblet on the ground, and as the earth drank, he brought the fire. And with his words ringing in the night, he lifted it high, spread it wide. Slowly, painstakingly, he drew the air in, winding it while the strain of holding all contained and focused ran sweat down his back.

The fire burned hot and red, then blue, and at last white and brilliant as it compressed. As it formed the door between the worlds.

"And with the words I have spoken, I ask locks to break and door to open. Grant me passage this night with my oath to carry the light from world to world to keep them free. As I will, so mote it be."

With faith, he stepped forward into the whirling light, the licks of flame. And hurled himself from one world to another.

A flash of light, a slap of heat, and the portal snapped shut again at his back.

He found himself in a room in dim light with noise humming against the window. But none inside, he thought, no sounds inside the room.

He flicked his fingers for light, studied it. Colorful, he thought, and tidy. And empty. The floor creaked under his boots as he moved toward a small table and saw to his right a kitchen.

He'd seen others like it on his journeys and in books, though this one was very small and smelled, not unpleasantly, of something pretending to be lemons.

He heard a door slam, and voices—but outside the one here.

So, an apartment then, but he couldn't be sure, as yet, the right apartment.

He walked down a narrow hallway, glanced in the room on the left. He saw a bed, neatly made, more color, a guitar on a stand, pictures of people playing musical instruments on the wall.

It neither looked nor smelled like Breen, so he turned into the room on his right.

And there she was—or the scent of her, the feel of her.

The machine she used to write her stories stood on a desk along with the picture of her father, his, and the others, like the one she'd given Marg and his family.

A case on the floor held a few things as if she'd laid them inside or had yet to take them out.

But where was she?

"Bugger it."

Because he recognized the scrying mirror, he picked it up. Under normal circumstances he'd never have used another's magick tool without permission, but he couldn't wait on the niceties.

"Show me."

The glass darkened, then cleared.

He saw her, sitting at a bar. She held a glass of wine, and her lips moved as she spoke to someone he couldn't see. He thought she looked a bit weepy, and that caused him some discomfort.

Then she embraced someone, another woman, one with white-blond hair falling over bare shoulders.

No, not another woman, he realized, looking closer as they drew away to speak again. A man dressed as one—and well.

Sally's, he realized. She'd spoken of the place and the man often.

He set the mirror down to take a divining stone from his pocket. "Show me the way."

He started out, then remembered his sword. This world, he knew, would frown on a man wearing a sword, so he unstrapped it, set it down.

He kept the stone in his hand as he left the apartment, went down flights of stairs. Doors opened and closed and let out the sound of voices, the smell of food. Someone played a horn of some kind, and not well at all.

Outside the air cooled and clogged with the smell of the cars and the fuel they burned. Again, the colorful struck him. Not just in the clothing or the many hues of skin but in the city itself.

It was like rainbows, he noted, and couldn't fault it.

Again, someone played a horn, but this time very well indeed. Lamps pooled light on the streets and sidewalks, and many strolled as if in no particular hurry. Two men approached each other with smiles in their eyes, then kissed as he walked by them.

He made a turn as the stone directed and found himself outside a building. More rainbows here and the lights in that same color spelled SALLY's.

He stepped in—heat and music and color beyond even what he'd seen. But what he didn't see was Breen at the bar where she'd been in the glass.

The idea of hunting her through the city irritated, and still the place itself lifted something in him.

Three women—no, men again—stood on a stage in costumes that glittered like stars. They sang in exceptional harmony.

The air smelled as bright as the voices.

So he paused to take in what had pulled her back to this place, and consider what he would have to do to find the way to pull her away again.

CHAPTER THIRTY

Behind the bar, busy mixing the perfect martini, Marco noticed Keegan the minute he walked in.

Some people, in Marco's experience, had that power—the power to pull attention to them in a finger snap. It took more than looks—though, man, this guy had them—it took POW.

You couldn't fake the POW. You had it, or you didn't.

He poured the martini into the chilled glass, added three olives while he watched POW take in the club.

Liked the music, clearly, but then the Supremes never failed. And just as clearly POW looked for someone.

Lucky someone.

Tall and built, he thought as POW began to move toward the bar. Casually dressed—dark blue sweater, dark brown pants, sexily scarred boots. A sharp, angular face with a scruff that came off casual instead of deliberate.

The kind of thick, black hair anybody'd want to get their hands into. And with the kick of a single skinny braid running down the left side.

Something started to click, then POW stood at the bar, looking him straight in the eye. Marco had no shame admitting his brain fuzzed with lust for a minute.

"Welcome to Sally's, Tall, Dark, and Gorgeous. What can I get you?"

"I'd be looking for Breen Kelly. Would you know her?"

The Irish accent slayed. And completed the click.

"The Irish god."

Keegan's eyebrows shot up. "Not altogether, no. A redhead, she is," he began.

"I meant you. I'm Marco. Marco Olsen." He shot out a hand to shake.

"Marco, is it? She spoke fondly of you, so I'm pleased to meet you. And would Breen be about?"

"She went backstage for a minute. She'll be back." Meanwhile, Marco thought, I can pump you for information. "What can I get you to drink while you wait? On the house," he added, "from one friend of Breen's to another."

"That's kind of you." And easier by far, as he hadn't thought to bring any local currency. He glanced at the taps, nodded. "I'd have a pint of Guinness, and thanks."

"You got it. So . . ." Marco set the pint glass under the tap and began the process of building the Guinness. "You live near Breen's grandmother."

"I do."

"Breen's really happy she found her grandmother. It means a lot to her, especially after she found out her dad had died. Did you know him?"

"I did, and a finer man I've never known save my own father."

While the layers of the Guinness settled, Marco took an order for a Moscow Mule, a Cosmo, and a couple of house reds.

"Breen didn't mention you were coming."

"She wouldn't, as I didn't mention it to her."

"Surprise! How long are you in town?"

"Not long, I'm thinking. You know what you're about there," he commented as Marco filled the order. "A skilled barman's a fine thing."

"On-the-job training." With the order filled, Marco finished the Guinness, set it in front of Keegan. "Breen's more than a friend to me, more than a sister. She's more."

"And you to her, as I know from how she spoke of you."

"I figure you could take me down and out without breaking a sweat, but I'd still come for you if you hurt her."

Keegan kept his eyes on Marco's as he sampled the Guinness. "A true friend, one who'll stand for you no matter, is a treasure. I'm not after bringing harm to her."

"She bruises easy. In here." Marco tapped his heart.

"I met a woman of strength and will, and a fierce determination. And still I'm not after bruising her heart, or having her treasure of a friend come for me."

"And who do we have here?" Sally, in snug, spangly black with over-the-knee boots and a platinum wig, sidled up beside Keegan.

"Breen's . . . friend from Ireland," Marco told him. "Sorry, she never said your name."

"Keegan Byrne."

"Oooh, accents do it every time." Though Sally trailed a flirtatious finger down Keegan's arm, his eyes stayed steady and assessing. "Aren't you the surprise package? I'm Sally."

"Sally? The mother of Breen's heart."

The assessing eyes softened. "That's a sweet way to put it."

"How she spoke of you made it clear enough. I like your place here very much. It's good craic, and the performers have fine voices."

"Wait until you see Sally's Gaga," Marco commented as he filled another order.

"You perform as well?"

"Honey, I was born for the stage, but I've got a little time before I blow the roof off. Marco, still water. Keegan, let's you and I get ourselves a table, have a little talk.

"Hettie'll bring the drinks," Sally added as he hooked his arm with Keegan's to steer him to a table in the back of the room.

"Would you be planning to come for me as well?" As, man or not, Sally was dressed as a female, Keegan held out his chair.

Lips twitching, Sally sat. "Should I?"

"I've the warning from Marco on it, and expect the same from you. You're her family after all. Thanks," he added when the waitress set down their drinks. "My friend, another brother to me, had his eye on my sister, and she on him. And though my sister's more than a year older than I am, and Mahon as true a man as I know, I said much the same to him."

"And how did that work out?"

Keegan lifted his beer. "Well now, it didn't come to blows, which is fortunate for both of us, as Aisling would have kicked our arses for it. And they're expecting their third child."

"To happy endings." Sally lifted his water. "And is that what you're looking for with Breen? A happy ending, children?"

"What?"

The sincere shock had Sally's lips twitching again.

"An example only of my understanding of family. It's a conversation I'm planning, no more, in hopes she'll come back with me. She's family there as well. And . . . there's a need for her there. A place for her."

"You speak for her grandmother? Someone she didn't know existed until last summer."

Diplomacy, Keegan reminded himself.

"Marg kept her silence, which cost her dearly, out of respect for Breen's mother, and to give Breen herself time to make her own choices when the moment came. It's not my story to tell you, so I'll say only when Eian brought Breen here, at her mother's demand, he did his best to keep his family safe and whole, and to keep the family he left behind the same.

"No one will speak ill of Mairghread or Eian Kelly in my hearing."

"Fair enough. Though I will say I wish her grandmother had made herself known sooner, and given Jennifer less time to do a number on Breen."

"I'm aware of your meaning, and the truth of it. But the time of choices comes when it comes. And she had you, didn't she then? And Marco, and this place."

He looked around again as applause followed the trio offstage.

"It's a good place, as I said. One of love and shelter, beyond the fun of it."

With a huff, Sally sat back. "How am I supposed to grill you like a fish when you say something like that?"

He smiled. "It's what I see and feel for myself now I'm here, and what was easy enough to glean from how Breen spoke of you, of Marco, of here, of . . . it's Derrick, isn't it?"

"Yes. The love of my life."

"So a fine man he must be, as you've no reason to settle for less."

"Shit. Charm, looks, and the accent." Sally tossed his platinum locks. "What's a mother supposed to do?"

"Let her go back with me, if she chooses."

"I couldn't stop her, and wouldn't try to stand in front of something she wants. She's never had her heart broken—romantically," Sally qualified. "She's had her ego, her self-esteem, both always wobbly, shaken and dinged, but not her heart." He leaned forward. "Don't be the first."

"I'm not— This isn't about romantic reasons."

With a manicured, hot-pink-tipped hand, Sally patted Keegan's. "Whatever you say, handsome. And that's my cue. Enjoy the show."

It was hard not to, even with growing impatience—when the hell would she come out again?—when the place erupted with applause and cheers.

And Sally took the stage.

He admired performers, and quickly saw Sally had spoken true. He'd been born for the stage.

A presence was what it was, the movements, the confidence, as he sang about a bad romance with many patrons joining in on the chorus as they might at a pub sing-along.

And though he enjoyed, he knew when Breen came in. Just a tip of power in the air. It always amazed him people in this world couldn't feel it.

He turned his head, and saw her as she saw him.

When she started toward him, he rose.

"What are you doing here?"

"We need to speak. If you'd come with me back to your home."

Instead she sat. "We can speak right here."

"It's a conversation I'd rather in private."

"This is private enough."

Her self-confidence didn't appear so—was it "wobbly"?—as her heart mother thought.

He started to lean forward, but the waitress stepped up, set down a glass of wine. "Marco thought you'd like one. Can I get you another beer?"

"Thanks all the same, this is more than fine."

"Just send out a signal if you need anything." Hettie looked deliberately at Breen. "Anything."

"You'd think I'd come to drag you off by the hair," Keegan muttered.

"We look out for each other here."

"As do we," he reminded her. "You said you'd come back, but it's been more than a month."

"Not quite a month," she corrected. "I speak with Nan nearly every day."

"And she'd say nothing that might weigh on you. In any case, I've been at the Capital these last days. You need to come back. The signs are growing."

"What signs?"

"Of the dark that's coming. You gave your word you'd come when needed. You're needed."

"I didn't think you took me at my word."

"Bugger it, woman, I was well pissed off, wasn't I? This isn't about your feelings or mine, but of duty."

The music pulsed. Sally slid into "Born This Way." People crowded onto the dance floor. The lights glimmered.

Everything, everything in the moment was so familiar, so safe, so normal, she craved it like breath.

"Tell me the truth. If I go to Talamh, I could die there."

"Everything I have, everything I am will fight to protect you."

She looked at him; she drank some wine. "I believe that. But I could die."

He fisted a hand on the table, but didn't pound it. "As I could, as all could. And if we fail, as all here could in time. Odran won't stop with Talamh."

"I see the land burning. I smell the smoke and the blood. I hear the screams." She set down the wine.

He closed a hand over hers. "Will you do nothing, and let that happen?"

"No." She rose, looked toward the stage at Sally, then at the bar and Marco. After pressing a hand to her heart, she started toward the door.

"I have a flight on hold for next week," she said as Keegan came after her. "I told everyone who matters I was going back—to Ireland." Outside, she began to walk quickly. "I needed to tell them, needed to say goodbye. Now I have, so I'll see if I can book an earlier flight."

"You were coming back."

She rounded on him. "I said I would."

"I apologize." He grabbed her arm as she turned and hurried on. "I'm sorry. Truly."

"Doesn't matter."

"Sure and it does. I questioned your word, insulted you there, and that hurts you. I'm sorry for it. And three times sorry, so it should be enough for anyone."

"I'm afraid." She looked straight ahead as she spoke. "Everything here is what I know, and I have something I always wanted with writing. It's like, here's your chance to be happy, Breen, really happy, to finally find your place.

"But it's not my place, or not my only place," she continued. "When I think about the cottage in Ireland, or the way the air feels on my face in Talamh. What it's like to watch Morena's wings spread, or the scents in Nan's workshop, her kitchen. How her door stays open."

She sighed, closed her eyes. "And I miss it like a heartbeat. And I miss having a place there, being a part of something the way I've never felt here. I want the magicks, want to feel that joy inside me.

"And I'm afraid."

"You'd be foolish if you weren't afraid."

She paused outside the door to her building. "Then I guess I'm not foolish."

She went inside, started up the stairs. "I have Marco, Sally, Derrick, friends from Sally's, and they matter so much. But I don't fit here now. And I'm afraid if I want or need to come back, I won't fit. That's assuming I live through what's coming."

She got out her keys, unlocked the door. "Do I have to give up what I love here?"

He wanted to touch her, reassure her. And for truth, did neither. "I don't know the answer."

"Neither do I. Go ahead and sit down. I'll try to book a seat on your flight. When is it, what airline?"

"You think I came on the airplane? Why would I do that? Bloody awful things, they are. I've opened a portal, a temporary one. Opening it again from here, now with you joining, will be a much simpler matter."

As he spoke, he picked up his sword, strapped it on.

"How did your sword get— Here?" she realized. "You opened a portal from Talamh into my apartment?"

"It seemed the best place for it."

"What if Marco had been here?"

"He wasn't."

"What if I'd had company, or I'd been in the middle of a damn orgy?"

"You didn't," he said simply. "You weren't. And since you spoke of a quiet sort of life here, I didn't consider the possibility of an orgy. Do you have them often?"

"People knock before they come into someone's private home."

He fought for patience, and felt himself losing almost before he began.

"Considering the circumstances, I set good manners aside. You can flay me for the lack of them once we're back. You've said your goodbyes, so let's be at it and gone."

"I need to pack."

"Bloody fucking hell, there are clothes in Talamh."

"I'm going to pack. I'm not leaving without taking what I need. Go if you're in such a damn hurry, and I'll take the bloody awful plane when I'm ready."

She strode into her bedroom, and going with priorities, packed up her laptop, notebooks, research materials first.

"I need my work," she shot out because he'd followed her. "It may not seem important to you, but it is to me."

"Never did I say it wasn't important."

"You might as well have. Hurry up, Breen, don't inconvenience somebody else by taking time for what you need."

He watched her wrap a shirt around the photo of their fathers, another around the scrying mirror. She packed them, and the spell book he recognized as one Marg had written.

She pulled things out of the closet, out of drawers, and her movements were jerky. Not with temper, no, not temper now, but something more fragile.

He felt her grief as he opened himself to it.

And how, he wondered, could a man who'd believed he understood women as well as any have blundered so badly with two within a week?

"I'm entitled to my own damn clothes, not just things someone has to spare. And if I want the frog mug Marco made me in middle school, I'm taking it."

She dumped pens and pencils into the suitcase, then wrapped what might have been a grinning pink frog before adding it to the rest.

"And I'm taking my own toothbrush, if it's all the same to you."

He heard the tears in her voice as she crossed the hall, swept things into a small bag.

"My own stuff, however frivolous that may be. Because I'm going to have what's mine for however long I can have it. I don't know when I'll get back, or if I'll ever get back, if I'll ever see Marco or Sally or anyone here who matters to me again. And I'll do my duty, goddamn it, when I'm packed."

She started to cross the hall again, but he stepped in front of her.

"Stop now."

"I'm not finished!"

"I'll find another way." He put his hands on her shoulders, on the trembling. "This is wrong. I've been wrong, and I'll find a way, as it's for me to find it. The duty's mine, and has been even before I took up the sword and the staff. I've had my life knowing, and you've had only weeks. I'm charged to weigh the right and the wrong of things, to find the fair way, the just one. And this isn't fair or just."

He lowered his forehead to hers a moment. The weight belonged to him, he thought, and always had.

"You'll stay here in the world you know, the world that has your heart. I'll find another way to hold Talamh."

Because her legs went weak, she slid down, spilling out what she'd swept into the little bag.

He went down with her, crouched as she sat with her back against the wall.

"You're saying I don't have to go. And don't say it's a choice."

"Well, a choice it is, but we haven't given you much room for it, have we? And no doubt if you'd come back, I'd have driven you just as hard, more, than I had before. That's the way of it. The way of me. But it's not your way or your world."

"My father—"

"Died for it. I loved him like my own. I don't think he'd be thanking me for dragging his daughter back to risk all. This is for me."

He pushed up, started to reach down to help her up.

The door swung open.

Marco saw Breen on the floor, tears on her cheeks, and to his eye, Keegan looming over her.

"You asshole! Get away from her!"

Leading with his fist, he flew at Keegan. Breen heard the *crack* of knuckles against bone before her shock broke, and she shot to her feet.

"Stop, stop! Don't you hurt him," she ordered Keegan, and just flung herself at Marco to keep things from escalating.

"Get out of the way, Breen. Nobody's going to treat you like that. You think you can go around knocking women down, fucker?"

"He didn't." Breen clung tighter. "He didn't knock me down. He didn't hurt me. It was the opposite. I was emotional; he was being understanding."

"Didn't look like that to me. And I saw how you looked when you left Sally's. You were upset. You're still upset. That's why I came after you."

"I was upset. I am upset. But not with Keegan. I promise. Go close the door, okay? Before the neighbors call the police."

After giving Keegan another hard look, Marco stomped over, slammed the door.

"I want to know what the hell's going on."

"I was packing." She hunkered down to pick up what she'd spilled, and to avoid eye contact. "And I got emotional. Keegan said things—kind things—and I got more emotional. He didn't hurt me, or threaten me, or . . . anything like that."

"Okay." But that wary eye remained. "If it wasn't what it sure as hell looked like, I'm sorry I hit you."

"No matter. Friends stand for friends. And it was a good punch, well delivered."

"Yeah well, I'm pretty sure your face broke my fist." He looked down at Breen. "And this isn't the whole story. What the hell's going on, Breen? And don't try to bullshit me. I know you, girl."

"You do." She murmured it as she pushed up. "I'm going back."

"I know. We talked about it."

"I'm going back pretty much now."

"Now? You said next week."

"I know." She looked down at the bag in her hand, the one filled with things that had seemed so important only moments before.

Now, important meant the two men in the room, and the two worlds they belonged to. She stepped into her bedroom to set the bag down.

"Let's get out of the hall."

She walked into the living room, turned to Keegan first. "I'm not leaving until I pack. I'm not leaving until I tell Marco the truth."

Keegan only shook his head and paced to the window.

"Wait. Is that a sword? Why does he have a sword?"

"Let's just sit down for a minute." After urging Marco to a chair, she perched on the arm of another. "I wasn't just in Ireland this summer. It started there. Or no, here. It started here, sort of, after I saw Sedric on the bus. The man with the silver hair, remember?"

"Breen—"

"But I started to feel more in Ireland. Morena—with the hawk? How I felt so connected so quickly. Then at the cottage, I felt more and more. And I followed Bollocks through the woods, and he led me to the tree. I went through after him and into Talamh. Where my father was from. Where he and my mother got married. Where I was born. I met my grandmother."

"I thought she gave you the dog. Your grandma."

"She did, but I didn't know she did until she told me. When I spent time with her, I learned so much. I learned, and could feel, how everything's connected. How there's a power, two-sided—the dark and the light—that connects everything and everyone."

"What, like the Force?"

"No, Marco, not . . . Well, sort of," she decided. "And there are worlds—remember when you wanted to be an astronomer? How you used to say we couldn't be alone because we were too small to be the only? You were right."

"So, what, you're going to tell me he's from the planet Tulip, and you're going through the space-time continuum?"

"For a storyteller," Keegan said without looking around, "you're bolloxing this."

"I know it. Think multiverse. There's more than one world. We're one. Talamh's another. There are portals that connect some of them, like the tree connects this world and Talamh. Wait. I wrote it all down."

Marco got slowly to his feet as she rushed back into the bedroom. "You've been messing with her head. What did you give her?"

"She found her birthright, her birthplace. She found her history, and her destiny." Keegan glanced at Breen as she came back in with her computer case and a flash drive. "You said you wouldn't go without giving him the truth, so you mean to go. But you leave him more confused and angry."

"Read this." She pressed the drive into Marco's hand. "I wrote it out as it happened. I wrote down my thoughts, my feelings. It's all there. All about Talamh, the Fey. How they chose magicks over technology."

"Okay, great, so he's—what—a wizard now? He's Harry freaking Potter with a sword?"

"Enough. I am of the Fey, as she is. I am of the Wise, as she is. Breen Siobhan O'Ceallaigh, I, taoiseach of Talamh, release you from your vow to return. Your choice is here and now. Make it."

"I'm going back."

"Breen, this guy's a lunatic or a con job trying to get your money. I'm calling the cops."

"Stop." Breen shot out her hands, and every candle in the room sparked to flame. "This is who I am," she said as Marco dropped back into the chair. "Daughter of the Fey, a witch who carries the blood of the Sidhe and the curse of a dark god."

She snapped her fingers and held a ball of blue light. Waved the other hand and called the air to stir.

"This is what was kept from me all my life. This power, this gift, this duty."

"Okay, okay, did we all do a whole lot of drugs?"

"You know we didn't. This is who I am, Marco. Who I really am. And if you're afraid of me now, I think it'll break my heart."

His breath came fast as if he'd run a few blocks, and his legs shook. But he got to his feet. Then he stepped to her, wrapped his arms around her.

"You're a little scary," he managed. "And I'm whacked out, okay? I'm pretty freaking freaked. But you're still Breen. You're still my best girl."

She vanished the ball of light, then held him hard. "I love you so much. This, all this came from my father." She pulled back. "There's too much to explain. Read what I wrote. I need to go. I'm going to get my things," she said to Keegan.

When she hurried into the bedroom, Marco turned to Keegan. "I know what I just saw. I don't understand it, but I know what I saw. I still don't trust you."

"You've no reason to I can see. I'll tell you I mean her no harm. More, I will give my life to protect her. As you would."

"Do you love her?"

"She is the key to the lock" was Keegan's answer. "A lock that holds back the dark. One that would consume my world. And yours."

"Maybe you don't want to hurt her. Maybe. But somebody does. I know my girl. She's scared. I want to know why."

"Read the file," Breen said as she rolled the hastily packed, disorganized suitcase behind her. "It's everything. I've left things. I know I have. I can't think straight."

"Sedric can come for whatever you want, but we need to go. Give me that." Impatient now, Keegan grabbed the suitcase, shouldered the computer case. "If we join, the portal opens faster, easier."

"Bullshit on portals. Breen—"

"I'll call you from the cottage as soon as I can. The cottage is on this side. We'll talk." She hugged him again. "I'll answer all your questions. But I need to do this."

She turned away. "I don't know how to open a portal."

"I do." Keegan took her hand. "With me."

He focused, drew from her, and began to open what he'd already conjured.

Behind them, Marco watched light, a pinprick, spread into a ball. And grow, grow. He saw dark behind it, but a dark sprinkled with stars, a pair of moons, their light a kind of shimmer over shadowed hills.

"What the actual fuck!"

Breen looked back. "I love you, Marco."

She stepped forward.

Marco didn't think, only felt.

He leaped forward and, grabbing Breen's free hand, tumbled through the light and dark with her.

"Oh God, Marco. Keegan, stop, pull back!"

Caught in the flash of light, the whirling wind between worlds, Marco only gripped Breen tighter. "You go, I go."

"It's too late to stop." Risking a shift, Keegan pushed out power he hoped would cushion the fall as he glanced at Marco. "Hang on, brother."

And with no time, no choice, Breen clung to the hand of the friend who drew her to one world, and the hand of the man who pulled her into the other.

NORA ROBERTS

For the latest news, exclusive extracts and unmissable competitions, visit

f /NoraRobertsJDRobb
www.fallintothestory.com